I0659236

BOOK FIVE IN THE COIN FOREST SERIES

ETTI'S INTENDED

JANET LANE

Dreaming Tree Publishing, LLC
Littleton, Colorado USA

Etti's Intended
©2017 Janet Lane

This novel is a work of fiction. Names, characters, places and incidents are either the product of the author's imagination or, if real, used fictitiously.

Published by Dreaming Tree Publishing
P. O. Box 1070, Littleton, CO 80160-1070 USA

ISBN 978-1-945508-03-5

First Edition
Printed in the United States of America

Available on amazon.com and other retail outlets
Available on Kindle and other devices
Available as an eBook and print paperback
Available as an audiobook in winter, 2018

Pronunciation Key

Atira	a-TEER-ah
Circle	The hub of the camp, fires
Dody	DOE-dee
Dorina	Dor-EE-nah
Durrill	DURR-ill
Eiderdown	EYE-der-down
Erki	ERR-kee
Gadje	GAH-zhe
Gitano	Hee-TAN-oh
Hanzi	HAN-zee
Ito	EE-toe
Jardani	Jar-DAHN-ee
Jilé	Jill-AY
Kamav tut	Kah-mahv-TOOT (I love you)
Kennick	KEN-ick
Kumpania	Koom-pah-NEE-ya
Latcho drom	LAH-cho drahm (Good journey)
Marime	MAH-ree-may (Unclean, impure)
Melodia	Meh-LOW-dee-ah
Miri	MEER-ee
Misto	MEES-toe (Exclamation of joy)
Nais Tuke	Nice TOO-kah (Thank you)
Pesha	PESH-uh
Phuro Marko	FOO-roe MAR-koe
Rafa	RAH-fah
Rom Baro	Rahm BARE-oh (Tribal chief)
Roma	Roe-mah
Romanes	RAH-mah-ness (Roma language)
Rupa	ROO-pah
Ruslo	ROOS-low
Sabann	Sah-BAHN
Sandu	San-DOO
Ucho	OO-choe
Vai	Vie

DEDICATION

This is dedicated to my daughter, Jalena Penaligon, who has now designed eight book covers for me. Thank you, Jalena, for your patience and awesome creativity.

ACKNOWLEDGEMENTS

Thanks to my fabulous critique group for their encouragement and their keen insights and observations. Thanks to my husband, John, for his patience and sense of humor. Special thanks to Kay Bergstrom and Pam Nowak.

When her father, chief of the Gypsies died, headstrong Etti lost her status, but none of her spirit. She's the first woman to race her horse in Marseilles. She survives attacks by her drunken brothers, the very men who should have protected her, and she's turned the head of Rafa, a delicious Gitano Gypsy from Spain with a tantalizing sense of adventure and breathtaking passion. She dares to break all the rules to pursue Rafa--and the exciting life she craves.

Etti's Intended is a prequel to the bestselling and award-winning Coin Forest series. It's set in fifteenth century England and France during the so-called Gypsy Honeymoon Period, when Gypsies were welcomed, their travels even financed by the nobility in the western European countries in which they traveled.

Pronunciation Key – see last page of book for pronunciation of character names and Romani vocabulary.

Etti's Intended

Chapter 1
Cologne, 1401

Etti passed the Gypsy tribe's blazing bonfire, its flames lighting the musicians and dancers in the Circle. She passed the steaming stew kettles and the tight cluster of grown women who watched them, none of whom were her friends. She looked straight ahead. Had she met the women's eyes, she knew what she would see. Mistrust. Unease.

Censure.

Still, she stood tall as she passed them. She was the daughter of Danior, beloved leader of the tribe. Since his death last year, however, her family's standing had suffered, and she held her bloodline before her like the paper shield it was. She knew how quickly it could crumple—her brothers shared Danior's bloodline, too, yet they had been banished.

She took the path toward the river and her uncle's wagon, where she belonged now that her parents had died. Her pet hedgehog, Pesha would be there. Smaller than a rabbit with sparkling ebony eyes and quilled back, his whiskers would wiggle and his antics would cheer her. She would feed him, laugh at his lively spirit and playfulness, and allow herself to forget their displeasure. Unlike the people in her *kumpania,* Pesha was always glad to see her.

As she neared the wagon, someone exited from the rear canvas door. Shadowed from the afternoon sun, he carried something in his hands and hurried down the steps. She recognized his blackberry-stained tunic and torn green hose. A boy of 11, same age as her. "Pobi," she said. "What do you have there?"

Instead of answering, he darted away.

Etti's heart seized. She yanked the canvas door aside. In the corner of the wagon, the door to Pesha's cage yawned, open.

The empty pen screamed at her, stripping her bones of all warmth. She'd lost her parents, her friends, and now—Pesha was gone.

The only creature who loved her. "Pobi!" Etti cried out and lifted her skirts. She could outrun him, had proved it many times. She lunged toward him, screaming. "Stop! Give him back!"

Other boys were running with Pobi. "We're going to eat him for supper," they taunted. "That's what hedgehogs are for," another boy yelled. "Not for pets."

She chased them, shouting, uncaring of the stones that punished her bare feet.

Pobi slipped in a rut in the road and stumbled.

Etti took advantage, pushing herself to run even faster. She raised her fist, pounding Pobi's back. She grabbed his tunic with her other hand and they fell together in the mud.

Pesha had curled in a tight defensive ball, as hedgehogs did when threatened. He slid from Pobi's grasp. Another boy caught Pesha. The stiff quills on his back stabbed him. He cried out and dropped the little creature.

Pesha unrolled, his body the length of Etti's foot. He scurried into the bushes, his short, skinny legs racing.

"You snake!" Etti wiped mud from her face and punched him in the back again. "He's my pet."

"He's a rat, and you sleep with him." Another boy said. "You're evil."

"Now he's gone, and you can't sleep with him any more," Pobi said. "You know animals have secret powers." He narrowed his eyes. "Like they say, you're cursed."

"I hate you!" Etti raised her arm and smacked Pobi in the jaw.

"Hey, hey!" A man's voice behind her. He grabbed her under the arms and lifted her away from Pobi. "Enough of this. Stop now." He turned Etti to face him, and his eyes widened. "Just as I thought. Under all the mud, you're a girl."

"So?" Etti wriggled free. "Who are you?"

"I'm Rafa. I'm from Catalonia. I arrived yesterday. What's amiss?"

He smiled in amusement, his white teeth perfect, his face the most comely she had ever seen. His striking brown eyes smiled, and his thick black hair tumbled over shoulders bulging with muscles as he held her in check.

She had seen Rafa when he and his family joined them on their way to the horse fair in Cologne. His voice had changed, and she guessed he was a few years older than she was. He had looked attractive from a distance. Now closer to him, she found breathing more difficult. She had never seen such a magnificent man.

Pobi struggled from the mud. "She keeps a hedgehog in her wagon. It's not natural. She's cursed, so we took it away from her."

The setting sun lit his brown eyes a warm copper color. *Rafa.* His name sounded light as a summer wind. He was strong, and manly. He would protect Etti from the boys' cruelty.

"Were you cooking it for dinner, little bug?" He asked.

"I'm not a bug. I'm Etti," she said.

"Yeah, she is a bug," another boy said. "Strange as a one-legged spider!"

"They stole him from me. *Charros!*" she cried, calling the boys thieves. "And I wouldn't cook him. They know that. His name is Pesha."

"Whose name?" Rafa asked.

"My hedgehog. Pesha. He's my pet." She said it with defiance, even though she knew her people believed most creatures to be tainted. Cats, rats, foxes were all called "dirty dogs." Even the tribal pups were not allowed to enter the wagons or to ever lick one's face. Hedgehogs were revered in other tribes but in Etti's, only as a food source.

Rafa's eyes widened. He looked to Pobi and the boys and back at her. He tilted his head, silent for a moment, then laughed. Rather, he melted like fat in the fire, grinning at first, followed by an accidental burp that grew into ripples of laughter. He threw his head back cackling.

"Yeah," Pobi said. "And she sings to the moon—and fights like a boy. You saw her." His friends laughed, creating a taunting chorus of amusement.

Catching the look on Etti's face, Rafa covered his mouth and made a rude and obvious effort to recover. "You keep a hedgehog as a pet?"

His careless words stung her. He was rich with beauty, but vain, like a well-formed tree with no fruit.

Etti punched him in the gut, throwing her full weight into it.

Rafa saw it coming and braced himself.

Etti's knuckles stung, as if she had punched a tightly packed bag of flour. She tightened her jaw to keep from crying out.

"It's not your affair, *Gitano*," she said through the pain, using a scornful tone when calling him a Spanish Gypsy. "Go back to Spain." No point searching for Pesha now. She would return and find him later. Spinning on her heel, she shook the mud from her skirt and stumbled in the soaked, rutted path back to her wagon.

Later, when the moon had risen high, Etti rested in her *eiderdown*. She had placed her comfortable bed next to her cousin, Atira, under the stars. Nineteen, with the womanly curves Etti yearned for, Atira was the talk of Etti's kumpania. A marriage counsel followed the horse fair. Ruslo, their tribal king and his council, would choose husbands for the girls of marriageable age. Gossip charged the tribe as her Roma relatives speculated which lucky man would be chosen to be Atira's husband.

Atira was the tribe's best *dukker of the vast*. Her hands soared like doves in the air when she told fortunes for the peasants in the small villages they passed during their travels. Now, she was snoring.

Etti listened for sounds from her Uncle Dody and Aunt Ucho. They slept in their eiderdown on the grass a few yards away, under the wagon's awning. Her uncle didn't snore, but Aunt Ucho some of times did. Etti heard nothing, but she could wait no longer. She needed to find Pesha before daybreak or she would be forced to leave without him when the kumpania packed and left for Cologne.

Slipping from her eiderdown, Etti walked away from her uncle's wagon.

Wherever they stopped on their travels, they selected a place that offered water and shade. The camp always surrounded the main bonfire. Fire gave them more than warmth. It served to dispel the darkness, provide light for cooking, and warded away predators. Thus their tents and wagons formed a circle around the flames.

The tribe gathered in the Circle to eat, play games, share information and settle differences.

The Circle showed standing within the tribe. Ruslo's tent was great, so large it could hold ten horses. His tent was positioned at one end of the big fire, also site of smaller cooking fires. Ruslo and his closest advisors kept their wagons there. The food was more abundant at the great tent, so the tribal dogs most often slept there, as well. The young and new families and less important Gypsies camped farthest from the big tent.

Uncle Dody's wagon, next to the great tent when Etti's father, was chief, had been moved farther away after Ruslo became chief.

It was from this position that Etti crept away from the wagons. The tribal dogs were used to traffic as the women went to their treed area to relieve themselves during the night, so they did not bark at her now. She must find Pesha and get him back before dawn—and do it without waking anyone.

The night had a bite to it, colder than Marseilles, where they spent most of the winter when not traveling. Etti's feet sank in the mud, chilling her. Taking a wide path, she stayed outside the perimeter of the camp, checking hedgerows where Pesha may be foraging for food. Looking around to be sure she was alone, she called for him.

At the site of her struggle with Pobi, she heard a distant growling from the tribal dogs. Her heart hurried. They were good hunters. They would chase after Pesha, try to flush him from the bushes or hedgerows. She tucked her scarf high in a tree. If Pesha was nearby, he would smell her scent. Knowing how Pesha loved apples, she draped her shawl in the fork of a tree in an apple orchard some hundred yards from the river. She passed the time walking from one site to the other, softly calling Pesha's name.

The night spent itself and the sounds of the awakening camp startled her. "Pesha!" She raised her voice and hurried to the apple tree. No sign of him.

She plucked an apple from the tree and took a bite. It was not ripe, and so bitter she coughed. She spit the fruit into her hand and waved it, sending out the scent. "Pesha. Apple. Come little boy."

5

The sounds of breaking camp brought a new urgency. She crooned to him, following the curve of the hedgerows.

No response. Her vision wavered, distorted by tears. Someone must have found him. Killed him. His quills may not protect him from a badger. Chest heavy, she retrieved her scarf and ran one last time to the orchard for her shawl. "Pesha! Pesha!"

She saw a movement in the corner of her eye. "Pesha?"

Her pet scurried down the tree and scuttled to her.

"Pesha!" she cried. She picked him up and he rolled into a ball. His pink footpads and face appeared to float in the little bowl he created with his quilled back. Rolled up, he fit in the palm of her hand, making his tiny *cheske-cheske* sounds, whiskers wiggling. She kissed his nose.

"Etti." Her Uncle Dody's reprimanding voice reached her. "What in God's name are you doing? We're ready to leave. The whole kumpania is waiting on you."

The thin daylight revealed her uncle's scowl. She had been so distracted she had missed the early light of dawn. Donning her shawl, she hurried to him.

Her uncle stood, legs parted, arms crossed in front of his broad chest. His once black hair had gone to snow, as he liked to say, at the temples, but his mustache remained black. His ever-present toosticca stuck out of his mouth almost two inches. He whittled wooden sticks to clean his teeth, wider at one end and carved into a small tree at the other end. He'd taken to twirling it in his mouth during quiet moments when sitting by the fire or drinking ale. Now, the toosticca lay still in his mouth and he frowned at her.

"I found him, Uncle. He came to me." It was only then she noticed her uncle wasn't alone. Pobi stood near her uncle with his friends. Her Aunt Ucho, Atira and several more stood watching her.

And Rafa.

Her skin grew hot with a greasy sheen of guilt, as if she'd been marked as a thief. She had hoped to find Pesha secretly, not drawing any attention to either of them. Instead they stared, their gazes darting from her to Pesha, then to her uncle to see what he would do.

"What did I say about her?" Pobi's voice needled her, taunting. "You saw it with your own eyes. When did you ever, ever see a hedgehog run to you, willingly?" He made a vomiting sound. "And she kissed it!"

People mumbled.

"It's a spell," Pobi said.

Uncle Dody stepped forward, waving Pobi back and glowering at her. He removed the tree toosticca and slipped it in his girdle. "Move along! You have delayed the kumpania, and our arrival at the horse fair. Ruslo is not pleased. Atira stored your eiderdown. Get into the wagon so we can leave."

Rafa gave Etti a sideways glance, his brows furrowed in disapproval. "The roads have already delayed us. Now this. The more we linger the more likely we'll lose a chance to sell our horses." He glanced at Atira, stood tall and thrust out his chest. "We can't miss the buyers because of a…" He twisted his mouth and looked down on Etti as if she had two heads. "Because of a silly girl and her pet hedgehog."

Uncle Dody's face darkened, and he pulled at his tunic. "I know," he said, not offering any support. "Her father allowed her to bring it into their wagon, and she begged to keep it. He had a weak spot for Etti and allowed it, may his soul find joy in the afterlife." He shook his head. "But it's not natural."

The others disbanded and returned to their wagons, and Etti hurried past Rafa with Pesha. She cursed her earlier attraction to him. He was comely—so long as he didn't open his stupid, ill-informed, childish, bully mouth. Etti added the silent insults to the drinking, quarrelsome reputation of Rafa's tribe, all likely well earned. She burned him with her gaze, hoping his hair would catch on fire. She yearned to shoot a few of Pesha's quills deep into his careless, dumb neck.

"You'd do best to let it go free," he said.

She wouldn't give him the pleasure of looking back at him. "You'd do best to tend to your own business," she said. "You're too stupid to understand, Gitano. Stay away from him," Etti growled, surprised at the sound of her own voice, deep and guttural. "You stay away from Pesha, and from all of us."

Chapter 2
Six years later
Marseilles, France, 1407

"I can dance—but only if it's with you," Etti said, curving her mouth up on one side, showing her dimples. She winked when she said the last word.

Etti's cousin Melodia struck the wagon's driving bench and laughed, a musical giggle worthy of her name. "No, silly. You blinked both eyes again."

"Did not."

Etti fanned her face. "It's so hot, and we've been sitting here forever." Etti drove the wagon today, if you could call it that. Theirs and dozens of others clogged the road for a half mile ahead, all tended by people waiting to enter the Marseilles horse fair. The men had gone ahead to register, leaving the women to wait and swelter, and eventually settle the wagons.

Melodia had joined Etti's kumpania in Hungary several weeks ago. Melodia and her family were true Roma, but their skin was much lighter, and their hair and eyes a light brown. She was wiser than her fifteen years, wise enough to teach Etti how to charm the boys. "You're so much older than me, and you're so good with the horses," she said. "Why can't you do something simple like wink?"

"Because the boys fear me. If I winked at them they would shrink in fear they'd grow four eyes."

Melodia laughed. "The marriage council is only a fortnight away, and you're among the girls to wed this year. How will you show your preference if you can't wink?"

At seventeen, Etti would be matched to a husband this summer. "And who would I prefer? Pobi?" Etti shuddered. He had grown taller and even more condemning since the awful time in Cologne when she had finally found Pesha.

"This is a wonderful opportunity for you to meet some men here, in Marseilles. Before the matchmaking. They haven't heard the rumors," she said delicately. "And you're so pretty, Etti. They'll be watching. You need to show interest."

Because of the size of their kumpania, they met with several other tribes to make pairings of unrelated girls and boys. Horse fairs were well attended, so the chiefs scheduled marriage councils after the fairs.

Only the Gypsy kings and their closest advisors were allowed to pair couples. Since the men decided, the only hope for a Gypsy girl to be paired with the boy she liked was to let him know she favored him beforehand. Amorous gazes and playful conversations were forbidden between boys and girls, making it difficult to communicate interest, especially if the boy wasn't the brightest star in the sky.

A carefully timed, private wink allowed for a wordless message of interest that would escape the ever-watching elders. Once he saw the wink from a girl he liked, the favored boy petitioned support from his father. The father would then present the boy's case to one of the leaders, where the pairing was finalized.

When her father died over six years ago, Etti lost considerable standing as the daughter of a *Rom Baro*, their tribe's chief. Her daily habits were suspect, and without her father's protection, she was subjected to increased reproach. She slept with her pet hedgehog, a small animal traditionally destined for the tribe's frying pans, not a young girl's bed. She was so free-thinking many whispered about her, and she was considered undesirable. If she didn't want to be traded away to another tribe, she'd better learn some charming behaviors. Winking was one of them.

"All right, one more time," Melodia said. "Wink your right eye."

"It's suffering hot." Etti wiped sweat from her forehead. "I'm going to melt like cheese."

"Forget the heat. We're in Marseilles," Melodia said. "You'll see an army of men here! Come on. Show me you can wink your right eye."

"Oh, all right." Etti winked.

"No, that's a blink again. You used both eyes."

Etti sighed. "It's no use."

"Try again. I know. Here, watch this." Melodia looked up at the sodden, grey sky and pressed her finger to her left eyelash, trapping it. "See? Now it can't move. You do it. Good. Now wink with your right eye."

Etti did.

Melodia cried out. "Yes! Do it again!"

Etti repeated it three times. Each time, she relaxed the left eyelid and moved the right one, and she sensed the different muscles. "I think I have it! Look!" She winked.

Melodia clapped her hands. "You did it! You're ready for tonight!"

"Now all I have to do is horrify one of the boys by winking at him." Etti laughed.

"Etti, you're a good person. You're a good friend. You have much to offer."

Such kind words had not touched her ears in months. Etti's throat seized, and she bit back tears. She finally found her voice. "*Nais Tuke*, Melodia." Thank you. "I'm sorry to be so slow." She paused. "I'm worried. I don't like any of the boys in our tribe any more than they like me. And how am I to know which of the men I meet here are honorable, and would treat me well? Look at what happened to Atira." She shuddered, thinking about her beautiful cousin's bad match.

"Don't be sad, Etti. You'll meet someone here. I have a good feeling about it."

Later, the sun had broken free and they reached the fair gates, manned by two guards. Etti stood tall on the wagon as she faced the guards. "I'll be riding in the race. Which way to the stables?"

The taller guard looked skeptical. "You? You're racing in the Mile?"

"Yes." Etti smiled. The Mile. While Marseilles wasn't as big as the other horse fairs, the race was still a full mile, and it filled an important role in the fair. Women were a rarity in racing but Etti had proven herself, first to her uncle, and then to the tribe as an effective trainer and rider. She would be the only woman in the race. She would join the young men and race Red, a fine palfrey, a mare with speed and grace.

The Mile served a larger purpose than simple victory. Provided the winning horses passed physical inspections and weren't injured during the race, they would command the highest prices at the sale the next day.

The shorter guard raised a brow and gave her a smile. "I've never seen a woman in the race. If you're as nimble as you are beautiful, little lady, you'll win, too." He winked.

Etti sucked in a breath, and her face heated.

The guard gave her directions to the stables and camping areas. She thanked him and turned the team past them.

"Did you see that!" Melodia's eyes widened. "He winked at you."

Once they were far enough away, Etti fanned herself. She had never been winked at by a man other than her father. "Only because he doesn't know I'm odd." His flirtation stunned her. "He said I was beautiful." Etti considered herself quite common, and the men in her tribe reinforced that. They winked at women like Atira, but never at her.

"Did you wink back, Etti?"

"Nay. He's *Gadje*." It was the word Gypsies used to describe anyone different from them. "You must watch them. They're different from us in many ways besides their language and skin color. Remember our meeting?"

Melodia nodded. Before arriving at the fair the mothers and grandmothers had summoned the young women in the tribe and issued warnings about proper conduct. "We're to blend in, be not shameless, and not cluster.

Etti's tribe had traveled farther west than other Romani tribes. Most of the peasants and country people welcomed them for their skills with horses and metal work, and many others were fascinated with their music and fortune telling. Some of the monks and nobles would provide food and welcome them to their monasteries and manors. Over the years of traveling, Etti had learned a smattering of several languages. The people seemed more willing to look past the Gypsies' different clothing and ways when she spoke in their native tongue.

There were others, though, who could not, and they may pose a big problem. The *Gadje* feared groups of Gypsies so, before entering a large city or a fair such as this, Ruslo would split them up. Smaller groups were less threatening. He also warned the men about excessive drinking and fighting.

The elders warned the young women to avoid provocative postures and gestures. The musicians were to avoid the louder, faster songs, and the girls were forbidden to dance.

"We'll be good girls today," Etti said. "We'll find Aunt Ucho and settle the wagon, and go to the river where they're cleaning the horses." Etti knew much about horses and how to note their conformation, their weaknesses. She would scout them and learn which ones to watch and pace during the race.

Tents, merchant stands and tables poured over entire fields, now overrun with people of every size and garb. Children ran through the narrow roads that meandered through spacious sectioned off areas for camping, animal enclosures and horse pens. The workhorses were kept in these areas. The sale horses were in the larger stables to the north.

They joined dozens of tents and wagons camped in a series of circles, each one a different Romani tribe, each one dotted with fire pits. A network of paths threaded through each circle, and led to the next tribe's wagons, and the next.

Melodia's eyes grew wide. "It's so big. I never expected so many people."

"You saw Cologne, but you were too young to remember it," Etti said. "It's much bigger than this, but this is fine. Really fine." People, people everywhere, mothers and children and the elders, drawing water from wells, filling pots for meals, bringing tables from the wagons. "Look there, at that woman's hair."

Melodia followed Etti's gaze to the tall Gadje woman with short hair, almost as short as a man's, and all curls. "And her dress. Her arms are naked all the way up to her shoulder. Outrageous!"

Merchant stands sprang up like flowers throughout the camps, bursting with colorful fabrics, barrels of ale and wine, smoked meats, vegetables, and barking, begging dogs. Babies cried, monkeys screamed from their cages, and women hurried by, wearing bright scarves so long they almost brushed the muddy roads. Etti grew dizzy from all the sights and sounds.

She spotted wagons from her kumpania and guided the wagon into an available space between her Aunt Ucho and her cousin's sister, Vai.

"Etti! We're so glad to see you," Vai said. "We were worried."

"I couldn't count all the wagons in front of us," Etti said. "They should have had more guards at the gates to check us all in."

Aunt Ucho took Etti aside and lowered her voice. "Your brothers are here. We thought they had found you."

Etti's fingers tingled, and her mouth went dry. Durril and Jilé. They were over ten years older than Etti, hot tempered and violent. She remembered many nights of raised voices and fights. Etti learned later, as she grew old enough to understand, that when they drank heavily, they became brutal. It caused a rift between the brothers and her parents, and one night led to a full tribal brawl, with many injuries and hard feelings.

Ruslo banished Etti's brothers from the tribe, and nothing more had been heard from them since. Etti's mother lived with a broken heart until seven years ago. Both her father and mother had grown ill and died within days of each other from a sickness that took six others from her tribe.

"You should bow out of the race," her aunt said. "There are bad feelings, still, with those two. They're dangerous."

Dangerous in many ways. Argumentative and aggressive, they threatened anyone less powerful, and they could pose a big problem for Etti and her search for a good husband. No honorable man would want a couple of wild boars for relatives. "No!" Etti cried out, her voice louder than she had intended. "Sorry, Aunt Vai, but I won't let them take this away from me. I've worked too hard getting ready for the race."

Melodia ran up to them. "This is wonderful. All so wonderful. I can't wait to see the horses. Can we go now?"

Etti looked back at the wagon and thought of Pesha. He would be safe there. After almost losing Pesha in Cologne, she had improvised a drawer below the heavy chest in the wagon. Pesha loved hiding places and small spaces. Atira and her friends still thought Etti strange for befriending an animal that was one of their main summer food sources. They had never accepted her pet, and if any of them looked particularly hungry, she worried they might steal Pesha and cook him, as Atira often threatened to do.

They tethered the horses and secured the wagon. Etti hurried to her Aunt Ucho. "Will you watch the wagons? I need to prepare Red for the race."

Vai crossed her arms. "Don't walk alone here. And you must take Miri with you."

Miri, Atira's oldest child, was five and painfully shy. "Why can't Atira take her? She's her mother," Etti said.

"I'll come, too." Atira appeared from behind Aunt Ucho's wagon.

Atira. Etti shuddered. Her cousin had borne three babes since Cologne, and it had hardened her. After the last babe she sent her husband away from their bed. Rumors were she threatened him with a knife and cursed him with a spell involving his manhood. As if to support the tale, she had not become with child since, and her husband did not stray with any other woman.

"All right," Etti said.

They made their way through the roads and arrived at the river. She looked at every turn for her brothers until it occurred to her they were likely sleeping. From what she remembered, they were as nocturnal as Pesha. The afternoon suddenly seemed warmer and more inviting.

The men washed horses at a turn in the river where it widened to the size of a lake, then narrowed and deepened as it took the next turn, twenty-five yards away. Large groups of people sat on the gentle slope, watching the horses. Each horse was ridden by a young Rom. The men rode without saddles, controlling the horses with their thighs and voices.

A group of men standing on the shoreline looked their way. Accustomed to the way Atira caught men's attention, Etti glanced her way, but Atira was looking at Etti. Etti looked back at the men.

Melodia tugged Etti's sleeve. "They're looking at you, Etti. See, I told you you were pretty."

Her father had called Etti pretty, but he had a soft spot for her. Her grandmother, too, but she'd dismissed it because she was so old her eyes were fading. Etti wondered at that, and her face grew warm with the unfamiliar feeling of being desired. It was pleasant, but unsettling. How would she know if she'd found the right one?

What if she attracted a man who would be a bad match, as Atira had done? She lowered her gaze and returned her attention to the horses.

The water swirled around them. Horses entering the lake were dusty and muddy. Those who had entered the depths of the lake emerged cleaner. Still others stood patiently while the men scrubbed and rinsed them, revealing clean, sleek coats of greys and rich browns.

The men rode bare-chested, practical as the water grew deep enough at points that the horses were forced to swim. At that point, balance became a challenge and the men clung to the horses' manes to stay mounted.

Drenched in the lake water, the men's chests sparkled in the sunlight, muscles glistening under a dotted cape of diamonds. It was the most sensual of all the tribe's activities, a sight not wasted on the tribe's women. They sat in clusters on the riverbank. The horses on display and the public setting relieved the women of the tribe's strict rules about staring, and they took full advantage of it. Etti and Melodia watched their bug-eyed appreciation, looked at each other, and smiled.

Next to them, another woman couldn't resist staring. Atira, known for her disappointment in the marriage council's choice for her husband, was transfixed. Her posture, so often stooped as she dealt with her children, was perfect. She pulled her scarf back, which revealed her lush black hair and cleared her eyes so she could better see. She held her back straight, her head high, her breasts proud. Her brows were raised, and her light brown eyes held a burning, faraway look in them, a curious, deep longing. She watched the men with interest instead of her usual disdain.

Atira's hand drifted to the base of her neck and she softly rubbed her collarbone.

Something in her gesture registered with Etti. It revealed a side of Atira she had not seen before, one of vulnerability and wistfulness. Being so close to having a husband named for herself, as well, it took Etti's breath. Cruel though she could be, Atira had likely had dreams. She may have had her heart set on someone else in the tribe, only to learn Vano had been chosen for her. Etti resisted reaching out and embracing her prickly cousin.

A splashing disturbance distracted Etti. By the river inlet, a sleek stallion rebelled against the deep water. It reared up, trying to rid itself of the rider. The rider's long, black hair fell to his shoulders, the wet curls dripping water down his chest. The water continued to flow in rivulets, rolling over his lean body. Soaked from the river, his brown hose clung to his skin, revealing well-defined muscles. He squeezed his thighs around the stallion's flank, refusing to be thrown. His spirit matched the stallion's, determined, strong and powerful. His profile revealed a straight nose and clean, strong jawline, and his laughter in the struggle showed even white teeth.

Etti felt a strong pull deep inside and moved closer. *He might be the one.*

"What do you see?" Melodia's voice sounded muted, as if it came from an underwater cave, distant. After a pause, she must have followed Etti's gaze to the beautiful man who rode the stallion. "Oh. Oh, he is wonderful."

The stallion swerved in the water and its rider faced her. His cheekbones were high and well-shaped, his brows...

The pleasurable warmth coursing through her body dissolved. What had moments before enchanted her now stunned her. "It's Rafa."

Chapter 3

Rafa settled Black Tide and led him into more shallow water. He brushed the dust and mud chips from his mane. "There, there you are, big boy. You're going to shine, even if you tried to drown me, you grumpy runner."

His friend Jardani brought his horse near and started brushing it. "Did you see her?"

"I don't miss a pretty woman. Of course I did. Along with every other man with red blood in his veins." The tunic hugged her high breasts and revealed her full hips, sights he had admired until the damned stallion had made him bite his tongue.

Rafa usually preferred taller women, yet this one was a marvel. The finest painter could not capture the full effect of her softness, her beauty. Her presence stole the space between them, and his breath, as well. But it was her eyes—wide, crescent, innocent, yet lively and engaged. And her face—like an oval jewel. She wore no scarf, so she was as yet unmarried, though why she would still be unwed was a mystery. Mayhap in spite of her beauty, she was a viper. Or simple-minded. He wished he had possessed more time to watch her before she dashed away.

* * *

"Slow down. I can barely keep up with you," Melodia said.

Etti did not break her stride. They soon arrived at the sale stables and found Red I her stall.

"But I don't understand," Melodia said. "You met him years ago, and he made fun about Pesha. It is unusual to have a hedgehog as a pet. We all know that. It was the first he heard of it, and it was his first response. You never saw him again, so he didn't have a chance to give you his second response."

Etti would not reveal the particulars of her embarrassment. Her humiliation. "I don't have time for this. I need to get Red. Get her cleaned and ready for the race tomorrow." Rafa would be gone from the river by the time she arrived there. His bare chest, his legs still lingered in her memory, and her heart still thudded in a most alarming manner.

What was he doing here? She knew the answer, of course. He was related to some of her tribe members. His kumpania was also known for its accomplished horsemanship and racing. Of course he would be here.

I will not let him distract me from my race. She would gird herself for the next time they met. Remember how he fawned at Atira. *Remember how he laughed at your terror, made fun of your misery at losing Pesha.* Her disappointment burned, even after all these years. How had she thought of him? Ah, yes, a tree with no fruit. Pretty, but no heart.

* * *

Etti tickled Pesha on the stomach, her fingers running through his soft fur. His left leg kicked. She must have touched an itchy spot. She scratched it for him and he rolled out of his ball, showing his skirt of soft fur below his quill-covered back. He scooted into his drawer. Stuffed full with wood shavings, he burrowed his way in until he was no longer visible.

Not for long though. The sun had set, and Pesha would be active through the night. She attached his cage to the drawer to keep him restrained and safe. She placed two of his favorite toy balls in the corner of the cage. Normally she would enjoy his frolicking as he played, but outside the wagon her tribe was celebrating around the big fire. She covered the cage with a corner of her eiderdown and left the wagon.

Once outside, Melodia ran up to her, her thin thighs flashing in the firelight.

"Finally you're back." Her eyes sparkled, huge. "There must be a hundred people here, Etti. And the pigs! The horse fair people brought two for us. Two big ones! Wonderful. The younger boys were still picking at the carcasses until Vai and Aunt Ucho chased them away so they could strip it. The older boys are throwing stones but they're going to race ponies up the road soon." She stopped to catch her breath. "And the Gitanos are on their way. Etti!" She lowered her voice. "You'll see Rafa again."

Etti shook her head and walked toward the fires. The horse fair provided separate areas for the Gadjes and Gypsies. The Gadjes pitched their tents and wagons on the north side of the fair. The Gypsies settled on the south side.

Each kumpania had been provided its own site, complete with a grassy area in the middle that served as their Circle. Looking from the top of the hill earlier at sunset, between the Gadjes and Gypsies, there must have been twenty great fires. As Melodia had said, hundreds of Gypsies.

And among those hundreds, a tribe of Gitanos. And Rafa. She had silently replayed the rude comments Rafa had made in Cologne and recalled his callousness toward Pesha. He was a feast for the eyes, but he would not torment her senses again. Ever. "I have no interest in seeing him."

Melodia's laugh tinkled out again. "You're so silly, Etti. You should have seen your face when you watched him." She laughed again. "You should see your face now."

"You're the silly one. He's with the Gitanos. He won't be visiting us."

"Oh, yes he will. I saw his face, too, when he looked at you."

Etti waved her off and continued toward her kumpania and its guests. The bonfire blazed outside Ruslo's massive tent. The Circle had been expanded to make room for mingling, a favorite pastime during the horse fair. This Circle was as large as the lists where tournaments were held. Sparks swirled from the big logs and flew upward in small spires. Like glow flies, they meandered upward and burned themselves out.

The flames lit many faces Etti didn't know, likely visitors from the other kumpanias, scattered among her tribal families.

While the older boys threw rocks, the young men wrestled, stirring old ashes and hay as they tumbled on the ground, grunting and grasping each other.

Feminine laughter came from Vai's wagon. Candlelight cast shadows on the canvas, revealing three profiles. Atira's nimble hands gestured as she talked, and the high voice, short stature and upturned nose made it easy to identify shy little Miri. The third profile was Atira's husband's mother, Liza.

After Atira had incapacitated her husband, Vano, with her curse, she had left his wagon for her father, Dody's wagon. Concerned about Atira's destructive temper, Ruslo and the elders forbade Atira to be with her children after nightfall unless Vano's mother was present. Poor Atira, but she sounded happy now, with her daughter. They were huddled over the table, talking, and were close enough Etti could hear them.

"It's there." Miri appeared as a silhouette, pointing at something.

Atira slid something across the table. "And now?"

"There."

"How about now?" They were playing bowls, a guessing game with bones.

"Do you play bowls, too?" A masculine voice came to her from behind.

Etti's quick intake of breath surprised her as much as the deep vibrancy of Rafa's voice. She tried to recall the chants of denial she'd been practicing, and failed. Turning against a tide of jumbled emotions, she faced him.

"I'm sorry. I didn't mean to startle you," Rafa said.

"Hello. We saw you in the river today." Melodia covered her mouth, her eyes wide. "Um, hello," she repeated. "I... I have to help, um, do something." She abandoned Etti.

"I saw you, too," Rafa said. "At the river. Twice. Once when I was cleaning Dark Tide—my horse—and once when you were cleaning your horse." Rafa couldn't take his eyes from her face. She was even more lovely up close, with the firelight dancing across the soft curves of her generous, proportioned features. Her eyes reflected the flames, and the air thickened, drawing him to

20

her. "I wanted to congratulate you for qualifying for the race. I have never seen a woman on the horse program."

She looked uncomfortable, and he rushed on. "I am also taken by your beauty."

"This is most improper, talking alone like this," she said. She cast her eyes down, as a good Gypsy girl would do, but her features were strangely drawn in discomfort. He had given her two compliments and had expected at least a smile for his efforts.

"I respect you, of course. And I admire you," he added.

"Yes, well. Excuse me," she said. Her gaze darted like a colt being bridled for the first time. Rafa shifted his body slightly to the left to slow her retreat.

Her eyes were shadowed, revealing hurt. "I must go."

Her face was tense. He was driven to know her. "What is wrong?"

When she met his gaze, her eyes flashed with anger. "I'm worthy of flattery now? I told you years ago, in Cologne. Stay away from me."

"Cologne?" She must be confusing him with someone else. "I don't understand. Did we meet in Cologne?"

"You were favoring Atira with your attention, if you'll recall. When you weren't condemning me for having a pet hedgehog."

Rafa looked into his memory, trying to reconcile the bony little girl with the muddied face in Cologne, with this woman's beautiful face and perfect, flowing hair. "You have changed so much." His words stumbled out, awkward, but he couldn't think of anything else to say. He stated the obvious. "I'm sorry. I—"

"I was crying because the boys stole my pet, and you laughed at me. You even told me to get rid of him."

"I'm sorry," he repeated. Her silence continued, making the moment heavy. "It was a long time ago." He struggled to fill the silence. "I wanted to wish you well for the race tomorrow."

She fixed him with a stare. Something more compelling than her beauty made him hopeful. Would she at the least consider his apology?

"The more you look, the more you see," she said, waving him aside as she strode away from him.

* * *

21

Later, Melodia returned and joined Etti at the fire, but Etti refused to greet her.

"I'm sorry," Melodia said. "My tongue got tied up, and I had to go."

Etti glared at her. "You left me alone with him, after all I told you."

"Simply trying to help."

Etti shifted on the blanket, the words she and Rafa had shared echoing in her mind.

"What did he say?" Melodia asked.

"He apologized for being so cruel in Cologne."

"Wonderful! And what did you say?"

"I said, 'Thank you.'" And added an over-worn remark. What had gotten into her? *The more you look, the more you see.* It was a proverb her mother used to remind Etti when people judged the Rom harshly—at times when the nobility and priests were kind to Gypsies, but the peasants were hateful and distrusting. "At least he's gone. Don't leave me alone with him again."

At Melodia's contrite expression, Etti softened her voice. "There are many other fine men here—some from kumpanias as far away as Burgundy and Bohemia. Who knows who will be interested in me? I haven't forgotten the marriage council, so I will be looking. Thanks to you, I know what to do if I find one that deserves a good wink." She executed a perfect one.

Melodia laughed, and Etti turned her attention back to the fire, thoughts swirling. She hoped Rafa would return to his own kumpania. This was her chance to look for a man who pleased her. She needed to meet him soon enough to have at the least a few days to get to know him and learn about his reputation and temperament. She would look for a gentle, good-natured man like her father.

A disturbing thought chilled her, though, and she scanned the shadows with a sense of dread. The later it became, the more likely Durril and Jilé would seek her out, and they would bring trouble.

Rupa, Aunt Ucho and other women from Etti's tribe had gathered, getting acquainted with the ladies from Navarre. A group of children threw pinecones into the fire, squealing when the cones sparkled and ignited. Two older girls clapped hands and sang to Atira's young girls.

The men squatted in small groups or sat on stumps. The smell of roast pig still lingered. The feast had included pig, chicken and sausages, and more than a little ale. The tribal dogs growled, protecting their bones. Men from the other campsites had joined them. Uncle Dody arrived, slid his tree stick in his mouth and started the stories.

The ale barrels grew empty and new ones were tapped. The noise level grew in their camp and the surrounding ones so that the whole of the horse fair was pulsing with stories and laughter. Spirits grew light and free as only Gypsy spirits could.

Etti hugged herself, immersed in the pleasures of summer. It was the time of fairs and travel and making new friends—friends who may find Etti pleasing, not odd. Mayhap even an interesting man.

The night deepened, and the moon rose higher. Vai's son, Kem, sang a toast to the Rom Baro of the Dusseldorf kumpania. His song started the *patshivaki djilia*, the friendship songs, one of Etti's favorite Circle traditions, made even more grand by the number of Rom gathered. Kem's fingers caressed the strings of the gittern and his voice rumbled, deep and strong. Other men joined in with harmony, and from across the road, more men sang as they joined the Circle. They sang of an ancient Romani family everyone knew, and the shared story brought them together, spanning the generations.

Kem started a new song of Etti's father and his days as the Rom Baro of Etti's kumpania. He had led the tribe in safe travels through five great nations, and his horse training methods had brought respect and recognition to them throughout the region. Kem finished the song and asked Etti to stand. "The daughter of Danior is with us today. Etti. This is her summer for the marriage council."

Etti stood. The young men murmured their greetings and tactfully inspected her. One was tall, with light brown hair, but most of them were darker, with black hair and admiring brown eyes. Etti caught a glimpse of Uncle Dody, his eyes bright with pride, a little moist. Like him, Etti's heart swelled at the words to her father's song. He had been gone so long, she seldom had the chance to wear the cloak of pride at being Danior's daughter, worthy of respect.

Ruslo had likely asked Kem to sing it, to impress upon marriageable men Etti's exalted position in the tribe. They needn't know the tribe secretly thought her strange. Va, she kept a hedgehog as a pet. Va, she liked to sing, by herself, in the moonlight. But because none of the other women in her tribe did so, it did not make her strange.

These men looked interested. Etti smiled, but not too much. Her father had raised her to be dutiful and pure. Doing so honored her father's memory and made her feel closer to him. She also avoided looking at any one particular man and expressed polite pleasure at meeting them. She would give them a closer inspection as the evening progressed.

The singing resumed. This time the songs honored Baba Lolli. Lolli was the wise woman of Etti's tribe. Her white-streaked hair fell in disgruntled knots about her face. Her raisin-like skin shrunk around her mouth, behind which a few old teeth still held stubbornly to her jaw. She gave occasional counsel to Ruslo when he asked for it. She sat, warming her bones by the fire, her eyes sparkling at the praise given her.

Atira left the wagon, dragging the reluctant Miri by the hand, and started singing, too. Her voice was high and a bit shrill, but the harmony was good. She elbowed Miri to join her, but the young girl's eyes bulged so much with fear that Atira let her hide behind her skirts.

Rafa emerged from the night shadows. His gaze closed the distance between them, and heat centered in her belly. She feared the intensity of her reaction to him. Ongoing rejection had thickened her skin. He had judged her and ridiculed her, right along with Pobi and his harsh friends. Now she had grown into a woman and Rafa clearly liked what he saw, she had no doubt he regretted it. Suspicion leaked into her bones, though, and could not be ignored—was Rafa's earlier judgment about her now buried by lust? She looked away from him.

Rafa took a seat next to Etti's uncle. Dody gave him a warm welcome, and they exchanged greetings. Dody slapped Rafa on the back several times, obviously fond of him.

Meanwhile, the older boys abandoned their stone-throwing and joined in the singing. Some clapped. Others danced with passionate, strong moves, pounding the ground and leap-flying

24

over it. Their song quickly faded into yet another physical competition over who could leap the farthest.

Two more mature men joined the group and settled by the ale barrels. Deep vertical wrinkles creased the skin between their eyes and around their mouths, suggesting a lifetime of anger. Their jet black hair and big-boned, thick, muscular bodies reminded her of her father.

A familiar knot of fear settled in her stomach. *Durril and Jilé.* Aunt Ucho had warned her, and here they were, after so many years.

Their dark manner stole the joy and camaraderie from the air. To be banished was to die while living. No one was to speak to them, or especially utter their names. With subtlety, Etti's cousins and kumpania slowly pulled away from her.

"Well, sister." Durril approached Etti, reeking of too much dark-spiced mead. He wore a large golden medallion on his chest, and a horsewhip hung from his leather girdle. Her heart raced, but she held his gaze. Remembering her childhood training against fear, she refused to step back. He laughed, stretching a scar running a good two inches from the corner of his mouth. "Look you, Jilé," he said to his brother. "Little Etti has grown into a woman." He raised an eye to her neck and her hair, neither of which were covered by a scarf. "And still not wed?" He glanced sideways to Jilé, grinning broadly. "Mayhap she's been misbehaving."

Uncle Dody raised a hand and pointed at the brothers. "Leave her. And leave our kumpania."

"Simply wondering about the family, Uncle. Didn't mean harm," Jilé curled his lip up in a caustic smile. "Unlike you, Uncle, I don't mean harm." He slowed his speech, uttering each word purposefully. He raised his hand, showing them the unnatural angle of his broken thumb.

Etti had been forbidden to leave the wagon that long ago night, but had heard the story. Her uncle had prevented Jilé from stabbing his own father during one of his drunken brawls. In the struggle, Jilé's thumb had been broken.

"Still doesn't work," Jilé said. Resentment simmered at the edge of his words, and his glassy stare at Etti's uncle made her shift uncomfortably. He swayed and recovered. "It's good to see you again, Uncle Dody."

Uncle Dody slid the tree stick out of his mouth and onto the barrel that served as a table. He did not respond.

"I've been wanting to challenge you, and where better than at the horse fair?" Jilé smirked and rested his broken thumb on his girdle, also burdened with a horsewhip. "You riding in the Mile?"

Her uncle glared at them, but his visible swallow revealed fear. "No."

"No," Jilé repeated. "You're too old and fat to ride, so let's do something that doesn't take strength." He gestured with his arms to the crowd to retreat. They backed away, clearing the east half of the Circle.

The crowd murmured, and the young men's comments reached Etti. "They're Etti's brothers," one said. "Fie! How unfortunate for her," said another.

Etti's face heated in humiliation, for herself and for Uncle Dody.

Durril glanced around the fire as if assessing the crowd. "Let it go, Jilé. It was a long time ago."

Jilé ignored him. He had been holding a horsewhip, and he suddenly flicked his wrist. It lashed, hissing through the air and, at uncoiling, ended with a booming whip crack.

Uncle Dody jumped aside in time, and it cracked, piercing the air.

"Uncle!" Etti cried. He was no match for her brothers. He was a quiet, peaceful man.

The young men who had earlier smiled at Etti now glanced furtively at her and whispered among themselves. Two pulled knives and turned toward her brothers.

King Ruslo and his huge nephew, Sandu, strode over from the great tent. As often happened between kumpanias, Sandu had been traveling with his uncle for the summer months. Ruslo's hands fisted, muscles tensed, and his brown eyes narrowed in warning. As they neared, Sandu slowed his steps, allowing his uncle to advance and handle the dispute. "You have been banished, both of you," Ruslo said. "Be you gone."

Durril laughed, too drunk to be intimidated by Ruslo's size and ill-tempered stare. He tossed his horsewhip to Dody, challenge in his eyes. "This is but a contest between an uncle and his nephew, Ruslo. We have a story of our own to tell tonight," he said. "It's about this man, Dody. He interrupted a fair fight between my brother and father. He broke my brother's thumb—so badly it wouldn't heal. Now my brother has a lame thumb, but he still thinks it's a fair match. A lame thumb against an old, fat man." He glanced at the men. "Unless Dody's lost his ballocks."

Etti studied her uncle's face. His eyes focused on the fire, busy in thought. The muscle at his jawline tensed. This was now between her uncle and brothers. Ruslo would not interfere in a family dispute. Dody stood tall and tossed a few whip snaps toward Jilé.

"Oh, good. You'll fight." Jilé snapped his whip. It struck Dody on the neck, and an angry line of blood glistened. Before Dody could respond, her brother struck again, and a part of Dody's lower lip dangled.

Rupa and Melodia startled, even Sandu.

"No!" Etti ran between them. "Leave him alone."

Durril seized Etti by the hair and pulled her to him. "Stay out of it, bitch, or you'll be wearing a scar on your own face." He pushed her viciously. She staggered backward, falling on the ground.

Ruslo signaled Sandu to join him. Their chief appeared ready to stop the fight and evict her brothers again. Sandu did not come forward.

A booming whip crack sounded from Dody's left side, and Rafa advanced, his eyes hostile over a tooth-bearing grin that left little room for doubt. "Uncle Dody said I could play in his stead. If," he stressed the word, his voice weighted with challenge, "If you have enough ballocks to fight a man closer to your own age." He had taken the horsewhip from Dody.

Rafa. Etti had never seen a hint of anger from him. His tight features revealed it now. Rafa had never been with her kumpania, and Dody was not his uncle, but he did hold blood relation with some members. Ruslo and his men stood back.

Rafa cracked his whip again, ripping a line of fabric from Jilé's knee to his shinbone.

Jilé struck back, lashing Rafa's arm.

"Good hit," Durril said. "Do it again, Jilé."

Laughing, Jilé danced in front of Rafa. "And that was with a bad thumb, Gitano. Now step out of our family challenge and give Dody the whip."

"You are banished," Rafa said. "Ruslo has ordered you to leave. You are not welcome here." The whip hissed and snapped again.

Etti jumped, but stayed well back.

Jilé wiped at the red streak of blood near his eye. He raised his whip again, but cried out under a shower of rocks.

"Go away," one of the boys said. He and his friends threw hard and a large rock buckled Jilé's knee.

Another boy's stone struck Jilé on the chest. "We don't want you here." A group of boys intensified their attack, pummeling Durril with rocks. "You're drunk. Go empty your guts in the ditch and don't come back." A rock struck Durril's forehead, producing blood.

Durril wiped it from his face. "Come on, Jilé." Jilé looked at Durril's whip, still in Rafa's hand. He read the expression on Rafa's face, hesitated a moment, and seemed to decide against challenging Rafa for it. They left, ducking under the barrage of stones the boys continued to hurl at them as they chased them down the road.

Aunt Vai walked Uncle Dody closer to the fire so they could tend to his wounds.

Etti stood in a fog of confusing emotions. Though troubled at being drawn to Rafa, she was weak-kneed with relief when he had challenged Jilé and taken her uncle out of harm's way.

She approached Rafa and extended her hand to him.

He took it. His touch comforted her, and she noticed she was shaking. He did not embrace her. Instead, he simply kept her hand in his and placed his other hand on her shoulder, as if to steady her after the bloodshed. He squeezed her fingers, and his strength fortified her. "Are you all right, Etti?"

"Yes. *Nais Tuke,* Rafa." She thanked him and fought the urge to fall into his arms with relief and gratitude. "Thank you." Reluctantly, she broke contact and hurried to her wagon.

Chapter 4

The morning sun coaxed the chill from the air. Silver dew sparkled on the grasses, streaked green where the horses walked to the starting point of the race. Thirty-two horses gathered in an empty field leading to the road.

Food hawkers shouted about sausages and cheeses, their coarse voices blending with the shrill cries of the ale women peddling their fresh barley water and stout ales.

Race officials walked the track that ran the outside perimeter of the horse fair, shooing dogs and children away. The track ran past the stables, past the vendor areas and fields, and past the camps of Gypsy sellers and Gadje buyers.

The horse coursers were looking for sleek, fast horses, sure-footed and alert enough to race over uneven terrain. They would buy those horses and sell them to the royalty and nobility to carry messengers and scouts. Others sought sturdy geldings that could support merchants made fat with success and too many feasts, and still others sought dependable, loyal mares for wives and monks for their pilgrimages. Everyone wanted healthy horses and good prices.

Etti had recently walked Red. She was a sturdy palfrey, with legs strong but not too long, and sleek muscles without excessive weight, both traits desirable in racing. Red's previous owner had beaten her, as evidenced by the scars on her attractive, chestnut neck. Cruelty made Red aggressive and hostile, so Ruslo had been able to buy her for a small price. Etti had petitioned to retrain her, and Ruslo had allowed Etti to work with Kennick, their horse trainer. For two years Etti had strived to gain Red's trust. The filly had grown into a mare with an even disposition and fierce loyalty. Etti hugged Red, patting her shining mane. Using the mounting stool, she hopped onto Red's back.

This race could make a difference for Etti. She didn't expect to wing but finishing near the front would enhance the mare's sale price and Etti would be honored in the tribal celebrations. In spite of her meanness and bitterness, Atira had gained tribal acceptance with her fortune-telling income. Perhaps, in spite of Etti's strangeness, she could gain acceptance through her skill with horses. And that may cause one special man to notice her.

Later, when buyers gathered to bid for Red, Ettie aimed to be present at the bidding and make sure Red was sold to a good owner. Her tribe would appreciate a high price but a gentle owner was more important. Etti aimed to get both.

Rafa approached on his horse, Dark Tide, an impatient black stallion, smaller than a charger, a sleek, muscular show horse. He snorted, head high as he walked, pleased with himself, and glancing about as if looking for trouble. His nostrils flared and he approached Red, sniffing her. Aware she was a mare of breeding age, the stallion snuffled and crowded her. Rafa reined him away from Red and Dark Tide shook his head, scolding Rafa. Rafa led him with ease, clearly in charge of the feisty horse.

Etti shifted her gaze to the rider. Rafa wore a white linen tunic, the neckline open to his waist. An image blinked in Etti's memory of water sparkling down his naked chest in the river the day before. Her heart skipped. Her skin grew sensitive to his nearness, a sudden warmth, like the sun, rising from within her. A silent shiver worked its way to her belly. He noticed her appraisal, and she came to her senses enough to form a question. "How is your arm?"

"Only a surface wound," he said. "And how are you? Did your brothers stay clear of your camp last night?"

She thought of their cruelty to her uncle, and all the stories she had heard about their disrespect toward her mother and their brutality to her father. Etti wished never to see them again. "Yes. You're fast with the whip. Thank you again."

His nose, generous and straight, dominated above a clean, masculine jawline. He widened his smile, revealing perfect, white teeth, with a slight space between two of them at the side. Interest sparked in his brown eyes, and something akin to dragonfly wings fluttered in her chest. She pulled Red free of the flirting stallion and its equally inviting rider. "Good luck with the race."

"And to you." Rafa took her dismissal gracefully and joined the other horses at the starting position.

Melodia approached and tugged on her boot. "What did you say to him?"

"I thanked him twice now."

"The way he looks at you. He's interested."

"If that's true, a wasted effort on his part." She wouldn't soon forget the arrogance under all his fine features. To still her heart, she ticked off all the reasons she wasn't interested. He was Gitano, he didn't love animals, and—well, she couldn't come up with a third reason, but she knew there were many.

"You're so stubborn," Melodia said. "For once you turn a man's head—a very comely man, I should say—and you reject him." She gave Etti a crooked grin. "All those winking lessons for naught."

Etti rolled her eyes and smiled.

"You're difficult. But good luck with the race." Melodia patted Red. "And you, you little prancer. Run like the wind today."

"My thanks," Etti said.

Melodia left, and Etti took a deep breath. Disliking Rafa was infinitely more comfortable than liking him, but the man made it difficult. He had apologized. He had been daring last night, protecting her and her uncle. But he didn't understand about Pesha, and that made him a man she didn't want to know better. She wanted a man who understood her, one she could trust with Pesha, one who viewed him as more than a source of food—or the brunt of lazy, thoughtless jokes. She had seen the desire in his eyes—but desire was not the same as respect and affection.

Rafa accepted her dismissal and joined the other horses. He probably thought she would be fawning and attentive to him after

31

the horsewhip fight. He may not be as callous as she'd thought. Perhaps he wasn't callous at all—but was he caring?

Etti was all too familiar with heartlessness and rejection. She had grown up in the thorny terrain of her brothers' sarcasm and dirty tricks, and under the disappointed eye of her mother as Etti unraveled her bungled knitting or stumbled through her awkward, ineffective palm reading sessions. Her father had understood her, but he was in the spirit world now. Her uncle and grandparents—even her cousins thought her strange, cursed because she didn't fall in step with their rules and expectations.

Pesha had chosen to be with her. She felt cared for—even if only by a lowly hedgehog that no one else appreciated. Maybe that was her bond with the charming little beast. Etti had been an unloved daughter, an unloved niece, granddaughter and cousin. She refused to become an uncared-for wife, as well. "Come on, Red, let's show them."

Kennick joined them. Years in the sun had carved sharpness into his features, but laugh lines softened his eyes and mouth. He possessed a gentle understanding of horses and shared his knowledge with Etti. He would have ridden in the race himself, but he suffered a failing in his hands, an unpredictable paralysis that lasted for hours. She would repay Kennick and Red for their faith in her.

Kennick greeted her with a smile and patted Red. "Excited? Ready for the race?"

"Ready. She'll shine today, and we'll find an owner who will appreciate her for the jewel that she is."

"She's full of energy this morning," Kennick said. "Lively. She'll carry you all the way."

"She's alert." Etti had walked Red through the race route twice already. Red's memory was good and she would meet the dips and turns with an experienced eye.

Kennick sent them on their way with a gentle slap on Red's rump.

Etti reached the starting field. The horses and their riders milled around, waiting for the marshals to set positions. The more experienced riders maneuvered their horses away from the outside. Etti had heard their conversations earlier. They considered the outside track dangerous, with a higher risk of a challenging horse wedging into another horse's path.

Etti had been fascinated with racing and horses since she was tall enough to climb to the top rail of the fence to watch them. Over the years, she had discovered a pattern in the racing, not fool-proof, but predictable. While the outside positions increased the risk of another horse sliding in and blocking, they also allowed for more freedom, and helped the riders earn a better race position early.

The other riders didn't see those opportunities. Etti would ride today with a gem of a horse beneath her. Red had heart, and a kind of second sight. She seemed to sense aggression and closed it off. Etti hoped she would sense it again today. She guided Red past the congestion in the middle and settled outside. It wouldn't guarantee an outside start, but it would make it more convenient for the marshalls to place them there.

Spectators clustered outside the fence, checking out the horses. A tall Gadje mingled, accepting payments from other men, gambling on who would win the race.

"Hey, Etti!" Durril appeared from among the crowd, shouting. "Be careful. Your nag might have a lame leg!" He sneered at her.

Etti ignored his threat. After the ugly scene with the horse whips, Ruslo had posted a guard for Red through the night to keep her brothers from harming her horse. "Durril," Etti said. "How did you get up so early? You'd better go back to bed and sleep off all the mead you drank."

In case Durril harbored thoughts to harm her horse, Etti reined Red away from the fence.

Meanwhile, conversation burst from the buyers, a buzz of murmured questions and comments. Several cast sideways glances at Etti while conversing, and a portly man, a nobleman by his ermine trimmed surcoat, leaned past another man to peer at her. Mayhap they noticed a woman was riding in the race. They hurried over to her, pushing Durril out of the way. The gamblers edged in, asking about her racing experience. In what races had she competed, they asked. Had she ever won?

"This is my first race," Etti said. Their eyes dulled, and the gamblers hurried off to a more promising rider for their wagers.

Three marshals arrived with their assistants, and the crowd split to make way for them. They wore the official blue surcoats and black boots and carried themselves tall. With their power to position the horses or disqualify them, and everyone afforded them courtesy.

A tall, thin marshal cocked his head to the side. "So here you are," he said to Etti. "The fair has been noisy with talk about you, young lady. Are you ready to race?"

"Yes, sir," Etti said. "Where would you like me?"

"In his arms," one of the buyers said, chortling. His cohorts laughed along.

The tall marshal turned, giving them a stern look, and the laughter died. "Stay right where you are, little lady. You'll start on the outside."

The outside position. The boisterous men's comments may have worked to her advantage, and Etti breathed easier.

As the horses settled into their assigned positions, Etti sought Rafa out. He and his Dark Tide would start from front and center, an enviable position. Etti silently wished him luck again. He had, after all, done her a kindness last night. Etti scratched Red at the base of the ear, her favorite spot, one that Etti reinforced before every practice run.

The starting bell rang, and the horses were off. Red bolted ahead, setting a quick, early pace. Etti's legs tensed along with Red's, gripping his mane, falling into the rhythm of the horse's stride. She passed five horses. Up ahead, Etti glimpsed black in the middle of the racers. Rafa had surged to the lead.

They reached the stables and made the first turn. A roar came from the onlookers and, from within the racing herd, the thunder of hooves and labored exhaling of horses from their exertion. Clumps of mud thunked on Etti's ankles, and she heard Red's rapid breathing beneath her. Another rider guided his horse toward Red and bumped against her, knocking her off pace. "*Chavaia!*" Etti shouted at him to stop and give ground. "Run, Red! Go!" Red pressed on, refusing to yield. She shoved the aggressive horse back and held her position.

Red passed another horse. Etti moved with her, breathing and straining with her, and Etti thought of the ocean's tide, surges of energy and moments of weightlessness and landing, a kind of dance that made her hair fly and fall on her shoulders in a dream-like flow. Etti relaxed into it, trusting Red.

Of a sudden men were yelling and shouting and waving, and Red crossed the finish line. The marshals were directing the riders who had completed the race into a side field. Several of the gamblers followed on foot to cluster around three horses. Etti guessed they must be the winners. Rafa was among them.

Etti rubbed Red's neck, heedless of the heat and horse sweat. "You did it, girl. You're a queen today." Dismounting, she walked her, listening with satisfaction as the horse's breathing slowed. She couldn't smile enough, and even as she cooled her horse down, her heart was still racing. She had done it. Red had done it. They had placed—but in what position?

She continued to praise Red. They would get plenty of attention from the buyers. It pained her to think of parting with Red, but they would find a worthy new owner for her. The funds would sustain her tribe and allow them to find other horses worthy of rescue and training. She led Red to the watering tanks and dismounted.

Kennick leaped over the fence, running to her. "What a race!" He hugged her, and they jumped together on the hay-strewn, muddy ground. Feeling lighter than the banners furling around them, Etti laughed. Kennick had added an impressive win to his accomplishments and she would be honored in the Circle later.

"Etti! Wait!"

Etti turned to the direction of Rafa's voice. He was running to her. "You placed fifth, Etti. Misto!"

Va, it was very good, and his excitement was contagious. His hair, black and straight, flowed back from his face, settling in disarray over his shoulders as he ran. Excitement glittered in his dark eyes. He smiled so widely his back teeth showed.

Before she could protest, he scooped her up in his arms and turned her around.

She flew in joy, so sweet after their victory, delicious and dizzying. A tiny sliver of worry lodged that Rafa was so bold with her in public, but they were with the horses and riders and trainers, not under the watchful elders of her kumpania. All the winners were celebrating, so they did not stand out. Only Etti knew the intoxicating delight she was sharing with Rafa. She laughed again. "You won," she guessed.

"Yes," Rafa said. Catching his breath, he settled her back on the ground. "So did you."

She smiled broadly. "Congratulations."

"And you placed fifth. Fifth!"

Etti giggled. Hearing it the second time, it sounded more true, more wonderful. Hearing it from Rafa was even better.

"I saw you cross the line," he said. "I'll never forget the sight of it. Your horse. You, over her, learning forward and clutching her mane. Your hair, flowing like a river behind you. The look in your eyes. I wish you could have seen yourself."

His words washed over her, so much so she could almost see herself riding across the finish line. She blushed from his effusive praise. "I saw you taking the lead, and I wished you luck."

He cupped her face. "It worked. Thank you."

Etti's heart stopped, and his nearness, his eyes—for a breathless moment she wanted to close her eyes and fall into his arms and kiss with a passion she had only witnessed from afar in stolen glances.

Rafa sensed it. His smile vanished, and he looked from her eyes to her lips.

Magic swirled around them, and the sound of her beating heart pulsed in her ears. She fought the faeries in her belly and pulled back. "Tell me about the race."

At her hesitance, recognition lit Rafa's eyes. He realized the situation, too, and exhaled, blinking. "Dark Tide fought for the lead at every turn. He gave me everything. And you—how did you overcome being started on the outside?"

Pride filled Etti's chest. "I was happy to start there. I preferred it, and Red was so relaxed. All I asked of her she did, so easily."

Etti's skin tingled from Rafa's firm grip on her waist. Her face, where his fingers had trailed, was still warm. If she remained standing so close to him, she would most surely melt into the muddied ground. She dared one last look at his intense gaze and reluctantly retreated. *"Ashen Devlesa, Romale, "* she said. May you remain with God.

36

Chapter 5

Dody turned his tooth-cleaning tree stick in his hands, his fingers rolling the tiny branches. His lip was too tender to do anything else with it, so he slipped it into his girdle. He watched Rafa twirl Etti around and stroke her face. For all her complaints about Rafa, Etti appeared enchanted with him. And Rafa—the powerful Gitano had fallen victim to Etti's exquisite beauty.

Thoughts bubbled up in Dody's head, thoughts of the pressure he'd been feeling since Etti had grown up, and the cloud of rejection she' received from the young men of his tribe. Dody faced the burden of getting her married, made all the heavier by the memory of his dead brother, bless his spirit, and Dody's promise to him. He had vowed to take care of Etti, but each year brought more challenge.

He faced the unsavory task of finding the young man in his tribe who was the least wary and disapproving of Etti. He would need an even temperament and be least likely to beat her into submission to become more normal, with more acceptable habits like cooking, cleaning and raising children. Until Rafa had arrived, Dody had all but given up hope of finding such a man.

His niece was sweet, but strange. And Rafa, he was a strong man, capable of protecting her and providing for her. And God's blood, it was clear he wanted her. This surpassed Dody's hopes.

He would need to light a fire under Rafa, who had until now from marriage.

Why had Danior been so cursed? At ten, he lost an eye in a fight. At twenty, two sons out of the womb, one after another, hale and capable but vile as snakes, dark with hatred and rank with the liquor that poisoned their minds.

And after they arrived, his wife birthed a girl shadowed by strange behavior. Singing to the moon. Setting rabbits free when the tribe was hungry, and then the damned hedgehog. A chill went up his back, and he shuddered.

Etti had finally noticed a man, and she appeared to be smitten. And damned if Rafa didn't seem the same. Dody would need to convince his king to match them for marriage.

But first, he must cement their bond. Dody must act soon, before Rafa had a chance to see how odd she was. How fortunate Rafa's tribe was all the way west in Catalonia! Dody would keep Rafa away from the single young men, who would chatter at length about Etti's strangeness. He would keep Etti in Rafa's sight, for beauty was the girl's strongest trait—her eyes, cheekbones, lips, and an eye-pleasing body.

Marriage matching was coming soon. He would keep them together, and see Etti wed by the next moon.

He waited until she left and approached Rafa, congratulating him profusely on his first place win. He started to pat his horse, but saw the look in the feisty stallion's eyes and dropped his hand. "Fine animal," Dody said. He gestured to a group of buyers hovering nearby. "You'll get a premium price for him now."

Rafa rubbed the stallion's neck and stroked him all the way down his back, and the stallion snuffled, leaning toward him. "No, Dark Tide's not for sale. He's my partner."

"He's a magnificent animal." Dody noted Rafa wasn't looking at his stallion, but was following Etti's progress off the field. Dody followed his gaze. "She a beautiful woman. I saw the two of you celebrating."

"I apologize," Rafa said. "It was the excitement of the finish. I—"

"Thank you for last night," Dody said. "My nephews…" Dody trailed off to avoid referring to them as devils.

"Family can be like a roast pig, burned on the spit," Rafa said. "You don't want to waste good food, but the ashes are foul and stick in the teeth."

Dody laughed carefully, protecting his lip. "You are clever. That is true. But their sister is a sweet one, equally happy in the rain as in the sun."

"She's a gifted rider." Rafa nodded, adding emphasis to his words.

"I've seen the looks between you two this day," Dody said. "She is beautiful, and she is…" Dody searched for the more worthy attributes of his niece. "She's skilled with herbs, she's an early riser and a hard worker." He came closer. "She shares your love of horses. You're a fine young man. You should know she is one of our tribe's young women who will be matched this summer, after the horse fair."

Rafa's eyes grew serious. "She is the most comely woman I have seen. A man would be very lucky to call her his wife."

"Many think so," Dody agreed, wanting him to feel a sense of urgency. "Would you consider yourself lucky in that case?"

Rafa's eyes widened. "Indeed."

"Are you of a mind to wed?"

Rafa lingered on a final glimpse of Etti as she disappeared behind the stables. "I had not thought so."

Not the hearty response Dody had hoped for, but he wouldn't have Rafa leaving the horse fair early without planting the seed. "You're two and twenty. Why haven't you wed?"

"I travel too much."

Dody laughed in spite of the pain. "Of course you do. You're a Gypsy!"

Showing his good nature, Rafa joined in the laughter. "I mean the horse fairs. It was fun all my life, but now that I'm buying my own horses—breeding, training them—I don't want to miss any of the fairs. I'm away frequently, and for long periods, from my kumpania."

"I've seen women at the horse fairs with their men. Etti loves horses, too," Dody added. "High time you wed, but only if you find the right woman. If it's Etti, I would be happy to speak for you to our king."

Rafa leaned forward, not missing the implications of what, exactly, Dody planned to discuss with the king. Rafa blinked twice and met his gaze, his brown eyes intense. "My thanks. I'll give it some serious thought, sir."

Rafa's expression was thoughtful, and it encouraged Dody. He touched his lip, tender from laughing, thinking of life without Etti. No more mornings filled with her sweet disposition, but Dody would honor his promise to Danior and be freed from Etti's embarrassing habits at the same time. He need only place her with another tribe, with a man who cared for her. And if those devil brothers of hers dared return to his camp after she left, he would then be free to kill them.

* * *

Etti left the field and entered the road, churned by the race to the consistency of *boranija*, a bean stew. A pleasant spell surrounded her, one of heat and yearning and lightness. *Ashen Devlesa, Romale.* She had unthinkingly said "remain with God." She took a deep breath and a shuddering exhale. She did wish Rafa well.

The prospect of him leaving the fair brought a grey chill. She held her arms, hoping he would stay.

Melodia, Aunt Ucho, Vai, and her mother's relatives rushed to her.

"You did great!" Melodia shook Etti. "Wonderful. Congratulations!"

"Well done, Etti." Her mother's brother, Uncle Bo, spoke quietly. Over the years, he shared the same disappointments in Etti that her mother had. He had aged better than Uncle Dody, retaining the thick hair and strong chin of his youth. He smiled, almost easing the sting of his wide-eyed surprise that she had done something praiseworthy.

Her Aunt Shelta took Etti's hands and squeezed them. "The whole tribe is talking about you. I would never have believed it." She raised her brows. "Now if you can learn to cook and dukker the vast—and get those creatures out of your bed—we might be able to get you a husband."

Vexing though their half-hearted compliments were, Etti thanked them. She didn't bother correcting her aunt, who thought, with her fading memory, that Etti also owned a monkey and a chicken.

Melodia hoisted a basketful of clothes and a couple of empty buckets. "Pray come with me, Etti, and talk to me while I wash clothes." Her eyes were bright with excitement.

"I'll do mine, too." Etti hurried into the wagon. She changed back into her skirt and tossed her riding clothes into the basket. She and Melodia walked past the vendors and rowdy children playing leapfrog. The l'Huveaune River flowed through the site of the horse fair, pouring over tiered and clustered rocks. From the north, it flowed southwest, providing water for cooking, washing clothes and, below that, water for bathing the horses and further downstream, disposal purposes.

They walked upstream until they heard a noisy chorus of feminine voices and frequent slapping sounds. Many Romani women filled the shallow riverbank. They wore colorful scarves and had tucked the hems of their full skirts into their waistbands. They waded in the shallow water among water-worn rocks well suited for laundering.

Etti checked the skies, darkening in crumpled bundles of grey. "Hope it doesn't rain." They needed at least a couple of hours of sunlight to freshen and dry their clothes.

"Let's go over there," Melodia said, picking a place less crowded. "Here are a couple of good ones." She pointed to two smaller rocks with ridged surfaces. "They'll work." She pulled a bright red skirt from the basket and plunged it into the bucket. Using a chunk of soap, she rubbed the ells of fabric against each other. "What a wonderful race! I watched you and Red go by. Did you see me wave?"

Etti laughed. "I was too busy staying mounted, sorry."

Melodia rinsed her skirt in the flowing water and swung it in a high arc over her head. Streams of water trailed as the fabric formed a big, sparkling water flower. Grunting, she banged the linen on the rock. "Tell me now. All."

Etti recounted the race—her starting position, the buyers who teased the marshal, the blur of the race, Red's amazing run, and the thrilling finish.

"And Rafa won first place." Wringing the skirt dry, she raised a brow at Etti and smiled. "Did you see him finish?"

"I was guarding Red's position from another horse who was trying to pass us, so no, but I did see him take the lead."

"Did you see him after?"

"Yes. After Kennick came out, Rafa came over to me. I was walking Red, cooling her down." Etti sighed and told her about it. "He's so strong. He picked me up easily as he would a baby chick. My heart stopped." She laughed softly. "Or maybe it danced."

"Wonderful." Melodia clapped her dripping hands. "You should see your face as you speak of him. Then what happened?"

"He told me about Dark Tide. Do you know what he said? He said, 'He gave me everything he had.'"

Melodia cocked her head, brows raised, smiling. "Yes? So?"

Wringing her riding shirt, Etti picked off a small clump of mud and held it for a moment, thinking. "It surprised me. I didn't think he liked animals."

"So... did he say he liked them?"

"There was a look in his eyes. Oh. His eyes." Etti sighed and plunged her shirt into the water. "His eyes warmed when he said that about Dark Tide." At Melodia's blank look, she continued. "He gave credit for winning the race to his horse. He didn't go on about how *he* controlled his horse and *he* found openings and knew when to run him all out. He said Dark Tide did it. That his horse *gave Rafa* the power and speed."

"That's... um... exciting?" Melodia tilted her head.

"It is," Etti insisted. "I think he may have become smarter."

"Then what?"

Etti hesitated. After harsh judgment over the years, she had learned to keep her feelings to herself. If she left her thoughts unexpressed, she couldn't be ridiculed.

"He kissed you," Melodia guessed, smiling.

Her enthusiasm encouraged Etti, and she smiled, too. "No. But Melodia, he wanted to. I could feel it, so strong it tingled my toes and my head was all whirling." She stopped banging at the stubborn stain on her tunic and brought the image back. "His eyes were so intense. He smelled of his leather and horse sweat, and I could feel the heat of his chest close to mine."

"By the saints, Etti. You're in love!" Melodia gasped and covered her mouth. "Wonderful! And he's in love with you!"

Hope bubbled up in Etti's heart. "I never thought it could be, but—"

"But it isn't love." Atira stood before them, hands on her hips. They had been so engrossed in their conversation they hadn't heard her approach. "It's only lust," she said. "Men reek with it."

Melodia raised her chin and glared at Atira. "They do not. You're jealous because you hate Vano." She referred to Atira's husband.

Atira dropped her laundry basket and sat on a rock. Pulling out her yellow scarf, she lathered it up, punishing the fabric on the rock. "'Tis no different from the dogs when they breed. And the horses. I know you've both seen the mares when they back their bottoms up to the stallions. They raise their tails. 'Tis mating. Not love."

"I know what I felt," Etti said. "'Tis nothing like the distaste you feel for Vano. It's... beautiful."

"It's foolish." Atira wagged her finger. "Both of you. Get your heads out of the clouds, or you'll be like moths at the fire. Burned." She smacked her scarf on the rock, scraping her hand. Blood bubbled up on her knuckles. "You'll be ruined. Do you hear me?"

Chapter 6

Hours later, Etti's tribe gathered in the Circle to celebrate the day's victories. A misty rain started to fall, so light it merely steamed above the blazing bonfires. All were there, the tribe's men, the women, even the elders and babes. Etti's Aunt Shelta sat, mending a scarf. Rupa and Aunt Ucho laughed over cups of celebration mead. The two other girls who would be matched this year, round-faced Leyla and Mary, with her wide nose and big eyes, played with little Miri.

Lasho, a cripple with watery eyes, leaned on his walking stick, staying close to the ale barrels. Half of them had already been consumed, along with three spit-roasted pigs, fried turnips, and baked cherries.

Kennick joined the Circle, and he patted Etti on the shoulder as he passed by. "Methinks I'll be hearing your name tonight," he said. "Congratulations."

Etti smiled back. She'd looked forward to this night, had worked so hard, so long for it. She would be praised for her race with Red. She hoped her father could hear it from the spirit world, so he could know Etti continued the proud tradition with horses that he had started with the tribe. They would accept her now, and she would hold the finalist certificate, issued in her name. She

44

would be gracious, and would thank Kennick and Ruslo for giving her this chance.

And Rafa was here. The shadows had lifted from her heart, and she smiled, happy with anticipation.

Etti's Uncle Dody was sharing a long story with Rafa and wiry young Hanzi, whose Adam's apple danced like a huge marble as he laughed.

It was a story Etti knew well, of how her father saved three wagons of Gypsies from drowning when the ice cracked on the river they were crossing.

Dody continued praising Danior's keen sense with horses, which helped shore up the tribe's funds many times. Dody had his arm slung around Rafa's shoulder; clearly, he was fond of him. Watching the handsome Gitano, Etti knew she, too, was growing fond of him. When he was near, her body heated with excitement.

Ruslo emerged from the big tent, a collection of scrolls under his huge arms. "This is a great day for our kumpania." He faced his tribe. "I am proud tonight to hold winning certificates from the marshals—three of them! For our tribe's horses." Ruslo swayed, evidence of early celebration with his favored blackberry mead. One could not find fault, though, in light of the tribe's victories. "Winners of the Marseilles Mile: Tenth Place, Hanzi, who raced Chooter! Come up, Hanzi."

Hanzi shuffled to the front, swallowing and grinning. Ruslo handed him a paper, proof of Hanzi's participation and win. *"Nais Tuke,"* Hanzi said. "I'll learn to be even faster."

The tribe applauded him. Ruslo gestured to his nephew. "The next winner is not from our kumpania, but he is my beloved sister's son." All knew of Sandu. Ruslo spoke of his exploits and mastery often. "His horse, Grey Wind, was tripped and stumbled, but Sandu still managed to bring him to the finish line. Winner of the Marseilles Mile, seventh place, is Sandu."

Sandu loomed over Hanzi, big as a bear with a thick neck and forearms. Unbeatable when wrestling, running or fighting, he was Ruslo's pride and joy. Having fathered girls, Ruslo was sorely absent a son. Sandu filled that gap, and Ruslo presented Sandu's seventh place certificate with all the flourish of a first place win.

"Our next winner has accomplished a remarkable feat. All the buyers are talking about it, the beautiful winner and her horse. She is the first woman rider in the Marseilles Mile history." He laughed. "I admit her choice in pets is suspect, and she has some strange habits, but today she is a winner. Etti placed fifth in the race."

He gestured for Uncle Dody to come up. "Your niece has made us proud," he said. "Let all of you witness the great Roma tradition of family. Dody has raised Etti to be a dutiful daughter. He has honored his brother's name, and his memory. Uncle Dody turned his head, protecting the injured side of his mouth, and the big men kissed as Roma men did, a firm, chicken-like peck on the mouth. They followed it with a series of hard thumps on each other's backs.

Ruslo pointed his index finger at Etti and curled it toward himself in a gesture. "Come up here, *ves tacha.*"

A flush of discomfort ran up Etti's neck. Ruslo had never used that term of endearment with her before, *my beloved.* They were not related, and he had been annoyed with her more than pleased since Etti's parents' deaths. Etti had hoped her good performance would enhance her standing with the tribe, but such effusive affection exceeded propriety. *Too much mead.* She smiled enough to be polite and self-consciously joined him.

Ruslo beamed and welcomed her, placing his left arm around her. He also placed his right arm around Sandu, hugging them both to him. "Our stable of horses has become more valuable with these wins. We will demand the highest prices for our horses in the coming year. I am a proud king this evening." He raised his tankard, mead dribbling down the sides. "Let's drink to our winners!"

The tribe cheered again, and ale flowed from the barrels. Kennick stepped forward. "I trained Red, and Etti helped me, and she brought Red to victory today. Here's to Etti!"

"Here's to Etti!" Rafa drank to her success, too, his eyes shining. He gave her a special look.

"To Etti!" Rafa's friend, Jardani followed with another toast.

Pobi and his friend stood and toasted Etti. They smiled, friendly and praising.

It shocked Etti. They had not said two kind words to her in the last several months, only snide slurs and jokes about Pesha. At the fire, Ruslo whispered something to Sandu, who looked at her with approval.

Melodia rushed up. Hugging Etti, she pulled her away, fair bubbling with advice. When they were out of the fire's glow, she spoke. "My, quite the attention you're getting from the men now. Have you winked yet?"

"What? In front of everyone?"

"No. No," Melodia lowered her voice. "Not directly. You walk close by to him, so no one else can see, and you look at him a little sideways, and wink."

Etti looked toward the fire and saw Rafa still sitting there. He was watching them. Her heart skipped, and she felt at once bold and timid. "You'll walk with me?"

Threading her arm through Etti's, Melodia led her back toward Rafa.

Etti's heart pounded. She followed Melodia's lead, answering her breezy questions about the race. Hanzi stood next to Rafa. Melodia elbowed Etti and approached Hanzi, asking to see his certificate.

Etti's heart raced, and an insect seemed to have flown in her ear, making a soft, buzzing sound. Everyone talked, not noticing her, no one but Rafa. She managed a shy smile and executed a good wink.

Rafa lowered his thick black lashes, winked and gave her a slow, secret smile.

It set off a tendril of heat licking down her chest into the pit of her stomach where it burst, leaving her breathless.

"Hey, Etti." Melodia tapped her arm. "Here comes your Uncle Bo."

Her uncle approached her, nodding to Melodia. "I need a word with my niece," he said, dismissing her. He huddled with Etti, and she held onto his arm for balance. He lowered his voice. "I have just returned from checking the horses," he said, a discreet reference to the treed area where the men relieved themselves. "Of all the people to see—your good-for-naught brothers are still at the fair. Watch out."

* * *

The morning of the horse sales arrived, bathed in sunshine.

At the entrance to the main stables, a temporary shelter blocked the sun for the buyers. Lines of benches ran to the front door. "Here's a good spot," Rafa said. "Shade, and shelter if the rains come." He and Jardani took a seat to the side.

Jardani's stomach growled.

Rafa laughed. "Va, the bacon smells so much better than the horses." He inhaled deeply. "And the bread. I'm hungry, too." Rafa signaled the vendor and ordered both, along with barley water for himself and ale for Jardani.

"What happens now?" Jardani asked.

"We wait until the horses clear the inspection area." Rafa had already been approved as a buyer. He was looking for a brood mare for Dark Tide. He gestured to the large field that had served as the starting point. "Then they'll go back to their stalls, and we can walk through."

"Can we ride them?" Jardani asked.

"The buyers already have. Outside," Rafa said. "Once they're brought in the stables, they can examine them, get information from the owner and view papers confirming pedigree and records."

A bell rang, signaling time for the buyers to proceed to the stalls.

Buyers shuffled in, some carrying notes about each horse. Rafa needed no notes. He planned to walk away with only one good horse.

Rafa scanned the competition. He recognized some prominent Rom traders from Devon, and a couple more he met during the race.

Sellers congregated in the stables, visible through the wide doors. They paced, excited, and Rafa understood their anxieties. Rafa's Uncle Yojo entered, along with other men from Rafa's kumpania. He recognized Rafa and approached. "I finally see you again," he said, an edge of reprimand in his voice. Since the race, Rafa had been spending all his time with Etti. "Will you join us for the sale?" his uncle asked.

"Later," Rafa said. "After the next round."

"Anton is tired," Yojo said. "He could use some help with his horses."

"I helped him with grooming this morning," Jardani said.

"I saw his horses. They look good," Rafa said. Preparation took weeks. The horses had been given salt to stimulate their hunger and thirst. Their grazing was carefully monitored, and in addition to the bathing in the river, the horses were currycombed. Their hooves were checked, re-shod if needed, and polished. "I'm sure Anton will do well."

Uncle Yojo gave Rafa a grudging smile. "Luck be with you this morn, nephew." They left, threading through the crowd.

Rafa saw Ruslo and Dody enter the stables, and waved. "Over here." The men joined Rafa and Jardani, and a discussion followed about which horses would be offered first.

"Are you selling Dark Tide?" Ruslo asked.

"He'd be a steal at any price," Rafa said. "He comes from an excellent mare family. His dam is half-sister to Ulysses, and you know his record."

Ruslo nodded and glanced at Dody. "Champion at the stallion show in Ireland. And after winning yesterday here, you'll get a great price."

"I'll never sell Dark Tide," Rafa said. "Today I hope to buy a brood mare for him."

Dody fluttered his whittled tree stick between his fingers and leaned in toward Rafa. "Did you see Babik's mares? He has some good ones. He's in the back stalls, on the north side."

"My thanks, but I have my sights on Red." Etti's horse. "I'll race her for a couple more seasons, because she has such heart. She's a good athlete."

"Wish you would have told me last night," Ruslo said. "I could have taken her off the list."

"I decided this morning at dawn, when I saw Etti running her around the race course," Rafa said.

Dody's eyes widened, and his head came forward.

Rafa tensed. Did he think Rafa was spying on Etti? "I was up early to exercise Dark Tide, and noticed the fluidity of Red's gait." It wouldn't do for them to think his actions improper—and he respected Dody. He reminded Rafa of his own uncle.

Rafa also wanted to tread lightly with Ruslo. Negotiating privately for Red would seem at first glance easier, but it could have become awkward. From experience, Rafa knew sellers—himself included—always thought their horses more valuable than the market would bear. Had he bid casually for Red, no matter the amount, Ruslo would question the adequacy. It was better business practice to let the market dictate the price—which meant a public sale. This fair allowed buyers to make offers. If the offers were uncontested, the seller could accept right away and the sale was complete. If other buyers wanted the horse, however, they were allowed to bid, with the highest bidder being awarded the horse.

They approached the stalls of horses that had won the Mile race. A dozen potential buyers surrounded Red's stall. Etti stood at the side.

She spotted him as they approached and she lowered her lashes. A warm sensation flickered in Rafa's chest. She licked her lips. They glistened, plump and inviting. He remembered her demure wink last night, the mischief in her eyes that quickly faded to the most adorable bashfulness. A woman of contrasts—the woman who drove Red across the finish line held a single-minded determination that made her glow with vitality. Now, she looked gentle—and quiet. Her neckline fell at a prim level, but her breasts pushed against the fabric, rising and falling from her breathing. Desire streaked through his body. She had wanted him to kiss those soft lips after the race, and he had been regretting not doing so ever since.

She reached for Red and scratched the mare's ears. Distress pulled on her features, and she wrapped her arm protectively around the horse's neck. Etti had to know any one of these buyers could win the bidding and take her horse. He hoped she would approve of his wanting to buy Red.

He was prepared to offer all the coin he had to accomplish that.

Etti felt Rafa's gaze, and the heat within it. His white tunic hugged his chest all the way from his wide shoulders, down to his trim waist. Warmth radiated from his smile. She welcomed it, wanted to capture it like a shining florin and hold it to her heart.

Ruslo was speaking to a tall Gadje with deep wrinkles, greying hair and shifty eyes. She turned to her tribal king, shaking her head slightly. She did not trust this man to care for Red.

Ruslo dipped his head to her and addressed the man. "My apologies, sir, but that's not enough."

Etti exhaled a shaky breath, thankful Ruslo had agreed to help her with this. She scanned the faces of the buyers in the front of the crowd, hoping to find a gentle face she could trust with the faithful horse she had come to love.

Other buyers stepped forward. Having heard the grey-haired man's bid, they increased it. The price climbed to fifteen pounds.

"Twenty, Ruslo," Rafa said.

She pivoted and met his gaze. He was bidding for Red. Her thoughts froze. Then she remembered his statement about Dark Tide giving him everything he had. He understood horses, and she believed he would be good to Red. This was more than she could have hoped for. She started to nod to Ruslo when another bid was given. "Twenty-two." A woman bid.

Ruslo glanced at her, but Etti had grown comfortable with the idea of Rafa owning Red. She shook her head.

Ruslo looked confused.

"Twenty-four." Rafa increased his price.

"Thirty." A harsh voice bawled.

Etti searched the crowd, looking for the last bidder. A fellow Rom met her gaze, waving a bag of coins. She took in the familiar vertical frown lines between his eyes, the determined stare, full of trouble. His face was marred with a curved scab over his right eye, carved there by Rafa with Durril's horsewhip.

Her brother, Jilé.

Etti shook her head vigorously at Ruslo.

Ruslo looked to Rafa.

Rafa gestured, palms up. "Twenty-four is all I have."

"Sold!" Jilé yelled. "Here's my money."

Chapter 7

"No!" Etti's heart banged in alarm at the thought of Jilé taking Red. "Wait!" She cried to Ruslo. "I'll ask Uncle Dody and get you the extra money. Please."

Ruslo pushed Etti off his arm and pointed boldly to Rafa. "Sold for twenty-four pounds," he said under a tightly furrowed brow.

"My price is higher," Jilé said.

"You don't exist to me, or anyone in my kumpania. You were banished years ago. You cannot bid."

"Marshal!" Durril bellowed. "My brother bid the highest price for this horse. Laws of the fair say he gets the horse, isn't that right?"

"They have both been banished from our tribe," Ruslo explained to the marshal. "To us, neither one of them exists."

The marshal asked people in the crowd what happened, and they recounted the bids.

"I'm sorry, Ruslo," the marshal said. "Our rules prevail over any tribal rules. He made the successful bid. He gets the horse."

Ruslo cast an apologetic look to Etti and lowered his voice. "If we naysay him on this, we risk expulsion from the fair—mayhap other fairs, if word spreads."

"No!" Etti fisted her hands to her chest. "No!"

Ruslo's eyes narrowed. "Are you able to pay the thirty pounds you bid?"

"Right here." Durril raised Jilé's hand, which held a large, heavily soiled bag of duck cloth with circular lumps visible on the outside. "Give me the reins, Ruslo," Durril said. "Give him the coins, Jilé, and let's go."

"I'm sorry, Etti." Ruslo handed Durril the reins.

Durril and Jilé grinned at her agony. When she was very young, she'd seen their cruelty with the doves, pulling their feathers out, one by one. She'd seen them teasing the tribal dogs with bones and kicking them when they came within range of their boots. Outrage blinded Etti. She cried out, a guttural cry such as one would hear from a trapped animal. She snared the reins. They may try to drag her out of the fair, but she would never leave Red in their cruel care.

"I'll pay thirty-two," Rafa said. His friend Jardani's mouth dropped, and he grabbed Rafa's arm as if to stop him.

Rafa brushed free, shaking his head at Jardani. "Leave the horse, and I'll get you the money within the hour."

"Too late. As it is too late for my face," Jilé said, tracing the horsewhip cut along his eyebrow. "This scar will cost you. I told you, remember?"

Neither one of these miscreants could afford thirty pounds, let alone how much money was in that bag. Perhaps they gained the trust of a wealthy buyer. "Who are you buying horses for?" Rafa asked.

Durril sneered. "We have a very important customer who wants this horse. We have good instincts about horses, and their owners. This buyer will pay us anything for this horse. Even forty pounds."

"Or maybe fifty if he waits too long," Jilé mocked, his mouth stretched into a half smile.

Rafa lunged toward Jilé.

Jilé slid behind Red, laughing. "I said I'd get even. You bargain with me if you want to please my comely sister, but you're going to need even more coins." Jilé lifted his eyebrows and pointed a finger skyward. "An idea for you. Mayhap you'll trade for your horse—what's his name? Oh, va! Dark Tide. Give us Dark Tide, and you can have the bitch mare. Even up."

Etti reached up, pushing Jilé. "I hate you. I hate you both." She pointed a fist at Jilé and shook it. "May blood pour from your ears. May your arms wither and fall off your body. May you both die a violent death if you harm this beautiful horse."

"Enough." Ruslo pulled her to the side and lowered his voice. "The fair marshal is standing right there. You cause me disgrace."

Etti lowered her head. As big and strong as he was, Ruslo had been known to grow quickly shamed among crowds, and Etti had screamed curses in front of all these people. "I—"

"Be silent." Ruslo lowered his voice even more. "This is your fault. Why did I agree to this? I could have sold Red to the woman, but you kept shaking your head and distracting me so that I didn't see your drunkard brothers arrive."

"I'm sorry, I didn't think—"

"That's your problem. The way you think. You think a hedgehog is a pet, but he's only a stupid hedgehog. He's dinner. That's all! And you win a race with Red and you suddenly think she's yours, that she has a human spirit? Red is a horse. We bought her to heal her and sell her, like we do all the horses. You didn't buy Red. I did. You didn't train Red. Kennick did. Red is no more than a horse, but you talked me into bartering as if trying to find a sinless parent for an orphan child."

Ruslo's voice ground as he spoke, and tiny droplets of spittle struck Etti's face. She wished she would swoon.

"And now," Ruslo muttered, "your hellish brothers have her. The marshal is staring at me. I look the fool." He took the reins and shoved her toward the door. "Go back to your wagon and stay there."

Etti stumbled away. She ran out the door, but once outside, crept to the window and listened. She'd wait until her brothers left with Red, and she would ambush them. Could she kill them? No, but she would knock them out and take Red and Pesha, and she would go… where? She remembered their cruelty and her vision wobbled through tears.

Hesitant to barge into Ruslo's position as seller, Rafa remained silent, glaring at the brothers and recalling the previous night. They had arrived uninvited and unwanted at Ruslo's fire. Details came back. They had eaten ravenously, ripping greedy shares of pork off the pigs, and they had gulped down the ale. Even now, their tunics sagged at the seams from age, their boots old, their hats tattered.

How could these reprobate brothers rub two coins together, let alone a whole bag of them? Rafa tamped down his rage at their taunts about Dark Tide and considered it. Where would they get so much money?

"We gave the highest bid!" Durril snatched Red's reins, speaking loudly and attracting attention. Sandu had backed away, his face tense, mayhap even more embarrassed than Ruslo. Buyers from surrounding stalls gathered, curious about the strange affair at Red's stable. Durril loudly counted out the coins, and Jilé strode quickly, tugging Red toward the door. It became evident to Rafa— they had to have stolen the money, right here at the fair.

Rafa grabbed Jilé's wrist and and waved with his free arm. "Marshal!" Rafa called. "Arrest these thieves. They have stolen these coins."

Ruslo's eyes widened.

Durril turned to bolt, but Ruslo gripped his arm.

The marshal approached. "Do you have proof?"

Rafa did not. To save Red, he would have to stall. "These men are criminals." Rafa retained his grip on Jilé. "They have no money and represent no buyer. Ask them."

"We do," Jilé said. "It's William Spence."

"Waters," Durril blurted at the same time, offering a different surname.

"There, see," Rafa said. "Their lies expose them. By now, someone has to have reported that this money was stolen from them. Please, sound the alarm and let's learn whose money this is."

The marshal considered.

"Please," Ruslo said. "These men are vermin, 'tis why we banished them from our tribe."

The marshal inserted two fingers in his mouth and whistled. The sound was repeated outside the stable, and soon several marshals arrived. The stable marshal reached for the bag of coins from Durril.

Durril pulled the bag to his chest. "It's mine, I tell you. I sold some fine horses before I came here."

"It may be." The marshal swept his gaze over Ruslo, Rafa and the brothers. "All of you will remain right here until we learn more. John," the marshal pointed to another marshal. "Bring me the girl standing outside at the window. She's somehow involved, too."

Etti returned, and within minutes, a well-dressed man arrived, a jeweler by his clothes and the wealth of gold he wore. "Where's my money?"

Durril's eyes widened.

The jeweler looked at Jilé. "You're the man my wife described." The jeweler turned to the marshal. "I have a stand outside the west door of the stables," he said. "When the marshals came round and mentioned the bag, I checked our tent. I found her, beaten and tied up. She said that man," he pointed at Jilé, "came to her stand. While she showed them her leather bit collars, someone slashed the back of our tent and rummaged through it. When she heard him and ran into the tent to investigate, they beat her, tied and gagged her. That's my cash bag."

Durril pulled the bag close to his chest. "I sold her a horse. A great horse! You didn't want her to have it, but she bought it any way, and gave me this money. You must have beaten her yourself when you found out." Durril's eyes darted from one marshal to the other, reading their expressions. His eyes narrowed and he punched Ruslo in the throat and freed his hand. He reached in his tunic and pulled a knife. Shouting a garbled curse, he slashed Ruslo's forearm and snatched Red's reins.

Ruslo released his grip on Durril and watched blood flow down his fingers. A look of fury crossed his features.

"Here! Take it!" Durril yelled and tossed the reins to Jilé. He slit the money bag with his knife, slinging it upward.

The coins flew out of the bag, falling like rain in Red's stable, and all the way across the aisle.

For a moment Etti and the men froze, watching the money fall, shillings and florins and crowns. Assorted notes fell as well, drifting downward like autumn leaves.

Men dove for them, grasping and fighting for the more valuable ones.

The jeweler cried out. "Stop them!"

The marshals shouted for order and the men shouted back, refusing to stop scooping up the coins.

Durril flipped the bag upside down to stop their spilling.

Jilé slapped Red's reins in Rafa's face and turned to run. Rafa held on.

Jilé pulled a knife with his free hand and slashed at Rafa's chest.

Rafa pulled back. His tunic sagged, wet with blood.

Men pushed from behind, diving for the coins. The crowd swarmed for the money, and the marshalls grew tangled in the throng.

Jilé led Red for a while but became tangled among all the people. Cursing, he stabbed Red in the shoulder.

Red screamed and reared up, ripping her reins from Jilé's hand.

"Red!" Etti cried.

Rafa reached up, grabbing for the reins, trying to calm Red. When he turned to look, he saw no trace of either brother.

* * *

The afternoon sky had slumped into a dull grey. Storm clouds rolled in, making the stable stalls dark. Dody lit a second lantern and hung it high and out of the way so prospective buyers could better inspect Hanzi's horse, Chooter. Ruslo and Hanzi joined Dody at the side of the stall, out of the buyers' way.

Chooter, a tan palfrey, had retreated to the back of his stall. A girl almost entering womanhood gently approached the horse. Her calm manner suggested she knew horses, and she seemed beguiled with the white marking on the palfrey's forehead. It resembled an upside down quarter moon. She reached for the moon, talking softly to Chooter. He leaned in to her, and she smiled at her father. "He likes me."

"Looks promising," Dody said. He didn't care much for horses. They pulled his wagon and played a vital role in supporting the tribe so he respected them, but beyond proper grazing and health, he held little interest. After the episode in Red's stall this morning, though, Dody saw Red had achieved what he could not. Because of Etti's favorite horse, Rafa's virtues had been revealed to Ruslo. With the marriage council fast approaching, Dody now had some seeds to plant with Ruslo. He would find some private time with him this afternoon to do so.

Kennick arrived, a wooden mane comb in his hand to pull Chooter's mane straight. Seeing potential buyers in the stall, though, he walked past the horse. He noted the girl and her father getting acquainted with Chooter and joined Ruslo, Dody and Hanzi.

"How's Red?" Ruslo asked.

"Jilé's knife hit the bone and missed the artery. Could have been much worse," Kennick said.

"So why do you look so worried?" Dody asked.

"Infection. We cleaned the wound. It appears the knife was sharp, and we'll hope it was clean, too." Kennick ran his fingernail over the teeth of the comb. "Hanzi, please help me with Red while we tend to her wound."

Kennick and Hanzi left and the buyers wandered off to other stalls, leaving Ruslo and Dody alone.

Ruslo sank his big frame onto a stool, and Dody swung a foot onto the lower rung of the stall divider, relieving his back. "How is your arm?" Dody asked.

Ruslo held out his huge forearm, showing him the bandage. "All clean and sewn. I'm fine."

"I hope Red will be all right." Dody pulled out his tree stick, gingerly placed it in his mouth, but changed his mind and put it away. "Jilé would have killed her, had he more time. Heartless bastards, those brothers," Dody said, warming to the topic. "Jilé won't have to worry about his thumb any more. If they catch them, he'll lose his hand."

"A just punishment for him." Ruslo picked straws of hay off his tunic.

"Quite the surprise, Rafa bidding so generously on Red."

"Twenty-four pounds! When I hoped for twenty," Ruslo said.

"Wonder why he did that," Dody ventured further.

Ruslo laughed. "A man'd be blind not to see. He did it for Etti, not me, though he impressed me when he agreed to buy Red anyway, in spite of the stab wound."

"Yes," Dody quickly agreed. "He impressed me, too." With Ruslo's acknowledgement of Rafa's honor, Dody would seek a commitment from him. "I talked with Rafa yesterday." Dody weighed his words carefully. "He indicated a man would be very lucky to have Etti as his bride. He showed great interest." Not exactly, Dody admitted silently, but he would get Rafa to that point, and soon. Before the matchmaking.

Silence enfolded them, and Dody's thoughts returned to the morning fracas. Ruslo had become angry with Etti over the bidding. Perhaps he would now be more willing to let her leave the tribe with Rafa.

"I've seen his affection for Etti. I know his father, and others from Rafa's tribe. Rafa is a well regarded trainer for a man in his early twenties. You heard his plans for breeding, and—"

"I saw him race," Ruslo interrupted.

Dody pushed free from the partition and stood taller. "I humbly ask you to consider matching Rafa with Etti at the council."

Ruslo didn't respond.

"She's an odd bird, Etti," Dody continued. "None of the boys in our tribe like her, and the women are uncomfortable with her and the damned hedgehog."

At hearing of the hedgehog, Ruslo closed his eyes and shook his head.

Dody suppressed a smile. He had hit the target by speaking of the rodent.

"It will be a difficult pairing," Ruslo admitted. "Mayhap she'll grow out of her attraction to the hedgehog."

Having seen his anger at Etti's obsession with Red, Dody drove the next point in. "There's more to it than the rodent. She has a strange link with all beasts. Look you at the trouble she caused with Red. What kind of dark power do you suppose animals have over her that she would be so loyal?" He leaned in and lowered his voice. "She *sleeps* with the hedgehog." Their tribe—indeed, all Gypsies—believed animals possessed mysterious powers. They never allowed the tribal dogs to sleep with them, just as all dovecotes had roofs separate from where the Roma slept during the winter months.

Ruslo stroked his thin mustache. "This has to stop. I'll have to get one of the boys to catch it and throw it in with the other hedgehogs for supper. She'll never know."

"You think any of the boys will be brave enough? After the curse she screamed at her brothers today?" Dody raised his brows. Etti would never know? Sure as the moon and sun would rise, she would confirm her suspicions and wouldn't let it go unanswered.

In truth, the boys were afeared of Etti. Ruslo would have to steal the hedgehog himself.

Ruslo tapped the stall divider, lost in thought. Dody knew he had hit home with the animals. Now to hit the heart of it. "Consider Etti's brothers, too. They're probably on a boat by now, off to Tours or Troyes." Dody gingerly rubbed his lower lip, still swollen from the whip, hoping they'd pay dearly. "Etti cursed them, before many people. They didn't take it kindly. They'll be back, like they were for me. Who in our tribe would be willing to take Etti into their family, with swine like her brothers causing trouble? They're like a disease. After this morning, they may even be trouble for you and yours."

Ruslo pressed his brows together.

"Sure as winter's coming, they'll return," Dody said.

Ruslo rose from his stool. "You've argued well for her. The men will have their recommendations, but in the end, Dody, to honor your request, I'll match her for marriage to Rafa."

Dody drew a sharp breath. Ruslo's promise sounded much like the fine strains of Erki's viol, sweet and pure.

"Considering Etti's faults, and allowing what Rafa paid for Red today, I'll set the bride price low." Ruslo scorched Dody with a sideways glance, looming over him. "You will say nothing of my decision." His frown deepened. "To anyone."

Dody dipped his head in a subtle salute that spoke undeniably of gratitude.

He opened his palms toward Ruslo. "Not a word. Thank you, Pen." Dody used the affectionate term shared between the Rom.

Concealing his relief, Dody picked up the shovel to clean Chooter's stall and started scooping. Now he would get Rafa to embrace the idea of betrothal to one sweet but irksome woman by the name of Etti.

Chapter 8

"I'm done." Kennick rose. He dropped the needle and thread into the water pan and rubbed his knees. "Now we pray for her."

Red lay on her side, her breathing steadier now that Kennick had finished stitching. Etti stroked her neck, praising her, and stood. Lightheadedness made her wobble. She clutched the side of the stall, overwhelmed with the iron-like smell of blood, the stained hay, and the fear rising from Red's body. She could mend torn flesh, but was thankful Kennick had been willing to stitch Red's wound. Even with the herbs she had given her, it hurt to think of causing Red further pain by piercing her flesh.

Hanzi had become ill from the blood and left, and Rafa had arrived. He looked downward at his bloodied tunic. "I'm sorry. I've been with the marshalls. Haven't been able to change."

"How is your chest?" Etti asked.

Rafa touched the tunic. "Only a scratch. How's Red?"

A cold knot formed in Etti's stomach. "He aimed to kill her, but he was hemmed in by all the people. Jilé hit bone. It's a ragged wound—hard to clean and sew."

Red struggled to standing, shaking her head, and Kennick limped across the stall with linen strips, his walk becoming more smooth as his knees recovered.

"You rest," Etti said. "I'll finish here."

"Your salve will help her. Bandaging, though, will be difficult," Kennick said.

"I'll wrap her at an angle over her withers," Etti said. "We'll keep her quiet."

Kennick patted Etti's arm. "She's in good hands." He opened the stall's short door. "It will be busy all day. Along with buyers, there will be those curious about the fight. I'll see about moving her to a private stall." He left, closing the door.

Rafa brought the bandages over.

"Hold her for me, please."

Rafa took the reins. "She is so comfortable with you here," he said.

It pleased Etti that he noticed her closeness to Red. She reached into the deep folds of her skirt, pulling out a small jar. "Ivy bright," she said, crooning to Red as she dabbed the salve gingerly on the gash.

Rafa coughed. "It stinks."

Etti smiled. "It works." She glanced up to meet Rafa's dark eyes. "What you did today. I can't find the words to tell you how much it meant." A tear wandered down her face.

He brushed it away with his thumb. "I understand."

"You do? But you thought I was so foolish with Pesha."

"Forsooth, I still find it a bit… unusual. But I understand what it's like with a horse. When those filthy swine offered to trade and take Dark Tide…" He fisted his hand. "I'm sorry I couldn't stop them." He looked up. "And I'm sorry I called them that. They're your brothers."

Etti exhaled in loathing. "If I never saw them again, life would be sweet."

He gave her an admiring smile, his eyes twinkling. "After the mighty curse you shouted at them, they should stay away."

Her face warmed. Oaths and curses were meant to impose will or simply release anger, but they were not used outside the Roma Circle, and never in the presence of Gadje. "I'm sorry. I don't know what came over me."

"Did you see your uncle when you cursed them? He almost popped his Adam's apple."

The image he suggested, along with the twinkle in his eye, made her laugh.

"You share the same spirit, you and Red," Rafa said. "I saw it during the race."

"I was glad you were there to bid on her."

"I had to. I saw the fear in your eyes, fear for Red. I would spare you the worry."

His concern made her want to fall into his arms. Rafa was the first man besides Kennick who understood her distress over Red. Like the morning at the horse baths, she became mindful of Rafa's male beauty. The clean prominent line of his jaw, his broad shoulders, the gleam in his eyes—it was a look she had never seen from a man before. It closed the distance between them, warming her chest, and raced, along with her blood, all the way to her heart—and lower.

But there were buyers and marshals everywhere, so she stayed her impulses and only touched his hand. It sizzled where their skin met, a fire licking its way up her arm with a kind of magic, magic like the gentle breeze of summer on a warm day.

His hand covered hers.

The heat of his body, the scent of him, a mixture of horse sweat and man, all filled her senses. "I was glad to see you this morning. I am always glad to see you."

His fingers laced with hers, his eyes dark, intense. "And I, you."

Rafa watched her lip quiver. Her eyes bound him in a spell, liquid, gold in the lamplight, with black lashes feathery as summer grasses. The simple touch of her hand set him on a slow flame that threatened to burst into life. He wanted to pull her to his chest, feel her breasts against him, to caress her back, follow the curves beneath his hand, sense her desire.

Dody's mention of the upcoming marriage council came to him, her uncle's words burning in his ears, "I would be happy to speak for you to our king."

Her uncle's message echoed like an alarm. Rafa should have responded with more conviction. Etti was a morning star of a woman, lovely to the eyes, with a warm heart, and passion.

Behind her, a string of buyers approached. It was not meet to be seen thusly, not good for Etti's reputation. He gave her hand a squeeze and stepped a more acceptable distance away. "So." He took a shaky breath, gathering himself. "You have no sisters? Only those... brothers?"

"Would that my parents had not died, I might have, but no, it's me and… them."

"Dody mentioned them. I'm sorry. How did it happen? How did you lose them?"

"A sickness. Not plague, mind you, but a slow, painful sickness." She patted her heart. "May their spirits be happy together, forever." She shook her head. "Enough of that. Today you saved Red. You bought her, even after she'd been stabbed." She turned her attention to the wound and dabbed the remaining salve on the stitches. "I was so relieved when you walked out with her. Thank you."

"You brothers. Have they always been so… so—"

"Evil? As long as I can remember, yes. They're eight years older than me. From my earliest memories, I feared them. They were mean to the dogs, the birds, my parents." She paused. "And me." She looked down to the hay-strewn floor, and Rafa could sense her pain as she visited dark memories. "They used to pull glowing sticks from the fire and chase me. If I didn't run fast enough, my skirt would burn."

"Your mother didn't stop them?"

"She said it was my fault for teasing them. 'You should stay clear of them,' she said. I wish they would go far away, forever." She looked at Rafa. "How many brothers do you have?"

"None. I have three sisters. 'Twas a noisy wagon, ours."

She smiled. "Tell me about them."

"There's Tasarla, she's five. Elophia's eight. She loves to run in the sea, chase the waves." He smiled, looking past the bale of hay and feed trough. "We have a little game we play in the lake. We catch crayfish and see who can catch the white ones. They're faster, harder to catch."

"And what's the prize? For the one who catches the most white crayfish?" Etti asked.

"The winner gets to walk into camp with the big bag of crayfish, and everyone gives her a big cheer."

"And how often does little Elophia win?"

Rafa leaned forward and gave her a slow, lazy wink, raising a brow. "Every time."

Etti laughed. Still, a part of her ached at never having had a brother who loved her, who would have brought joy to her days, instead of fear. Of a sudden the twinkle in his eyes revealed the promise of this charming man. A future with Rafa, she realized, would include *laughter*. The discovery shimmered like fairy dust, warming her heart. She caught her breath. "And your third sister?"

"Tali's the oldest. She's twelve."

"Tali? Like the dice game?"

"Yes. My mother's favorite. She said it would bring her little girl a lifetime of luck."

Etti smiled. "Has it?"

"Tali's a bit like Dark Tide."

"Fast runner?"

Rafa laughed. "Va. The boys have found her hard to catch. She's comely, but none have caught her heart."

A smile curved her mouth. "That's best. She's but twelve years. And it would cause problems at the marriage council."

Her comment caused Rafa to pause. "Councils are always easier if the couple is pleased with the match. Why would that cause problems?"

"Some couples are attracted to each other." Etti dropped her lashes. "But in our tribe, the men decide which bride is suitable— the boy's father, other men in the tribe, but in the end it's the king's decision."

Rafa huffed. "How can men alone know if the match is right? In my tribe, women as well as men form the council."

"Forsooth?" Etti's expression was one of amazement. She told him of Atira's disappointment with her husband. "It was never her choice."

Rafa looked at her closely. "What mean you? That a man and woman may be attracted—strongly attracted, as I am to you and you to me—and they would match you with someone else?"

Etti inhaled sharply. She met his gaze, wide-eyed and silent. Her mouth curved into the softest of smiles. The look in her eyes— it was as if he had just kissed her.

Rafa started. He comprehended what he had said. It had slipped out, like a greased pig at harvest games. He could not unspeak the words, so he offered her a smile.

"You like me?" Etti's gaze was direct and beautiful.

Rafa squirmed in the moment he had created. Forsooth, if he didn't speak soon, he may not have a chance with her. He stepped closer and lowered his voice. "I see only you. Your eyes, your face fills my vision and my thoughts, like the warmth of the sun in the morning. Your smile... inspires me."

He stepped closer, driven by an intoxicating music in his ears, a growing hum in his body as she fixed those magnificent, shining eyes on him.

He tried to stay his hand but failed. He brushed her lush lips with his finger, stroking it over her soft mouth.

Her gaze melted and she leaned toward him.

He pressed his lips to hers. He lost all sense of connection to the stables. They were floating on a cloud, in a dream. She stroked his neck, stirring a song in his soul, a new exciting tune.

He pulled her close. Her soft body yielded to him. As his thoughts had roamed to this moment, so desire kindled and burned, and he deepened the kiss.

He heard a harsh intake of air, a gasp.

Melodia stood at the entrance of the stall.

Chapter 9

"Fie! Mind you both!" Melodia gripped Etti's arm and pulled her away. "By the falling stars, what are you doing?" She scanned the gawking crowd of buyers. "No other Rom here, thanks be."

Etti gasped, patting her chest as if to tamp down the flames.

Melodia hugged her fiercely and danced around.

From her fog of passion, Etti tried to make sense of it. "What are you doing?"

"Trying to give them something to talk about other than what they saw with the two of you," Melodia said. "You!" She cuffed Rafa. "You show no honor to her. Go. Take a walk… and cool down."

Rafa exhaled. "I'm sorry, Etti." He left.

"I came to relieve you from watching Red," Melodia said. Her light brown eyes flashed in anger. "Thank the saints I came. The marshals wish to see you about your brothers. Meet them at the entry gate. Go you to them, and I'll tend to Red." She pushed her toward the aisle. "Walk tall. Mayhap these men will think you are betrothed, to be acting so."

Etti left the stables, heading for the front gate, some 300 yards distant. Her body simmered from Rafa's kiss, and she couldn't breathe enough air. She had heard of the spell of love from girls older than she. In her innocence she had thought their tales exaggerated, but the trembling and wanting left her weak and melting. She had seen Rafa's passion, the softening of his mouth, and savored the slow fire that burst through her body from his kiss.

The men watched her intensely as she passed. What they had seen! Her, losing all traces of duty and control. She followed Melodia's advice and held her head high. She walked past the jeweler's tent, still swarming with marshalls and curious fair goers, wanting to catch a glimpse of his poor bruised wife, no doubt.

Ruslo and Uncle Dody stood at the entry gate with three marshals. They told her Durril and Jilé had escaped, but with the fastest horses from the fair, they would catch them soon. "We need to learn where they may go from here," one of the marshals said. "Which way do you think they would flee?"

"I've no guess," Etti said. "They arrived here alone."

"They didn't get word to you?" Suspicion narrowed the older marshal's eyes.

"Of course not," Uncle Dody huffed. "We expelled them years ago. We haven't seen them until now." He rubbed the stubble on his chin. "Troyes used to be one of their favorite places. Mayhap they're following the Rhone River to it, north."

"By the light of God, we'll find them," the older marshal swore. "They're thieves, and will be dealt with as such."

Etti shuddered, glad of a sudden that her parents were spared witnessing their sons' shame, and the punishment that was to come.

* * *

Rafa left the stables, walking swiftly. He passed some buyers who pointed and gave him a thumbs up, laughing as he passed them. One man looked familiar. He had been near Red's stall when Rafa openly embraced Etti. Rafa hoped he didn't know Etti or any other members of the tribe.

By gad, but she was warm. Sweet. Her kisses had melted him like a candle in the midday sun. He had forgotten all but her mouth, pliant and willing on his.

They had been seen. Such disgraceful conduct would harm Etti's standing, at the time she least needed more scrutiny. Dody— would he still support Rafa when he found out?

He shook his head at his lack of control. He savored the moments in life when he stepped to the edge—racing against strong, well-trained horses, any physical challenge with a worthy opponent, anything that tried the limits of his strength, grace or talents. A worthy adversary sharpened Rafa's wits and, in that moment when he embraced the unknown and dug deep to be faster or stronger or smarter—those were the sweetest moments.

But Etti. She kindled thoughts in him, strong instincts to protect her, to help her. He had been able to, in the Circle, when her brothers attacked Dody with their horsewhips. And again in the stables, during the bidding, when Jilé had tried to kill Red.

The gratitude in her eyes made him feel so much like a man, her protector. But then he had tasted her passion and lost all control.

She was a nectar he could not resist. He had known sensual pleasures with Gadje women, but having held Etti in his arms, there was no comparison. Well, mayhap. It was like the difference between running along the edge of the sea on a hot day, or charging into the depths of it, feeling it splash over his body, sea spraying his face. He could not touch Etti without wanting to dive in.

When Etti brought Red to the finish line, he had seen her passion, her spirit.

He stepped aside to let a wagon pass by. He must find Dody, apologize for the scene at the stables and ask him for forgiveness. It was important Dody know how much he cared for Etti. How much he would cherish and provide for her.

"Rafa!" Jardani called to him from the tavern by the hawker stalls. "Come join us."

Rafa entered through the open door.

Inside, men filled the benches and tables, and the smell of stale ale and sausages filled the air. Jardani sat with Rafa's Uncle Yojo, their primary horse trader. Anton, with his greying temple braids, sat with him, along with Cori and other buyers from Rafa's kumpania.

Rafa signaled the server for an ale and joined them.

"Good you found time for us," Yojo said. His wide mouth often formed a big smile, but now he seemed reserved. "We're tallying our profits."

"Not so good?" Rafa unclipped his tankard and hoisted it to the serving woman, who filled it from the large ale jug.

Yojo raised his brows. "Good. All but your purchase of Red. You overpaid by a mile with that one."

"Va. But I paid with my own funds," Rafa reminded him, wishing he hadn't ordered an ale. Now he would have to stay for a time. He would make this brief and leave to find Dody and apologize.

"So you did." Yojo presented a leather journal open to a summary page filled with sketches of horses and numbers. His kumpania had sold eight horses and bought six. Yojo explained the circumstances behind the sales. Cori, a younger Rom at his first horse fair, told of the horses they had purchased.

Rafa listened, nodding and interjecting approval when it was fitting. He took a last drink of his ale and hooked his tankard back on his girdle. "I need to check on Dark Tide and Red," he said. "See you later at the—"

Yojo put a hand on Rafa's arm. "We're done here. We'll be leaving in the morning for Catalonia, as we planned. I've settled our tribe's accounts." He gestured toward Jardani. "He's packed for travel, and we'll be ready to head out at sunrise."

"But it's four more days before the fair's over." Rafa stood, poised to leave and search for Dody. "We need supplies, too. And uncle, from here we're going to Carcassone." The citadel, the lakes—it was one of the most beautiful cities Rafa had ever seen, and his uncle's favorite.

"I know why you want to stay, Rafa." Yojo's generous mouth stretched into a bland half smile. "You've spent most of your time in Ruslo's camp since we arrived. Jardani has told us what's been happening."

Rafa shot a glance at Jardani.

"Don't be angry with him. He's worried about you—and has good reason."

Other men at the table grew quiet, listening.

Yojo noticed and lowered his voice. "You over-stepped at Red's stall today. The girl has troubles with her people. You like to solve everyone's problems, but you can't solve this one. Leave with us tomorrow."

Rafa signaled to the door. "Time alone to discuss this?" Rafa said.

His uncle followed him outside.

"I respect you, Uncle Yojo," Rafa said. "But I am a grown man, and I'm staying."

"The woman, Etti. She causes you to lose touch with your honor. You interfere with their tribal matters."

"Her uncle will speak for me at the marriage council."

Yojo's eyes grew wide. "Whyfore?"

"By cause I asked him to."

His uncle crossed his arms and rubbed his chin. "Whyfore this interest in wedlock? She is comely. Seems to like horses as much as you do." He held his hand out, palm up. "But she's not…" He made a circular gesture near his ear "… not right, they say. And the curse of hers at the bidding." He shuddered. "You swore to your mother you would never wed. You refused her last two matches."

"Etti is not like other women. I will not refuse her. Nor will I leave her now." Rafa punched his uncle's arm with affection. "I wish you'd stay. I must apologize, make amends with Etti's uncle over my behavior with her. Earn his forgiveness. Jardani and I will travel to Carcasonne with her tribe. If all goes as I hope, Etti will be with me when I returned to our tribe in a fortnight."

He hesitated. *If she accepts me.* Confidence bolstered his voice, but he worried. Etti had revealed her passion for him, but would she be willing to leave her kumpania for him? He had earned Dody's and Ruslo's acceptance, but when the counsel announced their betrothal, would Etti accept it? Rafa could not separate her from her familia—and her father's legacy—against her will.

"Your mother will be shocked, Rafa." From the tone in his voice, his uncle did not approve.

He remembered conversations with his mother about the gift of love. "Tell her I have found my wife—if she will have me."

* * *

Later, Rafa left the stables, still seeking Dody.

"Rafa." Jardani tapped him on the shoulder. "Are you leaving with us?"

"Na. And I need you to stay with me. Have you seen Dody?"

Jardani shook his head.

"I'm going to check on the horses," Rafa said.

Jardani followed him past the horses to the trenches dug to accommodate nature's calls. From there, they walked on the path following the bubbling stream.

"Come with us," Jardani said. "Etti is naught but trouble for you. You can't even enjoy the horse fair with all the trouble she's stirred up."

"Her brothers. Not her."

"Yojo's right about Red—you overpaid several times. You did it for Etti and see what happened. Now you're troubled again by cause you were caught kissing her." He paused. "There will be other girls."

"Not like her." *With her I find happiness, an unspeakable joy.*

To be close to her—it frustrated him to put in words the effect she had on him. The tinkling edge of her laughter, musical. The sensuous glance through her dark lashes. The raw determination in her eyes when she guided Red past the other horses to the finish line. And the simmering desire in her gaze that promised untold ecstasy.

"You're a man obsessed." Jardani's expression of sickened curiosity caused a heat to creep up Rafa's neck.

He kept the flood of tender thoughts unspoken. "I want no one else."

"This is good." Dody appeared from the nearby road. "Jardani, you will excuse us."

"Yes, Sir." Jardani stepped through the high grasses to the road.

Rafa and Dody continued following the stream. Rafa waited to learn what Melodia had told him.

"When we reach Carcassonne," Dody said, "we'll meet with seven other kumpanias."

"Have you been there? It is beautiful," Rafa said.

"I'm not here to talk about Carcassonne. I'm sure you know that." An edge of impatience sharpened Dody's voice. He slanted a dark look at Rafa. "I heard what happened n the stable," Dody said. "Melodia told me."

Rafa had feared that. "Please forgive me," Rafa said. "I lost control. We were—"

"Foolish. Had Ruslo or Rupa—or any Rom seen…" He shook his head. "You are well past the age when most Rom marry. We don't want Ruslo or any of his advisors to suspect your intentions are anything but honorable. If they do, all the good you have done for us would be moot. All I have done on your behalf will have been in vain. Etti will be expelled, along with her vile brothers."

"I hold a deep respect for her."

"Good. You must be more careful. And you would have me speak for you to Ruslo?"

The moment magnified, and doubts assaulted him. The magnitude of his feelings—was it too soon, too sudden? Rafa wanted Etti beyond all reason. He had never found a woman like her, and had no reason in the past to speak of marriage to his mother. She wasn't from their tribe, and he admittedly had learned little practical information about her. Had she displayed in the past a touch of her brothers' impetuousness? Was that why all the other men avoided her? What didn't he know?

"Rafa?"

He recalled her shy wink, her pride in her father, the trust in her eyes. He faced a lifetime decision—some hesitation was understandable. Certainty chased the doubts away. "Yes. I would have you speak with Ruslo if you are still of a mind to do so. I—"

Dody held his open palm to Rafa. "No need to explain. So long as you honor her, I can overlook this. When I met my Ucho, I felt the same way."

"I have thought much about marriage to her," Rafa said, floating a bit south of the truth. He had thought of her beauty and courage, and the spell binding desire—but not of their future. He embraced the thought of making her his wife. His heart swelled with the certainty of it, and a fresh anticipation of a new beginning.

"And you would take her to your tribe?"

"Va."

"Then I have good news for you. As I said, I saw the way you both looked at each other. Your kumpania is… different from ours, but your family is known and reliable. I know Etti will be well cared for."

Rafa sensed Dody had more to say. His scalp tingled.

"Because of all these things, Rafa, I can rely on you. I spoke to Ruslo already on your behalf. You can say nothing of this to anyone, but Ruslo has agreed. At the marriage council, he will accept other proposals from other fathers, but he promised me. For Etti's husband," Dody said, pointing at Rafa, "Ruslo will name you."

* * *

The man's arm trembled, his huge muscles shaking in an arm wrestling match. The merchants and traders in the alehouse roared, half supporting him, the other half supporting Sandu. Sensing his chance, Sandu gritted his teeth and summoned a final surge of power, forcing his will on the blacksmith, James.

James collapsed and Sandu slammed his arm on the table. The thrill of competition passed, replaced by the ever-sweet sensation of victory. Sandu savored it for a quick moment then sobered and nodded to James. "You're a strong man, James. Good effort."

The merchants and traders in the alehouse applauded. Several came over slapping Sandu on the back.

"There you are." His Uncle Ruslo pushed his way through the crowd.

"Did they catch them?" Sandu disliked his Uncle Lumas's boys, but he'd never seen such demons as Jilé and Durril.

"Nay, but they will." His uncle cast arrows at Sandu.

"What is it?" Sandu asked.

"I would have a word with you." Ruslo's mouth twisted, clumping his thin mustache. "Now."

Outside, his uncle strode past the lines of ale barrels and stopped. "Why did you not help me at Red's sale? The devil's whelp knifed me in the arm, and you didn't raise a hand to help me."

Sights and sounds flooded into Sandu's mind—the horse's wounded screams, the flashing knife, the blood. The raw evil in Jilé's eyes, the seeping cruelty. It had caused Sandu to suffer a rheumy sickness that mingled with the sweat of nightmares, of knee-breaking fear.

Sandu tamped it down and took a step toward his uncle. "What? You think I could not kill that little pig with my bare hands? Why didn't you say something to me, so I knew it would be acceptable to come between you?"

"You could have held him. Kept him from escaping."

74

"It is your tribe, not mine. You must tell me when you want my help."

Ruslo's shoulders dropped, and he exhaled a fast breath. "You are my nephew. I would have you be part of my tribe. We will talk more when we have time, you and I. And va, I would have you help me. You won't be meddling—you need not fear that."

Sandu's mouth thinned. "I fear... nothing."

* * *

The horse fair continued without further incidents. Good to his word, Rafa's Uncle Yojo had left with the rest of the Gitanos for Catalonia. Red continued to recover from her injury, and Etti avoided Rafa. When they met at Red's stall, she mumbled an excuse and left.

The fair concluded with a big celebration in the field near the stables. Etti did not make an appearance. Today they would leave for Carcassone, and the marriage council.

Rafa rose early. He had not been able to sleep after he heard Dody's news. In spite of his confidence in Dody, new questions and uncertainties had begun to surface. Would Etti be pleased when the council named Rafa for her? Va! He believed it, so why was he now plagued with worry?

Because it was so important.

He and Jardani slept farthest from Ruslo's tent, near Vano's wagon. Tendrils of smoke curled upward from the dying fire, and the sky had lightened with impending dawn. The earth sighed with her fragrances, moist earth and the sweet smell of clover. From the cover of his eiderdown Rafa slipped into his hose and tunic. Jilé had slashed his white tunic beyond repair. The new, blue tunic lay soft against the healing scab that ran across his chest.

The day would be meaningless if he could not see Etti. There was so much to say to her, so much to learn about her.

But how, when she traveled in Dody's wagon, and avoided him?

Carcassonne remained over a hundred miles northwest. Their route would offer pleasing views when it hugged the shores of the Mediterranean sea. It reminded him why he loved the traveling life of the Romani people, each day fresh as the sun, with exciting, different places to see. He wanted to see it with Etti.

Now they had left the horse fair behind, he hoped Etti would be less embarrassed, more willing to talk with him. Today he would apologize, reassure her about his feelings.

Rafa rode Dark Tide. Because of his stallion's attraction to Red, Jardani led her from a distance. The mare continued to heal and seemed comfortable with their pace.

Etti traveled with Atira and Melodia in Dody's wagon. Not trusting Etti, the Marseilles horse fair officials had sent a marshal to accompany her wagon, as well, in case the brothers sought her out. The fair was determined to protect its reputation by catching and punishing them.

By afternoon the road had veered close to the sea, the breeze salty and fresh on his skin. Rafa removed his hat and ruffled his hair free, welcoming the warm summer sun.

Dody signaled to Rafa. "Drive my wagon for a while, will you, Pen? Atira and I want to ride this afternoon with Ucho." It was common for the Rom to trade wagons as they drove—it broke the monotony of the miles.

For Rafa, it made the day sweeter. "I am glad to, thank you." Rafa welcomed the chance to talk with Etti.

"Good," Dody said. "And remember our talk."

Rafa tethered Dark Tide to the wagon and settled on the driving bench alongside Melodia and Etti. Etti retreated into the wagon, leaving Rafa with Melodia.

Rafa broke the silence. "I'm sorry about the… the incident in the stables."

"I told Dody." Melodia said.

"Va. I didn't think. I'm sorry. Dody and I spoke, and I reassured him I would not be so careless in the future."

She gave him a long, hard look. The young girl stood poised to pass the threshold to womanhood. She came from a Hungarian strain of Rom with skin so light she could almost be judged a Gadje, but only by those who didn't know the sometimes wide divergence in appearance of what they called Gypsies. Her light brown hair blew free in the breeze, and her brown eyes were intent on Rafa. She lowered her voice. "Dody told me he would speak for you to Ruslo. Is that true?"

Rafa answered without lowering his. "It is. I would have her for my wife." He met Melodia's gaze. "I think she wants me, too. Do you think so?"

"Does each day surrender to the night?" Melodia quoted a common Rom expression with a crooked smile.

Rafa returned it. "I'm glad." He wanted to reassure her, and learn more about Etti this day. "She is in my thoughts always, ever since I first saw her in Marseilles." They rode in silence. The sea sparkled in the sun. Seagulls swooped the shoreline, crying musically in the clear air. He laughed. "Look you at those little sanderlings chasing the crabs." Their black, stilt-like legs blurred as they scampered, ruffling like the edges of thatched roofs in a gale as they escaped the whooshing surf.

"Do you live by the sea?" Melodia asked.

"Some of my familia live in the mountains near Barcelona, and the sea. We avoid the cities because of the Plague, and because some people grow hostile toward us. Our tribe is well known for our horses, though, so we are welcome at all the fairs." Gentle grasses blew in the breeze, catching his eye. "Va, it is beautiful, like this."

Later, they encountered a traveling army, some seventy soldiers with wagons and supplies. Melodia leaned toward him. "Are they fighting England again?"

"Thankfully, no." England had been challenging King Charles ever since Rafa could recall. Even before his father was born, England had campaigned to conquer France and put their English king on her throne. "The truce has held. So far. Would that England abandon this cause and end the war."

The soldiers passed and Rafa steered the wagon and the conversation back on course. "So, tell me, if you please, by cause you know I'm earnest. At the council, will others be speaking for Etti?"

Under raised eyebrows, Melodia smiled. "Many will." She clasped her hands together. "Etti is the most beautiful girl in our tribe. Even at the fair I saw no one who comes close to her. Our tribe—all tribes loved her Etti's father. Respected him. Were it not for her brothers... in spite of them, I'm sure several will ask for her, and as soon as she arrives in Carcassonne, there will be more."

Rafa suppressed a smile. Melodia's guileless youth made her gushing testimony sound amusingly amplified, but her love and loyalty to Etti impressed him. The indifferent young men in Etti's tribe did not worry Rafa but, as Melodia said, other men would be as taken by her beauty as he himself had been.

Would that Etti were free to choose. She had shown him her affection and desire, but Ruslo alone had the power to decide her mate. "I must comport myself well."

"Indeed," she agreed.

"You are a good friend," Rafa said. "Will you help me?"

She gave him a skeptical smile. "How could I help you, when you already have Dody on your side?"

"Help me with Etti. She's uncomfortable around me now. I hope she knows I didn't intend to harm her. I… I lost my senses for a moment. Will you tell her I'm sorry, and I'm hoping she will no longer feel awkward with me."

"Va."

"And prithee tell me if you learn more about the pairings."

Melodia put her hand on Rafa's arm. "I will help you. Worry not."

Ruslo and Sandu approached on their horses, accompanied by several mounted men in brown livery. As they came closer, Rafa recognized the old, wizened marshal from the fair. "They're the marshals from Marseilles."

Melodia jumped up and disappeared into the wagon. "Etti. The horse fair marshals are here."

Etti pulled the canvas open. She saw the marshals and looked to Rafa. The marshal Rafa had earlier convinced of Jilé's guilt recognized him and pulled in front of the wagon. "Godspeed, Rafa."

"And to you, Benjamin," Rafa replied, recalling the marshal's name.

Benjamin and Etti exchanged greetings.

"They have news of your brothers," Ruslo said. "We can meet in my wagon, if you please, and—"

"I have no secrets," Etti said from the wagon. "What needs to be said will be, for all to hear." She paused. "You found them?" She moistened her lips.

"Aye. About ten miles from here. They had strong, new horses and still possessed some of the stolen coins. We'll return them to the jeweler, but he will be sorely put on by how few are left. Your brothers were tried. Found guilty and… punished."

"Are they…" Etti pressed on her chest as if to contain her fear.

The marshal lowered his voice. "No. With their several crimes, though, they won't be battering or stealing soon. They severed Durril's and Jilé's left arms."

Etti cried out and covered her face with her hands.

"Well deserved." The other marshal growled, glaring at Etti. Benjamin waved the other man to silence. "Be not cruel. She was no part of it." He turned to Etti. "They threatened you. Said they'd come after you. We told them they would go straight to the gallows if they try to seek you out. If you do see them, though, you are to report them to the reeve. Be assured, if they're seen in France again, they will be hanged."

Chapter 10

Rafa sat with Etti by the sea. He held her hand, limp in his, and did not disturb the sound of the waves, sighing gently as they brushed to shore. Mayhap they would help heal her from this latest shock. For two days after news of her brothers' dismemberment, she had remained silent, listless in her movements, her eyes vacant.

Further on shore Melodia and Atira waited, there to protect Etti's reputation—and to remind Rafa to rein his more base impulses.

Etti pulled her hand free and turned her gaze to Rafa. "It was my curse."

Rafa had thought of that, too. Her anguished curse at the horse fair had turned heads: *may your arms wither and fall off your body*, among other damnations. "You were afraid for Red. You remembered the birds and the tribal dogs—and how they tortured you, too—and you were desperate to stop them from hurting Red."

She drew her fingers through the sand and sighed. "Ruslo heard it. Uncle Dody, too. It was whispered throughout the fair. Everyone knows it, and now it's happened."

"Your curse didn't cause their disfigurement. Their actions did. They stole a fortune from the jeweler, and they attacked his poor wife, almost killed her. Their punishment was appropriate and not related to you."

Etti released a ragged sigh. "But I am related to them. They must think I am evil, too, to have wished such harm to them."

He pulled her close to him, and she rested her head on his shoulders. "'Tis certain the rest of your familia is thinking of you now, sorry for your constant suffering because of your brother's misdeeds. Sorry because they know—I am sure of it—that you regret your outburst at the fair." He gently turned her face toward him. "And they know your brothers brought their punishment upon themselves."

"I, too, have said things in haste, and wish I could unsay them. They will understand." He wished there was more he could say. If he could only brush her face and in the brushing, push aside her remorse and memory of it.

"Jilé will come for me," she said.

"They're crippled and penniless. Do not worry."

"They are vicious. Heartless. They would have blinded Dody with the horsewhip."

I stopped them then, and I will protect you now. You heard the marshal," he reminded her. "If they return, they will both hang."

His words made sense, and the confidence in his voice calmed her. Her brothers were hobbled, destitute and marked forever as thieves to whomever they met. *Rafa will protect me.*

She met his eyes. "I heard what you said to Melodia. How can you possibly want me?"

"Only thin canvas separated us. I hoped you would hear it." He laced his fingers with hers, his touch gentle, loving. "I would have you for my wife."

"I am naught but a burden. And it will never happen." Her brows furrowed. "Methinks they will pick a harsh man for me. He will take Pesha away, and he will make me bend to his will. He will crush my evil spirit."

He put a finger to her lips. "You love animals, and racing, and you sing to the moon. You are not evil."

She lowered her head. "You heard that? About the moon?"

"Yes, and you have had to live under a curse of your own for many years—those brothers. Come with me to Barcelona. There are no shadows for you there."

She didn't look convinced.

"You will miss your family. I understand. But my kumpania attends the same horse fairs as yours. You can meet them every summer, every autumn. And my people, they're different."

"How so?"

He thought about his parents, his cousins. Jardani. "We are not without our problems. But we face them together, and..." He struggled to express it. "I told you. Our women form our councils. Men, too, but the women lead them in matters involving marriage and children."

"What? They lead the councils? That's unheard of."

"They do. It is rare, and to avoid conflicts, our women don't discuss it openly with other tribes."

"What of your tribe's rules about purity and marriage?"

"We adhere strictly to the Romani ways and standards, but they are..." He searched for the word. "More gentle rules. You will not be condemned if you voice a strong opinion. Or if you wish to sing to the moon."

Etti shook her head. "Ruslo will never allow me a voice. He's furious with me after the fair, and now all the tribe will be talking about my Evil Eye, and how I cursed my brothers. Ruslo likes you. He will not burden you with me."

"Etti." Rafa caught a lock of her hair, one she liked to curl by her face. He ran his finger through it to the end, its glossy strands cool, and watched them bounce back to the curl she had made. "You have let their misjudgments about you sink into your skin, into your heart. They are wrong. I see your gifts, your abilities. Your Uncle Dody does, too, though he worries about what the tribe thinks. Ruslo knows—remember how he praised you. But he was embarrassed at the fair, and that made him angry with you.

"Look at Red, how she trusts you. In Marseilles, you talked about how she raced for you. The animals know, Etti. Man can be deceptive and traitorous, but animals can sense it, and they know. Even—yes, even your hedgehog pet knows you have a true soul."

Rafa saw the women approaching. He had run out of time with Etti. He had promised Dody, and at the time had believed he could keep the promise of secrecy, but it brought joy to him to know it, and he wanted so desperately to ease her mind, to give her some hope on this troubling day. "There's one more thing, and you must promise not to say anything to Melodia. Or Atira. Or anyone." He waited. "Hurry. They're coming."

"All right. I vow."

"Dody told me yesterday." A thrill ran through his body, settling in his heart. "Ruslo has promised your uncle. Though he may hear proposals from other fathers, Ruslo will choose me for your husband." He watched her eyes widen, her jaw drop, and he traced his finger across her sensuous lips. "Me."

* * *

The next evening Etti, Atira and Melodia leaned together against an ancient oak tree, so wide all three of them could rest against its trunk. A gentle breeze visited occasionally, dissipating the last remnants of the summer heat. The emcampment and the green, bountiful land so pleased Ruslo that he had decided they should stay yet another night.

The aroma of cherries drifted up from Etti's cup of mead, the potent beverage a parting gift from the horse fair. She sipped and indulged her other appetite, looking across the flames at Rafa. His teeth shone white, revealed by his broad smile and laughter at something Jardani must have said. His features, clean and symmetrical, glowed in the firelight. His new blue tunic stretched tantalizingly snug against his muscular chest. *He would have me as his wife.*

Happiness danced in her heart. Her eyes could not drink enough of him, could not breathe deeply enough to savor all the magic of the night.

Tendrils of aroma enhanced the woodsy, sappy tang of the fire, remnants of their supper of *blini*, bacon-filled pancakes, and *perzala,* scrambled eggs and herbs.

Along with her kumpania, Etti lay under a sky of stars. Soft, thin clouds hugged the full moon that cast a silver glow to the leaves of the ancient trees. They surrounded the camp like protective sentinels. Most of the children had fallen asleep, and bits of conversation hovered in the air amid the soft fluttering of wings as bats swooped down here and there, catching the evening insects.

Etti sighed. Ruslo would name Rafa for her husband. She
wanted to jump up and dance with joy, and sing her special song to
the moon and hug Ruslo and Uncle Dody and Melodia.

Someone nudged her, and she turned.

"Be careful," Atira said. "Your smile is cracking your face,
and I'm not going to help you put it back together." She raised a
brow. "What's happened? You've been moping like a widow, and
now you're disgustingly cheery."

"*Va.*" Melodia agreed. "What is it?"

She would do naught to jeopardize their secret. "I am
thankful Red continues to heal from her stab wound. She's
traveling well. And I'm relieved that my brothers must stay away
from me." She took another drink, the fruit-laden liquid making
her head feel as light as her heart.

"I saw you staring at Rafa." Atira shot a warning look. "I
heard about the stables, too. Watch your urges, or Ruslo will boot
you out along with your brothers."

Etti opened her mouth to answer, but Ruslo stepped up and
signaled for quiet. He lowered his ample body to his knees to meet
Old Lolli's gaze. The wizened widow sat on a stump drinking
mead and scratching gnat bites on her forearm. She was older than
the trees, it was said. Etti remembered her mother telling her that
she was grizzled and old, even when her mother wed her father.
Old Lolli nodded, and Ruslo signaled Erki to play.

Settling on his stool, Erki pulled the viol snug to his body,
crossed his legs at the ankle and poised his bow over the string.
The notes quivered low, thoughtful, almost sad as the song
progressed. It evoked yearning and loss, a tune Etti remembered
from her earliest memories of evenings by the campfire, back
when her father held her in his lap, his big arms keeping the chill
night air from her shoulders.

Lolli struggled to standing. She emptied her cup of mead,
swaying a little before gaining her balance, and she sang the
history of their tribe, to a time when the great sickness—the Black
Death—spread through the lands of Hungary and Bohemia.
Families died, and the children, horrified at their parents'
discolored, blistering skin, would hide among the horses and refuse
to come out. Hundreds died, and they burned their dead with their
possessions, and the Rom retreated to the forests with their
surviving family members.

Lolli's thin voice warbled through the years and reached the time of Danior. She told of the good countries, where their people were welcomed, and she sang of the mistrust in other places.

Erki's bow drifted across the strings, the music fluid, heartfelt and a little sad.

Old Lolli crept forward, still singing, and gestured for Etti to stand. She raised Etti's hand. "This is his daughter, Etti. She carries his courage in her veins. His sons are forever banished, tainted with sin, but we have our Etti."

Ruslo joined her. "We need not speak of the evil brothers. They are forever dead to us. We remember instead Danior, and the honor of his bloodline. May his spirit find peace in this, and in his daughter's goodness."

Tears welled in Etti's eyes. She had worried she would be rejected, even exiled, and Ruslo had honored her family this night, in spite of her brothers. *"Nais Tuke."* She choked out the words to Ruslo.

Sandu, standing next to his uncle, gave her a smile.

Across the fire, Rafa clasped his hands together. Watching her, he fleetingly kissed them, a movement so precise, so small only Etti could detect it. He blew the kiss over his hands, toward her, his eyes admiring and intimate.

More mead was poured—indeed, the barrel was half emptied by now—and Ruslo led his wife, Rupa, to a cleared area. He towered over her, tall and sturdy, and took her hand, starting the dance. At the end of the song, they formed a circle, picking people to join them. More musicians joined Erki, one with a flute, another with a drum, and the tempo grew faster and faster. Women joined in singing, and they danced, their feet flying, hips swaying, children following them from behind, hanging on their legs and throwing themselves on the adults' backs.

Rafa raised a hand, gesturing for her to come dance with him on the other side of the fire.

Etti covered her mouth, uncertain.

"Oh, come on," Melodia said. "Time to have fun. Let's dance." She skipped to Rafa, joined Etti's hand with his, grabbed Rafa's other hand, and collected the younger tribe members. Soon there were two wide circles of dancing, laughing Roms.

Two songs later, people had turned breathless and the dancers dwindled as the older Rom found their way back to rest at the fire. The boys drew a large box in the dirt, signaling it was time to wrestle.

Miri had taken Atira's youngest daughter, Kostana, to Vai's wagon, and her son Kem, four years old, joined the younger boys. They congregated by the horses, posturing for the girls by dancing around and tackling invisible opponents.

Hanzi stood in the Circle, waiting for Ruslo to pick the first contender. Etti turned to Melodia. "I see Hanzi has earned their respect."

"How so?"

"He's perfected his hip throw this summer," Atira said. "And he's fast." At first glance, Hanzi looked like an easy target, wiry and all arms and legs. But the young men who had gone up against him had learned quickly he was no pushover. With his height, Hanzi also possessed good reach and leverage.

"Look," Etti said. "Ruslo has chosen Jardani."

"Have you seen him wrestle?" Atira asked.

"No, but he's a little awkward. He's shorter than Hanzi."

Atira took a last bite of guzvara, her favorite strawberry pastry. "This could be over soon."

The men shouted taunts and encouragements, and the ladies cheered both men on.

Jardani demonstrated good speed, escaping Hanzi's big hands, but his own hands were sluggish.

They struggled for a while in a crazy kind of dance, arms and legs wrapped around each other, teetering as Hanzi grunted, trying to take Jardani down.

Hanzi spun unexpectedly, leaving Jardani clutching air.

Jardani charged. Hanzi's long arm shot out, snaring Jardani's ankle. He swept his foot to the left, jarring Jardani's foot loose, and he fell.

Hanzi threw himself on Jardani, his long limbs like a net snaring him. In moments, it was over.

Ruslo entered the wrestling box, raised Hanzi's arm, and everyone cheered. Both were given a glass of mead from the fair, and the men saluted each other.

Atira's husband, Vano, entered the box and waited for his challenger.

Melodia took Etti by the wrist. "This will go on forever. Let's walk by the river." She gestured for Rafa to join them. "Come on."

They ran to the river bank, and Melodia slowed. "I have to catch my breath. You two go ahead." She turned to Etti. "Now you can kiss him freely," she said. "I will vouch for you that I was with you. But when I whistle twice, you must come quickly. I'll meet you by the big rock. They'll never know we were separated."

The big rock. She and Melodia had washed their clothes there, a river that cut through the forest and meandered over flat rocks. Several dead trees had fallen across the river, and a rock bigger than the others rested just yards from where they stood. The trees would block the light of the full moon, affording them privacy. "Why are you doing this?" Etti asked.

"I saw him blow you a kiss. Why do you suppose Ruslo arranged for the stories, this night, with Rafa here? Our chief honored you, Etti. Why would he? Because you're all but announced as under pledge to each other. He wanted to let Rafa know you come from a good family, in spite of those rogue brothers of yours. You're a good girl, a pure girl, and Rafa will be your husband. Go to him. And when I whistle, meet me at the rock." She gave a sweeping motion with her hands, eyes sparkling with conspiratorial mischief.

Chapter 11

Etti ran to Rafa. Fairies took wing in her heart, fluttering against her chest. A dizziness made her stumble, and he steadied her. "Melodia will watch for us. We will meet—"

"I heard. At the large rock." Her held her hand and they ran to the river.

A kiss, just a kiss. The mead must surely have gone to her head. They would be punished if caught. Melodia, too, but she was right. Ruslo would declare Rafa her intended. He had promised her uncle.

The earth yielded, moist and soft under her feet, the grasses thick and lush. Each step brought them closer to the river, and her heart pounded in her chest. She was pure, a virgin, and a valued member of her tribe. Once announced, they would be allowed private moments, but that wouldn't happen for at least another week, and a dizzying current raced through her now. She would protect her virginity—she must still pass the purity test with Rupa—but tonight she would touch her lips to Rafa's again, something she had been burning to do ever since the stable.

They heard the river before they saw it. Like white cream, it flowed from rock to rock until it emptied into a shallow area some ten yards wide, surrounded by rocks and fallen trees.

They waded through the warm, shallow water. The smooth stones that covered the river bottom were uneven, and she stumbled. He steadied her, his hand around her waist. "We're alone. We're finally alone." He brought her to his chest, guiding her head to his shoulder. He caressed her hair, stroked her back. It calmed her, and she sighed.

"Let's sit here." A fallen tree crossed the river. They sat on a smooth section of its trunk between the tree's broken branches.

Bits of the moon could be seen through the huge trees that grew on the riverbanks. They sat in the moon shadows, and the river whispered to them. Etti listened, entranced. The river slid smoothly over the large rocks, bubbled in the eddies at the edge. In the center, it frothed and gurgled as it tumbled down. She put her hand in the water, letting it flow through her fingers.

Rafa lifted her hand high and let the water drip down his face.

She laughed, pulling her hand away, but he held on to it, and brought it to his mouth. He licked it dry, his tongue sliding across the tender skin between her fingers, leaving trails of pleasure.

She giggled. Her skin tingled where his tongue had trailed. The river's current flowed through her toes, warm and arousing.

Rafa kissed her hand, and ran his fingers up her arm. He brushed the side of her breast.

Her senses swirled with the water. She could swim, she could float, she could fly. A primitive pulsing claimed her body.

His marvelous hands slipped into her hair, cradling her head. His eyes appeared ebony, sparkling in the dappled moonlight. He lowered his lashes, and the pulsing increased. He closed the distance between them and his lips touched hers.

It was as it had been in the stables, a searing streak of desire. Parts of her she had never felt before came alive, throbbing in a steady beat. Knowing it was the two of them, alone, thrilled in her veins and she raised her arms, plunged her fingers into his hair, pressed her breasts against him and heightened the kiss.

He gasped, and his tongue parted her lips, tangling with hers. She joined him, sliding her tongue against his, hot and filled with a greedy longing, delicious and agonizingly urgent.

Rafa ended the kiss. He swayed slightly on the fallen tree, shaken by the overwhelming desire she stirred in him. He had had his share of romps with the village Gadje girls—'twas strictly forbidden to deflower a Romani girl—but a mere kiss had never seized him with such intensity. He released a ragged breath and put his fingers on her lips. "We must stop now while we still can."

Pleasure softened her mouth, and she implored him with her eyes, her lashes lowered with hunger. "One more. I want to stay here, in your arms."

His body thrummed, his pulse beating all the way up to his throat. "I would kiss you all the way to heaven, Etti."

She brushed his hand away and kissed his throat. "I wish you would."

"We must go back," he managed. He stood with difficulty. "They will be looking for us. I must protect you, Etti."

She flung her arms around his neck and kissed him again, bolder and more aggressive.

A fresh bolt of desire settled in his groin and he grasped her bottom, snuggling it against him.

She sucked in a breath, recovered, and pressed back.

He picked her up in the air, dangling her above his head. "Enticing little beauty, you are. Behave, you. While I still can."

Wiggling to be freed, she laughed. To Rafa it sounded like music from the viol, rich and resonant. Her eyes caressed him, shining with a heady mixture of desire and love.

"*Kamavtut,*" he said. I love you. It slipped from him as naturally as breathing.

"*Kamavtut.* I want to be with you forever," she said.

He kissed her hand. "We will be wed. We will be."

They walked toward the large stone. His words of endearment rang in Etti's ears. *He said he loves me.* The gentle breeze caressed her, her heart skipping as she thought of it. *Kamav tut.* This magic spell was love, not, as Atira said, only physical passion. Still, it was different. Etti loved her parents and her uncle, and Pesha, but it did not feel like this.

She loved Rafa. She had thought of naught but him since Marseilles. His eyes, his smile, the way he looked at her—it stopped her heart when he appeared. It made her heart race when he grew close to her. The heart was where love came from, she knew that much. She had suffered heartache when she lost her parents, and it had been a tight, burdensome pain.

Melodia waited at the stone. "Good you're back in time. Sandu is wrestling."

"Sandu always wrestles last," Etti said. "And always wins." As they neared the campfire, Etti took Melodia's hand. "Thank you," she mouthed silently.

* * *

The next day, Etti drove the horses and Atira sat on the driver's bench with her, little Miri in her lap. They ate a breakfast of *bokoli*, wheat bread with crumbled fried bacon stirred into the dough. They followed the river and passed the large rock where Rafa and Etti had met Melodia after their kiss. Small glimpses of the river blinked from between the trees, and she could spy the shallow pool where they sat. How many more days before Ruslo's announcement? Time could not pass swiftly enough.

Atira followed Etti's gaze and gave her a stern look. "You are building false dreams. He will leave soon. He is Gitano. He will not join us. He will go back to Barcelona and leave you with nothing but reminders here and there that life was once sweet."

"You are bitter, Atira."

"I got matched with Vano. He's as loving as a wet rock. He smells bad, he's not tender or playful. He mates like a stallion—selfish. Rough. The best thing is, it's over with quickly. He's lazy and stupid. There's nothing to talk about with him, which is why I never ride in his wagon. That's why I cursed him, and right glad I am that I did. You would be unhappy, too."

"I'm sorry. Because you are miserable, do you wish for me to be, as well?"

"I would spare you the disappointments I have had to bear. Ruslo will choose one of ours for you, not a Gitano. The more you see him, the more grief you build for yourself in the future."

Anger rose. "So. You know who Ruslo will choose for me?"

"No. I only know it will not be the shining boy you want."

She pitied Atira. She had seen the yearning in her eyes at the horse fair, the loss of something special. Had Atira known someone like Rafa? Fresh fear sneaked up Etti's spine, followed by anger. Atira's unfortunate match all those years ago was no reason to make Etti unhappy. She smiled, uncaring if she appeared smug. "We shall see."

Atira raised a brow as she often did to challenge Etti. On seeing Etti's face, though, her expression changed to one of suspicion and scrutiny. "Do you know who Ruslo will choose for you?"

Etti's heart skipped. She had given her vow to Rafa to keep it a secret. "No, no, of course not," she blurted. "There's no way I would know of such a thing."

Atira did not look convinced. "You know something. I can see it in your eyes." She wagged her finger at her. "You're not a good liar."

"We're not supposed to lie," Miri recited. "Not to each other. Only to Gadje."

"Right, Miri," Atira said. "Etti, what has Ruslo told you? Or what has my father told you?"

Etti's heart continued to rattle in her chest. She could have answered, "nothing" to either question and been honest, at least on the surface.

"Something." Atira shifted Miri in her lap. "If you don't tell me, I'm going to ask my father. And if he doesn't tell me, I'm going to ask Ruslo."

"They told me nothing."

"You waited too long to say it. You're lying."

"We're not supposed to lie," Miri repeated. "Only to—"

"Gadje, I know, Miri. They told me nothing, Atira. That is the truth. I vow."

They rode in silence, and the sun grew strong, the day warm. They stopped in the early afternoon near a sprawling lake. The women tended to their duties, setting up camp, establishing cooking fires, boiling water for strawberry tea.

Once the fires were established, Etti left to find Melodia. She followed a path taken by some of the older Roms. The men carried fishing nets and bags as they walked through the trees to a still, shadowed branch of the lake. She found Melodia wading in the shallow water, looking intently at the water by the rocks.

"Catching crayfish?" Etti asked.

Melodia nodded. "They're big, and plentiful by the weeds."

"Do you have another basket?" Etti asked. "I'll help."

Melodia handed her a basket and a spoon-shaped paddle. "Now you're here, so tell me. Tell me! How was your walk with Rafa?"

Etti told her about the river, the moonlight, and how Rafa had held her and kissed her.

In an hour's time they had caught a basket's worth of crayfish. They rested in the soft grasses by the lake, letting the sun melt their bones.

Melodia closed her eyes, smiling. She spread her arms on the grass and released a contended sigh.

"My thanks to you for giving us private time," Etti said.

"It won't be long and you'll be wed. This is proving to be wonderful, simply wonderful." Melodia clapped her hands. "Did he speak of Barcelona? Will you go there with him after you're wed?"

He will go back to Barcelona and leave you. Atira's cruel prediction ruined the moment. "I must tell you, Melodia. When I am in his arms, everything is as you say, wonderful, but when I am not, I have second thoughts. Is it all lust, as Atira says?"

"Fie!" Melodia slapped an ant off her arm. "Your happiness eats at her. She can't let you be happy. What does she know?"

"I remember the look on her face in Marseilles, watching the men in the river." Etti looked to the white clouds puffing their way across the sky. "For a moment I saw hope in her eyes, followed by pain. She was happy once. I think she may have hoped for a certain young man—before she was chosen for Vano."

"Va. And because she had bad luck, she wants you to have bad luck, too. Do not listen to her."

"Mayhap. But I'm uncertain about leaving."

Melodia rolled over and grabbed Etti's head, giving it a shake. "Is there something in there? What are you thinking? All the men in our tribe rejected you. The women avoid you. You were so lonely you took a hedgehog for a pet. Whyever would you want to stay?"

"You're here. You are my favorite cousin, and were I to leave, I would miss you so much. I don't know any of Rafa's kin. They're Gitano. They live in mountains. Women are on their councils. Women don't like me."

"Most of ours don't. Forsooth. All the more reason to try a new tribe. You do want to be with Rafa, don't you?"

"I don't know." Etti covered her face with her hands. "Why couldn't his tribe visit ours? I know none of them but Jardani, and all I know about him is that he can't wrestle. I am here. Here, with my father's people. He is respected, and thus I belong."

93

"Listen to me. You found a beautiful man who has confessed his love for you. He found you desirable when no other man did. He protected you from your good-for-naught brothers who would have blinded Dody and harmed you. How good does he have to be to please you?"

"He pleases me. But Atira might be right. What if she is right and we are wrong?"

Melodia stood. She paced. With a snort of disgust, she picked up the big basket of crayfish. "I can't suffer you any longer. I'm taking these back to camp."

In the silence Melodia left behind, Etti secured the lid on her own basket to keep the crayfish from escaping. She placed it in shallow water and sat on a rock, watching the clouds move innocently across the sky, too white to be threatening.

She tried to clear her confusion. Last evening, everything had been—wonderful, as Melodia said. Why, now, was she finding fault? Why must men decide everything? If women had a say, men would have to convince them why they should change their lives and take a blind chance that life with them would be happy, not sour and disappointing like Atira's.

* * *

From a distance, Sandu checked his nets. He had isolated another good spot, and three nice bass were lurking under a rock. He had sunk his net an hour ago at a bottleneck point on the lake. He would jar the rock, startle those big fish and raise his net before they had a chance to evade the trap. He had been patient. Netted a dozen so far, and now these. His heart hurried in a most pleasant way as he anticipated bringing in the most fish for the tribe.

He heard faint laughter, growing louder. Ucho, Rupa and the other tribal women were walking to the lake to kill and clean the fish. He needed to hurry lest they startle the fish before he was ready.

Securing the net, he raised his right leg and brought it down hard on the plate-sized rock. It created a splash, and the big fish curled and swirled away from it. The water churned, and they dashed right into Sandu's net.

"Look!" Sandu shouted. He fisted the net closed and hoist it high. "See these beauties! Over ten pounds right here!"

Ucho and Rupa hurried over, wide-eyed and appreciative, while the other women crowed over his dozen previous fish, still flopping on the shore. They scooped them up, lauding his skills, praising him so profusely that Sandu thought they may burst into hymns at any moment. He laughed, immensely pleased with himself.

The women set up their cleaning area on a long, flat rock good for the task. Men hurried over to see his catch, pounding him on the back. Sandu laughed and thanked them. 'Twould be a fine night at the Circle.

The men returned to their nets, eager to better Sandu's haul.

Sandu brought his nets in, cleaned them of debris and began the orderly process of folding his nets for storage.

A sound knifed its way into Sandu's ears, a savage assault, a cursed memory from the past.

Slap. Slap.

Slap!

It stole Sandu's breath, paralyzed his body. His fingers fumbled, tangling his perfectly folded net, trapping him in his own snare.

Slap. Slap!

He jerked his head toward the sound. It was the tribal women, banging the fish against the rock to kill them.

The years melted away, as did Sandu, shrinking in height and girth and power until he was the tender age of six. Ivan, older at ten years, towered above him. He slapped Sandu again and again.

Sandu's face burned. His nose bled, and his leg had slammed into a sharp rock when he fell from Ivan's blows.

Deep in his cups, Ivan's father laughed, slurring his words. "Stand up, baby Sandu!" he scolded. "Don't fail again. Don't let Ivan do that to you! Be brave. Slap him back!"

Sandu held up his arms to protect himself but Ivan, on his knees, stood on Sandu's arms, slapping him again. Sandu soiled his clothes. The long ago stench tainted his senses, an evil spirit returned to torment him.

"Sandu?"

A young woman's voice, sweet.

Sandu took a ragged breath and composed himself. He met Etti's eyes, full of life and color and concern.

"Va," he said. "Forgive me. I… choked." He reached for a story. "Cheese," he said. "Those Gadjes at the horse fair tried to kill me. Sold me peppered cheese, but they threw in some gravel for weight, curse them." He waved her away. "I'm all right now." He coughed a couple of times to support the tale.

"Thank the saints," she said. She was young, not mature enough to conceal recognition of his deception. She fell into silence for a moment. "I heard all the excitement and came 'round." She lowered her gaze and smiled. "We'll be eating well this night because of your skill at netting."

There was so much talk among the men of Etti's strange ways, but she was kind. She had allowed Sandu his excuse and hadn't pried, as many women would.

"Caught some big ones," he said.

"Congratulations on winning again at wrestling. You always do."

"Not always. You finished before me in the horse race. You beat me." Sandu managed a smile. "Congratulations to you."

Her gaze dropped to his fishing nets, now in tangled disarray. "Since you caught so many fish for the tribe, can I help you with your nets?"

"Thank you. Aye." Sandu forced the sounds of the slapping fish from his head and concentrated on Etti's graceful hands as they nimbly fed him the ells of netting to refold.

Chapter 12

The next morning, Ruslo ordered camp broken at dawn. He wanted to spend a night at a grand chateau on the way to Carcassone. He regularly visited Joseph, baron Lagrasse. The baron was one of a growing number of the nobility on whom Ruslo could rely to provide food and coin to fund their trip through France to the marriage council.

The children lingered, picking berries from the bushes lining each side of the road. Their fragrance mingled with the thick grasses in the damp morning air and drifted over the abundantly green fields.

Etti's uncle had summoned Rafa again to drive the wagon. Jardani led Dark Tide, and Rafa had tied Red to her uncle's wagon. Her wound was clean and healed, and both horses were fed and happy. Etti had picked berries, too, black, fat, bursting with sweet juice. She dropped one into Rafa's mouth. He lunged forward, sucking her finger. She withdrew it, giggling, and settled back on the driver bench.

From the moment Rafa took the reins, Etti's heart fluttered, and she felt a warm glow that didn't come from the first needled rays of the sun. Rafa had washed his hair, along with his blue tunic, which was still wet so he had hooked it on the wagon to dry and wore only his jacket, unbuttoned.

She hadn't seen his chest since the horse washing. It was as smooth and muscular as she remembered it, but a short, jagged scar trailed across it now. It bespoke of his courage, reminding her of his decency and the ways he had protected Etti and those she loved. It made him all the more masculine and beautiful in her eyes, and she couldn't resist subtle glances his way. His muscles flexed and relaxed as he handled the reins, guiding the horses over the well-worn road.

"Fie!" She stabbed her finger with the lower blade of the scissors she held. Etti raised her hand to keep any blood from dripping on Miri's skirt of grey flax, especially the orange flowers skillfully embroidered by Atira. Miri had outgrown her skirt since Michaelmas. Etti couldn't stitch her way through a purse. She had never conquered the challenge of even tension with her thread, so Ucho always gave her the task of releasing skirt hems when the tribal girls gained height. The scissors were impossibly small, as was the needle. She sucked her finger above the knuckle. "I did it again."

"'Tis the wagon," Rafa said. "This right wheel is warped. Gives a pitching ride. Here." He took her hand and kissed it, lingering, sweeping his lips softly across her skin.

The sensation buzzed up her arm, spreading heat.

Rafa's eyes shone playful under his black lashes. Her toes tickled when he looked at her like that. He had erased her troubling doubts about the future. She wanted to be with him, to share the same driver bench, and soon, his bed, forever.

From within the wagon, Atira and Melodia's voices grew tight in anger. Atira was complaining because Melodia had released Pesha from his cage and Miri was playing with him.

Etti chose to mute Atira's sharp words with her own conversation. "Tell me about your country."

Rafa looked to the horizon. "It's very large, many mountains. In the north, the summers are warm, and the winters are mild. Cloudy, with lots of rain. In the south, it's hot. In the Meseta, the center, the summers are hot and dry, and cold in the winter."

"Jardani said there are beautiful islands by Barcelona," Etti said.

Rafa stiffened, and he grimaced.

"They aren't beautiful?"

He took a deep breath and exhaled. "They are known to be."

"You haven't seen them?" she asked.

"I don't sail." His voice had turned brittle. "I…" He shuddered. "The rocking of the boat. I have never been so sick in my life." He shook his head. "I can't take you there."

"But we sat by the sea."

"So long as I'm on the shore. I can't travel by boat, though. I'm sorry."

She squeezed his arm. "I like the shore. Tell me about the mountains. Are they cold?"

"They are beautiful," Rafa said. "In summer, it's cooler, very comfortable. A mist covers the mountains at times, making them look mysterious and romantic. You enjoyed the moonlight at the river, si?"

"Va." *And being in your arms.* She shivered from the memory, intensely aware of his closeness and the soft hairs of his arm brushing hers.

"In the mountains the moonlight is enchanting. You will like it. And my mother. You will like her, too. She is like Rupa, talkative like her, but, hmm…" He thought for a moment. "Softer. She has a sweet voice, like you."

Relieved, Etti collected the answers to questions she had been afraid to ask. *Will she like me?* She savored her closeness with Rafa—his touch, their kisses—but had not the courage to ask him such questions. This unwelcome feeling of timidity and awkwardness kept her silent.

"Is something amiss? You're so quiet."

"Na. I'm wondering about… your family." There. She said it.

"My Uncle Tomas is our chief. Our family is respected, my parents are close advisors to him—well respected, but none have the grand reputation of your father." He stopped the horses to wait for Phuro Marko's wagon, ahead of them, to clear a deep rut in the road.

"Do you love your kumpania?" she asked.

"Va."

"It will be a whole new world for me."

"And for me, too," Rafa said.

"How so?"

"From the time we arrive in Barcelona, I'll see everything for the first time through your eyes." He kissed her hand. "Life must have been hard for you with your brothers," he said. He lowered his voice. "And I seek your pardon for saying so, but Atira and the others... they are... harsh to you." He paused. "You will find my kumpania more friendly."

"My parents are warm-hearted, pleasant. They will like you. You need not worry. And we will see mountains soon and I will see your smile." He reached out for her hand and held it in his, and she could feel the confidence in his touch.

He released her, still careful to avoid unseemly behavior when others could witness it. From the wagon, Pesha grew loud, chattering and ending with his special sound, a kind of cough followed by what sounded like "tut," the Romanes word for *you*.

"That's your, um..."

Etti smiled. "Hedgehog, you can say it." She met his gaze. "His name is Pesha."

"Ah. Pesha. He sounds like he's saying... words."

"What does it sound like to you?"

Rafa's smile faded, and he shifted on the driver bench. "It sounds like he said, "You.""

"I think it sounds like he's saying, "I love you.""

Rafa's back straightened, and he leaned away from her. "Forsooth?"

Etti laughed. "No, but it sounds a little like it. You'll hear him say it again. He gets talkative when he's played with, and Miri's become fond of him." She lowered her voice. "Which greatly annoys Atira."

A raised brow revealed Rafa's discomfort. "But he doesn't—"

"Tell me he loves me? Na." A thrill bubbled up at his discomfort, and she laughed. "He is not possessed. He is not evil. He's simply a little animal who makes me happy." In the silence, a mischievous thought occurred to Etti. What better time than now to introduce Rafa to Pesha? "I'll be right back."

She entered the wagon. "Pesha. Here." She patted her chest, her signal for him to come. Pesha ignored her. He skittered across the wagon, corner to corner, disappearing under the chest, and back again.

Rafa peered inside. "You let him loose?"

"To exercise, yes," Etti said. "When he's not in his cage, where I keep him safe. Pesha." She gave the signal again, and he stopped. She lifted him toward Rafa in the opened canvas door, staying in the wagon. "See?"

Rafa's eyes grew wide, wary over a thin smile, as if she held a handful of hornets. "Oh."

"Meet Pesha."

Pesha ran up her sleeve until it became too narrow, and settled in. "Come out of there, you shy one," she said. She squeezed him out and he curled his body tight. Nestled in her hand, he resembled a brown snowball, his tiny black feet sticking out, eyes black and shining, nose and whiskers wiggling.

"I… I have never seen one alive before." Muscles tensed, Rafa appeared to be ready to leap off the wagon.

Etti laughed again. "Isn't he fun? He's a little jester. Likes to play, especially at night." She poked her finger into his soft belly fur. "The quills can hurt if you're holding him tightly and he moves suddenly in the wrong direction. Make sure you don't startle him. His fur is really soft here though. Give me your hand and I'll show you."

Rafa froze.

"He won't hurt you."

"Does he have fleas?"

"Not a one. I bathe him. Often."

He raised a brow. "Why isn't he running away?"

"He's happy with me. This is how he came to me in the beginning. He crawled into the wagon." She met his eyes. "And he stayed."

Rafa looked at Pesha. He raised both brows. His hand shot out, and he touched Pesha's skirt, where the quills turned into soft, white fur. He withdrew his hand quickly and met her gaze. "There."

Warm with wonder, she met his eyes. "You touched him."

"His fur is very soft. It is strange, is it not? I never thought I would. But I agree with you. He is different."

"How so?"

"Less…" He turned his palm upward as if to catch the word from the sky. "I guess, because he is yours."

"The more you look, the more you see."

He angled his head and regarded her. "You've said that before. What do you mean?"

"My mother used to say it. It means to understand, one must learn and to learn, one must first observe. Watch how he runs."

She released Pesha on the floor of the wagon. "Will you watch him for me, Miri?"

"Va! Pesha!" Miri bounced her hand on the floor of the wagon, and Pesha unfurled himself from his ball-like defense position. Stretched out, he was about the length of Etti's foot, and his legs, like short blades of grass, moved stiffly, swiftly.

Miri laughed. Atira rolled her eyes.

Rafa smiled. "He runs like a sanderling—those little wading birds on the shoreline."

She watched him. "I can see the similarities. Amusing."

Etti returned to the driver bench and closed the canvas door. Warmth filled her heart as her fears about Pesha's future subsided. "You have shown more courage than any man in my tribe. Oh, you are his favorite now, all right," Etti reassured him. "Next we'll have you feed him an apple and you'll be friends for life."

Rafa laughed, and his shoulders relaxed. "He has enchanted you." He caressed her chin and rubbed his thumb across her lip. His touch was possessive and sure, and her heart startled. "I am jealous." He lowered his voice, keeping the conversation just between the two of them. The twinkle in his eye reassured her he held no animosity for Pesha. "We will have a man-to-hedgehog talk. I am a jealous man. He may entertain you now and again, but I—only I—am allowed to charm you henceforth." He smiled, attractive in his cloak of self-confidence. "Agreed?"

Before she could reply, his mouth quirked with humor and he whispered in her ear. "If not, you and I must have a talk. Under the moonlight again. *Convenido*?" He asked in Castilian.

Would she slip under the moonlight with him again? The look in his eyes, the tone in his voice lured her into a warm haze, like sitting by the fire, when the flames billowed and settled her into a dream-like trance. A shyness came over her and she covered her smile. *"Convenido."* Agreed.

She had feared he would ask her to give Pesha away. If she did, Pesha would find himself in the supper fires. Rafa's jest about her pet reassured her. She bit her lip gently, filled with happiness.

Her uncle approached on his palfrey, smiling broadly. "You're looking very happy this morning, Etti."

She returned the smile, wishing she could think of a way to thank him for arranging the match with Rafa. Some day she could tell him, but not now. Rafa had sworn secrecy to him and she would never risk damaging his trust. "That I am, Uncle." She offered him some berries.

"Na, I've been at them already." He held up his hands, stained dark from the fruit.

Something sparked in her uncle's eyes as he watched the two of them. "I see. I'll be on my way and leave you to your talk."

Rafa gave her a private smile, drawing her attention to his lush mouth and the memory of their moonlight kisses. How many days until the marriage council? Mere days, but too many, which would be followed by yet more days as she awaited the ceremony that would unite them. Then she could release the passion he stirred in her, a passion growing stronger every day.

Body humming, she returned his smile. It would not do to jump into his arms at this moment, with judgmental Atira so close, and her aunt in the wagon behind them. Her heart pattered an insistent beat, demanding she find a way to be with him again.

* * *

The sun turned progressively warm as the morning wore on. At midday Atira switched to Rupa's wagon, taking Miri with her.

Melodia had put Pesha in his cage and joined Etti and Rafa on the driver bench. The three talked of Red and her steady recovery, of horses and their strength and loyalty. Etti told Rafa of Pesha's loyalty how, from the first time he ventured into the wagon, they experienced a bond.

They turned inland, heading for the baron's manor. "Do you know this baron Ruslo is visiting?" Etti asked.

Rafa scratched his brow. "Joseph, Baron Lagrasse. Ruslo said his chateau is unusually great. Grand. It was built at least two hundred years ago. The baron has repaired it, added a and fortified the wall. It sits on a high cliff." Rafa laughed. "He probably didn't want to wake up to find his bed sliding off the edge of the cliff in the middle of the night."

"That would spoil a good night's sleep," Etti said. "At the fair Rupa bought gifts for the baron—copper jewelry and fine spices. He and Ruslo must be good friends. Rupa said we would be telling fortunes." Like so many of the Gadje women, the baroness and her ladies liked having their futures told, and only Gypsies could hear the voices in the sea shells. While they traveled close to the sea, the tribal women had gathered large, swirling shells for that purpose.

"Old Lolly will probably sing some history and travel tales, too," Rafa said.

"I so enjoy those."

"I do, too. I'll look forward to hearing more of your father's achievements."

"I am proud of him." She thought of her familia and sadness stole the moment.

"What is it, Etti?"

"When you talk of your kumpania…"

Rafa waited, watching her.

"It's different for you." She lowered her eyes. Her parents had died. Her brothers had become hateful thieves. Etti had only her aunt and uncle and Melodia, and her father's history.

The countryside stretched before them, a rich, green carpet under a blue sky painted with feathery clouds that slowly dissipated like lovely white dreams. Craggy rocks and cliffs punctuated the fields, giving way to neat patches of lavender, asparagus and barley fields, with an occasional field of honeysuckle, its sweet blossoms delicious in the gentle breeze. Rivers meandered through it all, blue veins sparkling from the sun, stealing one's breath.

By mid afternoon they approached a walled village that climbed up a steep hill. Etti climbed in the wagon and took Pesha from his hidden cage. He was balled up, his little face and tiny feet making her laugh softly. "Hey, sleepy little boy," Etti crooned, tickling his soft fur.

Pesha chittered, scolding her.

"Va, I know. 'Tis daylight, your time to rest, especially after all that play with Miri and Melodia." She moved him to her eiderdown.

Pesha burrowed into the soft covers until he was invisible. Etti cleaned his cage, found the bucket with the wood shavings and freshened his floor. Foraging deep into her eiderdown she retrieved him and with a soft kiss on his nose she secured him in his cage and returned to the driver's bench.

They had arrived at LaGrasse. Two large columns framed the gate, the baron's white banners flying with his family crest of fleur de lis, and plumes.

"What does it mean?" Melodia asked.

"The nobility trace their family histories on their crests," Etti said. "See how the squares get real small on this side? The paternal side of the baron's ancestry has more branches than the maternal side."

Rafa tilted his head and regarded her. "You're familiar with nobility?"

"Na, na, but I do like to watch the scriveners at the horse fairs. They copy heraldic tables and charts for the nobility there. They're artists."

They proceeded through the gated village. Melodia's eyes widened. "It's stone. All stone. No grass. No gardens." She turned from side to side as they climbed the steep, busy streets, nearing the chateau. They stopped to stable their horses and waited for Ruslo to return from the manor. When he arrived, disappointment etched his face.

"The baron won't receive us until the morrow," he said. "He has entertainers for his court already this evening. Gitanos from Andalusia. Ruslo turned to Rafa. You know of them?"

"Va." Rafa leaned to Etti. "Andalusia is in the south, far from Barcelona. Seville, Grenada are there."

Ruslo turned to Rupa. "We'll tend to the horses and wagons. Take the women about. Bring your shells, tell some fortunes and we'll sup in the markets with your earnings."

The procedure was familiar. Even though their tribe was small, villagers grew anxious when seeing several strange men of a sudden in their streets. If the women appeared first, however, the villagers were less suspicious. Buying wares from the markets also made them more accepted. Ruslo was a good leader. While he could be patient and thoughtful, she had also seen him ferociously defend his people, fighting off three men at a time. He would control the more vocal and aggressive men of his tribe, and they would be peaceful guests in the baron's village.

The older women stayed to watch the children, and Atira, Rupa, Ucho and the younger women left to explore. "We stay together." Rupa gave her usual instructions when embarking on a new village. "No stealing. Be polite and let Etti do the talking. She knows their language."

"I know some," Etti said. She would let Atira work her fortune-telling magic with the women, and Etti would translate when needed. Her stomach grumbled, anticipating supper. They began their upward climb through the narrow streets.

"The buildings are wonderful." Melodia spread her arms, encompassing the many cream-colored structures, almost identical in size and box-like shape, all covered with the same stone slab roofs. "What's inside them?"

"Families," Atira said. "They're homes."

"Homes?" Melodia grew thoughtful. "They're not at all like the Gadje huts. So huge."

Gadje children ran on a street corner, playing stickball. As Etti and the women drew near, the children clustered together, watching them. Etti smiled and waved, and Melodia greeted them in Romanes. The children spoke to each other and hurried behind the nearest house.

"They're not like the peasant farmers' homes. These buildings look like… churches," Melodia said.

"Larger and stronger than the peasant homes, but still, Gadje homes," Etti said with a smile. "Come. Let's see how close we can get to the manor."

Etti enjoyed fairs and markets, villages and crowds of people, and the abundant talk and activity that accompanied them.

The market was still open when Etti and the women arrived, the aisles crowded with people in the southwest corner of the market. Weaving through the people, Etti learned why.

Six young women hovered over tables of fabrics and jewels. They stood out in appearance from the village women. They had stained their eyelids and brows, giving them a brooding, sensual appearance. Coins sparkled in their shining black hair. Gold rings had been pierced into their brows and ears, and their hair was spit curled at their temples.

Andalusians. These were the Rom Rafa had mentioned, from south of Barcelona. Etti had heard they were a handsome people—known for their fast-paced music and dancing. One woman, more willowy than the others and more boldly painted, had singled Etti out. Her eyes, wide and expressive, assessed Etti and gave a knowing smile and a saucy tilt of the head that made her coins tremble. "You." She raised Etti's chin. "Beauty." She crooked her finger on which a startlingly long fingernail grew, so long it curved downward. She spoke Romanes with a heavy accent, merry to the point of bawd.

To be singled out in such a way—Etti felt her face heat. She stepped forward and introduced herself.

"I am Sinfi." She took Etti's hands and introduced the other women, all their names lyrical and light on the tongue, but so similar Etti had already forgotten the first three. *Sholtari, Mahari, Tomari...* They stroked Etti's hair, touched her face and her back.

The tall one reached for Melodia and pulled her to them, praising her clear skin and pretty smile. The woman with blood-red lips snared Atira and spoke of her womanly curves and beautiful hands. Another cornered Rupa and admired her eyes.

"Come with us," Sinfi said, gesturing with her overlong fingernail to the chateau. "We practice our dances there now. We will show you. Come!"

Melodia's eyes grew large with excitement. "Can we?"

Etti looked to Rupa, who had already begun walking with one of the dancers. Beyond them, the chateau graced the top of the steep hill like a castle, banners flying, stones the color of marble, reaching high, as in a dream.

A cloud passed the main tower, casting a shadow, and a cool breeze caused Etti to shudder.

"Please?" Melodia gave her an endearing, dimpled smile.

Sinfi raised a brow in playful challenge.

Etti laughed. It was just a cloud, and she wanted to see Sinfi's dancers. "Va." She took Melodia's free hand. "Let's go."

Chapter 13

They climbed higher, and the gatekeeper allowed the dancers to enter. They passed through the door of the high, white stone barrier surrounding the chateau. Inside, they climbed steep steps that hugged the wall. Several steps later, a stunning site greeted them.

The cliff ended abruptly after the chateau and gave way to a dizzying drop to the fields below. Etti's stomach fell, and Melodia clenched Etti's hand so tightly she cried out. The green earth, laid out like a sea of colors, each field a pretty skirt of its own— lavenders, greens, yellows, browns. The river, so far below and distant it looked to be a pretty blue ribbon flowing in a majestic curl and sway through the land.

Sinfi laughed. "I knew you'd like it. There's more. Follow me."

They were granted entrance into a green, reminding Etti of the cloisters of the Notre-Dame de Senanque Abbey. Guards gathered at a blacksmith's fire, and servants were busy setting tables with white linens and shooing sturdy, wiry dogs from the outdoor kitchen.

They entered a smaller courtyard where other Gitanos lounged. Familiar instruments waited on a table, gittern, viol, harp. "Come, lovely ladies," Sinfi said. "See how we dance."

Sinfi raised her curving fingernail to the musicians, and they fell into place. A comely young man, his jaw shadowed by stubble, plucked a tune on his instrument, a type of gittern Etti had never seen before. The tempo quickened, growing unusual and unique to Etti's ear. "Be wary, Melodia," she said. "Else your eyes will fall out."

Melodia laughed and released Etti's hand, and Etti shook the blood back, feeling tingles up to her elbow.

As the notes progressed, it became less disjointed. Etti sensed a pattern to it, a complex pattern, very enjoyable, and she began tapping her feet.

"Va! That's it! She has it!" Sinfi shouted something, and the women lined up. Within their raised hands they held smoothly carved wooden discs. Small enough to cradle comfortably in their palms, each disc anchored by two strings to their thumbs. Standing tall and proud, they tapped the discs together, creating quick crisp clicks that accentuated the rhythm.

Etti and Melodia tried it, but they could not make the discs flutter. Laughing, they handed them back to Sinfi.

Sinfi and her women discarded the wood discs and pulled brightly colored scarves from the folds of their skirts. They turned them in circles above their heads, all the fabrics flowing to their fluid movements.

Sinfi clapped her hands, tipping her head in an invitation to Etti and the others to join her. The clapping enhanced the melody of the gittern, and another man played drums. The song became a pulsing, living thing, and the women began singing. They gathered Etti, Rupa, Atira and Melodia and brought them into the dance.

Atira's hands moved with a flow and grace, and gone were the lines of anger and annoyance around her eyes. She smiled broadly, keeping up with the dancers.

Melodia shed her shyness and joined them. The music came faster, more frantic. The Gitanos started shouting, encouraging each other to move more boldly. Melodia raised both her hands high, shaking her fingers. Her movements resembled a bird crashing into a tree. The dancers howled, encouraging her.

Etti was sure others from the chateau would hear the noise, which could have been taken as a hue and cry, but no one came. Etti smiled. The Andalusians had probably been entertaining the baron long enough that their noise had become commonplace.

Sinfi signaled Etti again, and together they went under the arched doorway into a small room. The exotic woman dug through fabrics blazing with color. "Here, wear this." She slipped a gold silk skirt over Etti's plain one.

Rupa and the others crowded into the room, and the chatter grew louder as the dancers shared their fabrics and scarves.

Sinfi unbuttoned Etti's tunic, revealing her chemise.

Etti crossed her arms, covering her chest modestly.

"Here. You can wear this," Sinfi said. She gave her a long, silky scarf, soft black trimmed with a thin strip of animal fur and jewels that caught the candlelight.

The scarf fell through her fingers like water. "I can't be seen like this."

"Look, Etti! I'm wearing the same." Melodia twirled, flailing a long yellow scarf. Even Rupa was wearing a silk skirt, laughing as she tried to snap her fingers.

"Here." Sinfi slipped dangling, decorative rings around Etti's ears, and dabbed a red oil on her lips. "It's only us ladies. The court is private. It is where we practice. That's all." She gave her a broad smile. "We will teach you to dance. Don't you want to learn?"

"I do. I do," Melodia said. Rupa shrugged with a smile and followed Melodia out to the courtyard.

Caution buzzed in Etti's head. What did she know of these Gitanos?

Rafa is one. He seemed happier than most of the men in her kumpania, too, carefree, but not so happy as these dancers. She peeked out in the courtyard. Beyond the musicians and dancers and her own relatives, there was no one else.

She ventured out, following Sinfi's swaying hips.

The dancers taught them about body movements, and the important role posture and arm movements played in the dances. "Clapping of the hands brings the music into the soul," Sinfi said. "Snapping the fingers wakes the feet and brings energy."

They were taught to turn their heads and look sideways, and Etti remembered Melodia's winking lessons. They learned how to move their hands to bring attention to the eyes. Melodia became so excited she spun in dizzying circles. They laughed. "Slow down, sweetling, before you fall down," Sinfi said.

Atira moved with as much natural grace as the dancers. Sinfi shouted her approval when she executed a smooth turn.

Etti thought of the moonlight, and the river between her toes, and moved languidly. The music entered her soul, and she lost track of time. When she stopped, all the dancers stopped, too, and stared at her, smiling.

"Wonderful," Melodia gushed. "This music is wonderful. This dance." She shook her head, unable to find more words. Her face was flushed and her eyes sparkled.

Do I look like that, too? The music had swept Etti away into a magical spell.

Rupa froze in her dancing movements and regarded Etti. Her eyes had lost their merriment and now reflected reserve and a cool assessment Etti had never seen before.

Etti's hand went to her chest. "What is it?"

Rupa averted her eyes, laughing. "Nothing, Etti. The dance is good, va?"

But the spell had been broken, and Etti struggled with the cool air on her naked arms.

"Nais tuke." Etti thanked Sinfi. "You are fine dancers. But we must go." They had better get to the shells and their fortune telling so they could earn their supper this eve.

They returned their scarves and skirts, and cleaned the color off their mouths. They hurried down the steps, appreciating the lights of the village as they wound down to street level. And hurried to the village green and their duties.

* * *

Rafa entered the stables, a shady and a cool respite from the lingering heat. Many trees sheltered the chateau, but the treeless village that had charmed Etti and Melodia was wrapped in stone streets and tiled courtyards. They absorbed the sun's heat and reflected it back like an oven.

The stables, set in a cave in the hills past the village wall, remained cool. The crisp air refreshed Rafa after all the mead the men had shared at the alehouse. They were disappointed and restless at having to wait until the next night to meet the baron and learn how much he would donate to their travels. The baron had been most generous during their prior visit, so their expectations had been raised.

Red, Dark Tide and the other tribal horses had finished their grain and water and appeared content. Red's wound had healed nicely. Etti would be gladdened to know her horse could be ridden soon.

Her horse—his horse. The troubles and passions of the last several days mingled in a warm stew of affection, delicious thoughts of his lady lover, soon to be his wife. Her kisses, uncontrolled passion from an innocent, sent a thrill up his spine, igniting a powerful desire and a trust in her that made his chest swell.

Quántos días más? Too many days until they were wed. The thought made his mind burst like the grand daisy lion flower, a round, feathery cloud. The poetry of his thoughts made his face heat, and he glanced around to see if anyone could read his mawkish musings.

"God speed, Rafa," a masculine voice said. "Dreaming in the daytime, are you? And what of, pray tell?"

Rafa turned. Dody, followed by Sandu, Ruslo, Jardani and the rest of Etti's tribal men, leading their horses. Recovering, Rafa laughed. "My investment is intact. See you Red's wound. It's healed." He looked to Ruslo. "I told you." Rafa spotted Kennick leaning on the wall. "And my thanks to you for your steady hand with the stitches."

"You can exercise her soon," Kennick said.

"We rode around the village," Ruslo said. "The people are prosperous." He handed the reins of his own horse to a sturdy young man. "She's been fed, Charles, but she needs water and a good brushing."

"Aye," Charles said. A good part of his day must have been devoted to maintaining his ornate mustache. His thick neck framed it well, and his voice was a bit hoarse, as if he had been shouting for an extended period.

"Say, Charles," Sandu said. "We rode our horses up the back streets. They're steep, and there are so many stairs to the chateau. How many, do you know? Steps, that is. We have a wager." Sandu gestured to include the others.

"One hundred seventy," Charles said.

"I won!" Jardani said. "Pay up!" The men reluctantly exchanged coins, Jardani relishing the take as he stuffed them into his purse. "Imagine running them."

Hanzi laughed ruefully, his Adam's apple bobbing and his purse of winnings from the horse race lightened. "I can imagine Sandu running them, but not you."

"What? You cannot imagine me running them?" Jardani frowned. "I could take those steps two at a time."

Rafa fought the urge to smile. He was likely still harboring a grudge against Sandu for having beaten him so soundly in wrestling. He would defend his friend, make light of it and deflect the anger with humor. "Aye, but those bandy little legs of yours would fall off after the first hundred steps. You'd never make it."

"Hell, you say!" Jardani cast a stormy look of wounded betrayal at Rafa. "I raced the mile in Cologne."

"You ran fast," Rafa said. "But they weren't steps."

Charles tipped his head toward the back stables. "You want to race them? Talk to old Pierre, back there. He won the harvest step races twice. Some time ago, but he still runs them."

Rafa looked behind Charles. A spry old man looked up at hearing his name.

The men laughed and mumbled comments about his age.

Rafa did not. The old man's muscles bulged, not the supple muscles of youth, but smaller and stringy, but in all the right places, thighs and stomach and calves. He was trim and worked his body—Rafa would not be surprised if the man bounced up those many stairs.

Pierre laughed at them. "'Tis harder than you may think, young man. 'Tis not the one hundred seventy steps that challenge you. It's the five hundred."

Jardani cocked his head. "What mean you?"

"You run all the way up." Pierre pointed his finger and ran it up to the cave ceiling. "And down. Then up again."

"Na!" Sandu scratched his neck and studied Pierre. "And you won?"

"In my prime I would have beat you, boy," he said, his voice arrogant. "You're three times my size. You have to haul your big body up each and every step. You need endurance to do it. You're not too solid in the middle, get my meaning." He ended with a dismissive chuckle.

The stables erupted with noisy protests and taunts. Several men had gathered, each of Etti's tribal men certain he could win such a challenge, and a handful of French men boasting of their experience with stairs.

Jardani closed in on Sandu, even poking him in the chest at one point. Rafa slipped in between them to avoid a fight in front of the Gadjes, forbidden by Ruslo. Some heavily bearded stall mucker abandoned his shovel and hurried into the fray, proclaiming he'd finished third in the race once, and could show them his back most of the way if they dared try to follow him.

Ruslo raised his arms and whistled for silence. He looked down on Charles. "Can we race them? Tonight?"

Charles walked outside of the stables, checking the sun position. "Could be. My lord and lady will be at table, enjoying the Gypsy minstrels. Why not? Pierre, would you check to be sure the stairs are clear? The merchants at the fourth landing, you should get them to move, what say you?"

Pierre bolted outside and Charles turned to Sandu. "You'd better hurry. Start soon so you won't be interrupting my lord. You won't be welcome if he wants to walk with my lady and you're all grunting and sweating up and down the steps."

The Roms settled their horses for the night and hurried down to the village gate where the steps started.

"The bastard thinks he's so damned good." Jardani glowered at Sandu, his face distorted in an unhealthy dose of humiliation and frustration.

"Control thyself," Rafa said. "We are guests, and we are Gitanos. We carry our families' reputations on our backs."

Jardani looked down, shamed into remembering that wherever the Gitanos went, they represented their tribes. They may travel all over Europe, but their worlds were really quite small. They attended the same horse fairs, the same markets. Any misbehavior would saddle not only the men doing the misdeeds, but their tribes, as well. "Va. For now." Jardani looked to Rafa. "Will you race, too?"

Rafa nodded, already stretching his legs. "I'll see you at the start, friend." He watched Sandu's muscular back as he listened to Charles recite the racing rules. Sandu was a gifted athlete. It would be exciting to challenge him, and even more entertaining to win.

Charles beckoned them back to about twenty-five yards before the steps began. "Start here. Get your speed before the steps. Fastest at the dash gains the steps first. Be gentlemen. We'll have men watching at each of the three landings. Anyone who elbows another man is out. Anyone who falls on the steps is out. *Comprende?*

The men nodded.

Rafa studied the steep flight of steps. The stairs were generously deep and three men wide. They hugged the buildings to the left and ended at the right, at the outside wall surrounding the chateau. The landings were four feet deep.

Dody would watch for any cheating on the first landing. Erki would watch on the second landing, and a Gadje would watch at the top for the finish. Charles raised his hand. "Get ready!" He rang the bell and all twelve men bolted toward the steps.

Rafa ran full out, knowing whoever gained the steps first gained a real advantage. No one else on the steps to invade his route, no one to push or jar him from his pace. He stretched his legs full out, determined to reach the steps first.

Sandu's wide back slipped into Rafa's side vision, and Rafa stepped up his pace. Still Sandu rushed on, lumbering but powerful with his big thighs and wide calves. Sandu took the first step.

Rafa followed on his heels. The sound of bare feet slapping the stone reached him, along with huffing breaths and occasional curses. Rafa took the steps two at a time, stretching, breathing deeply, exhaling forcefully. A light, misting rain began to fall, so light the moisture floated in the air, tickling his face.

Forty-four, forty-six forty-seven… He kept Sandu in his sights, counting at the same time. Breathe, pump… He cleared the first landing, tight on Sandu's heels. Second landing. Oaths, cursing, cries of pain behind him as some racers tripped and fell. *Hundred two, hundred four, hundred five…* The back of Rafa's legs burned, and he could sense the diminishing power of his thighs.

Jardani cried out to him from behind. "You're close. Push off on the top and take the lead, Rafa!" His friend's words rushed out, breathless and spent.

"Thanks," Rafa managed. The light mist continued.

Sandu took the top step. A chorus of cheers came from the men at the top landing. Sandu turned and pushed off, following Jardani's pointer.

Rafa turned to descend, taking a conservative push, and skipped a step. His foot slipped on the second step, flying forward. Rafa's heart seized. He punched his back foot down, hoping to regain his balance.

Pain spiked through his foot and shot up Rafa's spine. To keep his feet under him, he must keep running. He took smaller steps and returned to his one stride, one step pattern, and three steps later he shakily reclaimed his balance.

Sandu kept his lead. The mist stopped, improving the footing. The first of the two landings came and went. Seventy-one, seventy-two. Rafa maneuvered past one of the Gadjes sprawled on the seventy-fifth step.

Up ahead, Sandu suddenly slowed. Another Gadje signaled to him, and Sandu stepped to the side and walked down the landing.

What? What? Should Rafa stop, or continue and win the race?

Erki signaled Rafa to stop as well. Rafa scanned the area. All the racers save the Gadjes, the slowest ones who had yet to reach the second landing on their way up, had stopped by now and were gathered at a wall, peering through a long horizontal slit.

Sandu was making no effort to return to the race. *What the devil?* What could be so important as to stop the race? *The baron.* Rafa hoped they hadn't angered him. He slowed to a stop, took the landing and joined the men at the pierced wall.

"Shh," Sandu silenced him. "Look you at that!"

Rafa looked through the opening, about five inches high. Below, in a sequestered patio, several women danced to the rhythm of two musicians. He looked closer. "Rupa," he whispered. She wore a silken skirt. Her hips were swaying to the fast-paced, frenetic music. She had her arms raised high in the air. She was laughing and clicking her fingers.

The dance was loud and energetic, nothing like the dances of their tribes.

He glanced around for Ruslo and spotted him. He was so flushed in the afternoon sun his face looked like a beet-root. His mouth twisted in an expression of quiet rage.

"Mi:sto!" Sandu didn't even bother to whisper, the music had become so loud. "Etti!"

Rafa's heart seized again. He looked down, and his lady love was wearing a similar silken skirt, short enough to reveal her ankles. Melodia was there, too, and she was dancing as if she were standing on hot coals, wild and frantic.

Rafa glanced around quickly. No Gadjes had arrived yet, thank the stars.

He returned to Etti, and her ankles. They were slender and lovely, her feet following the unusual music. She whirled like the wind, hoisting a liquid black scarf with some kind of sparkling trim. She dipped down, touching the scarf to the tile floor, and back up, guiding the scarf so it obscured her face. But in the obscuring of her face, she revealed the top of her breasts in... she wore only a chemise! Her neck and shoulders were naked, her arms, too. With a slow, hypnotic movement she revealed her eyes and looked up.

A mist of ash shadowed her eyes, making them dark and brooding. Her lips shone a dark red, so sensual that desire gripped him, engorged him, made him want to storm down to the stage and claim her. Her mouth curved into a slow smile, and he melted.

Another dancer approached her, applauding. She was Rom, but darker, older, more bold. She encouraged Etti to dance like her.

The woman cradled Etti's face with her hands, possessive and persuasive with her body language.

Rafa's neck prickled. This woman reeked of experience and sensuality. The way the other dancers looked to this woman—she must be the leader, and she was closing in on Etti like a hawk for the kill. Etti needed protection from this woman. He must help her.

But all the men were watching, entranced. "This is shameful, Sandu, and it's enough," Rafa said. "We are peeping into their private moment. We must leave."

Sandu remained motionless, transfixed along with the others.

Hot, possessive anger washed through Rafa's veins. "Ruslo!" Rafa raised his voice enough to be noticed, and Ruslo tore his eyes from his wife. "This is not proper, Ruslo. We must leave. Now."

Ruslo blinked, as if from a sleep. "Va." He punched a couple of men in the back. "Get you out of here, all of you. The women don't know we are here. We must leave." He whacked Hanzi on

117

the back of the head and ordered the rest of them away from the shelter and back on the steps. "Sandu!"

Sandu turned to his uncle's voice. His mouth hung open.

"Shut your mouth and go," Ruslo said. "Everyone. Now."

The Gadjes, confused the race had stopped, were waiting at the first landing. "Who won?" one asked.

"No one." Ruslo narrowly assessed them. "Did you stop at the second landing?"

Some shook their heads, others answered in the negative. "We were waiting for the racers to come back down. A few made it to the bottom and started up again."

"I stopped the race," Ruslo said. "It is not meet to race on the baron's lands without asking permission." He gestured to Vai's son. "Kem, return everyone's wagers. All of you—no more mead. Return to the stables and wait for the women."

* * *

An hour later, the fire crackled, sending sparks showering into the sky above the camp. A three-quarter moon shone brightly, lighting the white village and chateau that perched high in the distance. Rafa sat with Etti, Atira and Melodia, finishing their dessert.

The women knew the men had secretly watched them dance with the Andalusians. Rafa had not had a chance yet to talk with Etti about it. He had asked Melodia to help him so they could have time by themselves. The more the evening progressed, though, the less likely it grew they would be able to find time alone as they had at the river. Rafa had begun to feel an affinity with the horses when they pulled the wagons through thick mud in hot weather—frustrated, waiting for a chance to break free.

Erki played his viol, and Hanzi and Etti's Aunt Ucho sang a nonsense musical round about a witch with magic bracelets.

Ruslo and Rupa argued from their tent, their voices loud and carrying past the music. "No virtuous Romani woman would dance in that manner."

"And no Rom would sneak up on women in their private courtyard and spy on them!"

"We didn't spy. We happened to be racing—"

"—and you dragged half the tribe and a handful of Gadjes over to peek at us?"

Melodia grinned and covered her mouth, amused at Rupa's scolding.

Etti looked down at her hands, contrite.

Rafa touched her arm to get her attention. "I'm sorry," he said. "You did nothing wrong." She had enjoyed her dancing, and so had he. She should not have to feel remorse because of the men.

"It wasn't like that." Ruslo tried to defend himself to his wife. "I didn't—"

"And stayed silent all the while," Rupa said. "And you insult me, say I have no virtue, I, the mother of your daughters?"

"Well, I—you—where did you learn to dance with such gestures? And dare to dress so boldly?" Ruslo lowered his voice. "Those women."

"You say it like they are snakes. They were entertaining."

"They're from Andalusia. You know their reputation."

"You buffoon! 'Twas a lesson, in daylight, and a private one until you came along with all these men to gawk at us like a bunch of loons!"

Their conversation deteriorated to a shouting match of accusations and insults.

Rafa sulked. How was he to escape with his lady love if Ruslo and Rupa kept the whole camp awake with their arguing?

Old Lolli, seated across the fire, was closest to their wagon. Grunting loudly, she spat out the last of her dessert through her two front teeth. She struggled up from her seat, her ample breasts swaying her off balance. One of the older tribal boys steadied her. She pushed him away, grabbed a fire stick and wobbled to Ruslo's wagon.

She rapped the stick briskly on the entrance, beating black marks where it struck the canvas. "Who's in there, squawking like a couple of mad monkeys? This is Ruslo's wagon and he'll not be pleased you're throwing Rupa's pots around." She whacked the wagon three more times. "Be you Rom or Gadje, tell me!"

No further sounds came from the wagon.

Lolly returned to her spot by the fire, growling as she walked.

Melodia started giggling, a sound that rippled through the group as others joined in. Laughing, Hanzi and Ucho went back to their song, singing Lolli's name to start the next verse of nonsense syllables.

Lolli gave a grudging, crooked smile.

Ruslo and Rupa left their wagon and joined the Circle, and the group applauded the now reticent couple. Ruslo poured two cups of mead, handed one to Rupa, and they drank together. "To the most beautiful mother of my fine daughters."

Rupa accepted the mead and elbowed him. "You brute. I'm the only mother of your daughters."

"And a dazzling, virtuous dancer!" Ruslo kissed her hand, and she capitulated with a hearty laugh.

Ruslo hugged her, gave the signal, and the ale barrel was unstoppered. Cheers and spirits rose. Ruslo led Rupa in a dance, and not another word was uttered about the Andalusian women.

In the quiet following the dance, the horses whinnied. "Someone's approaching," Rafa said. He stood, helping Etti and Melodia up.

Ruslo signaled the men to scout, and they scattered toward the road. Other sounds reached them. Wagons. Other horses. Men. Women. Laughter.

Ruslo hurried into the darkness and returned, beaming, a happy woman on his arm. "Look who's here!"

"Mama!" Sandu rushed to her, and she disappeared as the big man embraced his small mother.

Etti came closer to Rafa. "It's Ruslo's sister, Darly and his brother-in-law, Ito. Sandu's parents," she said. "They're attending the marriage council, too." She laughed and lowered her voice. "Thank the stars Ruslo and Rupa settled their differences."

Rafa saw his chances for a private rendezvous with Etti flying into the air along with the fire's sparks. He sighed. "Va. Lucky indeed."

Noise stirred the camp as Sandu's family merged with Ruslo's kumpania. Their travels were smoother than they had anticipated, and they had arrived a day earlier than they had planned.

"And guess who beat us to the baron." Darly shook a finger at Ruslo. "Some Andalusians tonight, and your tribe tomorrow night." She pouted with charm, her pretty, full mouth drawn in feigned anger. "How can we ask for travel funds from the baron if you have taken them all?"

"No fussing now, Darly," Ruslo said. The baron can well afford to help us all. He believes in our pilgrimage."

Rafa nodded. More and more Gypsies had assumed the popular role of organized pilgrim groups, claiming and obtaining travel subsidies from the nobility.

Etti leaned toward him. "I'm happy for Ruslo. He and his sister are very close, one of the reasons Ruslo is so fond of Sandu."

"He is. To have all of them here. 'Tis good."

Ruslo's family drank and toasted and drank and toasted again. Stories flew like red leaves in autumn, memories of childhoods, weddings, funerals, and weddings.

"We have four beautiful Rom girls for council this year," Darly said.

"Indeed," Rafa agreed, but none could match his Etti. His arms ached to embrace her.

"But you know what they say about beauty," Ito said, hugging Darly. "It won't fill a man's stomach or keep a child healthy. Our girls are good Gypsy girls who know duty to their families. They can cook and tend children."

"Come here, girls," Darly said. "Here they are, Ruslo."

The girls stepped forward, careful to avoid lingering eye contact and carry themselves as proud, good Rom girls.

"Do you know them?" Rafa asked Etti.

"I know Camanda, the tallest one. She is Sandu's sister." Etti gave her a big smile as she walked by, and Camanda smiled back.

"We have three fine girls here for council this year," Ruslo said. "Girls, stand up. Here is Leyla, Mary and Etti."

Etti smiled demurely, and Rafa's chest swelled with pride. She was the most beautiful of the brides-to-be. He had no doubt she was the most beautiful of all the girls at this year's matchmaking. And she would be his.

"Etti here," Ruslo continued, "She placed third in the Mile Race at Marseilles. First woman to ever race there! She helped train the horse she rode, and we got a fine price for it at the sale."

As Ruslo praised Etti, Rafa took in the sight of her, eyes luminous, golden brown in the firelight, skin smooth, with perfect woman's curves and shining, healthy hair tumbling to her waist.

He couldn't believe his good fortune. She was chosen for him, and, most wondrous of all, she cared for him. With her skill at riding, they would make a powerful pair. The horse fairs had never seen a training, racing couple. Etti possessed the same fierce competitor's spirit as he did. They would give their children those talents and strengths, and they would become famous for their horses. He would know physical pleasures with her—and in a matter of days, he would hold her in his arms as his wife.

Etti kicked him and gestured for him to stand.

Rafa rose, in a fog. They had been talking. What had been said…?

"Ruslo said you won the race, and have been a most welcome visitor since the horse fair," Etti prompted.

"Please pardon me," Rafa said. "I was recalling the race. It was a good one. And now I have Red. She's a fine horse. I'll race her again once she's healed."

"Healed?" Darly said.

"Long story, for another time," Ruslo said. "Give me the honor of this dance, sister. It's been months since I last saw you, and I promise to not step on your toes." He signaled Erki, who positioned his viol and beckoned the drummer. They began playing. In no time, members of the two kumpanias were visiting and dancing with each other.

Etti and Melodia joined hands. They took Rafa and Atira into their group and it grew to over twenty. They danced faster and faster, following the increasing beat of the drummer, until the song ended and they collapsed on the grass, gasping for air and laughing.

Etti stood. "I must leave you now," she said. "I need to feed…" She looked around at Ruslo's sister and her family and hesitated. "I need to check on my cousin, and it's late."

"I'll help." Melodia followed Etti to the wagon.

Melodia pulled the drawer to the right spot and released the hidden catch, freeing the wood, and pulled it the rest of the way out. A thick carpet of wood carvings filled the drawer, and a big lump in the middle of the deep drawer started wiggling.

"Come out of there, you little goose," Melodia said. She cupped the big ball and lifted it out.

"Pesha. Oh, Pesha, Pesha." Etti called him in a sing-song voice he liked.

The hedgehog started throwing bits of shavings away, and his head appeared. He shook, and the shavings flew, revealing all of him.

Etti picked him up and he shrunk up into a ball again. "Oh, you bashful little boy, you. Come on. Come out and play with us."

True to his nocturnal self, he was quickly awake and scurrying on Etti's eiderdown. She crumbled bits of his dinner for him, scattering them, tossing them here and there for him to chase down. His nose wiggled and his fine whiskers shook as he chewed, and Etti laughed. "I never get tired of watching him eat. He's so funny."

"I never imagined how much fun a hedgehog could be. They were always just dinner." Melodia met Etti's widened eyes. "Oh, I'm sorry, I didn't realize what I was saying. I... I never knew a hedgehog could make such a loyal pet."

Etti stroked Pesha's head, continuing over his quills. "I wonder how long they live. I hope for a long time." She looked up and smiled at Melodia. "Not that I would go 'round the camp, asking anyone. They'd laugh and answer, 'Only until dinner!'"

Pesha scurried up Etti's arm, chittering and sputtering. "Hear that? He's saying, *Kamov-tut*, do you hear it?" *I love you.*

"Well... if you say so," Melodia said.

"I do. And thanks for humoring me," Etti said, patting her arm.

Pesha ran away, disappearing in the pile of eiderdowns. He lifted his head up by the table, burrowed away and appeared up again near the tool box. He blinked several times, his tiny lashes batting.

They rolled on the bedding, and he chased after them, running over their arms and backs, and they laughed to the point of tears. "Enough, Pesha, enough. I need to clean your cage." Etti set to her task. She'd need to clean it again in the morning because Pesha was messiest at night, but this would make her morning work faster on the morrow.

Etti added new wood shavings. "Melodia, would you mind if I asked you a favor?"

"Va. I will."

"But I haven't asked you yet."

"He has been miserable all evening, wanting to talk to you. I'll tell him to meet us at the turn in the river."

Etti waited with Melodia. The sound of Pesha's scratching proved he was healthy and running the length of the large drawer, filled with nocturnal energy. She would have liked to have given him run of the wagon, but had not forgotten when he roamed out of the wagon, years ago. It distressed her to keep him so confined, but it was too dangerous to leave him unattended.

A rock landed on the driver's bench, followed quickly by the sound of another one. *Rafa's signal.* Etti counted the quickening beats of her heart. "Let's go."

Chapter 14

A soft roar came from the campfire, the sounds of music, laughter and conversations. "We won't be missed," Melodia said.

They walked under the almost-full moon until they reached the trees. At the bend in the river, Melodia settled on a smooth rock. "If you need to come, I'll whistle."

"I'm sorry you have to wait here, alone."

"I brought my stringing bag to keep me busy." She raised the bag of beads from the folds of her skirt. "The moon gives light enough. I'll be busy."

Rafa appeared. His blue tunic appeared grey in the moonlight, his hair as black as the river. It wasn't as wide here, about ten yards, gurgling softly and smelling of moist earth, rotting wood and fish. His fingers curled around hers, warm and big. He waved to Melodia. "Thank you."

They disappeared into the shadows of the trees and followed the riverbank until they found a welcoming boulder. The moisture from the wet banks settled on her skin. He held her hand, but made no move to hold her. Etti tensed. Was he, like Ruslo, angry at her for dancing with the Andalusians? How much had he seen? She realized she had been twisting her braid with her free hand, and stopped. Would he judge her as unseemly, uncomely for having danced in such a manner? The kumpania's judgment of her had disappointed her, but Rafa's judgment—Etti shrank from the mere thought of it.

She felt thirsty of a sudden, and swallowed. "You saw the dancing."

He nodded.

"They carried us all away with the music. I had never heard such sounds from drums, and Sinfi was so spicy, so happy, that we fair forgot ourselves, and—"

"You were graceful as a deer." The moonlight played on his smile. "Melodia's arms and feet were flying; she looked afflicted with a nervous disease, but you...I could not tear my eyes from you. You are so beautiful, I could not breathe." His voice deepened to a most arousing rumble. "Your breasts are so lovely. When you bent down you offered the most enticing sight, and the way you moved your scarf." He inhaled and released it as a sigh. "Until I realized the other men were looking at you, too. I was ill at ease to be seeing you without your knowledge or permission, 'twas a private moment. The men angered me, staring. I wanted to strike them down so they could not see you thus, so womanly, so desirable."

"I heard your voice." Etti touched his face. "You were the one who stirred Ruslo to order them away."

"Not in time to protect you from their eyes."

"You are not angry?"

"Only at myself for my slowness to protect your privacy."

"I will dance for you when we are wed."

Rafa groaned. "Don't speak of it. I'm trying to control myself." He kissed her, his mouth soft against hers. "I want to touch you and kiss you and..." His tongue nudged her lips open. His hands cradled her head, pushing deeper into her mouth. Longing heated her, and her toes tingled.

He pulled away, releasing a ragged breath. "You do not want to know all the things I want to do to you, with you."

Etti's breath was ragged, too. "Oh, but I do. Pray tell me."

"I want to reach into your chemise and touch your breast."

"Do. Pray, do." Something had happened to her voice. It sounded older, deeper, husky, as Rafa's sounded. She lifted her chemise and brought his hand to her breast.

A helpless moan escaped his lips. He cupped her breast, softly squeezing it, and rubbed his palm over her nipple. "Oh, Etti. I must protect you from me."

She swallowed and moaned from his touch, her breasts feeling full and she shamelessly arched her back when he tried to pull away. "I need no protection from you. You are my intended. We will be wed in a few days, Rafa." She kissed him with zeal, pressing her breast against his hand. "What can be gained from waiting?"

He stood and crushed her to him, rubbing himself against her. Etti molded herself to his body, her senses falling off the side of the cliff, heart racing, skin humming. This was the fire inside Rafa. Rafa, the man who saved her from her brother's cruel whip, who saved Red from abuse, who spoke of his desire for her in such a way she could see herself as he saw her, as a beautiful, desirable woman. He had spoken for her to Dody, that she would be named his bride. She felt the hard bulge in his hose. "I don't want to wait."

"I can't love you in an open forest like this. We're only yards from the camp." He freed himself of her embrace. "There is an old aqueduct—of course it's old; it's very old. It's Roman." He shook his head, laughing softly. "It's crumbling, but there is a section still standing, and a walkway at the base with small chambers that offer privacy. It's about a hundred yards from here." He lifted her chin. "But no. We won't hear Melodia whistle. I can wait for you. We don't have to do this now, my love."

She took his hand. "We'll listen. Let's go."

They walked to the ancient aqueduct. The moon lit the stonework, golden in some places, bleached white in others. "Water used to flow on the upper tier," Rafa said, "Way up there. The next level down once served as a bridge." Rafa gathered branches from a dead tree and pointed. We're going in here." He guided her to a lower structure with an arched entrance, and a path inside wide enough to accommodate a small cart.

The surface of the walls was punishingly sharp and raw, with some kind of thick deposit on the sides that narrowed the hallway. Every twenty feet or so, a high window was cut into the stone.

As they walked, Etti had become skittish. She looked around, as if to fill the silence. "Why did they need windows for an aqueduct?"

He eyed the windows. "They look big enough for a man to crawl through. These water channels are hundreds of years old. Mayhap the work crews needed ventilation, especially if these things became clogged. Water can get brackish, putrified. Or if the top tier collapsed, water would rush in here and fill up quickly. Mayhap it was for the men to escape. As it is, it lets in the moonlight so I can see you." He smiled wickedly.

She didn't respond. Rafa placed the dead branches across the entrance.

"What are you doing?"

"If someone comes, they'll step on these. We'll hear them, and won't be surprised."

If someone comes. Etti's earlier courage left her, and her face heated. They walked through two more hallways that ran until a pile of rubble sealed the pathway.

Condensation collected on a sagging portion of the ceiling, and an occasional drop fell in a small pool on the floor. Rubble on the dry side formed a gradual ledge. Rafa removed his tunic and covered the stone. He brought her hands to his mouth and kissed them, slid his own hands up her arms, his touch a whisper on her skin.

Her pulse quickened, and passion climbed as Rafa claimed her with his caresses. He continued up to her shoulders and boldly moved his palms over her breasts. "You have stolen my heart, Etti. I'm keen with an awareness of you, the smell of your hair, the way you walk." He bent down, slid the chemise aside and took her nipple in his mouth. She gasped as desire leapt from her breast to somewhere in the depths of her stomach, heat spreading.

He kissed her, caressing her ear. She lifted her arms and stretched her body close to his, frustrated with the chemise and tunic that kept her from feeling his skin against her. Taking his cue, she rubbed his naked chest with her palms, feeling his nipples harden against her skin.

"Come lie with me, Etti." She settled on the rock, cushioned by her ample skirt. She lifted her hips. "Here. This will be more comfortable." Shamelessly, she slipped out of her skirt and spread it out. She lay on her back, looking up at him, his hair silver-black in the moonlight from the window.

He settled next to her and helped her out of her tunic and chemise. She lay naked before him, simmering in the pool of sensuality they created. *So this is how it feels to be loved.* She was giddy with the magical sensations the two of them created. She kissed him with a passion she never knew she possessed, her hands running through his hair, pushing herself closer and closer to him.

His breathing became raspy, his voice even deeper, like velvet caressing her ears.

He skimmed his hand over her stomach, causing another streak of desire to flare up. He deepened the kiss and explored her nether curls, sliding his fingers between her folds.

New sensations ignited, and she lifted her hips. All shame had disappeared, and raging desire consumed her body, all from his touch, his kiss. An overwhelming hunger stole her breath. "Take me, Rafa."

She released the front points of his hose and reached inside, finding him large and hard and pulsing.

"We cannot, Etti. We cannot. The tests. Surely your women test the bride."

Why was he talking? Yes, Rupa and Ucho would conduct the bride's test to prove she was pure for her wedding night. "We are named for each other. Others have ignored the rule when they were announced."

"And we haven't been announced. We can wait."

"I cannot." Etti swallowed. "I am ready for you." She felt the length of him, caressed the tip.

Rafa gasped. "We cannot—"

"I have seen the stallions," she said. "I know what happens."

"Stallions are not good lovers," he said. "They're selfish. They bite the mare." He kissed her deeply, his fingers finding a new part of her that fair exploded with sensation.

"Like this?" She panted. She sank her teeth into his neck at the base, feeling the cord move as she did.

A sensual sound filled the ancient stone hallway, somewhere between a gasp and a cry. "Va," he said, his voice a hoarse whisper. He moved his fingers faster and bit her neck. She cried out, and he bit a little harder, sucking the tender skin. She was falling, falling, losing control.

"Stay with me, Etti," he moaned. He thrust against her. He was hard between her legs, and he rubbed himself against her, not entering, but moving faster, harder, still biting and sucking her neck.

Something burst inside of her. A delicious series of spasms rocked her body.

Rafa kept thrusting until he, too, began rocking out of control, and he shuddered against her.

She had felt no pain, only pleasure. "You—you didn't—"

He laughed. "No, my little dancer. I love you. I said I would protect you from me." He kissed her softly, lingering on her lips, caressing her face. "And you will still pass the examination."

Two sharp whistles sounded, urgent, much louder than Melodia ever had given.

Etti gasped and stood.

Rafa gathered the many folds of her skirt and handed it to her, jerking the strings of his hose into a quick knot.

Etti threw her chemise on and smoothed her braids.

"Hurry!" Rafa took her by the hand and they stumbled over the uneven floor and out onto the soft river bank.

Voices. Men. Melodia. Atira.

"Let's separate," Rafa said. "Hurry, you stay with the river bank, I'll walk away from it."

Who's coming? They could not be seen together like this. What had come over her? Rafa had been right. She unhooked her necklace and hurled it forward. She would be looking for it.

Rafa raced away from the river. Must protect her. He should have been more responsible. Poor Melodia, and woe to Etti if they found out.

"Etti?" Ruslo's voice.

"Is it you, Etti?" Dody's voice.

"Na. It's Rafa."

"What in Saint Christopher's name are you doing, Rafa?" Ruslo's voice was edged in anger. "What kind of fool are you? They aren't here, any way."

They? Rafa couldn't imagine what he referred to, but he'd better respond or risk being damned. "Well… I didn't know."

"It doesn't surprise me that Etti and Melodia would do this, but you? You're a man. You're supposed to have common sense."

Rafa accepted the lecture, desperate for a clue to what he was talking about.

Melodia and Atira approached them. "I'm sorry, Rafa. I shouldn't have asked you to help me find a hedgehog."

"I should have stopped you," Atira said. "We don't need any more rodents in our wagon." She looked around. "Where's Etti?"

"We—uh…" Rafa's mind raced. Melodia or Atira had come up with an excuse for them. He'd follow it best as he could. "We found a couple of them, and we almost caught one—"

"How?" Dody asked. "You have no net or can."

Yes, the tribal boys used those to catch hedgehogs, a stick to knock the hedgehog off the upper branches, and something to trap them until they could kill them. "I had a… um… a big piece of bark from a fallen tree, the right size." Rafa's speech came faster as he developed the fable. "We knocked one off, he fell, and I covered him. Etti helped, but he bit me." He sucked his thumb. "Not hard, but it startled me and he got away."

Etti approached, too late to hear his excuse and with question in her eyes.

"I'm sorry I couldn't catch a hedgehog for Melodia."

Etti looked quickly from Rafa to Melodia, who gave a grimace of a smile. "Thank you for trying. I should never have asked you. It was wrong."

Dody's jaw muscle was pulsing, and his eyes flashed. "I've put up with Pesha, but I won't stand still for another one. I've a mind to cook him up tonight and get this whole hedgehog affair behind us."

"No! Please, Uncle." Etti choked, fear gagging her. "We won't try it again. Please don't hurt Pesha. Punish me. It was my idea. I'm so sorry."

"And where in Hades have you been?" her uncle demanded.

"I lost my necklace." Etti lifted it to show them. It was short and held a cluster of carved wooden stars, each stained a different color, suspended from a black leather cord. "The one my mother gave me. The clasp is loose. It fell off. I felt it, but it dropped into a bush and I didn't see it right away in the dark."

Uncle Dody took it from her and examined it. He hooked it and, shaking his head, returned it to her. "Get all three of you back to the wagon. You may not come to the fire again tonight. And you." He turned to Rafa. "You have an eye for Etti, but don't let it blind you to common sense. Of all the fool things to do." He spun away, joining Ruslo as he strode back to the festivities.

The girls returned to the wagon. Once inside, Melodia explained. "Ruslo sent Atira and Dody to find us. I saw them coming, and whistled, but you didn't come. Atira sent Dody to look for you at the river. I told her, and she said the truth would hurt, so she made up the story about the hedgehog." Melodia exhaled. "It was a good story, Atira. Thank you."

Etti grasped Atira's and Melodia's shoulders. "Va. They're angry with us, but nothing like they would have been. Thank you for helping me, both of you. I'm so sorry I got you involved. I'm so ashamed." She dropped her face into her palms for a moment. 'Twas a good idea about the hedgehog."

"It was Atira's idea. I lost my tongue in fear. I whistled for you. Why didn't you come?"

Atira shook Etti. "Yes, why? I know. What did I tell you?" she hissed. "I told you he'd use you, and still, there you went tonight, prancing in the forest with him." Her face darkened. "He had you, didn't he!"

"Na. Na!"

"Hells' bells, you say." Atira held her lantern up to Etti's face. "Your lips are bruised, and…" She gasped. "And your neck! By the gods, it looks like raw meat! Thank the stars it's dark and they sent you here." She dragged Melodia near. "Look you at her! He chewed her like a strip of dried fish!"

Chapter 15

The campfire had died down, and Ruslo and Sandu sat close to it, poking at the coals with Ucho's kettle hooks.

Ruslo stretched out his big legs, letting the warmth melt his bones. He was pleasantly drunk, and being with his sister and her husband—it was good. "I haven't seen your mother for almost a year." He smiled. "She was always getting me into trouble when we were children. Did I tell you about the time she cut off my toes?"

Sandu laughed. "Va, and she didn't cut them off. I got her story, and it was an accident, and you still have all ten."

He grinned, and Ruslo enjoyed the sight. His nephew had his mother's smile, with small, even white teeth. He eschewed all facial hair, and why not? His clean, square jaw, even features and thick hair had attracted Mary, their oldest bride this year, from the first time Sandu had traveled with his kumpania. Though smitten, she couldn't turn Sandu's head. Ruslo had hoped, but Sandu remained negligent of her flirtations, focused only on wrestling. He didn't even like horses much. He hardly seemed Rom at times.

But he was Ruslo's nephew, and he wanted Sandu to succeed him. He'd talked with his sister about it earlier tonight, and she thought it was a good idea. He would make a fine tribal chief, and she felt it would be good for Sandu to have his own tribe. A shadow crossed her face when she spoke of him leaving. Ruslo had tried to pursue it—she was guarding a secret, he knew her too well—but she closed the door with finality.

So be it. Tonight, Ruslo would plant the seed for Mary. "The marriage council is days away. The young men are already fighting over Mary. She is pleasant. Cheerful. Her laughter always makes me smile, and her big eyes are a lovely, honey brown." He leaned toward his nephew. "I have seen the way she looks at you. It's good."

"It could be even better," Sandu said.

"How so?"

"I remember your talk. How you'd like me to join your tribe. There is a way I would."

Ruslo sat up, not believing his ears. Sandu had avoided talking of it since Ruslo brought it up weeks ago. "Va? And?"

"Mary is a nice girl. Pleasant. But I have had many Gadje girls who laugh and titter. A lifetime of it would make me grind my teeth. I want a woman who feels deeply, as I do. A more sober woman."

"Leyla?" She was the third young woman who would be considered at council this year.

Sandu shook his head. "There's a woman I've had my eye on. She's lovely to look at, nice, womanly hips, pretty hands. A bit strange, and sometimes sharp-tongued, but she has passion. When I saw her dancing, I swear, Uncle, she reached out to me and took my heart. I have thought of naught but her since."

"You cannot have that one. She's dangerous. She has uttered a wicked curse that has come true."

"She's kind, and sensitive," Sandu countered. What I want in a woman."

"Kind?" A word few if any would use to describe that one. "Verily, she and her husband will never be reconciled, but she is taken. You cannot have Atira."

"I don't want Atira. Well, in some ways I do. She would be a challenge, but she is too old for me." He paused and met Sandu's eyes, a thoughtful smile curving his mouth. "I want Etti."

No, no. No! "Etti is naught but trouble," Ruslo said. "Even this eve she disrupted the camp, chasing after yet another hedgehog to coddle. She is as odd as a snowfall in Marseilles. And forget not the curse she slapped on her brothers, and look at what happened! Both of them lost an arm. You don't want to share a bed—and your private parts—with a woman like that."

"I want a woman who can bewitch a man." Sandu spoke slowly, deliberately. "I want her."

"But I've already talked with Dody," Ruslo said. "We're matching her with a man from a different tribe. It's time she left us."

"The marriage council has not even begun. He has to know it's not final. Tell him you have loyalty to me." Sandu cast him a determined glance loaded with purpose. "You do, don't you?"

"Va. Which is why I'm against this in every way."

"I am your direct family," Sandu said. "Dody is unimportant in the tribe. Listen to this, uncle. You want me to join you. Do this one thing—this small thing for me, and I will leave my mother for you. I will join your tribe." Certainty flowed through his words. "I vow it to you."

"You would join me? Permanently?"

"Va."

Ruslo tossed the kettle hook on the grate. It clanged and rocked slowly to stillness. "You would wed the silly girl, even after you've seen her strangeness?"

"I don't think she's silly. She's comely. She has a magic about her. She has bewitched me, without so much as a touch." He held the pot hook with both hands and dropped his gaze. He seemed to fold into himself, and a shadow fell over his features. "I have given this much thought."

The dance was only yesterday. In this, Sandu was a victim to impulse. It would not do.

"Do not make me beg, Uncle."

"That's not my intention. I vow to consider it. But I think it's wrong."

Sandus' face contorted into a mask of anger, and he stood. "Good night then." He gave Ruslo his back and left, his stride long and forceful.

Ruslo watched the fire, the coals glowing into mist. A single flame licked up the side of one of the last logs, dancing its way along the grain of the wood, frivolous and of no purpose to the greater, hotter fire.

He would let Sandu cool off.

Ruslo left the Circle and checked on the horses, thinking as he walked. He liked Etti. Hell, he admired her. But he was torn. She was ambitious, a fascinating trait that she wore well as a woman. It gave her depth and interest, and there was the crux of the problem. What made her more valuable, more interesting and more worthy, was at the same time her downfall.

Women were—well, women. They were *mahrime*—mysterious, unclean and to be controlled. They produced children, but they caused trouble and distractions. They could make money for the tribe, but burdened with unpredictable emotions, they could not plan or lead.

Aging helped the older women think more clearly and control the jealousies and violence that frequently broke out. The last thing he needed as tribal leader was to see other young women adopt Etti's independence and odd visions. Little Melodia demonstrated signs of corruption just this eve.

He finished, straightened his tunic and threaded through camp, making his way to his wagon. Ruslo carried a burden, remorse for his past actions. He had succumbed to Etti's unseemly fierce spirit and will, allowing her a voice in approving Red's buyer. Whenever animals were involved, she stepped over the edge into madness, beyond logic or control.

Her shrieked curse still haunted him. She had the Evil Eye, and Jilé and Durril had suffered, as she had foretold. Fie! Embarrassed to admit it to himself, she had even woven a spell on him, too, but he would die before admitting it to anyone else. 'Twould be better to send Etti off with Rafa, away from this tribe.

But he wanted Sandu with him. He had been hoping for years that his nephew would become the new Rom Baro. Here, right in front of his nose, was the chance he needed to make it happen.

Problem was, Sandu was out of his head with desire for her. His mother, Ruslo's own sister, was strong-willed. She hadn't chosen her mate, but over the years she had bent him to her will. Ruslo didn't want that for his nephew. The tribe needed a strong leader, not a milksop. Damnation!

* * *

Ruslo entered the great hall, leading the members of his kumpania who would entertain Joseph, Baron de Lagrasse. Attractive in a meager way, the baron had light brown hair, a short forehead, small eyes, and a small, perfect mouth. Like his sumptuous hall, the baron's tunic glittered with medals and trims, and he looked down from his grand table, giving Ruslo a tepid smile in welcome.

Supper was over, and it was time for Ruslo's people to entertain the baron. It appeared Lagrasse wasn't taken with Erki's music. Unfortunate they had to follow the Andalusians and their wild drums. Ruslo could imagine the look on the baron's face when Sinfi and her dancers wiggled their way to his high table. Would that his people could have performed before instead of after them.

They couldn't match the color and excitement of Sinfi's women, but they had prepared well. Ruslo dressed in rich attire. He was known to the baron as King of the Gypsies, and Atira was *Princess* Atira, from Little Egypt. The Rom had learned the importance of wealth and position, so they dressed and invented lofty titles to convince the noblemen that they, too, came from families with power and privileges.

Atira followed behind him, beautiful in her palm reading gown, a shining, rich red fabric the women had sewn. Only inches behind her, Atira's husband, Vano, followed her. He had brought his trained dogs to charm the baroness, and would show them after Atira finished her readings. She glanced sideways at him, her lovely face tense, brows furrowed. Like the moment before lightning strikes, the air crackled with tension between them.

Ruslo scanned the hall. At the high table sat the baroness, a priest, a woman who resembled the baron; and the steward, Ethan, who had shown support to Ruslo's tribe last year.

They walked past the lower tables, filled with Gadje peasants. Ruslo pitied them. Controlled by the liege lord who lived in splendor above them, they were an agonized, fearful bunch, sharing their cots with livestock and wary of earthly pleasures.

The nobility "owned" the land and the forests, along with the wildlife within. Both were alien concepts to the Gypsies. Who could own the earth? The air? Or the rain, and all the plants and trees that grew on it?

Still, they were guests here, so Ruslo would be respectful. They would please Legrasse, gain travel funds and sell him their best horses.

He passed the guest tables, where his Rupa and Ucho sat, along with Etti, who was casting sheep's eyes at Rafa, a row away from her. He gave her a stern look, shook his head and continued walking.

They reached the dais and the baron welcomed them. He invited Atira to sit and read the baroness's palm. Lagrasse stood, looking over his wife's shoulder as Atira settled in.

The nobleman stood taller as Atira predicted events from clues in his wife's palm. Atira gave a loud read as she worked. Her voice rang, an enchantress's song, so different from her normal, harpish speech. Her rich silks flowed and her gold bracelets tinkled as she gestured with her graceful hands.

Vano listened from below, a smitten expression on his face. Ruslo wondered anew how an otherwise good Rom could be so effective at training dogs, yet so awkward with his woman.

But someone else was taken with Atira, Ruslo noted with satisfaction. The baron had earlier homed in on her gown's low neckline, but now he watched her hands with an expression of wonder, as if in a daytime dream. He followed her graceful movements as she gave an animated forecast of his wife's future.

Vano grunted, interrupting the moment. He was supposed to be preparing the dogs, but instead he lingered, making no effort to conceal his jealousy. His face grew dark with anger.

"Vano. Leave her be. She's reading." Ruslo jabbed his thumb toward the side door, where the dogs were. Where Vano should be.

He did not move.

The baron gave Atira an admiring smile. He held her hand and asked her to read his sister's palm, as well.

Atira leaned toward him.

Vano glared at the baron and bounded up the steps to the high table.

"Vano!" Ruslo said.

A guard jumped forward, club drawn to protect his liege lord.

Vano grabbed Atira's arm.

The guard struck Vano on the head, and he crumpled to the floor.

Lagrasse shouted something in French. He pulled Atira to him, protecting her.

Ruslo hurried to the base of the steps to the high table. "Pray don't kill him. It's one of our kumpania, Vano. He had an accident with his horse." Ruslo tapped his head. "He suffers with his thinking. Please forgive the interruption."

"I most certainly will not," the baron growled. He released Atira. He pulled at the neckline of his tunic, his forehead dotted with sweat. "Dump him in the garderobe pit," he said to the guard. "And if he tries to come back, kill him."

The guard kicked Vano. When he didn't react, the guard snapped his fingers, and two big men came forward. Grabbing Vano's hands and feet, they lifted him and hauled him toward the nearest door out the hall. Vano groaned as they crossed the threshold.

"My apologies, my lord." Ruslo held up his open hands to the baron, and bowed to Lagrasse.

Atira's face had blanched white. She fanned her breasts, giving the baron something more pleasant to think about. "Oh! That startled me, my lord. Might we start again with the reading?"

The baron looked toward the door where Vano and the guards had disappeared. His eyes narrowed, and he made a dismissive gesture. "We have heard enough. Thank you, Princess Atira."

The moment was spoiled. Ruslo turned to Kennick. "Cancel the dogs." No amount of Vano's dog tricks would undo the harm he had caused. Ruslo shook his head. "Bring in the horses. Let's hope they impress the baron."

"We'll present our horses now, if it pleases you, my lord."

LaGrasse gave an impatient wave of his hands, and Ruslo chose to interpret it as consent. He nodded to Kennick, who signaled to his men.

Outside, men whistled, a special signal for the horses to urinate before they came inside. Then of them trotted in, stomping the rushes covering the floor. Their hooves released the sweet fennel and lavender as they approached the dais. The steeds were elegant in silks and feathers. Kennick, dressed almost as elaborately as Ruslo, rode the first horse, a white Arabian mare. She was followed by two lively palfreys, ridden by Hanzi and Pobi. Kennick danced the Arabian, rearing her up so she pawed the air, and the other two steeds performed a stately bow to the baron.

Ruslo signaled his approval to Kennick. The horses had performed perfectly.

But the baron applauded blandly, and signaled Ruslo to approach. "That will do, King Ruslo." His mouth twisted into a scowl. "In the future I trust you will better control your people."

"Aye, my lord. I am deeply sorry. He will be punished."

"Your people will leave now." Lagrasse dismissed Ruslo and signaled his minstrels to play.

* * *

Etti's heart pounded as she waited in the courtyard with Rafa, Uncle Dody and Ucho. Atira arrived, telling them of Vano's aggressive lunge toward the baron. It bordered on madness. Vano was lucky to have been spared death.

Etti stole several glances at Rafa. Over years of entertaining the nobility, her tribe had extended naught but courtesies and a desire to please the ruling leaders. The sole purpose was to gain favor, funds and sell their horses. This would doubtless affect the baron's financial support.

"What did the baron say?" The tree toosticca had found its way back into Dody's mouth. He rolled it restlessly, revealing his distress.

"He chided Ruslo and dismissed me," Atira said. "All thanks to that donkey for a husband I have. Fie! Pease for brains, that one."

"He's lucky to have his head. 'Tis a wonder the guard didn't run him through," Dody said.

"Did you say something to Vano, Atira?" Etti asked.

"Na! I was sick to have him walking that close to me, bah! I was giving my reading, when of a sudden he's up at the high table, glowering at the baron." Her breath came fast and labored, her breasts surging at her low neckline. "I thought we were all headed to gaol. What a *dilo*! He makes the Gadjes look smart!"

"What did he say?" Dody asked.

"The guard cracked him before he had a chance to say anything He stormed up those steps, angry, I tell you. The baron jerked so that he must have hurt his back." She shook her head. "Vano frightened him."

"All our work," Ucho said. "With your palm reading, preparing the dogs, the horses."

Dody swatted gnats off his arms. "And funds for our travel—by the saints, we can't lose that."

Atira slapped her father on the arm. "I told you he was dull-witted. He should never have been allowed in here. You should never have forced him on me in the first place. The only thing he's good with is dogs."

They neared the camp, and Dody stopped them. "Rafa, will you help me fish Vano out of the pit? We'll need to wash him in the river before he makes it back to camp. Say nothing of this to anyone. Tell them Atira did good readings for the baron, and that the baron liked the horses. Let Ruslo decide what he wishes to say to the tribe."

Rafa squeezed Etti's hand and left with Uncle Dody. She had hoped for time with him tonight, but now the night seemed empty, newly complicated after what had happened. Would their departure for Carcassone be delayed because of this? That would delay their arrival at the marriage council.

The camp was active. The horses were fed and settled in for the night, and the men were playing tali, the painted bones rattling at four tables. The women were engaged in a game of speculation, hushed predictions about Mary and Leyla's future husbands. As Etti approached, all conversation ceased.

Etti looked away and turned toward her wagon. She had long ago become accustomed to the younger women's distance. They weren't cruel, but sometimes obvious and awkward. Mayhap they were thinking how to console her when no man stepped up to ask for her. Could they be speculating that she would be humiliated by Ruslo passing a message to the other kumpanias—that he had an unwanted Gypsy girl, and would they like to take a look at her?

Etti found Melodia in the wagon. She lay on the pile of eiderdowns, cooing to Pesha. She had opened his cage, but he had burrowed deep in the wood shavings.

"He won't come out," Melodia said. "I tried to pick him up and he hissed at me. And scratched me."

Etti looked at the scratch, kissed it. "He gets that way sometimes. If I spend a lot of time with him, he's happier. I've been busy lately."

Melodia gave a crooked smile. "Busy with a certain comely Gitano with flashing eyes." Her gaze traveled to Etti's neck. "You must be hot tonight with that scarf on."

Melodia had seen the bites—no use trying to avoid it. Etti giggled. "Rafa looked uncomfortable, too."

"So tell me. How was tonight? I've been thinking of you in that beautiful castle. Is the baron comely? How old is he? Are there gold statues and fountains inside?"

Etti honored Ruslo's request, and told Melodia about the good parts of the evening—the horse tricks and the baron's admiring gazes at Atira.

"She is comely. If she weren't so surly ... but poor woman, she did get stuck with Vano." Melodia shuddered. "Did Rafa ride Dark Tide?"

"Na. Ruslo chose only horses the baron could buy tonight." Etti turned to the cage. "Pesha, come here, baby boy."

Pesha shook free from the shavings and came to the front of his cage.

"See, he comes to *you.*"

"'Tis not you, Melodia. Even after all this time, he's unpredictable. He's not dependable like a dog. Has the independence of a cat at times."

Pesha frolicked through the bedding, wanting to be caught. He disappeared for some time. "Pesha?" Etti called.

He didn't appear.

"Pesha, boy. Come here."

He didn't. Mild alarm needled Etti. "He's been out of sorts. I brought some apples home for him from the baron's table. I'll coax him with this." She held a generous chunk in her hand, blowing the aroma around to lure him. He eventually appeared and grabbed the fruit.

Melodia laughed. "His little whiskers are so cute when he eats."

Pesha turned it around as he nibbled. After the last bite, he scurried the length of the beds, jumped through the tie-down wagon entrance and disappeared.

"Pesha! He doesn't do this. He must be upset." They hurried outside. The hedgehog had climbed to the top of the wagon.

"Come down, Pesha. I have more apple." Etti tossed a big chunk to him.

Pesha scooped it and retreated. He raised his head, sniffing the air, and looked toward a copse of trees fifty feet away.

"He seems interested in those trees over there." Etti thought of the tribal dogs and glanced around. Between the glow of the fire and the now full moon, it was all clear. "No dogs around, thank goodness."

"He can always roll up in a ball," Melodia said. "His quills will keep them at bay."

"But there are many dogs, and they can be stupid," Etti said. "They could hurt him, but they're not here. They must be begging. Good. Pesha, come."

Pesha's eyes twinkled. He took a step toward her—and stopped.

Etti's heart hurried. "Pesha? He always comes to me. Always."

Pesha chattered and spit.

From the trees came similar sounds.

"By the saints—he's talking to other hedgehogs. Pesha!"

He took another step toward her.

She reached for him, and he backed up again. He watched her intently, clicking and stuttering.

"He's saying it again, *Kamav tut*," Etti said. She couldn't breathe.

Pesha scooted down the wagon and dashed toward the trees. A chattering chorus sounded from the high branches.

"Do you think he's going with them?" Melodia asked.

"Na! He would never leave me." Etti's heart skipped. She ran to the trees, fighting for her breath, her ears ringing. "Pesha! Pesha!" Her cry became more sharp in her throat.

"I'll get Rafa. He can help," Melodia said.

Etti stopped and looked up at the cluster of trees. "Pesha, come down." She waited, listening, but if there were more hedgehogs up there, they would be silent now, with her so close, unwilling to reveal their position lest the tribal boys arrive with their killing clubs.

Swallowing became difficult. Her vision wavered. "Pesha. Bad boy. Come to me." Her voice broke.

"I'm here to help you," Rafa said. "Where is he?" He raised his lantern and jumped into the crotch of the tree.

Three hedgehogs fell from the branches, all about the same size, a hand and a half long, dark quills on the tops of their bodies with wiggling, white fur skirts along the bottom. Their little legs hurried like the ocean terns at the shoreline, fast and laughable.

"Which one is he?" Rafa asked.

Etti blinked. They scattered so quickly. "I—I don't know. Wait!" One of them was carrying a small piece of fruit. "There he is, with the apple. I was feeding him."

"But another one has a chunk of apple, too. See there." Rafa pointed.

"And it's not an apple tree." Etti ran toward the first hedgehog with fruit, and they all scattered.

Rafa saw her tears and his smile faded. "Don't worry, Etti. Pesha wants to…to play a little. He'll come back to your wagon to sleep."

Etti thought of his recent behavior, his restless running in the drawer at night. He hadn't climbed a tree in years. She had kept him locked up. "He's lonely. But I had to protect him." She'd feared the dogs, and the hunters—the badger, along with her own tribal members. "I love the little boy."

"He's enjoying their company. He'll come back later. Let's go back to the wagon." Rafa subtly pointed behind him.

Etti followed his glance. Many were watching them—her aunt, her cousins, and Sandu and Hanzi's family. Their expressions were similar—fascinated repulsion.

Chapter 16

"Etti! Come now, come here!" Melodia poked her face past the canvas opening and into the wagon. "It's a most wonderful castle."

Inside, Etti swayed to the wagon's movement, stretched out on the stack of eiderdowns. With great effort, she lifted her head. It was so heavy, her whole body so heavy, her bones cold. Her heart was gone, left at the little copse of trees where she last saw Pesha.

He had not returned last night. She had listened in the dark, wanting to hear the little animal's clicks and chatters, hoping to feel his skitter across her arm as she lay under the stars, wishing under a blanket of loss that brought silent tears sliding down her face.

She had risen before the sun and climbed the tree where Pesha had run, staring at each of the branches as if she could will him to appear. She had called to him, softly lest anyone in camp heard her. She chattered her teeth, trying to mimic his sound. He hadn't responded to the apple she waed in the air, hoping to lure him back with the aroma.

Her misery deepened. She remembered the awful moment when her Aunt Ucho had climbed down from her father's wagon, pity in her eyes, loathe to face Etti. "Your mother…" Ucho's voice had faded as words failed her, and Etti knew. Even as they had prepared her mother for the pyre, Uncle Dody had approached, sympathy tightening his features, too, and she had known her father had joined her mother, and Etti was alone.

An empty hole had settled in her heart. Pesha had filled it, cuddled next to her, warm and wiggling, his happy scurrying and chasing and chattering adding color and purpose to her life.

Melodia pulled on her arm. "You must look! Get you out here."

"It's Carcassone, you fool," Atira said. "Come see it."

Etti dragged her feet under her, took wobbling steps to the canvas and wriggled through to the driving bench. She followed Melodia's pointing finger to the right.

A Roman aqueduct stretched across a wide, briskly flowing river blue as the sky, with green grasses waving like feathers at its banks. Sweet memories shivered up her spine, thinking of the abandoned aqueduct and Rafa's passion. This aqueduct rose tall and in good repair, though, its stones creamy in the sun. A crenelated wall climbed up the expansive hill to the city walls. Beyond that, the castle rose like a dream, nigh touching the soft clouds.

A castle—nay, a sprawling series of towers and crenels and turrets so sweeping it could be ten castles. Fortified magnificence, all hugged by a wall of golden stone as far as her eye could see from the left to the right, all bathed in the glow of the sun.

Pennants flew atop the castle, but the air was still, and they hung quiet from their poles like the curls of an angel's tresses.

Etti gasped.

"See, we told you," Melodia said. "And you could have missed all this."

"Will we go there, Uncle?" Etti asked. He had not asked Rafa to drive the wagon this morning. His eyes were as filled with wonder as her cousins. "Nah. Ruslo wants to get to the council. We have another half hour to reach it."

The grand city shrank behind them, and Etti crawled back to the feather beds to think of her beloved Pesha and wish for a miracle.

Hours later, she awoke. As she gained her senses, she smelled the campfires and heard many voices. Darkness had fallen, and the smell of food on a spit wakened her empty stomach. She smoothed her braids, adjusted her scarf on her neck and unstoppered the bottle of mint ale.

Before she reached the Circle, Rafa appeared. "Etti." The way he said her name, soft and caring, made the back of her eyes tingle. "I've missed you," she said.

"And I, you."

Aware of propriety, she guided him to the wagon, gesturing for him to sit on a barrel while she sat on the driver's bench. Should anyone happen by, she tossed him a bucket and some pegs. He could improvise an excuse, but at least he was busy and acceptably distant.

His kerchief still covered his neck, and his tunic afforded a small glimpse of his chest. She lingered there, then met his eyes.

"I've been thinking of you all day," he said. "When we approached Carcassone, I could imagine the look on your face as you beheld it."

"It was like a dream," she said. "After the baron's chateau and his lovely village, I didn't think I would see such beauty again, so soon. But Carcassone! It's the most grand city, ever."

"I missed that, Etti. I want to be with you for every wonder you see, for all our days." He paused. "I know you had a sad day because of Pesha. I'm sorry you lost him."

"It hurts." Her voice wavered and she struggled to control it. "Now everyone thinks me more strange. The way they looked at me." She shivered.

"They understand, a little." He pulled a knife and whittled the peg, smoothing out the top so it wouldn't snag the fabric when hanging the clothes to dry. "They hold their dogs and horses dear to them. They hurt when they lose them. It troubles them, though, the way you cherish a hedgehog. I heard Hanzi say it's like growing fond of a pig, or a chicken, when they're no more than dinner."

"I've always been different. I can never please them."

"You please me," he said, his voice soft. "You have a tender heart and care more than most of us, that's all."

"They will never accept me." She put words to the fear. "Your people will never accept me, either."

Rafa tilted his head and halted his whittling. "Have your people disowned you, shunned you?"

147

"Nay. But they haven't accepted me, either."

"Ruslo praised you when you did so well in the race at Marseilles. Your family looked proud. They expressed good will to you for that. They don't approve of everything you do, but that doesn't mean they don't care for you. Look at Atira."

"What about her?"

"She's unhappy. She got saddled with Vano. And her children—Vano's parents are raising them because they think she cursed their son out of his manhood. Atira is mean to you, but she saved us when we were almost caught at the aqueduct. I've noticed your annoyance with her—but I've also seen you two share laughter and understanding."

"She surprised me."

"Others will surprise you, too. Give them a chance." He lowered his voice.

"I wish I could hold you. I would tell you that you accept your family for their shortcomings, but you don't accept your own."

"That's silly. Why would I bother to accept myself? I have no choice. I am in my own skin."

"You care for Red. She's crabby in the mornings, you must know. She needs to be up and fed before she can be ridden."

"Va. She often bangs the feed can with her head. She hit me with it once."

"But she's a fine horse. We all have our bumps and shadows. I've learned yours, but that doesn't stop me from caring about you. You're much more good than bad. And your bad isn't bad," he rushed to add. "Only different."

She smiled. "I have seen nothing bad about you."

"For sure? You, who were so angry at me that you wouldn't give me a smile for two days?"

"You some of times speak before thinking, it's true."

He laughed. "And I don't ever want to anger you again." He sobered. "Had I not come to Marseilles, some other man would have claimed you and I would never have known how special you are." His voice lowered and deepened. He glanced around and, seeing the opportunity, approached her, reached up and took her hand.

It was warm over hers, his lifeblood pulsing in his fingertips, sending a thrill to her heart. "Each minute is a year, my sweet Etti, endless days until I can call you my wife. What we shared in the aqueduct—at the river—that was the beginning. On our wedding night I will love you 'till dawn and after." He leaned toward her, and she could feel the heat from his chest, his breath on her arm.

He stepped back. "I can't wait to make you happy. You will never, ever be lonely, Etti." He handed her the pegs and pail. "I must go before I lose all control with you again. I'll see you at the Circle."

Etti waited a few minutes before following Rafa. She couldn't stop herself from checking the wagon again, pulling out Pesha's drawer. His wood shavings were still there. She picked them up, letting them sift through her fingers, drifting down.

Kamav tut, little boy," she whispered. "I miss you so much, but I saw you with the others. I know you're not alone, Pesha." She traced the frame of the drawer, skimming the smooth sanded edge. She had seen the love in Rafa's eyes, heard it in his voice. "Nor am I."

* * *

Angry voices filled the Circle when Etti approached. Her spine stiffened with apprehension. There must have been a hundred, maybe more Roma around their fire. Families from another kumpania pressed close to Ruslo and Sandu.

"We are not at fault." A Rom with a deep cleft in his chin and a viciously torn tunic stood, hands on hips, legs parted. "We have been traveling for two sennights. We didn't know what it was."

"They have buboes!" Ruslo's voice cut through the air, deep and forceful. "You carry death with you! You must leave. You are not welcome with your disease."

"We have seven girls of marriageable age," the Rom shouted. "We cannot delay a year."

"You must, and you must leave." Ruslo clutched his tunic, almost pulling the ragged garment off the Rom's chest. "Your children have the plague. Get you out. This night, or we'll file complaints with the *Kris.* "

The Rom stepped back, mouth slack. "You wouldn't." The *Kris*, made up of a group of volunteers, governed all the kumpanias. They met each year to settle differences and force retributions for wrongs committed by one Rom to another.

Silence fell. The visiting Rom read the expression on Ruslo's face and backed down. He gestured for his tribe to stand. "We must leave."

The ousted tribal members filed past Etti. Some of the men looked downcast, others angry. A few of the mothers' faces were tear-stained, likely from having heard the dreaded word spoken: plague. Marked by their red bracelets, the young, would-have-been brides passed by, giving each other wide-eyed looks of disbelief.

Seven fewer brides than planned. Would that cause an increased interest in the remaining ones? Etti stamped out the grass fires of worry that burned at her heels. Her husband had already been chosen. All was well.

Ruslo joined the other chiefs and the singing began, accompanied by the clapping of hands. Hero stories were sung. Lolli honored their kings again, and darkness arrived with louder celebrating.

Lolli rang a bell, and more families settled in until the Circle was as crowded as a horse fair. Erki drew his strings over the viol, a sweet, slow song.

The brides gathered, signaling the processional, the formal walk that opened the council.

Etti held hands with Leyla and Mary and walked to the fireside. Eve, Jeta and Ludu did the same. Sandu's mother hugged them and sent them to join the remainder of the marriageable girls. The completed line grew to over twenty young women. They walked, eyes cast down, some smiling, others looking solemn, even grave.

Lolli sang, her voice cracking with age but her eyes shining with love. She sang of the goodness of the Gypsy girls, the purity with which they would enter the sanctity of marriage with their Gypsy boys. The old woman sang about health and strength, which would help them bear many children. They came from good families and possessed strong character and even tempers. All of them were able to tell fortunes, and had become accomplished singers or a dancers.

When Lolli mentioned singing and dancing, the young, unmarried men started talking, their voices increasing to a hum, and Etti felt eyes staring at her as she passed. Word of their dancing in the baron's chateau must have circulated. She squirmed under their scrutiny. She suffered no insulting comments or laughter, though, for that type of behavior was strictly forbidden.

The married men clustered in groups on the grass. Etti dared glances at them, wondering which ones were part of the council. She hoped Mary and Leyla would get husbands they would come to love as she loved Rafa. The elderly men sat closest to the route the girls walked. Perched on stools, logs and buckets, their ancient eyes twinkled with appreciation and mayhap some memories of their own youths, and their early wedded years.

Etti dared not to look for Rafa, for she could not conceal the love she felt for him, and he had not proved himself successful at that, either. Her heart beat so furiously under her chemise that she was sure it could be heard over the music.

Finally, Lolli's song was over and their walk was completed. In the silence, the moment became awkward. The girls separated for their wagons, Etti to her uncle's. In the next tradition, the brides would be attended by their mothers or sisters, who would wash and braid the girls' hair. On this night, Etti had declined the stern attention of Atira, and chosen Melodia to attend to her.

Melodia chattered all the while she braided, a pleasant hum of gossip, speculations about the pairings, and which girl would command the highest bride price. "Are you nervous?"

"Excited," Etti said. "The waiting has been so hard."

Melodia laughed. "For Rafa, too. I can't wait until the morrow!"

"I don't think I'll be able to sleep," Etti said. "And I slept all the day. Let's play Tali."

Melodia cleaned her comb and set the water aside. "I'll get the bones."

* * *

Ruslo entered the large tent and settled on his stool, joining the five other Gypsy chiefs. He placed his ceremonial cane behind his feet and accepted the goblet of mead as it was passed. The liquid burned its way down his throat, potent and rich with the aroma of blackberries. He passed it on to Woodlock, another chief.

While the Romani kumpanias traveled most of times and didn't claim any one country as their home. They seldom roamed beyond certain areas. Ruslo's area ranged from Hungary west to

France. Woodlock's people covered the more northern lands in Poland and Swabia. Tribes preferred to keep their members together, but they made exceptions when faced with a surplus of young women or men.

The time for decisions had come.

Ruslo had slept little since Sandu's request. He held his postion of chef dear, considering it an honor to lead his people.

He was still fit, and settling into his responsibilities, but Danior had been fit, too. It had alarmed him, earlier in the evening, to see the young children with the bubbles of death on their small bodies. He had shaken their father's hand. Had that tainted him with death's kiss? Fear chased up his spine, fear and a deep concern for his tribe, should he die. If it were to be, Sandu would make an able, thoughtful successor—gentle, but strong enough to protect his people. He may have a strange, dark side, but only where Etti was concerned.

Ruslo wanted Sandu with him. Needed him. Ruslo must protect his nephew from Etti, as Ruslo must protect himself from her eery influence. The best way to do that would be to get her gone. His last chance to do so would be at this council. With support from his advisors, he would not fail with this.

Sandu approached Ruslo, giving him a purposeful gaze. His height and muscular build drew attention from the others, and Ruslo felt warmth anew, pride of his strong nephew.

Sandu presented goblets of mead, a fiery blend of apples and the buds of the gillyflower, the silver goblet looking small in his nephew's huge hands. The aroma of cloves tickled his nose, and he drank. They partook of their fellow Rom's liquors, enjoying the rounds that would continue through the night or until they were done.

A fresh-faced young man introduced himself as Alexander, their scrivener. He sat at their feet, settling journal and ink on a crate tilted at an angle for writing. He sharpened the nib of the quill and waited.

Kaven, chief of a kumpania that traveled Bohemia and Bavaria, had been chosen by a roll of the dice to lead the pairings. "We have four girls this year. Who is Tawni's father?"

A dozen fathers sat on stools toward the back of the tent. To retain their dignity, the girls were not allowed to be present. To avoid brawling, no more than one immediate relative of the brides could participate. Because one could assume the family member would offer only compliments about the bride, her fellow members' comments on her character, reputation and skills carried equal weight. A mature man with a heavy beard and big stomach stood. "I am Thomas, Tawni's father."

Kaven led him through the negotiations. He questioned the father about Tawni's attributes and shortcomings and opened the discussion to others. Tawni sounded to Ruslo like the typical good Romani girl. She was a virgin, pure and maidenly in her manner. She could cook, her legs were strong for work, her hips wide for child bearing, and she held her tongue even when provoked.

They discussed three potential husbands for Tawni, considering their strengths and weaknesses. One of the young men beat his horse, a damning trait the Rom did not tolerate. They took an early vote and eliminated him. Tawni's husband was eventually named and a bride price agreed upon.

Alexander finished with a flourish and sharpened the nib of his quill, ready for the next girl.

Ruslo breathed easier. With over twenty brides, they may finish by dawn.

Hours later, the sky had taken the hue of a bluebird's egg, powder soft, signaling impending dawn. The men had negotiated all the girls but those in Ruslo's kumpania.

Ruslo assumed the role of questioner. His eyes met Dody's, and he was glad to see that he refrained from chewing on that damned tree stick during the council. Ruslo took a deep breath. A chill settled in his lower back, rising slowly, and he leaned closer to the fire. He hoped Etti's weird actions the night before—her superstitious, dreadful conversation with the hedgehog—had convinced Sandu that she was possessed. Evil.

Ruslo would not have Sandu bypass the doe-eyed Mary and stubbornly keep harboring sheep's eyes for Dody's niece. He planned to match Etti first.

"Our first girl comes from a good family. Daughter of our esteemed Danior, our brother, our tribal chief taken from us by disease, but living ever in our hearts. Etti has proven herself capable with horses, both in the tending and racing of them." Ruslo scanned the gathering. Only council members were included in this tradition, but he checked in case the Gitano, Rafa, had crept in.

Given the look on his face whenever he beheld Etti, it would not do for him to hear this. The lively young man was not to be seen.

"Etti's main strength seems to be her horse sense." Ruslo continued the discussion, rehearsed beforehand with key members of his tribe. "Even you, though, Dody, as her uncle, you have seen her troublesome behavior." Dody nodded, and pity stabbed at Ruslo to do this necessary stripping of his niece's reputation in front of all the leaders.

Ruslo launched into a lengthy, negative discourse about Etti—sleeping with rodents, harboring them in her wagon for years. The way she kept to herself, even kissing that hedgehog. Singing to the night skies during a full moon.

The men shrank back, murmuring to each other.

Sandu's mouth took on an unpleasant twist.

Ruslo prepared to drive the stake deeper. "She is a sweet, even-tempered girl most of times, but she has demonstrated moments of ill temper." He paused, eyes downcast, as if it hurt him deeply to say more. Sadly, it did, but he must. "I myself witnessed the moment in Marseilles when Etti cursed her brothers. She entered a spell. Her eyes grew wild, and she struck out and cursed them with a heinous fate, that they would be torn from limb to limb." He paused for effect in the now-silent tent. "Within two days, both of them lost their arms."

The tent buzzed with gasps and exclamations of surprise.

Sandu's expression grew dark and dangerous.

"Mind you, Her brothers upset her. They're evil. They tried to blind Dody with horsewhips a couple of sennights before that, and they bought a horse Etti had trained. She had an unnatural attraction to the horse, too, and wouldn't let it go."

"They were thieves," Sandu growled. "They deserved what they got."

"Va, as I said, Jile and Durril are evil. And a woman who can curse is to be watched, especially when vulnerable, during the night. When sleeping. That is all I am saying. Other than those incidents, she is an industrious girl." He paused, letting all the facts settle in. "Who harbors interest in Etti?"

"Rafa, the Gitano," Dody said. "Rafa admires her ability with horses, and plans to race with her and breed horses for the fairs. They have worked well together, healing Red—her brothers stabbed her mare. That is why she was so angry." Dody explained,

154

facing the other men. "Etti and Rafa have developed the type of close friendship that will blossom in marriage."

Sandu leaned forward. "But if he weds Etti, he will take her to Barcelona. We do not wish to lose Etti's skill with horses. She can train, race and sell them to our tribe's benefit." His words flowed smooth as warm butter. "We do not wish her to leave our tribe." Sandu stood, emphasizing his strength as he hovered over the other Roms, his big legs spread in defiance, his muscular arms crossed. "I want Etti, Uncle. I am strong enough to protect her. If I am to stay with you, I will have her."

"Rafa protected Etti from her brothers. No one else stepped forward to help her that night," Dody said. "Rafa is prepared to offer a generous bride price for her." Dody rushed on. "That will more than make up for any extra pounds she might make at next year's horse fair. She will not ride or train any longer once she is with child, so it's a moot issue."

"Whatever Rafa's price is, mine will be better," Sandu said. "Much higher."

"Etti is not a horse to be sold to the biggest purse." Dody's face reddened. His held his hands at his side, fisted, and an unusual chill hung on his words. "I recommend Rafa." Dody narrowed his eyes at Sandu, who was still locked in his grim, formidable stance. "Rafa comes from a good family. I highly recommend him." Dody shot spears of determination at Ruslo. *You agreed,* his sour expression relayed. *Stay true to your word.*

Ruslo rued his position. He had taken the debate as far as he could, and he could not elevate Rafa at the expense of Sandu, not when his nephew's muscles flexed beneath his tunic, itching for action. Ruslo did not doubt that Sandu would fight for Etti. Curse that he saw her dance! Curse that Ruslo himself had not pulled the men from the dancing.

"Etti is mine," Sandu said. "I am your nephew. I, too, come from good family." He relaxed his stance and offered a smile. 'Twas not a smile of happiness, nor a smile of affection. His eyes did not narrow in anger, but his lids lowered, and it was as if he had slipped into darkness. The quiet control, the sudden withdrawal seemed otherworldly. Ruslos' stomach clenched, a strange sensation creeping along his skin, as if he were knocking on the door of his sister's secret about her son.

Sandu lifted the goblet of mead from the table, one of the many he had poured and drunk through the night. He drained it in one gulp, but his nephew's tongue remained clear. "I come from a good family. A loyal one." He walked closer to the scrivener, signaling him to pick up his quill, and glared at Ruslo, a probing challenge in his dark eyes. "Now, uncle, you must decide."

Chapter 17

Rafa waited all night by the fire with Jardani. Rupa and Ucho boiled fruit water and prepared wheat bread with bacon, but the camp was quiet. "Why aren't they back yet, from the pairings?" Rafa asked the women.

"There were many girls this year," Rupa said.

Rafa noticed the Circle, deserted but for women and children. "Where are the rest of the men?"

"They left for the village blacksmith, remember?" Ucho said. "For the wheels, and shoeing the horses."

Of course, Rafa thought. The roads had taken a toll on the wagons. He accepted the corn meal cakes from Ucho. He had no appetite, but refusing food constituted an insult for Gypsies. He chewed slowly, forcing a swallow. In past years he had watched the young men of his own kumpania suffer through the slow wait for results from a marriage council, but he had never had a personal stake in one before.

Until Marseilles, when he had seen Etti at the riverbank while washing Dark Tide, he thought of marriage as something he would do many years hence. Until he had seen her smile, the joy of life in her eyes. When he held her in his arms he found a feast for the senses, saw rich new opportunities for a life of physical pleasures.

He suffered from an insatiable hunger to discover every delectable part of her.

But he had also discovered a quiet joy at watching her from afar, as she stroked Red's mane, the way she lowered her lashes and laughed—even as she performed ordinary tasks, as when she hung her washed clothes with pegs to dry. Their interests fueled his hopes for the future—her love for Red, her zeal for racing, and the eager affection and longing in her eyes that launched nights filled with dreams of her in his arms.

The dawn stretched on like a festering wound in his stomach.

"You look terrible," Jardani said. "Why don't you try to sleep?"

"Can't. I've had friends wait through a council before. The men talk about the girls beforehand, and most is settled before they enter the tent. What can be taking so long?"

Jardani punched his arm. "Why so nervous? Dody is on your side, and he said Ruslo likes you. The two of you have been together for two weeks, pining for each other. They would have to be blind not to notice."

"I need to know." Rafa's nerves scraped, as if he were being dragged by a horse over sharp stones. He was tired, hungry and too upset to sleep.

Dody finally appeared from behind a wagon. He signaled Rafa to join him.

Rafa jumped up, spilling his beverage. "'Tis time."

Jardani stood and rested his hand on his cousin's shoulder. "She will be yours, Rafa. I'm sure of it. Worry not."

"My thanks," Rafa said. He hurried to Dody, eager to read his face to learn sooner than the words could escape his lips. "Well? Was I—"

"Let's walk." Dody's mouth was free of the tree stick, and he walked briskly. He wouldn't meet Rafa's eyes.

Rafa stopped. "I don't want to walk, Dody. I need to know." He was Gitano, and that might have caused problems. But Dody had assured him that he and Ruslo would support him. "Was I named?"

Dody grimaced, as if a handful of fire ants had taken residence in his shirt. "Na."

Rafa's feet stumbled on the earth, and his legs refused to move. "Na? What happened?"

Stroking his mustache, Dody shook his head slowly. "I spoke well for you, Rafa. As did Ruslo." A profound sadness pulled at his features. "I wanted this for you. I wanted this for Etti, a new beginning. Many of us have been too harsh with her, but then, Etti is a strong woman and would not bend to their wills."

Rafa's breath left him in a painful jolt. If he wasn't named… "Who?"

"Family blood is stronger than friendship. Sandu demanded his uncle name him to wed Etti. Ruslo tried to talk him out of it," Dody hurried on, "but Sandu became so angry. He's never been so forceful."

"Sandu." Rafa could not swallow. Or breathe. His mouth was so dry his words came out in a croak. "He gave his word to you. You said so."

Dody remained silent, and the moment heated, a silent protest that consumed Rafa. "He can't do that. She loves me. I love her."

"Sandu ordered it written. It is official."

Rafa clenched his teeth, unable to control the fury that tensed his muscles so tightly he could no longer stand still. He paced, trying to release the pressure. "I'll kill him."

"You have not seen him when he speaks of Etti. He is, I think, out of all reason with it. You are young and strong, Rafa, but Sandu is… you would not want to fight him."

"But I do. I will. I must."

"Do it, and you'll be banished, like her brothers. Is that what you want?"

"Na. Na." Rafa turned to him. "Did someone mention that I was a Gitano? Reluctant to marry? In my twenties and yet unwed?"

"I presented your strengths. Not one person listed a fault against you."

Rafa slogged through the choking disappointment. "I want only what I was promised. I want Etti."

"You were not promised Etti. I should never have told you. Ruslo has the right to change his mind, and he didn't know Sandu wanted her. He's very fond of Sandu. Ruslo has no son. Sandu is the closest he will come to that."

"I'm sorry. Your friend, Jardani, will give you counsel. Go. Talk to him about this. I must go now, and tell Etti."

"Na! I must tell her myself. Do not take this from me, too."

159

Dody considered a moment, and faced him. "You will walk with me to my wagon. You will sit outside the wagon and talk with her."

Rafa held his ribs. A knife must have lodged between them, making it hard to breathe. His heartbeat pounded in his ears, roaring in a pulsing, bleeding grief. *I have lost her.*

"Do nothing foolish. Do you hear me, Rafa? Say it, say, 'I will do nothing foolish.' Etti is a dutiful niece. She will not defy her chief, or me. Nor will you. Do you agree?"

Rafa released a ragged breath. "I will not embarrass her, or do harm to her reputation with the tribe."

Dody's eyes misted. "Let us go to her now."

Etti slid from her eiderdown, her thoughts blurred from a restless night. The council had stretched through the night. Eventually the Gypsies left the central fire and returned to their camps, too tired to wait for the announcement of who had been named to wed the young girls.

For one very special man, Etti knew the answer to that question. She was careful to not wake Melodia, who had fallen asleep after many games of Tali.

Etti stood, shaking the wrinkles from her skirt. She had waited so long for this day. Joy bubbled in her chest, little butterflies of excitement fluttering inside. She suppressed an urge to giggle. She could not wait to see the happiness in Rafa's eyes.

My hair! Her braids had become hopelessly tangled from her tossing and turning in bed. Etti rushed to the water basin and washed her face. She chewed mint and rinsed her mouth, straightened her kerchief so her love bruises would not show.

Her fingers shook as she released her hair and combed it. She wanted to be beautiful for him. Rafa. *He will be your husband.* She hummed a happy tune from her childhood.

The camp was quiet. She heard her uncle's voice and glanced down the line of wagons. Uncle Dody and Rafa approached. He was looking for her.

She waved, laughing. She smiled so broadly it hurt. The earth beneath her feet was soft and moist, and sunshine warmed her. The air, light with a gentle breeze, caressed her hair. She closed her eyes, wrapping the moment close around her.

"Good morning!" Her voice was high and silly, but she had no care.

As her uncle drew nearer, she saw trouble framing his eyes. Sadness. Profound sadness. As if bringing news of death. The air grew too heavy to breathe.

Rafa—his shoulders slumped. He approached her with hesitating steps, his skin pale. Hurt and longing lay naked in his eyes.

Etti's thoughts scattered like swallows before a storm. The warmth vanished. Heart pounding fiercely in her ears, she swallowed, trying to find her voice, but a suffocating thought seized in her throat.

"Na. Na!" It had been too wonderful, too dear. She held her hand up to them, refusing to listen to what they would say.

Melodia jumped up, struggling to escape her eiderdown. "Etti! Are you all right?"

Etti waved her to silence, and Melodia froze, her eyes widened in concern.

The men grew closer. Rafa said something to her uncle. At the least she thought so because his mouth moved, but she could not hear for the ringing, the nightmare in her head. Dody stayed focused on Rafa. "I'll give you a moment, but I won't be far. I'll be here." He turned and walked toward the open field.

The question rested uneasily on her tongue. Her breath was caught in her throat as she turned to Rafa. "What is it?"

His silence crushed her. He avoided her eyes. "There is no easy way—"

"Say it. Just say it."

"Ruslo named Sandu."

"Sandu?" She fair screamed the name. "Sandu?" This could not be true. Some other mishap, surely. "Named him for what?"

Rafa closed his eyes, as if it was too painful to put into words. He shook his head. "He tried to talk Sandu out of it, but—"

"Out of what?" The words scraped their way off her tongue as she clung to the crumbling edge of her future.

"Wedlock."

The path spun beneath her feet, and an inky sickness chilled her veins. She swallowed, gagging. "He's never looked at me in that way. Never."

"He saw you dancing. He pressed Ruslo hard, saying he wouldn't stay with his kumpania if he was denied you. He—"

Etti covered her ears. "Na! I'll hear nothing of this. Naught, do you understand? Sandu is a big, old giant. Like an ox. How dare he think I would want him?"

He reached for her, but she pulled away. "Ruslo must change his ruling. He promised he would choose you."

Rafa lowered his voice. "He swore Dody to secrecy. Forbade him to tell anyone. Dody told me in the strictest confidence. You will hurt your uncle if you mention it to Ruslo."

"So I'm to wed Sandu? You would allow that?"

The muscle at his jaw pulsed, and he grit out the words. "It has been decided."

"Let's leave then. Leave with me, Rafa."

"We need time to think. If you leave, there will be penalties."

Banished. She would be banished. Her family, Melodia, Atira, Uncle Dody—all would be forbidden to even look at her.

He took her hand. "Let's talk with your uncle. And Ruslo. Dody can remind him of his promise."

Uncle Dody approached and joined them. "You must leave now, Rafa. Your presence here is… unseemly now."

Unseemly. Panic welled in her throat as her uncle's words echoed. There would be no more gazes. No more smiles, no more touches and talk with Rafa on the wagon bench. Ever. *Our time together has ended.* Cool tears chilled Etti's face. She wiped them away and faced her uncle. "You must help us. Please."

"I spoke for Rafa." Her uncle cupped her face in his hands, his brows drawn in sorrow. "I tried every logical argument for him, and against Sandu. He is Ruslo's favorite. You must accept the decision."

"Why?" She shrugged his hand off. "I don't care for Ruslo or Sandu, or any of those men on the council. I care for Rafa."

Uncle Dody's voice softened, and he gave a sad smile. "I, too, thought it good for you to be with Rafa, but you must accept their decision. You are a good Gypsy girl—"

"I am *not*, and you know it. I need you to fight for us. You counseled your own daughter when she was matched with Vano. It broke her heart, and she lost her children, and—"

"She did not lose them. They're with her during the day. Because she is dutiful, she is still part of her family. She will always have a place with us." Dody released a tired sigh. "You're upset. You need to think. Rest."

"I need you to help us." With a last lingering gaze at Rafa, she turned away. "All of you. Leave me now." She strode past Melodia and into the wagon, tying the door shut.

* * *

An hour later, the heat had become oppressive in the wagon. Etti tore her gaze from Pesha's empty cage, where she'd been staring. Her father had given it to her when Pesha first invited himself into her life. It was actually an eel cage, with an oval shape similar to a jug of the finer French wines. Turned on its side, it fit neatly in the large drawer. Pesha enjoyed running up and down the sides during his nightly frenzies.

There would be no furry movement any more. Outside, the camp stirred to life as the sun rose higher in the sky—the scrape of the kettle hooks as cooking pots were settled above the fires, the indignant tones of the mothers as they shamed their children out of their beds, the horses banging against the feed buckets.

Inside the wagon, though, quiet reined. No scurrying little feet in the cage, no laughter, only echoes of memories with Rafa. Whispered flirtations, velvet words of endearment, the masculine scent of him, the breathlessness of lovemaking. His smile when he described how she appeared to him when she finished the race.

She loved him. She cherished the reflection of herself that she saw in his eyes. And the confidence he had in her, the dreams of their future, racing and breeding horses together. Building a new family to replace the one she'd lost.

She hoped they could not see her misery now.

I'll never give him up. The spirit of resistance in her words collided with truth. The contradiction sank like a fish hook into her heart, and she bled slowly, her dreams leaking from her, staining her hope. She moved mechanically, cleaning Pesha's cage of all its wood shavings. She removed his yellow toy ball, scratched from his tiny claws, and the leather collar he had outgrown. He would not be back. Nor would Rafa.

The thought weakened her, making her arms heavy. Through a dark haze she filled a bucket with the shavings and swept dirt and grasses from the wagon.

She stiffened her back and her resolve. She would not let them ruin her life as they had Atira's. Dody didn't have the courage to stand up to them, but she would. She would not live the rest of her days without Rafa. She would not!

A soft knock at the wagon entrance startled her. "Who's there?"

"Sandu." His smooth, mellow voice invaded her reserve, and she swallowed a reflexive gasp. "Godspeed, my future bride."

She closed her eyes and took a deep breath. She must start by dissuading him from such thoughts.

She dreaded leaving the wagon and facing him. She decided in that moment that she would appeal to his generosity, his good-natured side. She would explain how she could never make him happy while loving Rafa as she did. She would convince him he deserved better than her; she was so odd, after all. Her fingers sluggish, she untied the canvas and left the wagon. She turned toward him, unwilling to meet his gaze. "God speed, Sandu." She forced the anxiety from her voice, and it sounded neutral, calm, as she had hoped it would.

He shifted his huge frame from side to side, an ox trapped in a ditch of mud. Beads of sweat had formed on his forehead, and he pulled at the hem of his tunic. "Your uncle told you of the marriage council's decision. I am to be your husband." He cleared his throat. "Of this I am pleased."

"I'm sorry you drew my name," Etti said. "You deserve better than me."

"Oh, it was not by chance. I wanted you." His eyes homed in on her, a slow, heavy-lidded focus. "I told my uncle. I wanted no other."

She slipped past him and gathered her eiderdown.

He hastened to her, helping to lift the puffy bed.

"Let go." Etti jerked it out of his hands. "It is my bed. I can do it myself."

The bed was awkward, flopping this way and that, an unruly squid wiggling out of her grasp.

Sandu laughed. "It's too big for you, little girl." He grabbed an end.

Etti worked quickly, getting the other end through the canvas door, and pulled the last corner from his hand. "I have not been a girl for years, and I can handle this now, thank you."

She shoved it inside, a giant cloud of feathers and quilted linen. She wrestled it in place over her uncle and aunt's bed, making it as neat and orderly as she wished her own life could be.

Outside again, she gathered Melodia's smaller bed. She had left, honoring Etti's need for time alone.

"I know well you're a grown woman," Sandu said. "You are comely. I... I saw you at the baron's chateau." He lowered his voice, and it grew thick. "Dancing. After seeing you that day, I will never look at another. " He wiped the sweat from his brow with his hand and dried it on his hose. "It is only you I want."

Her thoughts tangled into hopeless knots. He'd watched her dance. She avoided his eyes and stuffed Melodia's bed through the canvas, careful to not snag the eiderdown on the hooks that held the canvas in place.

Repulsed, she bit her lower lip to keep the groan from escaping. "I am nothing. You deserve much better than me."

The lust in his eyes made her stomach turn. She gave him her back. "You chose the wrong one. Mary wants you."

"She has been chosen for Hanzi."

"She was the right one for you. Not me, do you understand, Sandu?" She gestured a cutting motion with her hands. "Not me."

He gave her a small, tender smile. Stubborn as the ox he resembled, he was not listening reason. Etti abandoned her plan for gentle persuasion. "I love Rafa. Not you. He loves me."

"But we are betrothed now. You are mine." He took a step toward her.

"You cannot force me."

That stopped his advance on her. His face darkened. He stuck his chest out and, impossibly, he appeared even more brawny.

"Ruslo has ordered it. You have no choice in this. We have decided."

Etti returned to Melodia's eiderdown, stuffing it into the wagon with a vengeance, snagging be damned. The linen ripped down the whole left side. "You have no right to decide for me. I will not wed you."

Sandu trapped Etti's shoulders in his huge hands. He pulled her away from the wagon. "You will do your duty. In time you may love me, the chief of your tribe." He turned her around and crushed her to his giant chest. He ran his hands through her hair. "Etti, my queen. Together we will lead our tribe, as your father and mother did. Our kumpania sings his praise now, and in the future, they will sing mine, and yours. For all time."

"She pulled her dagger and stuck it under his chin. "Release me."

Sandu snatched her wrist, squeezing it until the knife fell from her hands. He laughed. "We wed in three days." He gave her a lustful grin. "You will like our wedding night."

She twisted out of his grasp and stepped up on the wagon.

He grabbed her.

She reached for the broom and struck him. The torn eiderdown burst, and a soft white rain of feathers fluttered to the ground.

"Let go of me!" She cried out and struck him in the face again. Clutching clumps of the down, she yanked them out and threw them at him, as if hurling mud. Feathers flew, snowing down on them, on the wagon, on the ground.

Women gathered around them, her cousins and others, their expressions curious and excited. Ruslo broke through them to reach Etti. "What goes here?" He reached his nephew and stopped, looking from Sandu to Etti for an answer.

"He's hurting me," Etti cried. "You broke your word, Ruslo. I love Rafa, and you know it. So does Sandu." She threw feathers until the bed emptied and tears blurred her vision. "I will not wed Sandu. I will not."

Chapter 18

Etti's throat ached with unreleased anger and pain. She felt trapped, mortally wounded, helpless prey soon to become supper.

"Where are you going?" Melodia's breath came in fast huffs as she caught up with her.

Etti considered her question. She walked in a cold darkness now, an unfamiliar, unsettling place, one without escape. One without Rafa. "Away. Anywhere away from here," Etti said.

Melodia trailed her across a field of fennel. Etti's feet sank in the moist soil as they walked.

"What will you do?"

Etti stopped, covered her face with her hands and sobbed. "I don't know. I never dreamt this could happen."

Melodia held her, and they sank to their knees, the mud coating their skin.

"I can't wed Sandu. I won't. I would rather die." Her heart ripped like the eiderdown, and she sobbed.

"You're not going to die." Atira's voice reached them from behind, sharp with a brash edge. "Curse you for walking in the field. You should have at least walked along the hedgerow where there's a path." She caught up with them and her tone grew more gentle. "I heard. I'm sorry."

Etti's nerves flared. "No you're not. I don't need you here, telling me how you suffered and warned me about all this. I'll not wed Sandu, and I won't leave Rafa."

"Easy to say, Etti. How much courage do you have?"

"What mean you?"

Kindness filled Atira's eyes. "I've been harsh with you in the past. For that I'm sorry, but you're so strong-willed you overpower the other women, one of the reasons they avoid you." Atira touched Etti's arm, her hand warm. "We have spent much time together. You're like a sister to me. I would never wish ill for you, and va, I am truly sorry. I saw you with Rafa, and he with you. Let's walk. Over there, on the path. We'll go to the river. We'll talk."

At the river, they tucked their skirts into their waistbands and dipped their feet in the water, rinsing off the mud.

Tall willow trees clustered on the riverbanks. Like a maiden's hair, the branches swayed lazily in the warm breeze. Patches of white flowers released a citrus-tinged fragrance, and the sun-baked mud at the river's edge smelled rich and earthy with mushrooms.

Wading in the shallow water, Atira paused. "Please don't hurt my father. He tried to match you with Rafa. You must have noticed. That is why he had Rafa drive the wagon for him so many times. Giving the two of you time to know each other. He believed Ruslo when he said he'd match Rafa to you."

"Rafa is my choice. Not Sandu."

"So you say." She paused. "Are you prepared for what will happen if you refuse Ruslo's match?"

Etti lowered her eyes, poking her finger into a failing seam in her skirt. "How could he change his mind as he did, choosing Sandu instead of Rafa, and still punish me? I will go with Rafa."

"Against your chief's command," Atira said. "And wed him in Rafa's tribe?"

"Va. And do not tell me he doesn't love me. I know he does. I'm sure of it."

"But what about Sandu?" Melodia chewed on her thumb, her brows furrowed.

Atira crossed her arms. "I'm going to tell you what you must already know, Etti. You're too upset right now to think clearly. You should never have challenged Ruslo like that."

"I didn't challenge him."

"You accused him of breaking his word, and you did it in front of all of us."

Etti shook her head. "My temper. Fie!"

A portion of Atira's skirt broke free and fell in the river. She walked to the shoreline, wrang out the water and shook out the wrinkles. "If you refuse Sandu, Ruslo must save face. He cannot admit to us that he promised my father, then broke that promise and changed his mind to favor his nephew, which is exactly what happened. You will be banished from our tribe."

Her mouth grew dry as Etti considered it. "That would be like... like death." Her mind raced. She would leave the tribe. They would never speak her name. It would be as if she had never existed. She would not be able to visit with Atira, or Melodia, or her uncle, or her Aunt Ucho—none of them. At the horse fairs and festivals throughout the year, all the people she cared for would be ordered to shun her.

"The Kris would be told forthright," Atira said.

"The Kris." Melodia hissed air between her teeth. "They decide issues for all the tribes, right?"

"Always," Atira said. "Other tribes will shun you, Etti. Even Rafa's. He will not be granted the right to wed you."

Etti's heart sank. "Na!"

"Va!" Atira countered. "You should know this. Your brothers were banished. If they visit other tribes—any tribe—they are expelled. It will happen the same for you, Etti. Banishment is not done lightly, and there will be talk and speculation of why you refused Sandu. You will be judged as soiled."

"Stop! Why do you torment me like this?" Etti's voice broke. "I have lost Rafa and now you're scaring me with this."

"Is this all true, Atira?" Melodia asked.

"Va. I say this not to hurt you, Etti. Before you act rashly, you need to be reminded of your duty."

"The men needn't follow such harsh laws."

"Not so. The Rom must be dutiful, as well, or live with the consequences. Some are pleased with their marriage matches, some are not. My Vano is as unhappy with me as I am with him."

The branches of the weeping willows swayed with a sudden movement.

Etti's hand flew to her throat. "What—"

A horse emerged from the trees, then another.

Jilé. And Durril. They each led their horses with only a right arm, their left sleeves sewn short.

"Ah," Jilé said. "Sister. You're surprised. Did you think we'd forget what you did to us with your curse?" Anguish strained his voice and the languid cruelty that always lit his eyes had been replaced with glassy-eyed fury. He raised his remaining arm. "We're taking *yours* this day."

Etti gasped. Sure that they would not risk death by remaining in France, she had let her guard down. Like the darkest visions in her dreams, they loomed over her on horseback. She crossed her arms, covering the terror that hammered in her chest.

Atira spun away and darted down the path.

"Get her!" Durril shouted, "Or she'll bring help."

Atira ran, crookedly, hobbling over the uneven path along the hedgerows that divided the fields. She risked a look back. Jilé was gaining on her, but his horse also struggled with the rugged ground, mis-stepping and uncertain. Jilé wobbled in his saddle, using the stump of his left arm to stay mounted.

A peasant tending the fields saw them and shook his hoe. "Cursed Gypsies," he cried. "Get out of my fields!"

"Help!" Atira cried. "Help me!" Gadjes either welcomed or loathed Gypsies, and he showed no concern at her plight. Atira didn't break her stride.

Jilé reined his horse and waited for a moment, considering. He looked from Atira, who had now gained distance, to the angry peasant, and at the challenging path itself.

At no hoofbeats pounding behind her, Atira stopped, noticed Jilé's hesitation. He could manage riding with one arm, but not running it full out in pursuit. He turned his horse around and worked his way back to Etti and Melodia.

Must make haste. Atira ran toward camp, stumbling over the stones and clumps of grass. She spied Sandu, relieving himself in the cover of tall bushes. No time for courtesies. "Sandu!" she rushed up to him.

He ducked, straightened his clothes and stepped out, anger pulling at his features. "Shameful, Atira, interrupting—"

"Etti's brothers. They have Etti and Melodia. We need to help them. Come on!"

The color left Sandu's face, and he ducked his head as if dodging rocks. "Where?"

"The north field." Atira pointed. "Jilé and Durril. Hurry."

Sandu hesitated. "I have—there is something I must do right now."

"What? Did you not hear? Their lives are in danger. Those brothers are mad. Hurry!"

He raised his hand, his palm toward her. "I'll be there posthaste. I'll be right back." He disappeared, running into the trees.

Atira stood, frozen in her steps. "Are you angry about this morning? Their lives are in peril with those brothers, Sandu," she shouted. "Get you back here!"

She counted to five. Nothing. She spun around and broke into a run for their camp.

She saw two men collecting waer for the houses and shouted. Coming closer, she recognized them. "Rafa! Jardani! Help!"

They ran to her. "What is it?" Rafa asked.

"Etti and Melodia. Etti's brothers. They're here."

"Where?"

"The north fields that lead to the river. I came as fast as I could."

Rafa and Jardani ran for their horses.

Atira chased after them. "There's a peasant in the field. A Gadje. He may have seen where they went."

Rafa grabbed a length of rope, patted his dagger to be sure it was there, and swung onto Dark Tide.

Atira watched them leave, praying they would make it in time, and wondering what in devil's name had happened to Sandu.

* * *

Etti and Melodia stood together, holding each other. Durril flashed a long, brutal dagger at them, and a bulky Gadje that Durril called Sabann had arrived shortly after the brothers had surprised them. Sabann had relieved them of their daggers and threatened to kill them if they tried to run as Atira had.

Melodia's face had turned even lighter than normal, blanched with fear, and her brows were raised high.

Etti closed her eyes and slowly nodded, praying to give Melodia hope. She chanced another glance at Sabann and spied his horrifying disfigurements.

Sometime during his dark history, he had lost his nose and both ears. Etti thought back quickly over the stories told in the villages and at festivals. Mutilation of the nose was common for those who had uttered defamatory words against men in power, men like barons or high-ranking priests. Or instances of rape or adultery. Caution rang loud in her head. A consuming fear squeezed her throat, making her light-headed.

Another image sent her off balance—his ears—the lack of them. Etti's mind raced to gather clues about the hideous man behind them. Had he lost his ears due to heresy? Sodomy? Burning?

The sound of an approaching horse made them turn around.

"Lost her," Jilé said. "And there's a stinking Gadje peasant in the fields. Let's get out of here." He slapped Etti on the back of her head. "You ride with me, and I warn you now. If you try to take control of my horse—or throw me off—Sabann will catch you." His eyes narrowed. "Imagine the look on that pig Gitano's face if he finds you drawn and quartered."

Etti's struggled to keep the fear from her voice. "Where are you taking us?"

Jile laughed. "Away. We promised you would suffer for your curse."

Sabann tossed Etti onto the horse, in front of Jilé, and did the same with Melodia, settling in the saddle behind her and squeezing her into his chest.

* * *

Rafa and Jardani had been riding about ten minutes when they encountered the peasant. He raised his hoe and cursed at them to leave his fields.

Rafa shouted to him. "We're searching for a man—two men—both missing one arm, both on horseback. The women's lives are in danger."

"Filthy Gypsies! Be gone with you! Tearing up my land and taking our water for your horses. Thieves!"

"The water's still flowing in the river." Rafa pulled a gold coin from his money bag, held it up so it flashed in the sun. "Did you see the men? The women?"

The Gadje plodded through the mud to get closer, holding out his hand.

Rafa flipped the shilling to him.

The Gadje pointed along the path at the other side of the river, showing their travel to be westerly.

"Be there a bridge?"

"Past my house, there's a turn in the river. Shallow enough to ford."

"My thanks." Rafa urged Dark Tide on and they left.

* * *

Etti held on, terrified if she fell, he would trample her to death with his horse. Jilé was seated behind her. He squeezed her left shoulder with his stub for balance, and he rode steadily. He used a saddle, probably for stability after having lost his arm.

"Where is Durril?" she asked, worried about Melodia. They had been behind them, but had disappeared.

"He's hunting. He'll catch up with us after."

Jilé's horse stumbled and Etti tightened her grip on the horse's mane. *Hunting for what? Or whom?*

They had crossed the river at its low point a few miles back. The road had become more level and smoother. Etti wanted desperately to look behind. Had Atira escaped? Would she noticed Melodia again? Would Rafa find her? Jilé's stump slipped and grabbed, slipped and grabbed her, and memories of his cruelty stirred terror in her throat.

She clutched the clasp of her necklace. If she could just get it off, maybe drop it in the road. The stars were colorful, would be noticed against the dark soil. She gave it a hard jerk.

The chain held true, and she rued the lie she'd told about the faulty clasp, her dishonesty catching up with her. She braced herself and tugged again. Nothing.

"What are you doing up there?" Jilé growled.

"Naught. I'm... nervous."

"You should be, bitch." He spat on her neck. "It was hard tracking you with one arm, but we're eager to repay you for that curse."

She released her grip on the sturdy leather collar. Lowering her hand, she gathered the clump of stars that hung from the necklace. Maybe they would break free from the collar. She waited for the horse's next step and jerked hard.

Pain shot up to her head but she was rewarded with a palmful of stars. She resisted the urge to toss them until she determined the least obvious way to release them.

Jilé leaned to the left as they rode. Judging by the horse's gait and the angle of his body, he had learned to compensate for his left arm stump. She transferred the wooden stars to her right hand and slowly released a few of them.

Shortly after, Sabann and Melodia pulled up beside them. They left the road and returned to single file. When Jilé's horse stopped to dump, Sabann and Melodia took the lead, giving Etti the opportunity to release the rest of the star beads. She let them trickle out of her fingers and down the horse's flank, falling to the road along with her prayers.

Jilé's horse continued, and she sighed in relief.

Jilé pulled the reins.

The horse stopped abruptly. "Hold up, Sabann." Jilé turned his horse around.

Etti tried to swallow.

"What did you drop back there?" Jilé yanked her hair, pulling her head back to face him, his eyes flat with dark intent.

The deception was a huge mistake, and she couldn't undo it. He would see the beads. "My necklace. The clasp is worn." Her scalp burned and he pulled her hair even harder. She was about to fall off the horse. "Mama gave it to me." She rushed on, hoping to convince him that she hadn't done the stupid thing she had done. "Look you at the clasp," she managed, her voice pinched from the painful angle of her neck.

"What's amiss?" Sabann's words gurgled from his loose jaw.

"The little whore tried to leave droppings so we could be followed."

"No," Etti said. "My necklace broke, and he thinks I'm casting spells."

"She's not satisfied at taking my arm. She wants me to die."
Jilé jerked her hair again, and she cried out. "Family love," he
sneered.

"Don't hurt her!" Melodia's voice dipped in desperation.

"Na, Melodia. Say naught." Etti waved toward her cousin.
The man who held her captive bore proof of his violence—
someone had lopped off half his face for his crimes. "Jilé." She
held her unclasped necklace. "Look."

His gaze lowered. "Wood beads. Sabann," he said, showing
them to his friend. "See how many beads you can find. Back there,
right where we left the road. Make the girl help you, and if she
tries to run, kill her." He turned to Etti. "How many beads were in
it?"

Etti's thoughts raced. She knew not how many of the twelve
she had pulled free, nor how many were left.

"Well?" Jilé jerked her again. "You've had it for years. You
should know."

Twelve. She'd ripped perhaps eight or nine beads free.
Dropped four or five the first time, followed by three or four when
they left the road. Or was it five? The numbers collided. Her scalp
was on fire. Pain stabbed her back in the unnatural position he had
forced her into. She remembered her early training about fear. She
would not let her see it. She would be strong.

She summoned strength and found it. "Eight," she lied,
grabbing an answer he may accept. "Eight, for my eighth
birthday." If there were any left, he'd have to do the mathematics.
She worried. He was far from stupid; his intelligence was what had
brought him to so much trouble all his life.

Jilé's eyes narrowed. "I don't remember this necklace."

"You wouldn't," Etti replied. "You had already left our tribe
by then."

Sabann and Melodia returned. "We found four." Sabann
reached out to give the beads to Jilé, and paused, likely
remembering of a sudden that Jilé had only one hand. He avoided
Jilé's eyes and wordlessly slipped them into his saddle bag.

"There are three left on the necklace," Jilé said. "Fie! I should
kill you now."

"Not yet," Sabann said. "The beads are small. We put two sets
of eyes on the search. If the girl and I didn't spy that last one, no
one else will, either."

Jilé peered at Melodia. "And she didn't trick you while you searched?"

"Nay. She's so scared she peed. I can smell it on my saddle."

From her awkward position Etti could not see what Sabann may be doing to Melodia, but her cousin released a shaking, mew-like cry, and Sabann's voice grew smoother, more suggestive. "Let's get on with it, Jilé. Time for your revenge—and my pleasure."

Jilé yanked Etti's hair, and she fell off the horse onto her back. He leaped on her, his knees gouging her shoulders and pinning her hands, rendering her helpless. He fisted his right hand and drew back. "Here's your reward for trying to trick me." Pain shattered her jaw.

* * *

Rafa pushed Dark Tide on. Progress had been slow on the hedgerow paths. He had wanted desperately to race his stallion, but he couldn't risk a stumble or fall. Their travel had improved since they'd spied the peasant's hovel and crossed the river.

They were in a heavily farmed area with few roads. The forest encroached here and there, fingers of dense pine and oak around which the peasants worked to grow their crops. One lonely sign, small and crudely carved, announced a village thirty miles distant. The isolation may work in their favor, with less roads from which to choose, but it would also mean no pilgrims or troops, or even merchants would be traveling the roads who might rescue Etti and Melodia.

His chest burned with worry for them. He knew Etti's anguish over the council's decision. And his own. He had made a mistake, and wasn't sure, even now, how he could have done things differently. Her uncle had ordered Rafa away from Etti. He had gone to Ruslo, tried to reason with him, but to reveal he knew of Ruslo's promise to Dody would ruin Etti's uncle, so Rafa chose not to challenge Ruslo.

What Rafa struggled with was the fact that if he didn't curb the impulse to scoop her up and take her away from all this, he may become the sole person who dismantled Etti's life, leaving her banished from her tribe. Not only her tribe, but the whole Romani community, which encompassed the entire Continent—including his own tribe. If Rafa tried to force the issue with her tribal king, Etti would be shunned, despised by her own people.

It all mattered, but what mattered now was what cut to his heart, making each beat painful and filled with fear for her and what her vicious brothers would do to her in the name of vengeance.

"How far ahead are they?" Jardani asked.

"We must not waste our time speculating. Let's keep hope and stay in pursuit. We have the better horses."

"But the brothers would buy good horses. They must have robbed someone else after they escaped the horse fair," Jardani said.

"Va, and they're known for their cruelty. They've had plenty of time to punish any good horses they may have bought. As they say, horses with broken spirits have weak legs."

"Who said that?"

"All good horse trainers," Rafa said. "Let's stop talking and gain time here." He urged Dark Tide ahead.

"Wait. Wait!" A man called out from behind them.

Rafa turned. Racing from behind came Ruslo.

* * *

Etti moaned, awakening. She was tied to a tree. Her neck hurt, her face throbbed and pain pulsed up her arms.

They were in the forest, and from the filtered light it appeared to be dusk. Five feet away, Melodia was also propped against a young tree, arms tied behind her.

"Where are we?" Etti asked, her lips so swollen the words came out all mumbled.

"I don't know. We rode about an hour more after Jilé beat you for dropping your beads." Melodia's voice was dull, as if she'd used up all her fear and was left with no more emotion. She twisted against the strips of cloth that held them. The pattern of the fabric was familiar.

"Your skirt." Melodia's skirt was torn to shreds. "They tied our hands with fabric from your skirt," Etti said. She glanced around, wary. "Where are they?"

"They were waiting for Durril to return. He was hunting." Melodia's voice broke. "They're going to eat before they kill us."

"Oh, Melodia. Please don't give up. Atira ran for help. Someone will come for us. Rafa." Saying his name brought fresh hope.

"He can't help you now. Sandu will come. And Ruslo." Having said the words, Melodia sat taller, and she looked like she had inhaled a breath of fresh hope, too.

"Yes. They'll crush my brothers, and they're even bigger and stronger than Sabann. They will find us."

Etti wished for help to arrive. It had been foolish and dangerous for her to drop beads, but they may still alert someone. "At the least, four of the beads are there at that first turn after the peasant's cottage."

Melodia smiled through her dried tears. "I saw the fifth bead. Sabann didn't because it was hidden under a dandelion. I moved it to the top so it was visible."

"Melodia! That was so dangerous. What if Sabann had seen?"

"He'd searched that area already, so he didn't suspect." She gave a conspiratorial smile. "Since you risked your life tossing them, the least I could do was help."

"So. Two chances for us," Etti said.

The sound of approaching horses silenced them.

Jilé rode to Etti's tree. He swung a black and grey animal aside and dismounted, tethering his horse. "Got us a badger for supper, ladies."

"But there's only enough for us men." Durill said, and Sabban laughed, causing the indecent remnants of his nose to spread.

Etti held her breath. From what she remembered of her childhood, the two brothers were typically meaner when together.

Durill approached. "My, and what has happened to our sister's face, brother?"

"I thanked her for the curse. Because it worked so well." Jilé waved his stump. "Guess she didn't expect us to visit again so soon, huh, Durill?"

"Yeah," Durill said. "She probably thought we'd slink off into a cave and die in agony. She'd never expect us to find a friend like Sabann. But here we all are, together. A new family. So now, Etti dear, we're going to return the favor." Durill pulled a short-handled hatchet from his saddle pack. "You'll lose two arms today, sister. One for me, and one for Jilé here."

"No!" Melodia screamed. "No! No!" She screamed again and again. "Help us, someone help us for God's sake."

Sabban struck her with his fist, and her head lolled to her chest.

Jilé dropped down, pinning Etti's ankles with his knees and hand. "I'll hold her legs. You should have tied them so she doesn't try to kick us, the witch." He met Etti's gaze. "We don't want to miss and cut off your head by mistake. We—"

The sound of approaching horses interrupted Jilé.

"Let her go."

Etti looked up, following the voice. "Rafa!"

Chapter 19

Rafa took in the bruised and bloodied women and dismissed any concerns about attacking one-armed men. He drove Dark Tide toward Durril. *Must get that axe out of his hands.*

Durril saw Rafa and looked up at Dark Tide. He dropped the axe and ran. Jardani reined his horse and followed Durril.

Taking advantage of the distraction, Etti freed her ankles and kicked Jilé in the chest. He fell backward, and she scooted out of his reach.

Rafa dismounted and grabbed Jilé by the throat.

Sabann stepped in, picked up the axe.

By this time Ruslo had dismounted, and he ran to Sabann. Muscles bulging in his back and arms, Ruslo kicked the axe out of Sabann's hand.

Sabann scanned Ruslo and tensed at seeing the tribal king's brawn and height.

Ruslo's fist connected and Sabann fell back. He rose quickly, ready for more, and the two big men pummeled each other, blood spattering as they rolled in the matted grasses.

Several feet away, Jilé recovered and pulled a long fighting dagger, slicing it at Rafa. "Big hero, fighting a crippled man," Jilé taunted.

"Bigger than you," Rafa countered. "I don't batter defenseless women."

"Defenseless? She's a witch. She cursed me. She did this." He waved his stump.

Rafa came closer, tempting Jilé to strike again. "She was always better than you, Jilé. Always will be. You're nothing but a skunk, fouling you own nest. You and your brother brought this on with your thieving. You might as well have cut your arms off yourself."

"Bastard Gitano!" Jilé wound up, turning to strike. He put all his strength in it and swung himself off balance.

Rafa shot out his fist and struck Jilé's eye.

Jilé crumpled to the grasses.

Rafa pounced and continued striking Jilé. "This is for Etti." He swung again "This is for Etti." He was being pulled away from behind. "You'll kill him, Rafa," Jardani said. "Enough."

"Did you get Durril?" Rafa asked, panting.

"He's on foot. We hobbled their horses. He won't get far. I'll find him." Jardani mounted and led his horse in the direction he last saw Durril.

Rafa dragged Jilé away from Etti. He spied a large scrap of torn, flowered linen on the ground and tied Jilé's right hand to his right foot. He hurried to Etti.

"Etti. Oh, Etti." He touched a part of her cheek still unravaged. "Let's get you free." He cut the rope and held her arms for a moment. "How long have you been tied like this?"

"An hour?"

"Two," Melodia said. "She was knocked out for a while."

Rafa examined her. She was bloodied from her struggle against the rough pine bark. "Bastards. Your arms will hurt when I lower them."

Etti cried out as he released her. "Swine Gypsy," he growled to Jilé. "You don't deserve to be called Rom."

Later, they sat by the fire and finished the roasted badger. Durril was right—there wasn't enough for everyone, so there was naught but boiled mint water for the brothers and the faceless Gadje named Sabann.

They traveled like Gadje now, with a saddle. They tied the men as they had tied the women, binding their feet as well for good measure, and had persuaded them to be silent.

Ruslo sat on a rock near them. He would watch them through the night, he said, and they would get an early start back to their camp the next morning. They would send messengers to the village to the north where the Rom waited for the blacksmith to finish repair to the wagons. The marshall would take the brothers and Sabann. They would likely have a short trip to the gallows.

Rafa soaked the ragged strips from Melodia's skirt in a nearby stream. The women cooled their faces with it.

Their injuries made Rafa ill. The men had hired this—this monster—as a guard, to be their missing arms. Their saddle packs overflowed with stolen goods. Coins from the Marseilles jeweler, modest gold and silver rings and brooches, silver chalices bearing the marks of monasteries. All evidence of the suffering and losses these criminals had wrought in their travels.

Etti's head rested in Rafa's lap. He held her tenderly, rueing the suffering she had endured. "Sure you can't eat something?" Rafa held her arms gently.

She shook her head. "Tired. So tired."

Rafa shifted his weight, feeling a sharp object in his purse. "Oh." He retrieved the star-shaped beads and held them out. "I found these at the second road. I remembered beads like these on your necklace. I saw that single bead, too, at the next turn. Had they not caught my eye, I might still be searching for you." He kissed his fingers and touched her swollen mouth. "That was bold of you."

"Stupid. It was stupid. I was beaten for it, and Melodia was, too, for trying to stop them."

"But had you not…" He exhaled loudly. "Oh, Etti. I don't know what I would have done had I lost you."

She lowered her voice. "Did you talk to Ruslo? Will he release me from the council vote?"

Rafa told her of his failure to convince Ruslo, frustrated as he formed the troubling words and sentences. "Etti, he's resolute. I don't know how to sway him."

"You must," she said. Tears slid down her bruised face. "Rafa, you must."

"Ruslo is your chief. Your king. I cannot claim you if doing so will leave you bereft of your family. Your kumpania. Of everything. The risk to you is too high."

"Let's leave together."

"You know we can't. Our actions will follow us. We will be banished."

"But he broke his word to Uncle Dody." She whispered through her tortured lips.

"I want to take you in my arms and leave with you, this moment. I want to take care of you, and present you to my mother and father, and all my relatives, so they can see you and know how beautiful you are. I want to announce my intentions to wed you, to make you my wife."

He sighed, gently stroking her hair. "But I can't intervene without hurting your uncle, either. If Ruslo knows Dody broke his promise of secrecy, he may banish him, too." He paused. "You must find a way, Etti."

"I can't. I'm only a woman. The men decide everything."

"In my tribe, women have a say. If they won't give you that liberty, take it quietly. Talk with Dody. Ask Atira. She has proven to be your ally."

"Am I alone then?"

"Do not think that for a moment. I am with you." He swallowed hard. "I want you for my wife. We are meant for each other. I've heard that said by other men in the past and scoffed at it, but I understand it now. It's—it's hard to explain but having met you, I feel like I have a new life. The air is fresher, warmer when you are with me. The sky is brighter. I'm happy in my own skin and want naught but to touch you, to experience you, to live with you. I want that for the rest of my days."

Etti's voice was soft as a morning dove's flutter of wings. "But?" She raised her head from his lap, waiting.

He said the words he'd been dreading to think, let alone utter. "If loving you destroys your family and your life, I want you to send me away, Etti. I can't bear to be responsible for laying your life to ruin."

"So you're—you're leaving me." She choked as she said it.

"Na." He kissed her hair, careless of Ruslo's presence, keenly aware this may be their last time together. "You are the daughter of a famous Rom Baro. Your father's courage and strength are sung by all. In spite of that, Ruslo can banish you."

He turned to meet her gaze. "Are you prepared to discard your familia, your tribe, your Romani heritage? It's who you are." A tear streaked down her face. "Isn't it? Or do you want me to lift you up on Dark Tide and we can laugh in Ruslo's face, and I will whisk you away?"

She didn't answer.

"And I will leave my tribe, and we can be Gadje."

Her eyes widened, her mouth twisted with disgust. "Body of God, Rafa," she cried, tortured. "Na."

"Your people have decided that we are not to be together. I have no voice in it. It must be you who decides. You who acts."

* * *

They arrived in camp mid-morning. A breeze came off the river, cool despite the sunny day. Rafa and Etti had ridden together, Jardani with Melodia, and they had tied the two brothers together on one horse. Sabann and Ruslo had ridden alone, Sabann tied securely.

Rafa held Etti close to his chest, her velvet skin and tender vulnerability making him want to roar like a deranged bear, sweeping a mighty arm at her brothers for hurting her, ripping Ruslo from the shade where he stood, sending him to the spirit world for taking Etti from him.

She touched his hand, squeezed it. He wanted to hold her forever. Hell, he wanted to throw Ruslo the reigns to Etti's hateful brothers and the deformed ape, Sabann, and ride as fast as Dark Tide could take them, far from here and Etti's intended husband, Sandu. He wouldn't stop until they reached Barcelona's mountains.

The thought drew a fresh fire to his belly. He no longer cared one whit for honor and tribal rules, or the Kris and their laws and prohibitions, or even to his family's sense of tradition. *I was so wrong.* He knew he loved her, knew they were meant to be together forever. He had trusted Dody, trusted Ruslo, respected their traditions, and now... He wanted to be with her so badly. He bled inside for her, sick with a desperation that grew stronger every minute.

But her Aunt Ucho and Atira were running to meet her, arms outstretched, their faces strained in those first throes of relief after a night of agony, wondering if she was still alive. He understood. They loved her, too. He dismounted and held her gently, helping her down.

Atira held them both, and they broke into sobs.

Rafa's throat constricted at her suffering, but he admired the strength that had brought her through this trial. It gave him new hope.

Rupa came running to meet them. She ran to her husband and touched his bandaged hand. "You're safe. I was so worried. We all were."

Ruslo held his wife's hand briefly. "Get you Vano and Hanzi. Ask them to pack food and water and bring extra for Rafa."

Rupa turned to the girls. "My stars. My poor *chavis!" My poor girls*. She held Melodia's and Etti's hands. "I'll send your Aunt Ucho to your wagon to help you."

Ruslo turned to Jardani and Rafa. "I'm grateful for your help. Thank you for saving our girls. Jardani, ask Baba Lolli to check that eye."

"He was no match for this Rom," Jilé said, smirking.

"He has honor," Ruslo said. "You're the sorriest example of a Rom I've seen in my lifetime." He punched Jilé in the ribs. He wobbled in the saddle, hanging on with his one bound hand. "Your father was a great man. You two are naught but *charros*. Thieves. A corruption of his blood."

"And you're a big-ass, stinking boar," Jilé said. He spat in Ruslo's face. Durril laughed.

Ruslo narrowed his eyes in disdain. "You'll soon find laughter awkward when swinging on a rope." He stepped aside to speak with Rafa. "You fought well back there, even when you were outnumbered. I trust you to take these thieving dogs to Villasavary, a small village south of here." He gestured at the brothers and Sabban. "Turn them over to the marshall there. Will you do this for me?"

"Va. They richly deserve to hang." He would enjoy permanently ridding Etti of her thieving, murderous relatives. He wanted her safe, and he didn't trust Sandu to protect her.

"Vano." Ruslo signaled for Vano to join them. The left side of his face had turned a dark blue from the LaGrasse guard's harsh blow. Rafa remembered helping Vano out of the hole, of washing away the stench from the garderobe waste pit.

Subdued, Vano stood before Ruslo.

"Because of you, we lost our travel funds from the baron," Ruslo reminded Vano. "I'm going to make this as plain as a pikestaff for you. You will ride with Rafa." Ruslo pointed at Jilé and Durril. "You will keep these leeches from escaping, and you will show, by your actions in Villasavary, that you respect and honor your tribe."

Vano took a deep breath. "Pray forgive me. I will, Ruslo."

"Good." Ruslo returned to Rafa. "Remind the marshall of their sentence in Marseilles. There's no need for a trial. You were there last night and can serve as witness to their crimes. Make damned sure he hangs them. Mayhap you'd like to help if he asks."

"Na. I simply want to be done with them."

Rafa got directions. He approached Etti and took her hand. Ruslo gave him a sideways glance.

Rafa stared back, pumping a potent message in his gaze. The marriage council and Ruslo's wavering judgments be damned! He had risked his life to save Etti, and her *legally appointed* husband was absent. He lifted her hand and kissed it. "I'll be back, Etti."

Her hand tingled where Rafa's lips had brushed it, but the abuse from her brother had unnerved her. A taste of metal lingered in her mouth, and she felt sick to her stomach. Her face throbbed, her scalp burned with every slight swing of her hair.

Her hopes had died—indeed she had almost died with them. She still lived, but she had lost Rafa. Pain claimed her body, yet she shivered in unimaginable joy that she still possessed two arms.

"Fie!" Atira cried out and hurried to Etti and Melodia, gasping at their bruised and swollen faces. She took them to the wagon and settled them on Etti's eiderdown under the canvas that sheltered them from the sun. Atira's children, along with many other tribal children, clustered around them, little birds chasing tiny seeds of excitement. Atira sent them away. "I'll be right back."

She returned with a poultice for their scrapes and cuts, and a basin of cool water and cloths for their faces.

Etti dipped her cloth and wrang the water out. "Here, Melodia." Etti held her cloth gently to the swelling. "Please forgive me for all of this. I should have known they would wreak revenge on me for my curse. I should never have walked so far from camp."

"We all walked along the river," Atira said.

"But because of me we left camp."

"Who would have thought they would find a friend?" Atira said.

"Fie!" Melodia cried. "Friend? He's a branded criminal, a grotesque monster. Guilty of unspeakable cruelties, faceless from his punishments."

"Did he…" Etti's question died on her lips, so afeared she was to give it voice.

"Na." But he touched me all over." She shuddered. "Please Atira, do you have a skirt I might wear? He ripped my clothes to shreds." She lifted what was left of her skirt, so short it revealed her calves and thighs. "He used it to tie our hands."

Atira busied herself in the chest and helped Melodia change. "You needn't fear him any longer. Rafa will take him to the marshall. I'm sure they'll be marched promptly to the gallows."

"I worried I would never see this day," Melodia said.

"Or if I did, I would face the sunrise without arms." Etti released a shaking breath. "Rafa arrived in time to stop Jilé." Etti spoke over the wet cloth at her mouth. "He saved my life. I want to leave with him. I never want to come back here." Etti realized how it sounded. "Oh, fie! I dread ever leaving you, Melodia, and Atira, you've been so good to me, but—"

"We know," Melodia said. "You love Rafa and want to be with him."

"We understand." Atira patted her arm.

"But Rafa wouldn't leave. If he loved me, he would leave with me." With each mile of the trip, Etti had become more and more frustrated that Rafa could so easily give up on them. "He said that he doesn't want to ruin my life." A tear rolled slowly down her face. "But he has."

Atira shook her head. "Etti, trust him. What he's saying is that he doesn't want to drag you away from us to Spain. If he did that, he wouldn't be any better than Ruslo and his cruel marriage council. Rafa wants you to be free to decide what you want—life here, or life with him, in his tribe. You don't want Ruslo deciding your husband, and you shouldn't want Rafa making that decision for you.

"What do you want, Etti? What is your wish? That's what he wants you to do."

What did she want? Rafa. Always, Rafa. "He should be the one to decide, not me."

"He explained all that to you yester eve." Melodia dropped her gaze as soon as she said it. "Forgive me. I listened." She turned to Atira. "Rafa does not wish to be responsible for her banishment. For ruining her life. Because the decision is so difficult, he feels she must make it, herself."

"We should run away," Etti said.

"Then you have no choice," Atira said. "Be prepared to abandon your Romani blood. Your people. Everything. Live as a Gadje."

"A cursed existence with Rafa, or life with my family, but no Rafa? I cannot make that choice."

"Do nothing, and Sandu will be your husband." Atira paused. "That's what I did. I refused to choose, so in not choosing, I chose. I know that is not what you want. Think of Rafa."

Rafa. The magic of his eyes, his hands, his body. The way he saw her, the true Etti she was—without shame, without apology—with him.

Etti pulled away from them, curling herself into a ball under the covers of her eiderdown. The weight of it crushed her, and she sobbed. Every loss she'd suffered leaked past the fluffy down, stinging her like Jilé's savage blows. Her mother. Her father and his pride in her, his doting attention and patience. Her standing in the tribe. Pesha, and his playful joy and loyalty.

Etti hugged her knees to her chest. Choose Rafa, and he would gain a tainted bride, humiliated, shamed, condemned, unwanted by both her tribe and his. Choose honor and duty, ideals she had always valued, and she would lose Rafa.

"Whichever path I choose, I will lose all."

Chapter 20

Etti sat with Atira by the fire. Melodia still rested at Uncle Dody's wagon. Her cousins had applied poultices and cold cloths to her swollen face and the cuts on her arms and legs.

Etti's impulsive dash from the camp had put Melodia in such danger. Etti hoped she would some day forgive her.

She felt eyes on her. Aunt Ucho had ceased staring at her bruised face, but a hum still rose from others in the tribe whenever Etti appeared. They proved again how adept they were at sideways glances.

Ruslo sat with his advisors, and with Darly and Ito, in front of the large tent. Sandu laughed easily with his father while Dody slumped, staring at the fire. Sandu had not approached her since her return; indeed, he had avoided her gaze and kept distant without being obvious.

For Ruslo, it was merely another night at the fire with his family, not an evening of agony, as it was for Etti as she sat, bruised and defeated, feeling her life unravel as they toasted Sandu's upcoming wedding.

To her. Disgust coursed through her veins, and a growing desperation. She would find a way out. This eve, she would force Ruslo to rescind the council's decision.

He left the dirty work for Rupa. She had squatted down in front of Etti after supper, sitting on her heels. She spoke so softly Etti had to lean forward. "You will wed Sandu. Two days hence." Rupa left abruptly, leaving no chance to learn more.

Etti pushed it out of her mind and fondled the last three stars on her necklace, thinking of her mother, and her mother's sons. She sent a prayer to the stars that Rafa and the others had by now safely delivered her brothers to Villasavary. Had Jilé and Durril met their end yet? She could stir no sorrow in her heart for them, but she wished they might learn compassion in their journey to the spirit world.

Before her, a great log burned brightly over the glowing coals. Flames flowed upward over it, like waves crashing on the rocks at sea, the flame embracing the wood, intense and all-consuming.

Time passed, and the moon rose, a sliver in the star-strewn sky. Conversation was subdued. Va, it had been a sobering day. Bits of conversation floated her way from the elders of the tribe. Her brothers' names were spoken.

Jilé. Durril.

They likely recalled them when they were babes, esteemed offspring of their tribal chief. Mayhap they were telling stories of when they laughed and played, little pony boys prancing through the grass, all their lives before them. Before the hatred destroyed them.

The time had been set for her union. To Sandu. With Rupa's message, her new role was waiting, only two sunrises away.

Atira wore a concerned expression, revealing fine lines of worry and anger that had slowly hardened her face. *She knows how I feel.* The thought brought no comfort, but instead a brooding, painful kinship. *In time, that will be me.*

A crackling in the fire made her turn. The middle of the large, long log had been consumed. Now glowing, its sap bubbling, the log surrendered. It broke in two and fell into the coal bed below.

A rich stream of sparks flowed upward into the sky, burning out, turning grey.

A sign. A divination. She—Etti—was worth more. She had been treated as little more than a good horse to be traded for personal gain. Men and their weaknesses. Ruslo's duplicity. Sandu's refusal to rescue them yesterday, a childish way to pushing her for refusing him. Uncle Dody's faintheartedness that prevented him from protecting her. It all pointed to the futility of duty and the feminine custom of yielding.

Her life would change because she had changed. She would never again be the little girl, begging for a scrap of love and attention, of acceptance and understanding. That little girl was gone. She was a woman now, and she deserved more.

"Atira." Etti grabbed her arm. "I need to talk with you. Anon."

In the wagon, Etti, Atira and Miri settled on the piled eiderdowns. "I need a spell to defeat Ruslo," Etti said.

"I... I—" Atira curved her mouth down on one side and glanced deliberately at Miri.

"Here, Miri, would you like to play with the Tali bones?" Etti asked. "Can you roll three ones? Try it in the corner there."

Miri grabbed the bones. "I can! I'll show you."

Etti faced Atira. "I need a spell to learn the secret. How I can change Ruslo's mind."

"Why not Sandu's?"

"He's too adamant. Deep down, Ruslo has to regret breaking his promise to Uncle Dody. Help me, Atira."

"Regret. 'Tis a vague thing."

"You cursed Vano. Please."

"I can't." Atira shook her head. "But I can work a spell for you. For clear sight."

"Me?" Etti swallowed. She'd seen how Vano had been brought to his knees with Atira's spell. "What if something goes wrong?"

Atira swung her legs over the side of the stacked eiderdowns, preparing to leave. "Spells are not certain. They can be dangerous."

Miri rattled the bones and squealed. "I did it!"

"Misto! Misto!" Atira gave Miri a big smile and clapped her hands. "Now try to roll three twos. If you can, we'll make mud pies together tonight."

Miri squealed and began rolling.

"I cursed Vano because I was desperate. 'Tis best we don't try."

"I am desperate, too, Atira. Let's do it. Quickly. It must be tonight."

"You won't hold it against me if it doesn't work, or goes awry?"

"I promise," Etti said. "I believe in you."

"I'll need these things." Atira counted off the items.

Later, Etti hurried past the fire. Ruslo, Sandu and the others were all still there, by then heavy in their cups, their voices and words looser, louder.

She carried the bag of ashes, lavender, rosemary and other ingredients she'd found in Atira's case. She held them carefully to her breast as she entered the wagon.

Inside, Atira placed oil, leaves, ashes and two owl feathers in a small silver firecup. She plucked a short hair from Etti's temple and added it. A quick poke of the needle brought Etti's blood to the surface of her finger, and Atira squeezed out three drops. She positioned the candle flame under the cup. It burned the silver black and brought the oil to bubbling. The dainty feathers sank, and Etti's hair swirled around it all. Atira chanted.

> *Sight to the blind, strength to the weaker,*
> *Stir in the pure, untainted beaker,*
> *Render thy blood, invest in thy heart,*
> *Thus secrets and insight doth impart*
> *To the good heart, the pure heart,*
> *The one who breathes*
> *Hope and love for she who believes*

Atira removed the candle from below the spell spoon. "Now you say it, Etti."

Etti hesitated. "Why?"

"By cause it was in the chant. You must believe. Chant it so it might reach your soul." Atira paused. "So you may achieve *clear sight.*"

Etti's ears rang in the silence. Slowly, she repeated the words.

Atira blew on the spoon and removed the hair and owl feathers. "Drink it now."

Etti sniffed the murky oil. "It smells like a wet chicken." She quailed from Atira's glare, pinched her nose and finished it in one swallow.

Soft laughter from the Circle floated into the wagon.

"Let's go back," Atira said.

Etti swayed, light-headed, her heart thudding heavily, a drum inside her chest. Thump. Thump. Thump.

She bit her lip. She was poised, she knew, on the threshold of something life-changing, and the moment knocked, insistent, demanding to be answered.

* * *

Etti and Atira returned to the fire.

Ruslo and Rupa had settled on benches in the front of the big tent. They had moved back to adjust for the heat of the growing flames. Sandu sat next to him, along with Sandu's mother and father.

Phuro Marko, the elder, sat with them. His presence sent a cold chill down Etti's back. The formality of their seating, their posture—this may be when Ruslo would announce her wedding day.

Etti sat next to Atira in the warm summer grass. Doom settled in, a heavy yoke.

She studied Sandu with new eyes, her vision sharper, seeing... deeper. *The spell was working.* This was a different Sandu. Big, powerful, but at the same time muted, neutral, like a beach with no footprints. Images wandered in her mind. A hollow tree. In its branches, an empty nest. She shook her head. What did it mean?

She shivered and wiped her wet brow, more sensations washing over her, reminding her of childhood day dreams. She perceived Sandu as mushy, like green strawberries after a freeze, tasteless.

"What is it?" Atira asked. "You look as if you smelled rotting fish."

"Must be the oil," Etti said. "Your spell." She paused, checking to be sure the earth was still beneath her. "I'm having the strangest thoughts." Why was Sandu most of times so... so dull, but in these last few days, when it came to her, so domineering and demanding?

Lust. All men. As Atira had said.

Or something else? As though it had taken wings, her mind soared, high and clear and...

"I have it," Etti said, insight touching her. "I know what I have to do. Will you support me?"

Atira put her hands out, smiling. "Va!"

Courage coursed through Etti. She stood. Horns of alarm sounded in her head, but still, she faced Sandu squarely. "Sandu," she said, clearly and loudly, across the fire.

There must have been challenge in her expression or stance because, while Sandu remained seated, Ruslo stood. To remind her of her duty, she thought with disgust. Of her honor, of which Ruslo had so little.

"What?" Sandu asked, not sounding particularly eager to learn more.

"After the marriage council decision yesterday, you told me you wanted no one but me. You told me I was your bride. But when my brothers took me away, Atira ran to you for help and asked you to save Melodia and me." Etti turned, meeting the gazes of the other members of the tribe. They were quiet, watching her. "But you didn't come to save us. You ignored Atira and walked away, into the woods. And stayed there until Rafa and Ruslo left to bring us back."

Sandu's face hardened, and surprise blanched Ruslo's features.

Atira pulled at Etti's skirt. "Sit down!" When Etti refused, Atira shot a furious gaze at her as if to say, *How could you?*

Etti fixed Sandu with a stare. "Atira told you our lives were in danger, but you didn't come, Sandu. Why not?"

Ruslo pointed at Etti. "We will speak of this privately." He jabbed his thumb toward his wagon for her to follow him.

"Na." Etti held her ground. "I think everyone here would like to hear his answer. Sandu, why didn't you save your bride?"

"You will come to my wagon to discuss this. Now!" Ruslo snarled.

Etti gestured with a wide sweep of her hand to include everyone. "And Ruslo, Rom Baro. My king. Is it not true that you promised my Uncle Dody you would name Rafa to be my husband, not Sandu?"

Ruslo's hands fisted at his sides, and his face darkened. "You speak falsehoods," Ruslo shouted. "You consort with animals in unnatural ways. You cursed your brothers, and they were mutilated. I excused you because of your father, but I am out of patience with you. You are henceforth banished."

Gasps and murmurs swept around the Circle. Wide-eyed relatives turned to Etti. Baba Lolli sat on a short cask, watching, unblinking.

Tradition required Etti to drop her gaze and pack her things. Banished meant shunned. She would have naught to do with the kumpania, and no one would speak to her from this point on.

Her blood stirred again, an oily fury at the injustice of it. She stared at Ruslo with insolence. "I have spoken naught but the truth, my king."

Ruslo gave her his back, his signal that all tribal members must do so, as well.

They turned away, but remained within range so Etti continued. "When Sandu decided he wanted me, you broke your promise to Uncle Dody. And do you know why he wanted me of a sudden, Ruslo?"

Rupa and Aunt Ucho remained with their backs turned to her, but several other tribal members turned to face her.

"Let me tell you." Etti raised her hands, palms up. "There are tribal members here who seek the truth." She took a breath. "Sandu wanted me because he peeked in on me—and Atira and Ucho and Rupa—when we were dancing in a private area at the baron's chateau."

Ruslo's expression tightened into deeper outrage, but he had already banished Etti. To follow the rules of his tribe, he could not address her so he turned to Atira, who stood next to Etti. "Atira, you have become tainted, as well. You've spent too much time with her." Ruslo did not use Etti's name. He had already engaged the rules of exile. Having been banished, neither he nor anyone in her tribe would ever again speak Etti's name. A numbness swept over her.

"You, Atira, are banished, too."

Chapter 21

"What?" Atira bounded to her feet. "I have been dutiful. I wed Vano. Bore his children."

"And cursed him," Ruslo said. "Because of you, he is no longer a man. All know of this."

"I spoke the truth! Do you hear me?" Atira screamed and scanned the tribal members. "I told Sandu that Etti and Melodia were in danger, and he... he walked away into the forest. Then I found you, Ruslo, and you left to help them."

Ruslo's Sister, Darly, stood. "Wait! Say no more. Please. Wait." She placed a hand on Ruslo's arm, and she leaned in close to her brother, speaking long and earnestly. Ruslo's expression changed from annoyance to surprise, to disbelief, and finally to anger.

He pushed her away and conferred with Phuro Marko, ignoring Sandu who had decided to stand and show interest in their discussion. Ruslo pointed at Ito. He spoke words she could not hear, and Ito nodded gravely.

"Etti. Atira," Ruslo spoke their names. "Come to my wagon. Sandu and Darly, you come, too."

Etti gave Melodia what she hoped was a reassuring smile, and she and Atira left the Circle and all the staring relatives.

At Ruslo's wagon, Ruslo, Darly and Sandu were seated around the table. A residue of anger hung over Sandu. Ruslo appeared wounded beyond the bruises he sustained fighting Sabann. Darly's brow was furrowed, her eyes sad, moist with tears. Sandu stared at his hand and picked at the skin on his thumb.

Etti absorbed their expressions, reading the signs. Her thoughts came quickly, with a sharp, keen edge. Whatever Darly had told her brother had sorely disappointed Ruslo. Something vital had shifted in their relationship. Feeling her life in the balance, she waited for the next clue.

"I have been betrayed by my own family." Ruslo had reined in his anger, leaving only a jot of his usual strength and confidence. "As you said, Atira, you have been dutiful. On your vow that you never say another word about Sandu, or anything related to this matter, I will revoke my judgment on you and you can remain with us."

Relief softened Atira's features. She turned to Etti. "My babies." She shook her head. "I'm sorry for you, Etti, but I love my children." Blinking tears, she repeated the vow he demanded of her.

"Break it, and you will be exiled. You may go back to your children now."

Atira left, avoiding Etti's eyes. Etti was alone.

Ruslo took a deep breath and exhaled. "Etti, Sandu is leaving us and returning to his own tribe."

"Na." Sandu slammed his fist on the table.

"Va!" Darly cried. "Silence! A bug won't fly into a mouth that's shut!" Ruslo's sister ground out an old Romani proverb at her son—if he remained silent, he would court no more trouble.

Ruslo regarded Etti. "What I said to your uncle about Rafa was not final. Naught is final until the matchmaking."

Etti's swallowed a new dose of despair. She had dug herself a deeper hole. Instead of wedding Sandu and staying with her tribe, now she would be forced to wed Sandu and leave her tribe.

Like a wheel without spokes, her hopes collapsed. She had dared to fight Ruslo and had made matters even worse. They would hold her captive until the wedding. Sandu would claim her, the bridal sheets would be bloodied, and he would drag her away to his tribe.

She looked up. Ruslo was still talking to her. "…and since Sandu is leaving, I am overturning the council decision."

What had she missed? "What does all this mean, Ruslo?"

Ruslo turned to Darly and Sandu. "Sandu, I release you from the council match."

Sandu's face darkened and his hands fisted, but he glanced at his mother and remained silent.

"You are to leave in the morning with your mother, Sandu," Ruslo continued. "Go back to your tribe. We will meet again next spring at our rendezvous. Darly, go you to your wagon now. I will visit you yet this eve."

They left, and Ruslo faced Etti across the table.

"You have not been dutiful. You are divisive and you possess your brothers' contempt for authority."

"I meant no disrespect."

"Shesti!" Nonsense. Ruslo uttered it through thinned lips. "You always do as you wish. You are a dangerous woman." He leaned toward her. "But you seem to retain a trace of honor. I need your silence. Speak no ill of me or anyone in this tribe. Vow you will not judge, condemn or curse," he added emphatically, "anyone. Go quietly, dutifully, with Rafa. Wed him and remain with his tribe." He stood. "Promise this, and you will not be banished." He straightened. "Speak your vow now."

Etti choked on her breath and coughed. What was happening? What had happened? If she didn't speak of it, she could wed Rafa and leave? She hurriedly repeated the vow. "May I go now?"

"Va." Beneath his sparse mustache, Ruslo's lips curled in simmering disgust. "I should have matched you with Lasho."

Lasho—the old cripple with the watery eyes and big walking stick. Etti pulled back.

"It's what you deserve for your lack of respect. You, with your perverse habits—I treated you better than most would have done. It would bring me pleasure to watch Lasho whip away your impertinence. But that would mean I would have to see your god rotting face every day." His eyes burned with hatred. "Pack tonight. Be gone by daybreak."

"But Rafa has not yet returned." She paused, her mind a bird's nest of broken twigs, anger and tangled changes. "And what of our wedding?" Ruslo had not banished her, which kept her rights in the kumpania intact. "You would not send me away to travel to Barcelona, alone with Rafa."

Ruslo lowered his chin. His mustache almost disappeared beneath his big nose, and his eyes were dull with disdain. "Being alone with Rafa never bothered you before. After your night in the woods with him, I fully expect you won't be wanting to submit to inspection to prove your purity."

Etti gasped. He was accusing her of being unchaste, guilty of unlawful intercourse. While banishing destroyed all social life as a Gypsy, being called impure was the deepest insult a Rom could give a woman. "I am not afraid of the examination."

"You don't deserve one. At first light on the morrow, take Red, and any other belongings Rafa may have left here. Jardani will escort you to Rafa. And never—never, do you understand— discuss Sandu's refusal to help you. To anyone."

Etti swallowed. Ruslo's fury had eroded his thinking. She must leave him before he thought of worse fates for her. "Yes, of course, I...will you make the announcement?"

"Va. And if you interrupt me, I shall change my mind about Lasho."

She had cared for Ruslo, been dutiful—until Rafa. A protest stood poised on her tongue, but she covered her mouth. She recovered and nodded. "As you wish."

* * *

Atira was waiting for her in Dody's wagon, lying forlorn on the pile of eiderdowns. "I'm sorry, Etti. My babies. I can't—"

Etti showed her the palm of her hand and shook her head slowly. "Worry not. I understand." Etti smiled thinly, recovering from Ruslo's hurtful words. "Ruslo changed his mind. He's sending Sandu back with Darly and Ito." She paused, holding her hands under her chin, leaning forward. "And he chose Rafa for me, after all."

"Na! Na!" Atira's mouth dropped in the middle of a huge smile.

Etti threw herself onto the bed, and she and Atira rolled around, kicking and laughing.

Breathless, Etti panted. "I leave with Jardani in the morning to meet Rafa. Ruslo is so angry." She sobered. "He won't allow our wedding. We are to leave, first thing tomorrow."

"No wedding?" Atira sat upright. "That will reflect poorly on you to Rafa's people! Why is he being so cruel to you?"

"I don't know," Etti said. "It's about Darly. She was crying."

"I saw."

"And about Sandu. Ruslo is sending him back to his mother and father's tribe. Because he didn't come to save me."

"So why would he be angry with his sister? What's amiss?" Atira scuttled off the feather beds. "Let's go."

"Where?"

"Where is Ruslo?"

"He said he'd visit Darly."

"Let's go to Darly and Ito's wagon and listen." She put a finger to her mouth. "Shh. We'll be quiet."

"But it's not dark yet. We'll be seen," Etti said.

"Fie! It's getting darker. We need only get close enough to hear." Atira hurried outside. "Besides, after your argument with him at the fire, there'll be others listening in."

Sounds of anger reached them as they approached Darly and Ito's wagon, brother and sister's voices sharp and cutting.

"He's your nephew. You vowed to help him," Darly said.

"Help, va," Ruslo said. "With tribal rituals, and learning to lead the tribe. I knew nothing of your secret. Why didn't you tell me?"

"He was too young! Only six, but he was so big for his age they tried him too early."

"Don't play me. If a boy doesn't pass the test, it's given again. And again. He had to have failed many times."

"Va!" Darly splayed her hands. "Because they scared him the first time, he dreaded it. They ruined him."

"A man doesn't become a coward overnight," Ruslo said.

"Don't call him that!"

As it became darker, the candles in the wagon created silhouettes. Ruslo whirled around. "Ito! You're not saying anything. I trusted you, too. Your son is faint-hearted, and you had to have known about the test."

Etti and the hovering tribe members knew. They tested Gypsy children during their early years. It was a lesson of transcending fear, of learning courage.

As part of the Romani courage training, a younger child was required to say and repeat a coarse insult to anger an older child. The older child would slap the younger child being tested. The younger child was not allowed to back down. Instead, he was told to repeat the offending word or phrase until he was struck again.

The young one would get slapped increasingly harder until the supervising adult called an end to the trial and congratulated the younger child. If the child became too afraid of the punishment and quit annoying the older child, the lesson would be repeated at another time until he or she finally overcame the fear of punishment and passed.

Many a mother cried when their child collapsed from the test. They also knew he would have to face it again. The test was that important. Timidity would not help them through the trials Gypsies would face as they traveled, and travel they must. The Gadjes reluctantly accepted the Gypsies' wanderings, but they would not allow them to settle in their villages. To survive in the face of danger and mistrust, even the children must be strong and defiant. With all the hostilities and challenges the Rom faced from Gadjes and local officials, they would not suffer cowards. All Gypsies believed fear was Evil because it killed a man's soul.

"Sandu failed the test. Va," Ito said. "But it was so long ago. He is big. So strong. No one has ever challenged him."

"You hid it from me. So strong. So big," Ruslo scoffed. "But he ran from Jilé and Durril," Ruslo said. "He failed to protect the woman I named to be his bride. Everyone knows now of his cowardice. He was to succeed me! By the saints! I won't have my tribe led by a coward! A Rom Baro must defend his people—not crouch down in fear!" His deep voice wavered, stricken, disappointed. He had been cruel to Etti, but his anguish caused her to flush with embarrassment for him.

"He's not weak!" Sandu's mother cried. "You said yourself he wins against all in wrestling. What man would be foolish enough to challenge him?"

"Any who heard Etti's accusations tonight!" Despair tightened Ruslo's voice. "Two women from our tribe were in danger, and he ran like a rabbit into the woods."

Silence filled the wagon, matching the deep quiet outside of it. A prickly cape of guilt fell on Etti's shoulders. She had fought bravely for herself, but not without wounding her Rom Baro.

"Darly," Ruslo said. "Had you told me, I would have worked with him."

"Good. You can teach him," Ito said.

"At his age? His patterns are deeply rooted by now. There are reasons we train our children young. Your deception has ruined him."

"Fie! You're wrong," Darly cried.

"You must lower your sights for Sandu. Take him back into your tribe. I can't look at your faces. You have shamed me. Made me the fool in front of my own people."

"We did no such thing," Ito said. "Etti did that to you."

"You're a Rom! Where were you when your son needed you?"

"At least my people don't question my leadership," Ito said.

"Why you—" Ruslo swung and connected with Ito's jaw.

Ito stumbled and crashed into the side of the wagon, breaking the grommets that held the canvas in place. They continued to scuffle, cursing and grunting.

"Stop! Fie! Remember yourselves," Darly cried.

Ruslo retreated, panting. "For you, Darly. I will. But be gone by morning—you, Ito, Sandu."

The wagon rocked and lurched as Ruslo stomped down the steps.

Etti and Atira ducked behind the water barrel, but Ruslo had already spotted them. He raked the eavesdroppers with an angry gaze. "Get you gone, all of you. To your wagons. There will be no more songs this night."

They hurried away into the shadows.

Back at Dody's wagon, Melodia was waiting for them. "I had a hard time getting away," she said. "My cousins are worried about me, being with you until your brothers are ..." She swallowed. "I'm sorry."

"Rafa will deliver them." Emotions overwhelmed Etti as she realized she would be safe from them. Her hands trembled, and she burst into tears.

"Oh, Etti. I'm so sorry for you."

"You don't understand, Melodia," Etti said. "Of all the times for you to miss the gathering." Her tears turned to soft laughter, a lilting madness, all the hopes and fears and tensions spilling out of her at once. She looked to the stars, and back at Melodia's dear, puffed-up face. "Ruslo reversed his decision. I'm to wed Rafa." She cried out the news.

"Etti!" Melodia managed to smile past the swelling—it had to have hurt—and she started dancing around. Her bruises reminded her of her ordeal, and she stopped, opened her arms and hugged Etti, rocking her. "I'm so happy for you!"

"But there's to be no wedding ceremony." Etti shook her head.

"What?"

"Come," Atira said. "Let's get in the wagon, and we'll explain."

They told her of the night's events.

"Etti asked me to create a spell for her. And it was a good one," Atira said. "Fie! I have never heard a woman talk like that to Ruslo. Besides Rupa, I mean. By the saints, I thought we'd both lose our heads when you confronted him." Atira told Melodia of the sharp exchange, and how loudly Ruslo had shouted.

Etti turned to Melodia. "My pairing with Sandu has been annulled. Ruslo has denied me a wedding, and we have to leave in the morning, but I'm free to wed Rafa now! And it's all because of that special spell of yours."

Atira shrugged. "It was simply oil and pigeon feathers, Etti. A common spell."

Etti put her hands on her hips. "You gave me a common spell?"

"It was you Etti. All you!" She laughed.

"But I felt it. A dizziness, and I saw through Sandu, what he really was."

"Call it a spell of knowledge if you prefer," Atira said. "I was there. You were brave. And determined. It was you."

They told Melodia of the argument, of Sandu's cowardice and Ruslo's decision to send his sister and Sandu away.

"What a time to be stuck in the wagon," Melodia said. "I missed so much. So—I understand why Sandu's fear would embarrass Ruslo, but why did Ruslo change his mind?"

Etti played with the door to Pesha's cage. "Ruslo wanted Sandu to be our next Rom Baro, but he learned he could not trust Sandu to defend our tribe. It's clear to me now," Etti said. "Ruslo wanted to get rid of me—what better way than to send me off with Rafa, all the way to Catalonia."

"Then Sandu saw you dance," Atira said. "Ruslo made all those concessions with Sandu to keep him here—only to learn his favorite nephew was unfit to rule. By defying Ruslo—by revealing to the tribe that Sandu shirked from rescuing you and Melodia—you forced Darly to confess Sandu's cowardice." She gave Etti a gentle push. "It was your courage that exposed Sandu."

Atira slid the special bolt under the corner cabinet, and opened the door.

"What are you doing?" Etti asked.

"Last of the berry mead," Atira said. "Father's been hoarding it."

"We can't." Etti said.

"It's our last night," Atira said.

"Last night?" Melodia repeated, looking from one to the other.

Etti sobered. "If Rafa returns before dawn, he and I will leave together for Barcelona. If he is not yet back, I leave with Jardani for Villasavary, and we will travel from there. Ruslo is so angry with me. He doesn't want to see my face again. He even threatened to match me with Lasho if I ever spoke of Sandu's cowardice."

"Lasho!" Melodia shuddered. "Fie!"

Atira unplugged the bottle. "Here's to my spell."

Etti laughed. "Common spell, indeed. You will some day be the tribe's wise woman. Baba Atira."

"Whose words will be heeded by all in the tribe." Atira raised her chin. "So shall I be."

"And I will be the teacher of love spells," Melodia said. "How to capture a man's heart forever with one wink of an eye."

Etti held the bottle up to them, emotions spilling over. How would she get by without Atira's caustic wit and Melodia's good cheer, and the deep trust and support these two had given her? "I'm so happy Rafa and I will be together—but it saddens me to lose you. How can I thank you for all you've done for me?"

Atira took the bottle of mead and swallowed twice. "We're Gypsies. That's what we do. And we travel. We'll be at the same summer horse fairs and have many stories to share. I expect you will have learned new dances you can teach us. Next time, though, we'll dance inside, where the men can't spy on us."

Etti passed on the second round. She would need her wits about her for these final moments. Ruslo had denied her a proper ceremony. Traveling unwed and unchaperoned would damage her reputation. What would Rafa's family think of him wedding a soiled woman, for without the rites, that would be their assumption.

They passed the mead for the last time, finishing it. "I'll thank Father for sharing this," Atira said.

Melodia pulled her own and Etti's eiderdown off the top of the pile. "Let's put the featherbeds outside, so we can watch the stars."

"Good idea." Atira gathered hers and they laid their beds in a clearing that gave them a good view of the sky.

"The stars will look the same in Catalonia, won't they?" Melodia asked.

"I think so," Etti said. "Should we pick a star for us?"

"Va." Atira pointed upward. "See those three? It's a crowded, skinny triangle—there. That's us."

"Va." Melodia pointed to the uppermost of the three stars. "That's you, Atira. Teller of fortunes and spinner of spells."

"Va." Etti selected one slightly lower, to the right. "That's Melodia, dancing in the sky and winking at her favorite young man."

Melodia giggled. "I have no one in mind. Nothing like you and Rafa. But there, the star below, that's Etti, in Catalonia, far from Atira and me, but bright and always in the sky with us." She turned to Etti. The campfire danced across Melodia's battered features. "I will talk to you at night, Etti. Next summer, you can tell me if you heard me. My thoughts."

"Thank you for the stars. It will be a comfort when I'm missing you."

Atira laughed. "You're being polite. You'll be too busy with your comely Gitano husband to be missing us."

Etti gave Atira a playful push back on the bed. "And Melodia, take my eiderdown, since I destroyed yours."

Atira's voice lowered, tauntingly seductive. "Methinks Rafa has plans for you to share his."

"I can't take your eiderdown," Melodia said. "Your mother made it for you. I rescued enough feathers yesterday to get by until we stop at the next market town."

"Thank you." Exhaustion drew a curtain over Etti's eyes. She turned away from the sparkling night sky, nestled into her comforter and drifted off to sleep.

Chapter 22

In Villasavary, Rafa looked up at the stars. He wished he had not agreed to this errand of death. He didn't do it as a favor to Ruslo, not after his betrayal. Oh, he understood why. To the Rom, family is vital, and Sandu was family, not Rafa.

But a man's word—that was vital, too.

A star fell in the ebony sky. He ached with need to be with Etti, especially now. During this short time before Etti was wed, his place was with her—last embraces, last wishes, last kisses. He had sacrificed all that to lead this mission of death, not because of Ruslo, but for Etti. He needed to witness Etti's brothers hang so she would finally be safe.

Rafa, Vano and Hanzi shared a second floor room on the outer border of town. The gallows stood just behind the inn, an unfortunate location for them.

Some men harbored dark instincts. So it was with the marshall. He had agreed to allow a Romani funeral, but in vengeance against Gypsies, he had ordered the executioner to leave the dead hanging until the next day. Curious townfolk had gathered to see the executed criminals. Young boys poked sticks at the bodies. They swayed, and the gallows creaked. The taunts and laughter sounded more like a night at the campfires than a mocking diversion of deviance and death.

"*Dinili*," Hanzi jeered. "Stupid Gadje. We should make them stop."

"Va. Jilé and Durril are Rom." Vano turned over to face them, his straw mattress crackling from his movements. "Even after all they did, they are still Rom."

"Sabann is Gadje," Rafa said. "They disrespect him, too. The marshall will allow us their funeral on the morrow. For now, get thee some rest; we rise early."

Rafa closed his eyes, hoping for the oblivion of sleep. A stone of disgust lodged in his throat, making swallowing difficult. During their lives, Jilé and Durril strutted in a cloud of defiance and cruelty, but they had been all that was left of Etti's immediate familia.

A wretched loneliness seeped into his bones. Ruslo's unanticipated move to name Sandu had strangled all their dreams. As if to torture himself, he remembered her alluring dance, the teasing smile that ripped the steps out from under his feet as she swayed, her earrings brushing her neck, and her black scarf swirling around her delectable body.

Etti, soul of his soul, now bound to Sandu.

* * *

They burned Jilé and Durril under a grey morning sky that spit moisture like tears. The flames licked high into the air, hot and hungry on the funeral pyre. It had been burning several hours. The villagers had helped them gather the wood, relishing their task of adding fuel to the fire. By midday, though, most of the people had grown disinterested and drifted away to their homes and chores.

Vano added pitch to hasten the process. The flames darkened to angry black fingers that clawed the brothers' flesh, burning the hatred and releasing it into the damp wind.

"What do you think?" Vano asked.

The shrouded bodies had collapsed. "It's time to meet with the marshall," Rafa said.

They found him in in his office, dusting the ink on his report. He looked down his nose at the Gypsies. "Can you read?" He made no effort to disguise his disdain.

"Some," Rafa said.

The marshall showed him the large page."Enough to sign as witness to the execution?"

Rafa snatched the vellum from his hands. He wandered through the heavily flourished letters. He had learned several words from monks in the monastery south of Barcelona, but he only recognized an occasional familiar word. Loathe to admit it to the smug marshall, he asked for his pen. "I imagine you can't read many of our Romani words, either."

"I'm sure I don't know." The marshall's mouth twisted. "I have never before laid eyes on a Gypsy book."

Rafa accepted the pen, choosing not to stab his eye with it. Instead, he wrote, in Romanes, *"On this day we witnessed the deaths of Jilé and Durril, sons of the departed and distinguished Rom Baro, Danior."* He signed his name with a flourish and handed the pen to Hanzi. He and Vano wrote an X.

* * *

Etti awakened before dawn to a dark sky laden with moisture. She pulled the eiderdown over her head, her body aching everywhere. Memories jolted her upright. "Rafa!" Today she would go to him.

She found Aunt Ucho in the wagon. Baba Lolli stood next to her, leaning on her silver-knobbed ceremonial cane, her white hair a tempest of wayward locks escaped from her braids.

"Godspeed." She greeted them. "You heard...?"

"Va." Her aunt cupped her chin, smiling. "You are to wed the man you love."

Tears welled in Etti's eyes. "I am to leave this morning. I—"

Lolli embraced Etti, humming and rocking her. "Darling Etti." She stroked her face with her wrinkled hands. "You are the little chick who wandered from all the others." Her voice lilted with affection. "You always sought adventures the rest of us only imagine." Lolli held her at arm's length. "The women of our kumpania have not been deliberately unkind in keeping their distance from you. Because you are… unlike them in many ways, they fear you."

"I have tried—"

"Your father was lenient, but the hedgehog…" She shook her head. "I will not have you leaving on horseback, turned out— disgraced as a soiled woman." Lolli's thin, brittle voice dipped in indignation. "You are a treasure, the daughter of a Rom Baro, and you will begin your new life with grace." Her white brows rose. "I have talked with Ruslo. It took most of the night because he is big, and thick, and pigheaded."

Aunt Ucho and Etti laughed.

Lolli's soft laughter creased her dimples. "It is settled. You will wed Rafa here, in your father's kumpania. You deserve that."

Fighting the urge to cry out in joy, Etti covered her mouth with her hands. "Misto!" The ceremony would validate them as husband and wife. She would go to Rafa's family with dignity. Etti released a soft moan.

Lolli took Etti's hands and squeezed them.

Her ancient face. The roads of joy and sorrow she had traveled had etched their way onto her skin, marring her beauty, but not her spirit. Her smile spoke of her affection. Her eyes sparked with life, and more than a little mischief. "The ceremony will be small and brief, I'm afeared—it was the best victory I could attain with Ruslo; he's very—unsettled."

Overcome, Etti bowed before the old woman. *"Nais tuke,* Baba Lolli. My deep and heart-felt thanks."

Lolli tapped her cane on the wagon floor. "Let's make haste. We have much to prepare, and precious little time. She pulled the canvas door open. "Girls! Wake up!"

Outside, Atira and Melodia grumbled and crawled from the eiderdown.

"Take Etti to the river. Wash her hair with this, annoint her skin with this." She handed Atira a twisted bundle of boiled herbs and gave Melodia a vial of oil. "And hurry back." She pointed to Ucho. "Bring her eiderdown in here. We will prepare for the examination."

Etti hurried out to join Atira and Melodia, and they strode toward the river.

"This is not good," Atira said.

"What?" Etti asked.

"The test." Atira glanced pointedly at Etti. "After your night with Rafa." She slanted her mouth, saying no more.

Atira's words sank in. Each bride was inspected before her wedding. Conducted by an elder woman and one relative, the test proved the bride's purity—or lack of it. Combined with the wedding sheet, which revealed the blood of her lost maidenhead, the groom and his family would be assured she was pure. If the bride was found to be unchaste, woe would beset her and her familia, for the Rom believed such a fallen woman, if tolerated and kept in their midst, would bring strife. Infighting. Years of bad luck.

Etti stopped walking. "You think—"

Atira rolled her eyes. "Va! You're mad for each other and you were in the aqueduct—alone—for over an hour, so va, I think. What will you do?"

Fie! If they knew the pleasures she and Rafa had shared there! And how desperately she had wanted him to join with him. She would give him a multitude of kisses and be forever beholden that he had controlled himself. Etti raised her chin. "You do me an injustice. Rafa, as well. I am proud to prove myself."

They all washed in the river, using the ash and herbs on their hair, and spreading the sweet smelling oil on their bodies. Atira and Melodia pranced around, skin shining, making feminine gestures and uttering soft sighs. Etti laughed, as immersed in the light moment as she was in the water.

Returning, Etti joined the women inside the wagon and Atira and Melodia held guard during the examination. Etti emerged minutes later, wearing a demure smile. She glanced at Melodia and winked.

Lolli followed, offering her hands to the girls for help down the steps. "Our bride is pure." She pointed at Etti. "You'll need a better skirt."

"She can take mine," Melodia said. "My mother will sew me a new one."

"And I will braid her hair," Atira said, nudging past Melodia.

"You will enter Barcelona with dignity. You will greet Rafa with your wagon, your eiderdown, and your dowry."

"But I have no wagon." It was burned as part of the ritual during her parents' funeral.

"Travel in your uncle's. We have no time to get you a new one," Lolli said.

The morning evaporated with preparations and warm congratulations from the women.

Ucho, Vai and Rupa tied black ribbons along the front of the wagon and on the sides. Aunt Ucho presented her with a small chest holding her *sumadji*, her family heirlooms, the only possessions not burned with her parents' wagon after their deaths. Among them was a long strand of gold coins. Atira braided the necklace into Etti's hair, applying gentle pressure after Jilé's brutal yanking.

"Wonderful!" Melodia clapped her hands. "You look like a princess!"

Etti touched her mouth. "Except for the swelling."

"It'll go down more every day," Melodia said. "Here." She handed Etti a bundle of folded cloth. "My dress. It's my wedding present to you."

Etti kissed her cheek. "Thank you. It's lovely." She slipped into Melodia's dress, made of yellow linen. Delicate white flowers swirled throughout the full skirt, and the tailored bodice was of a shiny black taffeta. "It fits well, Melodia. It's too pretty for me to keep. I will return it to you when next we meet. In Marseilles." She looked toward the canvas door. "Any sign of Rafa?" She was finally ready to be his bride—but where was her groom?

Chapter 23

Rafa, Vano and Hanzi rode out of Villasavary and into a long, narrow valley bordered by forest on each side. "The marshall," Hanzi said. "We should have put a viper in his bed."

"Gadjes," Vano sneered. "We're nothing more than sheep to them."

Rafa thought about the many ways Gadjes admired, envied and loathed the Rom. "They would never admit it, but they need us," Rafa said. "We tell their fortunes. Stoke their dreams. Give them something besides themselves to fear." He reflected on the cruelty of some, the generosity of others. "We unite them, as they unite us."

The wet sky seeped into Rafa's bones. Of a sudden he held Dark Tide back, loathe to make this last trip to Etti's kumpania, dreading the moment when he would kiss her beautiful hands for the last time. He doubted he could ever utter, *"Latcho drom"* to her. *Good journey,* the traditional Romany farewell.

"It's breaking up," Vano said later. A patch of blue sky grew in the west. After a while, sunshine broke through, mocking Rafa. Its warmth didn't reach his heart. How dare the sun shine so boldly?

Ahead, the forest closed in and the path veered left. Rafa recognized the last sharp turn before they would arrive at camp. He slipped into a brooding, painful silence, resenting each step closer to a farewell.

Hanzi reined his horse and held up his hand. "Listen."

Pulled from his dark thoughts, Rafa stopped. The strains of a viol and singing reached him. "Music." Would Ruslo be so cruel as to celebrate Etti and Sandu's wedding before he even left? Ungrateful snake—after he did Ruslo's bidding and delivered Jilé and Durril to the gallows.

The music grew louder. The aroma of roasted chicken filled the air. "The bastard. He wouldn't wait so I could say goodbye to her."

"Let's hurry then," Vano said, compassion in his eyes. "There may still be time for you to see her... before."

Rafa nudged his horse into a trot.

He spied Etti, coming out of her wagon. Atira and Melodia were with her, and the old woman, Lolli.

Etti wore a wide skirt, yellow as the sun with a black bodice that hugged her curves, revealing the tops of her breasts. From her braids, a shower of gold coins winked in the sunlight. She was walking to Sandu. *I must stop her before she meets him.*

He pressed his thighs, urging Dark Tide to a run. She was so beautiful and she was his great love—but no longer his. The thought seared him, and he strangled from lack of air.

She saw him and cried out, smiling. She spread her arms wide open, welcoming him. The joy in her bearing further shredded his soul.

He reined his stallion, tossed the reins to Vano and rushed to her. Mid-stride and mere yards from her, he stopped. Chest heaving, he closed his eyes, fisting his hands at his side. Etti was no longer his. It was early afternoon. All the tribe would be there. Watching. He must do Etti honor and block the ocean of passion that pumped in his veins.

She ran toward him, a dream, a fairy from the Gypsy tales sung 'round the fire, coins jingling, breasts bouncing in the low-cut, tightly tailored tunic, skirt swirling at her feet like high surf.

But she was promised to Sandu. She must have lost her composure; surely she had been driven as mad as he with the reversal of their fortunes.

She crashed into him, and they fell together to the earth, she on top of him.

"Etti. Etti, you're slaying me." He fought to contain himself, but his arms moved of their own accord, embracing her. Her hair smelled sweet and clean, intoxicating him. The braided coins assaulted his face like so many pebbles, striking his eyes, his chin, his forehead.

She straightened her arms, raising halfway up from him, laughing.

"Sandu. My god, if he sees us—"

"He's gone." Etti's laugh rose from deep within her.

"What mean you?" An unexpected sound surrounded them. Rafa raised himself as well, propping himself on his arms. Atira and Melodia were by the wagon, pointing and smiling. Etti's uncle and aunt and the old woman Lolli and Atira's children, and the young boys and men, and the younger wives and Rupa and Vai—all of them, amused. Clapping their hands.

Rafa froze, confused. Surely the earth had rumbled below him and it would soon tumble into the sea and no one had warned him. "What is it?"

"'Tis our wedding, Rafa. Ours!" She kissed him. "We have been waiting for you," Etti said. "Walk me to the Circle and I'll explain."

* * *

Rafa stood with Etti in a group that included Baba Lolli, Phuro Marko and Vano, and a surly, scowling Ruslo. He refused to perform the ceremony, deferring to Lolli. She asked them to repeat the vows, simple statements affirming they were willing to wed, and would raise their children in the Romani traditions.

Rafa repeated them and stroked Etti's face. *"Ves' tacha."* My beloved.

A single tear slipped down her cheek. *"Ves' tacha,"* she repeated. *"Kamav tut."* I love you.

Bo, Atira and Vano's young son carried the *pliashka*, the wedding mead. It was contained in a silver bottle wrapped in a red kerchief and tied with a string of gold coins. Dody stepped forward for Etti's departed father, Danior, and Jardani stood on behalf of Rafa's father, Marcos. Jardani and Dody drank the mead, formalizing the ceremony and the union.

Rafa watched, confused. The sequence of events for the ceremonies was out of order. Given, Etti's people may celebrate differently, in small ways, from Rafa's kumpania, but the wedding ceremony was more or less the same from familia to familia. For their wedding, everything was happening all at once, instead of over several hours, or even days. *So be it,* Rafa thought, more than a little superstitious and most unwilling to stop and ask why. Given what had come before, Rafa was anxious to complete the rituals as soon as possible before Ruslo changed his mind again.

Little Miri came forward with the dowry satchel, handing it solemnly to Rafa and placing a brown tile on the ground in front of them.

Rafa's head still spun with all the news of Sandu, Darly, Ito's fight with Ruslo, and Etti's wedding. His wedding. He turned to Etti, his lovely, joyful Etti. "Ready?"

"Va." Her smile, so brilliant, stole the rays from the sun.

Etti and Rafa jumped. The ceremonial tile gave a satisfying crack, and it was done.

Applause and cheers followed, and Erki's bow drew on his viol, strains of celebration. The sound of came after, and people crowded around the bride and groom.

Ruslo stalked away without so much as a farewell.

Rafa kissed Etti, gently pressing his lips to her bruised mouth. "My wife. I love you."

"Husband." She put a finger to her lip. "But we cannot call each other thus until our first child is born."

He drew close to her ear. "I will whisper it to you when we make love." He swooped her into his arms and carried her to the fire. There, the ceremony continued and Etti's Aunt Ucho, Rupa, Lolli and Atira unbraided Etti's hair. It fell in shining waves past her waist.

Baba Lolli tapped forward to a table, the silver ball of her cane sparkling in the sunlight. She rested the cane and offered them two wooden drinking cups, carved with a quarter moon kissing the sun. "Dance under the sun, and love under the moon," Lolli said. "And drink this for your wedding night." She blinked in the bright sunlight. "Your wedding *day,*" she corrected.

The cups held a special drink. The Rom insisted the potion calmed the bride on her wedding night, but Rafa suspected it was to relax the groom, as well, from the strain of witnesses to the union. They didn't watch, but the canvas-top wagons afforded little sound privacy, and the women were expected to suffer. Many a bride chose to further prove her virginity by drawing attention, crying out so in pain that the entire camp could hear. Many a Rom complained of the difficulties of sustaining a husband's performance when his bride was screaming and pulling his ears.

He gave a conspiratorial smile to Etti. Moments ago, Rafa wed the most comely woman he had ever seen. Her body, supple and hale, brought him to his knees, sensual, lush and eager. The tribe would have evidence of Etti's purity with the wedding sheets, but he would be patient and gentle—he would not make Etti cry. He wondered where she would touch him with those graceful hands of hers. His body responded with the thought. She may utter moans—likely several, but no cries.

"Rafa?" Etti had raised her cup and waited for him to raise his so they may drink.

Rafa pushed his lusting thoughts aside long enough to get them to the privacy of the wagon. He lifted the cup, saluted Etti and brought it to his lips. The beverage was frothy, and the rich aroma of cherries tickled his nose.

They finished the drink, and they all escorted Etti and Rafa to Dody's wagon. Once there, Etti and Rafa entered it, waved to everyone, and tied the canvas shut.

Inside, muted daylight lit every corner, and a single candle burned on the table. The desk, chest and Pesha's drawer and cage had been moved to the side, and Etti's eiderdown had been placed on the floor.

Rafa slid into it, careful to keep the marriage sheet in place, and undressed.

Etti slipped out of her skirt and climbed in.

They kissed and slid into an embrace.

Rafa laced his fingers in hers, settled her head on his shoulder and simply held her. He sensed her discomfiture and turned her away from him, her back to his chest. He held her virtuously, playing with the profusion of ebony curls that spilled over his arms. "I must surely be dreaming. Only hours ago I thought I had lost you forever."

"I know." She pressed closer. "These last two days seem like a year, they've been so long. So dreadful."

Her chemise rubbed him, soft and warm. "I struggled, trying to imagine how I could bear to say goodbye to you." He sought her hand under the covers, brought it to his lips. "Knowing I would be kissing your lovely hands for the last time."

"And now we are wed," she said softly. "And you must take my maidenhead."

He laughed, relieved he didn't have to mention it. "And we must do it in the daylight, with the whole kumpania gathering near the wagon."

Her laughter was forced. "Let us moan for a while, and I'll cry out, and then we can be gone on our way."

"You forget the sheets," he said. "And your heart is too soft to sacrifice a pigeon."

She laughed, loudly this time, and Rafa was glad to have found her good humor. A few brides, in an effort to prove maidenhead when it had already been taken, used pigeon blood for the marriage linens. If word got out, her name was spoken about camp as the "pigeon bride."

She turned, a knowing smile on her face. "I'll bite your neck again."

"The Rom laughed at me, wearing my kerchief in the summer heat."

"And the women stared at me, and pointed at their necks."

Silence descended, a blanket of awkwardness Rafa had never worn before. He turned her so they faced each other, placed her hand on his shoulder and closed his eyes.

She tapped his chest. "What are you doing?"

"I'm exhausted. I'm going to take a nap."

"What?" Etti watched him. His features were perfect Gypsy, a delectable Rom as divine as a dream, his long lashes jet black against his skin, his chest muscular. Its rise and fall was fast, though, betraying his pretended sleep. "M-hmm," she murmured, her voice low and breathy, like a moon goddess. Now, what had made her think of that? Oh, yes, the bridal cup. "Enjoy your nap," she said. "Oh, but what is this long, hard object pressing against my leg? She reached down and encircled his rigid shaft with her fingers, stroking the velvet skin.

He gasped and his eyes flew open, dark with desire. His neck thickened, his pulse visible there, throbbing.

A sudden hunger slammed through her veins, landing in her core and melting her bones.

He reached for the hem of her chemise and pulled it over her head.

A recklessness came over her, and she laughed wickedly. There would be no rushing, no shameful discoveries, no condemnations, no penalties. This delectable man was her husband now, and they were free to love each other. She grew hotter, wetter, remembering how he had taken her over the edge at the aqueduct.

She pushed him onto his back. Memories drifted to her, and she followed her instincts. She kissed his ear and, knowing the tenderness of his neck, she licked it like a juicy chicken leg fresh off the fire. She used the tip of her tongue at first. Propping on her arms, she lowered to his chest and licked as if cleaning off the final remnants of a spoonful of custard. She swirled her tongue on his nipple, enjoying the catch in his breath.

He cupped her breasts, rubbing the nipples, his big hands on her, a gentle massage that brought heavenly sensations and a moan to her lips.

Returning to his neck, she bit and suckled. He squirmed under her, growing even harder with desire.

He rolled with her in the eiderdown, positioning her below him. He grabbed the top of the cover and disappeared toward the bottom of the bed.

His hands moved from her breasts, down her stomach, soft, trailing kisses. He touched her thighs, squeezing them, a teasing kiss here, a feather touch there. He spread her legs gently.

She tried to close them. "Na." She was deep in her cups from the frothy wedding drink and the intoxicating closeness to his naked, beautiful body. Her breasts were heavy with want. Her nether parts were burning, and everywhere her greedy skin cried out, "Touch me here. And here. And more here."

He sensed it. He was eating her up, devouring her. His fingers slid into her curls, and the tent his head had formed with the comforter collapsed as he lowered to her. The touch of his tongue as it swirled deeper drove her to a madness she had never known, a desire, unencumbered by shame or fear or caution, a total freedom with the man she loved beyond any love she had ever imagined.

She squirmed beneath him, and he held her, suckling and nibbling. The sounds of heavy panting filled the wagon—her sounds—and she grabbed his muscular shoulders, trying to pull him atop her, into her.

Waves crashed within her and she shuddered with ecstasy.

Rafa emerged from the covers and turned her so she faced away from him again. Both of them on their sides, he fondled her nipples and bit her neck. Like summer lightning, the sensation raced to her core, and she was needy for him again. He embraced her, his chest smooth on her back, and his hand skimmed down her stomach to her pleasure point.

She turned. "I can't see your face in this position."

"This way I have both hands free." His fingers rubbed and massaged, two of them taking great liberties, entering her, paralyzing her with want. She groaned and moved against him, lost in a physical ecstasy she had never known. His hot breath warmed her ear, and he was saying something.

"… going to take my time. Not hurt you." His voice grew husky. "Pleasure you through your first time."

He guided his shaft through her folds, sliding it against her. His velvet skin rubbed against her like a key, and she opened, inviting him.

"I'll be slow. Gentle," he managed, his voice deepening.

The candlelight faded and the canvas walls blurred. Etti sank into a glittering, gem-encrusted well of liquid, pulsing desire. She thrust her bottom toward him, wanting him inside her.

"Easy. Easy." He grabbed her hips, stilling her.

Pressure, and a delightful friction as he moved, his fingers still stroking her. She moaned, wanting more. As he thrust gently forward, she arched backward, taking him in.

A sharp pain, then a burning sensation. She gasped.

He stopped moving, held her. "I'm sorry."

"Touch me again," she said.

He fondled her, and the good feelings returned. "Move slowly, my love. As you wish, only so long as it's pleasant."

She thrust carefully, small, pleasing movements, enjoying the fullness and the rich sensations from their union. His fingers moved faster, and he rocked his hips side to side. It lifted her higher and she grabbed him, pulling him closer.

She began falling, falling, and reached a sudden crest. "Rafa!" She found release, holding him.

"I can't hold back. I'm sorry." Rafa thrust powerfully, his eyes closed. He released a massive groan and and a sharp cry that sounded like something between pain and joy.

She breathed through her pain, thankful the thrusts were short-lived. They lay, joined together.

"Are you all right?" she asked.

"Va. Va!" He said, raining kisses on her shoulder. "I am well… my wife," he whispered. "And you?"

"Truly." She disengaged and rolled around to face him. "My husband." His black hair was tossed every which way, some of it hanging down over his forehead. He watched her intently through his dark lashes, his eyes shining with possession, a man content. She remembered his previous expression, and relished her newfound power to drive him over the edge with pleasure as he had done for her. "I thought I was the one who was to be crying out," she teased.

Rafa kissed her face, her eyes, her mouth. "I heard a fair bit of noise from you, my wife." They drifted in the down, skin to skin, melting into each other, the most intimate moment of her life.

He brushed her hair from her face, pulling her from her love dream. "Ruslo made it very clear he wants us gone. Please dress and step outside." He held the eiderdown open for her. "If you'd be so kind, limp a bit from the ordeal of having survived my lust and vigor."

She laughed.

"I'll hang the marriage linen, and we'll be on our way to Barcelona."

She put a finger to her chin. "Can't we rest?" She rubbed her hand on his chest. "Take that nap?"

"Does a blind man wish for sight?" He helped her up. "But speaking of sight, we need sunlight to travel."

She dressed and stepped out of the wagon, her body still humming. Rafa hung the wedding sheet and joined her.

Melodia and Atira waited outside, standing at a respectful distance. Atira's children clung to her skirt. Jardani, wearing a black eye and scraped knuckles, held his horse and Dark Tide. A canvas bag rested near his feet, his and Rafa's possessions.

Kennick held Red. Etti approached him. "Thank you for teaching me how to train horses."

"You have a gift with the animals, Etti. You will win your next race." He patted her hand. "Much happiness to the both of you," he said. Of all people to send her off, Pobi stood next to Kennick. He had grown two feet since he snatched Pesha out of his cage and tried to drop him in the cooking pot six years ago. Mayhap he had grown in other ways, too. Her old adversary gave a hint of a smile and waved. *"Latcho Drom."* Good journey.

She returned his smile. *"Nais Tuke."*

Dody approached her, arms out, and she ran into them. "'Tis a joy to see you happy, Etti."

"Thank you, Uncle, for your sacrifices. And you, too, Aunt Ucho, for your wagon. We'll never forget how you helped us."

He ended the embrace and looked in her eyes. "Tried to. 'Twas you who stood up to Ruslo," he said. "Your father is proud of you in the spirit world." He kissed her cheek. "Latcho dram. I'll see you in Marseilles."

In the grassy clearing directly behind the wagon, dozens of her familia and kumpania had gathered.

Lolli approached, holding a yellow kerchief. She kissed Etti and placed it over her hair, helping her position and knot it. "Now all will know you are a married woman. Godspeed, my dear."

"I'm beholden to you, Baba Lolli. Thank you for pleading for my wedding."

Lolli tapped her cane on Etti's arm, affection in her eyes. "Off with you now."

Everyone rushed in to wish her well—Uncle Bo and Aunt Shelta, Aunt Ucho, Aunt Vai. Hanzi and his new bride, Mary; and Yoska with his new bride, Leyla.

The women gave Etti small parcels. "Thank you, she said. She hugged them, accepting their gifts. She smelled the packages, wrapped in linen. "Mmm, strawberry bread. Walnut cakes. This will taste so good on our trip."

"Godspeed."

"Latcho drom."

"Baksheesh!"

They wished them happiness, good fortune and safe travels. The good wishes swirled around them, warm as the summer sun.

Most of them waved their farewells to Etti and Rafa and returned to their wagons.

Vano and Erki harnessed the horses to Dody's wagon, now Etti's. The black celebration ribbons fluttered in the breeze, and it was time to go.

Etti turned to Melodia and Atira. She found it difficult to swallow the rock in her throat.

"Oh, don't get weepy on us." Atira's voice was thick, despite her words. "You're running away with the comely Gitano, remember? And you're taking my wagon."

"Uncle Dody's," Etti said.

"Still." Atira's dark eyes flashed, her mouth curved in a teasing smile.

"And I'd go with you, but my father forbade me to," Melodia said. "Besides, you know how to wink now. You're ready to fly the nest." She wasn't as successful as Atira at staying her feelings. Two big tears slid down her cheeks.

Etti embraced her friends.

"Latcho Drom," they said. Good journey. "I wish you happiness," Atira said.

"And a long life with Rafa," Melodia said.

"*Kamav tut,*" Etti said simply. "I love you both. See you in Marseilles." Etti joined Rafa on the driver's bench. Uncle Dody, Atira, Melodia and the others clustered nearby. Laughing and grunting, they gave Etti and Rafa a good-luck push to the wheel of the wagon that would take them into their new life together. The horses took over, pulling away from the Circle. Etti waved one last time, and they entered the road.

Rafa offered her his arm, and she slid close to him, nuzzling into his shoulder.

"I can't believe it," she said.

"Nor I. This morn I was in the deepest misery of my life, and here we are now. Married."

His brown eyes caressed her. "You will dance for me, my bride?" He licked the tender skin between her fingers. "Tonight?"

"Va." Her heart burst with love for this man who saw her in such a special light. *Kamav tut.* She so loved him—his sense of humor, loyalty and deep passion—all Rafa. "Husband. My husband."

He stopped the wagon and kissed her, softly cupping her face. She reveled in his embrace. Sensual, unhurried and gentle, the kiss of a new beginning. The look in his eyes filled her with hope and a delicious anticipation for the days to come. He ended the kiss and winked at her. "My wife."

THE END

IF YOU ENJOYED ETTI'S INTENDED

Please consider sending Etti, Rafa and the rest of the cast some love in the form of a book review. Here's the link: Quick Review of Etti's Intended. Just scroll down to "Write a Customer Review." Short or long, it will be very much appreciated by me and by other readers looking for new historical romance adventures.

Thank you, and happy reading!

Upcoming book release news at:
www.janetlane.net
Join my newsletter there – new book releases, contests, free books, hot deals!

It's About Time – short story in "Mistwillow" anthology, RMFW Press
For Book Club Readers

About the Author
#1 Amazon bestselling author Janet Lane writes "history, made passionate" in fifteenth century England and France.

Her heroines carry the spice and spirit of Gypsies in their blood, and they're strong and resourceful as they confront the turbulence of that century, be it war, prejudice or yes, romance. Her novels have won the 2015 and 2017 international IPPY Award, the 2015 international Next Generation INDIE award, the 2015 EVVY, the 2015 HOLT Medallion, and the anthology, Broken Links, was a finalist in the Colorado Book Award.

Janet lives in the Colorado mountains with her husband and a fiesty Chihuahua. She very much enjoys hearing from her readers, and will always thank you for a review if she has a way to reach you. Happy reading!

AWARDS FOR THE COIN FOREST GYPSY NOVELS

TABOR'S TRINKET
International Awards: IPPY, INDIE
National Awards: RMFW

EMERALD SILK
National Awards: EVVY, RMFW

TRAITOR'S MOON
National Award: HOLT MEDALLION

CRIMSON SECRET
International Award: IPPY

Free previews of all these books follow after the Author's Note!

Author's Note – the Gypsies

Over the centuries, Gypsies (Romani) have been romanticized, feared, tortured, and expelled.
Yet these nomadic people for a brief time enjoyed a social honeymoon in Europe. In a time span of several decades, royalty, the church, and nobles in many countries not only welcomed the Gypsies but also willingly financed their journeys through their lands.
Records of their travels (and recent DNA evidence) suggest that India is their land of origin, but these nomadic people more often claimed Egypt as their homeland. During their exodus through Western Europe, the clever Gypsies ascertained that nobility had its privileges. Always adaptable, they assumed titles

such as "King" and "Count." Harnessing the popularity of pilgrimages, their story evolved: they claimed to be of noble blood, ejected from their lands in Little Egypt. They traveled on a pilgrimage of penitence by order of the pope himself, who directed them to roam the earth for seven years without sleeping in a bed.

Dark-skinned and handsome, riding choice steeds and dressed in exotic clothes, the Gypsies dazzled peasants and royalty alike. Gypsies gained papers ensuring safe conduct from such dignitaries as King James IV of Scotland and Sigismund, Holy Roman Emperor (1411–37) and King of Hungary (1387–1437).

BOOK CLUB DISCUSSION TOPICS

Hedgehogs

Hedgehogs live around two to three years in the wild, with mortality most often caused by predators. In captivity, they can live up to ten years. To stay healthy and happy, hedgies need frequent, kind handling and exercise. They become stressed and subject to illnesses if denied either.

Are hedgehogs too "exotic" to be kept as domestic pets?

Courage training

Throughout the centuries, many cultures have addressed the issue of timidity, bullying and cowardice. According to personal accounts of Jan Yoors in *The Gypsies*, the Rom believed that fear was the symbolic attribute of Evil because it destroyed men's souls. They would hold mock battle "lessons" repeated until the child broke free from fear. Contemporary martial arts programs include "courage training." U. S. Navy SEALS are trained into fearlessness through habituation, a process whereby trainees are repeatedly exposed to something they initially fear. The more repetition, the less fear will be felt until eventually they become immune to it.

Is this type of training appropriate for children and, if so, at what ages, and under what circumstances?

Assimilation

Roma fear assimilation with Gorgio or Gadje societies because they dread being corrupted by those societies' influences. America is known as the land of immigrants yet, when viewed in terms of historical continental migrations, European countries have also received waves of immigrants. Is it possible for a people to integrate in a new country, without assimilating?

Dispelling Myths about Gypsies
From a site endorsed by the National Association of Teachers of Travellers and Other Professions, here are some popular myths about the Romas.

Myth: Gypsies and Travellers are work shy.
Truth: Gypsies and Travellers often start work young. Traditional skills are passed down from generation to generation. There is a strong work ethic, based on the need to survive. Many Gypsies sacrificed their lives for this country in World War I and World War II.
Have you seen Gypsies at work? What are some commonly known professions and occupations for them?

Myth: All Gypsies live in caravans.
Truth: Romani Gypsies and Irish Travellers are recognized ethnic minorities with their own culture, language and beliefs. Historically they lived nomadic lives, but now 90% of Gypsies across the world live in houses. Being nomadic is more common in Western Europe, but even there only 50% of Gypsies live in caravans. Gypsies also live in houses, but they take their culture indoors with them.
What are your concerns associated with nomadic living?

Myth: Gypsies are endowed with special supernatural powers, including the ability to curse and see the future.
Truth: Some Gypsies may well have psychic powers, but no more than anyone else. But some myths can be turned to a community's advantage. A nation without an army is forced to defend itself with curses and superstition. Some Gypsies have capitalized on this myth and earned a living telling fortunes, cultivating the mystery that has always surrounded Gypsy culture.
Have you ever had your fortune told? Was the fortune teller a Gypsy?
Have you or your children had your faces painted at a Renaissance Festival? Was she a Gypsy?

Janet Lane

* * *

Free sample pages of Janet's other books in the series!
All these novels are available on amazon.com and other major retail outlets

Tabor's Trinket –Book One in the Coin Forest Gypsy Series – Sharai dances to survive after slavery

Tabor's Trinket

Lord Tabor wants to wed an escaped Gypsy slave, but if he defies the king by doing so, he may as well fall on his sword.
It is 1435, and Tabor doesn't mind playing the Arranged Marriage card in order to save his lands--until he's enchanted by the beautiful escaped slave-turned-dancer, Sharai, who's bright and observant enough to know life in a nunnery would be safer than being his mistress. While Sharai avoids a possessive Gypsy king who lusts for her, Tabor navigates the treacherous political waters preceding the War of the Roses in an effort to save their love.

Tabor's Trinket
(Book 1 of the Coin Forest series)
Copyright 2006, 2014 by Janet Lane
Chapter One

Marseilles, France, 1426
The sound of strangers' voices woke Sharai. Ropes binding her feet, she stumbled upright and stood on tiptoe, peering outside the forecastle at the bow of the slave ship.

Dawn. Seagulls called, circling the limp sail that flapped around the main mast. Below that, a blackbird pecked at the body of the slave, Zameel, draped over a coil of ropes, his forehead white with maggots. His neck bulged, black with grotesque knots, more proof that this was no nightmare, that she was in fact an unwilling passenger on a ship of slaves and death.

Sharai's mother stirred, her eyelids red and swollen. "Ves' tacha," she rasped in Romani. My beloved. "What is it, my little Faerie?"

"Shh." Sharai put her fingers gently to her mother's lips.

". . . and touch nothing!" A man's voice commanded from outside the ship on the port side. Heavy footsteps sounded as men jumped on board. "If anyone still lives, kill them."

Fresh terror seized her chest. All the crew and slaves had died, all but Sharai, her mother, and the captain, who lay still at her feet. He had been delirious these last few days, but still able to navigate to Marseilles where he had planned to sell forty healthy slaves.

Sharai checked the captain but he didn't stir, nor did he breathe. He must have died during the night. She pulled his dagger from a sheath at his side. Its blade had been recently sharpened and its ivory handle had been delicately carved with a bird in flight. She gripped it tightly.

Footsteps sounded on deck and she knelt by her mother. "Feign dead," Sharai whispered. Not a hard task, for they were close to it. The bug-ridden biscuits had run out days ago, and they had been living on ale, wine, and rancid meat.

"Mother of God," exclaimed a man. "Slaves. Gypsy slaves, dozens of them."

"There's more below deck," said another. "What stench!" He gagged and retched, and the dull splashing of vomit followed.

Sharai's throat constricted from the sound and a cockroach crawled up her neck, but she willed herself to remain still.

"See the lumps. Plague!"

"Get off the ship! Burn it!"

Liquid splattered on the deck, followed by a whooshing sound. The rope ladder creaked and the men's voices diminished.

Sharai risked checking. "They have gone." Using the captain's fine dagger she severed the ropes that bound her and her mother's feet. "The shoreline is but a hundred yards away. We must swim to safety."

"Curse Murat," her mother said of Sharai's uncle, who had betrayed them. "I cannot swim, Faerie," she said. "I have no strength. Go without me."

"Never!" She lifted her mother's chin. "Let me help you."

"You are but eight summers. I will drown you. Go!"

Sharai half-carried, half-dragged her mother down the ladder from the forecastle to the main deck. She grabbed a small wine barrel and dumped it, and the musty odor of tainted wine filled the air. "I cannot leave you here," she told her mother, and handed her the empty barrel. "Hold onto this and you will stay afloat."

Wind whipped their faces with the stench of burning flesh and the heat of hell. Rushing past the flames, they climbed over the railing. Sharai slashed the last remnant of rope from her ankles and dove into the water, imploring the good spirits for safety.

* * *

Hampshire, England, August 1430

His chest wound throbbing, Richard Ellingham, younger brother of William, Baron Tabor, leaned against the metal gate leading into the armory. The tang of blood and burned hair blended with the odor of rusting metal. Coin Forest Castle was under siege, and uncertainty burned into his flesh as surely as the pitch-laden arrows had. He fought the darkness that came in waves and threatened to carry him away.

Cyrill, his knight, fell against Richard, his lined face creased in pain. "The Hungerford knights have breached the curtain. God's blood, and your father barely cold in his grave."

Richard steadied him. "Their claim is false, but their swords are not."

Richard's brother, William, hurried down the steps to join them, his expression lacking all traces of his usual confidence. At twenty-one, he was short but able-bodied, a fitting lord of the castle. "All is lost."

Richard rested a hand on his brother's armored shoulder. "We did our best. We must leave. To the tunnel," he said. "Now."

"Can't." William backed against the stone wall. "They've cut us off."

"Then the armory." Richard opened the gate. "Come on!"

William rushed ahead and a dozen of their men hurried into the armory, the sight of their gold and green livery reassuring.

Aurora, his brother's wife, ran to Richard, grabbing his arm. Her red hair tangled past her shoulders and fear glittered in her eyes. "They've taken the keep!"

A rush of forbidden love pulsed to the surface. Richard would wrap his arms around her, shield her from the fear, but as always he honored his brother and held back. He took her arm to guide her. "You must hide." Despite her protests, he pushed her behind a shelf of broken armor, stuffing the folds of her skirt behind the wood.

She struggled. "I'm going with you."

"We're outnumbered. Stay here. Be silent."

Across the chamber, Cyrill and his men swung the gate shut.

Behind them the enemy's footfalls echoed in the stairwell as they clambered down from the great hall. One knight slipped on the stairs, made wet from the rains. The knave recovered and joined the rest of them, a wall of black and white liveried knights. They turned their shoulders against the gate, ramming it to keep Richard's men from homing the lock. The black and white devils broke through and the gate collapsed. Grunts and shouts of pain from both sides echoed in the damp chamber.

Three of the attackers advanced into the armory, downing four of the defending knights, leaving less than a dozen to hold the castle.

From the adjoining, smaller chamber William appeared, driven backward by Rauf, Hungerford's son, more evil by far than his father. Metal clanged and Rauf's sword struck William's flesh with a wet thud. William's armor broke free at the shoulder and exposed his hauberk, glistening with blood, and a second knight advanced on him.

A primitive shout filled the chamber, and Richard recognized it as his own. He ran to his brother, sword at the ready, but the narrow doorway offered no room to swing it. He shoved his sword sideways, blocking the tall knight's attack on William.

Richard drew his dagger and cleaved it into the tall knight's neck.

The Hungerford knight froze. His sword, poised to strike William, dropped from his hand and he fell.

The meaty-faced Rauf swung again at William, missing.

William smashed an armored fist into Rauf's face, driving him back. "Thanks, brother." William lunged forward, following the press of enemy knights to the fireplace.

Richard saw movement out of the corner of his eye. He turned and a swinging mace rushed toward him.

He ducked.

The mace grazed his face, shaking his skull and jolting Richard into a dull senselessness. Blood pumped down his face. He fell, and the stone floor punished him, cold and unyielding.

Death would come to him on this day. Blackness overwhelmed him.

A firm hand pulled at him. "Richard. We must away." His knight, Cyrill.

Richard managed to lift an eyelid. His stiff limbs made movement difficult, but he was still alive.

He listened, hearing no more clanging of armor. Torches hissed, and somewhere nearby metal scraped on stone. The sick sweet smell of blood mixed with the stench of sweat, and pain throbbed like devil's fire in his ears and teeth.

The fighting had stopped. Gingerly touching his left eye, he found it swollen shut. Of the Coin Forest men, only Cyrill was with him. Richard looked past him, deeper into the chamber. Black and white clad bodies littered the floor, but there was one, a stout one, in gold and green. One of theirs. Richard crawled to his side. His brother, William.

"Nay!" He gestured to Cyrill. "Give me light!" He raised his brother's head, but William's gaze was unseeing. A part of him had hated William for taking Aurora from him, but Richard loved his brother. Gone in his arms. *Sweet Mary*. Richard closed his eyes to stop the pain.

"Help me." Aurora's voice was tight with pain.

Richard gently rested William's head on the floor and hurried to the skirted form on the floor in the corner.

Aurora rolled to her side. Her hair pressed against her neck, matted with blood. In the torchlight he caught the muted green in her eyes, framed with a sheen of tears.

He propped her with his left arm. He moved her hand from her side, saw her life's blood pumping down her bodice.

Fresh pain sliced through him. Not her. No.

She shook her head. "I'm sorry."

"No. No apologies." Despite his love for her, she had chosen William instead of him.

She offered her hand and he took it. A tremulous sigh slipped between her parted lips. Her head dropped, and her hand relaxed in his.

He felt love slipping away, and his breath caught. "No!"

Her suffering over, she sank back on his arm.

Richard tried to swallow the pain that stuck in his throat like a sharp rock. He smoothed Aurora's curls back from her face and closed her eyes, laying her head gently on the stone floor. He took a breath so deep it caused his chest to throb again.

He looked around the keep, at the blood soaked bodies and fallen swords. Could he have prevented this slaughter? He'd sensed trouble coming from that pig Hungerford and had tried to warn his brother. "I should have been more insistent that William increase the guards. I should have kept after him."

Footsteps clamored on the stairwell above. More men coming.

"Don't blame yourself," Cyrill said. "We must go."

"I cannot leave her."

"You must. Hungerford's men were called above, but they'll be back soon. We can access the tunnel now."

Richard stumbled down the circular steps, past the storehouse and treasury and into the dungeon.

Just a handful of his men were waiting there.

Richard gestured toward a small, inconspicuous hallway. "Follow me." The hall led to an inner chamber. Aided by the knights, Richard moved the stone that blocked the doorway. He met the loyal gazes of his four remaining men, their brows glistening with sweat and blood beneath their armor. "Go."

They squeezed past the stone, their torches flickering in the revealed passageway. Behind them, they pushed the stone shut, closing the exit.

The low tunnel smelled of wet earth and mildew, and a chill brushed his face with each step.

Cyrill stabbed the torch into the darkness.

Spider webs snagged Richard's face. He brushed them off, moaning from the pain of touching his burned skin. He stumbled again, and sharp stones tore at his shoulder. "My eyes." Even his good one had swollen shut.

Cyrill placed Richard's hand on his shoulder. "Hold on."

One foot in front of another. Uneven steps, slippery footing, floor muddied from the heavy summer rains.

Occasional drips of water, the light splattering sounds of scurrying rats.

"The passageway is narrowing. Take care," Cyrill warned.

Richard fought the dizziness. Through the pounding of his head he sensed the tunnel dropping steeply.

Cyrill halted. "Bloody pox."

Richard pulled his eyelid open to see. Ahead of them, water sparkled off the torch's light. "God's bones. The rains have flooded the passage."

"We're trapped." Cyrill walked knee deep into the water. "'Tis a steep bank down."

Richard looked back the way they had come. "Hungerford's men are closing in. There's no going back." Richard removed his damaged breastplate, then his helm and leg guards. He nodded to Cyrill and the others to do the same.

Shed of their armor, they stood facing the lazy sparkle of light that wriggled, mesmerizing, on the black water's surface.

Cyrill's breath came in shallow puffs. "How long before the path rises again so we can breathe?"

Richard stared at their inky obstacle, swirling, taunting him for his hesitation. "I don't remember."

The youngest knight, John, stepped forward, his yellow hair matted with blood and sweat. "Don't try it. William's gone, so you're Lord of Coin Forest now, Richard. We can't lose you, too."

Cyrill stepped forward. "He's right, my lord. You're the last son, the last hope." His knight rested his hand on his shoulder. "Richard, Baron of Tabor. Lord Tabor."

Tabor. Richard felt of a sudden older than his nineteen years. "If we don't escape soon, we'll be dead and in a place where titles don't matter."

His greying eyebrows furrowed, Cyrill looked to him for a decision.

The sound of clanging armor echoed in the darkness from which they'd come. Enemy knights swarmed closer, thick as hounds on a downed boar. To remain would be suicide.

Torchlight danced across the water, a winking surface that masked the perils that might lie beneath. Guards routinely checked the tunnel, but they had never reported flooding. The skies had spilled rain for more than a sennight, and now this. He regarded his sword, the curved handle, crafted for his large hands, the fine blade. "This will weigh me down." He placed it in a niche above the rough stones and hoped to reclaim it someday.

He gave what he hoped was a reassuring smile to his knights. "Time for baptism, men." Taking a deep, painful breath, he sank into the dark water.

* * *

At next morning's first light, they reached St. Giles' Fair, just outside Winchester. Cyrill led Tabor to a bed in a large storage tent near the Gypsy dancers' wagons. Three knights had refused to swim the flooded tunnel and stayed back to fight to their deaths. Tabor, Cyrill, and John made it through the tunnel to safety and then traveled through the night to the large fair where desperate men could disappear amid the crowds of buyers, sellers, and thieves.

Cyrill pulled the blanket from the bed and gestured to Tabor to lie down. "Rest now." At thirty and five, grey had claimed Cyrill's temples and brows, but his eyes reflected strength. And raw worry.

Though the ceiling tarp dripped and the ground had been muddied from the rains, the tent was spacious, with a small fire pit in the middle of the floor. Crude ropes strung at eye level sagged with the burden of colorful fabrics. A half dozen chests cluttered the corner, apparently moved to make room for the bed that awaited him by the far wall. The air smelled of wet wood and the faded evening's ashes.

"Rest? When Hungerford's men are at Coin Forest?" Tabor protested.

Cyrill gently pushed Tabor, who was taken aback at how quickly his knees buckled. He fell back on the bed with a groan, and Cyrill prodded the wound in Tabor's chest.

Tabor drew a sharp breath.

"'Tis deep. How would it be to tell your mother you died, as well?"

"But the king . . . " Tabor paused, as all men did. England's king was but eight years old. He might understand that Tabor's holdings had been unlawfully seized, but he was off in France and even once he was notified, the child wouldn't grasp the need to intervene before the knave Hungerfords stripped the castle of its riches. "Regent Bedford must be notified, but he and the king are away at Rouen." England's war with France plodded on and Bedford was looking out for England's holdings in Southern France.

"We'll get word to Gloucester, the Protector. In a few days you can return and we'll rout the vermin."

"Thanks be my mother is at Fritham," Tabor said. "But William." Memories of his brother formed in Tabor's mind— William's arrogance, prancing his horse after winning at tournament. The time they scared the Hawkridge girls by bursting pig bladders when they were in the garderobe. He'd spent his youth in William's shadow, but held no ill feelings, only admiration and deep camaraderie. Fresh grief ripped through him. "Hungerford will pay."

"But what of the three knights left behind?"

Tabor's gut wrenched. Secrets spilled under the pressure of torture, even with the most loyal. "The treasury—"

"They won't find it." The hesitancy in Cyrill's eyes betrayed his words. He squeezed Tabor's arm in sympathy, bade a hasty goodbye and left.

A woman entered the tent. Etti, his friend and head of the dancers. Her black hair fell well past her shoulders, brushing his hand. She nudged Tabor onto the bed, forcing him to lie down. "Fie! Tabor, your face." She shuddered.

Above high cheekbones, her ebony eyes flashed. Lines clustered at the corners of her eyes and mouth, leading Tabor to believe she had lived at least forty summers.

"Thank you for safe harbor. I'm in your debt."

She laughed. "Ah, now I have a landed noble in my service. Music to my ears." She produced a small vial, forced his eyes open, and splashed a liquid in them.

It stung. "Agh! What is it?"

"Just eyebright and ground ivy." Etti was one of the dark skinned souls who came from a place called Little Egypt, a handsome people with a talent for horses, music and healing. She removed the crude bandages on his chest and gasped softly. She sprinkled liquid on linen and dabbed gently at his chest wound. "I'll be back to stitch this closed." She poulticed it and handed him a small blue flask. "Here. Swallow this for the pain. And spare me your thoughts on the taste."

"I need to go."

"Ha! You'll stay until you can travel." From a chest she pulled an armload of crude linen. "With that face no one will know you, but your clothes will draw attention. Here." She held up a shift of russet cloth and rolled him to his side, helping him change. "There. You'll be taken for a commoner now, Lord Tabor." She winked in that playful way her people possessed, and tended the fire.

She'd called him Lord Tabor. Hearing his new title reminded him of his loss, and fresh pain stabbed him, a pain no tincture or bandage could heal. His brother, William, was dead. And Aurora. In the quiet that followed, Tabor thought of her. Like the sensation of inhaling smoke from a torch's fire, a sharp pain burned in his chest, below the gaping wound. He turned his head toward the wall. She had never been his. She'd only played with him, used him to get close to William, heir to the title and lands. Though she sought only station and wealth, his love had been real. He heard a soft moan—his own—and then sleep overwhelmed him.

* * *

A clicking sound awoke him. The herbs Etti had given him made his mind blur. How long had he been sleeping?

A woman knelt in front of a chest of clothes. No, a child; a girl not yet upon her womanhood. She hummed a hymn, her voice a light velvet, her tone as sure as the monk singers at Winchester. Her arms were thin, her skin lighter than Etti's but still swarthy, like a ripe walnut. She twisted her long black hair into perfect rolls then slipped into a formal headdress, using a polished metal mirror in the chest lid to adjust the veil.

"Ooh," A tiny voice purred, and pudgy fingers grabbed the edge of the chest. The golden curls of a child's head appeared and a hand reached upward, short fingers grasping for the veil. "Mine. Mine!"

The older girl laughed and handed the child the veil. "Be gentle, Kadriya." Scooting a bucket to the overhead lines of clothes, the older girl pulled down a smock, slipped into it, covered it with a gown and tied the laces. Standing on the stool gave her enough height for the flowing skirt, though the bodice sagged on her flat chest. Tabor smiled at her slightly believable illusion.

Kadriya squealed and placed the large veil over her head like a blanket.

"Lovely, Lady Kadriya." The older one straightened her back, lifting her nose toward the tent top. The movement made the lace of her veil dip past her tailbone. Tabor caught a glimpse of her silhouette and her raised eyebrows. Too entertained to interrupt, he remained silent.

She held a rag in her hand and waved it like a fine kerchief. "You fancy my necklace, do you? 'Tis a family heirloom." Aiyerloom. Her tongue twisted around the phrase, leading him to believe she may have just learned the words. 'Twas a gift from the king himself." She turned a few degrees and dusted the air with her rag. With great flourish she offered her hand to the tiny girl. "Come, Duchess. Sit with me in the great hall and we shall have a feast." She shrank from an imaginary enemy. "Away with you. Such a knave you are, and me a fine lady. Guards, protect us. Take him away." She turned from her imaginary knave, leaving him in the custody of her equally fanciful guards.

She spun too quickly and the long skirts caught under her foot. Her arms swung in big circles and she tilted out of balance. With a cry she stumbled off the bucket, landing in an inglorious heap on the hay-strewn floor.

... end of Tabor's Trinket Preview Pages ...

Emerald Silk – Book Two – Kadriya's bigoted lover and their search for a priceless chalice
Emerald Silk
Copyright 2008, 2014 by Janet Lane

Chapter One The Emerald Chalice

England's Applewood Horse Fair, September, 1448
Kadriya paused on the hill above the gentle valley where swarthy-skinned men groomed horses and children squealed with delight in a game of tag. Their bare feet skimmed the earth, their cheeks flushed with the breezy freedom of innocence. Watching them run, Kadriya's own feet yearned for escape from the tight English shoes and the confining life they represented. Soon she would feel the rich, earthy grass between her toes. She savored the aroma of fried apples and campfires, and the prospect of returning to a life without barriers, under the stars. The thought stirred the Roma side of her heart. It was here she belonged.

She hoped.

Shifting on her horse she spread her arms, palms to the sky, and inhaled the crisp September air. The sun had finally broken through and tall willows wept at the banks of the meandering Parrott River, sprinkling leaves of gold on the surrounding valley floor.

Below, her Spanish-bred stallions nuzzled and nickered in their corral amid scores of other horses offered by competing Somerset breeders. Her patron, Richard, Baron of Tabor, was away fighting in France, and she was handling the sale on her own. She would do Tabor proud and return with a fat purse. Then she would begin her new life.

Maud pulled alongside her, reining her horse to a stop. She filled her saddle, a tall, stout woman with copper hair, ample breasts and a heart just as large. Maud's gown rode up her thigh, revealing a collection of knives big enough to slay a dragon. Her eyes twinkled with good humor. "You look happy as a fox in a warren."

"I am." Kadriya smoothed her skirt, a light yellow wool, and adjusted her own dagger. "Today Teraf announces our intention to break the tile together." Teraf, handsome, bright, and fiery king of

1

the Roma, was offering her marriage and a home. With him, and with her mother's people.

Maud's blue eyes reflected a soft sadness. "Sharai will miss you."

Sharai. The woman who, as a young child herself, had raised Kadriya after her mother died. "I wish she could be with us." A fresh ache grew in Kadriya's chest, as of a delicate web being wrenched from its mooring, forever breaking connections. Sharai was everything to her—mother, sister, friend. The prospect of life without her... Kadriya adjusted her scarf. wishing the airy linen weave of lavender, pink and yellow could shield her from that aspect of her future.

"I can no longer abide the whispers, Maud." Twenty, unwed, her mixed blood alienating all prospects among the nobility. "I must make my own way. With Teraf." She would finally be wed. At last she had found her place.

John Wynter peered through the sunset's gloom, separating the bushes to keep the heathens in his sight. Their campfire leapt higher, illuminating the frenzied swine as they danced at the river's edge, oblivious of the mud dripping from their feet. They had left the civilized section of the horse fair, where good Englishmen congregated, and moved to their own camp some hundred yards distant, a camp with several small fires and a community blaze where they all gathered. Two dozen tents, the larger ones flying colors of red and yellow. Gypsy flags. Devil's music leapt from their strange instruments, and they danced as if plagued with St. Vitus' disease, the women swaying their hips in an unholy bid for attention from all who watched.

John rolled his cross between his fingers, tracing the dent on the right crossbar, damaged during battle when it saved his life. The smooth surface of the gold reminded him of his faith, of his friendship with and duty to the abbot.

It had been two long, miserable days of riding from the monastery in a torrent of rain that had stopped just today. All because of the Gypsy thief, Teraf. He had stolen a priceless chalice from the abbey, a chalice with a history involving the most prominent bishop in England, a history that would cause his abbot embarrassment and loss of funding if it wasn't found, and soon.

These foreigners looked to Teraf as their king and he held a court almost as colorful as himself, a swaggering peacock, wild-eyed, hair bound in a yellow scarf and flowing past his shoulders like an ink-stained curse.

Roger, one of the five knights who rode with John to seize the thieves, joined him. "Still no sign of the other one, Erol."

"The abbot wants both, but by the saints, I'll not let this one get away. Erol must not be here, and their ceremony is over. The Gypsy king has won his prize hen." John watched the beautiful Gypsy tart who stood so proudly at Teraf's side. He had treated her like an ornament all the day, while she eagerly welcomed any shred of attention he gave her.

He noticed her large almond eyes with lively, expressive brows—none of that infernal plucking that the woman at court practiced—none of the outrageous ells of linen that cloaked the noblewomen's heads and necks like a hornet's nest. Her hand swept to her breast just then, a woman's enticement, but the gesture betrayed the hesitance of a girl. Her generous mouth curved with a delightful smile as if to conceal it, but she was a maiden.

She had tied her light scarf high, hugging her forehead and temples like a crown. It flowed down her back, fluttering from her movements, touching her neck, her shoulders. Her steps, sure and effortless, stirred her skirt as it flowed over the matted grasses. In spite of her excessive obeisance to the thief, she seemed to possess her own spirit.

With a toss of her head her exposed hair swung back. Garish hoops of gold hung from her ears and her clothes shifted, shamefully loose at her shoulders.

Never had he seen a more captivating woman.

Leather sandals held her small feet and strapped up her ankles and higher, peeking out when her skirt rolled softly from her movements.

An arrow of lust pierced him. How high, he wondered, did the leather lacings climb?

Cease. He pulled his gaze from her, and chipped a scale of mud off his armor with his thumb. He was here to serve his abbot. She was nothing more than one of them.

Foreigners.

In moments she would learn her peacock was just a pigeon, and a black one, at that.

John turned to Roger. "Are their ponies hobbled?"

"Aye."

"Good. Now we strike."

Teraf offered Kadriya a broad, white-toothed smile. His cream-colored cotehardie hugged his chest, and he moved with unfailing certainty, flamboyant and charming. The fine fabric was mud-stained and smelled deeply of male and horse sweat, though judging by his gaiety, it didn't matter. Who else would dare to wear such a light hue when riding horses in muddied fields? His raven hair spilled past his shoulders, reminding her of an unbroken stallion, his untamed eyes flashing with challenge and natural charm.

Of all the tribal kings in Marseilles, Teraf was the youngest, just two and twenty. Though impetuous and sharp-tongued, he was respected among the tribe. She admired his intelligence and self-assurance—in spite of his limited command of English, he negotiated fiercely, relentless until he extracted the most coin possible for his tribe's horses. He accepted her, as if she were a rare jewel, as if she were true-blooded rather than the worrisome, mixed-blood woman she really was.

Teraf nuzzled her. "When I'm through with you, my queen, you'll spit in the eye of any nobleman you meet." He hugged her with an enthusiasm that stole air from her chest.

She coughed and pulled away from him. His laughter had grown steadily louder since their announcement, his normally gentle touch now more bold, more controlling. Up to this point her day had been serene, like a pleasant float on the river. Then, after their betrothal announcement, she had been stung by the narrow-eyed assessment from the young tribal women who had vied for and failed to gain Teraf's attention. Teraf had changed before her eyes and that peaceful river had become a tossing ride on a restless sea, with no sight of land with which to regain her bearings.

But she did not feel unwanted. If anything, he seemed ravenous. Likely the mead was pickling his brain, and come sunrise he would be groaning.

4

"I'll purge that dusty English blood from your veins." He kissed her, his lips not tender, but hard and purposeful. "And fill you with pure Roma fire." His dark eyes flashed in the large campfire, and he swung her, too forcefully, in a circle. He lost his balance and they fell together in the mud.

It soaked through her tunic to her spine. Kadriya gasped from the shock and pulled away from him. "Let me go, Teraf. You have drunk more than you should."

"Do not whine, woman."

A horse whinnied. The musicians stopped. Startled gasps sounded from throughout the camp, and Kadriya scrambled to her feet.

Three mounted knights rushed in on grand destriers. From the riverbank two other knights rushed in, swords drawn, their horses' hooves plopping through the wet earth then sucking free in the sudden silence.

The tribal dogs sprang from their begging positions near the fire, fangs bared. Many Roma surrounded Teraf, daggers flashing.

The knights urged their mounts forward, one bumping Kadriya.

"Fie! Rein your steed," she said in reprimand.

The knight rammed her again, spitting on her skirt. His gaze settled on her chest and he reached for her.

She spun away and returned to Teraf's side. Her mouth went dry. Since childhood she had been accustomed to Lord Tabor's protection, traveling with knights and escorts. But here, limited by law to carrying only daggers for protection, Teraf and his men were at the mercy of these heavily armed knights.

They loomed over them now, swords drawn. "Stand back," the older one said.

She turned to Teraf.

The moment grew large, each man frozen, weighing his next move as the dogs rumbled menacing growls.

Dots of sweat glistened on Teraf's upper lip, betraying his fear and offering no reassurance. He signaled to the dogs. "Ho. Lie down." He turned to his men. "Do as they say."

A sixth knight lunged out of the darkness, yanking Teraf's daggers from his belt. "You'll come with us, thief."

Teraf's stout, muscular build offered no match for the burly, sword-wielding knight. "You make big error," he said in broken

English. "I am Teraf. King." He gestured to include all the Gypsies. "Pope give papers of protection. Grant free travel. We--."

"Papers." The largest knight spat the word like bad meat. "Bring them with you then." He wore armor but no helm. A gold cross stretched across his wide neck, held by a leather lanyard, its right crossbar bent at an odd angle. His dark blond hair lay flattened against his skull. The stubble of several days' growth shadowed his face, gaunt with high cheekbones, his blue eyes cold as a fireless night. "I am here on authority of the church," he said, "and we know who you are. A foreigner. A heathen. A thief." His hand played over the hilt of his sword, his breath heavy, as if he were struggling to resist the urge to run Teraf in at any moment. "You availed yourself of work and coin at the abbey, and you repaid that kindness by stealing an altar chalice. A special altar chalice. You will bring it to me now."

Teraf struggled to free himself. "You are fool." He looked toward Kadriya. "These are all lies," he swore in Romani. "I have been to no abbey, but here. With my tribe." His yellow scarf had been loosened in the scuffle, releasing his long hair. It fell, obscuring his eyes so she couldn't read them for truth.

Kadriya's heart pounded in her ears. He was looking to her, but the church's authority was sacrosanct.

"Kadriya?" Teraf stared at her, waiting for—what? Her confirmation that he had been here? But she had just arrived from Coin Forest. She didn't know, couldn't bear witness.

But she must respond. *He's your betrothed. He's too smart, too dedicated to his people, to steal treasures from an abbey. He must be innocent.* Teraf needed her to support him. "It's a mistake. He is no thief," she said as much for her own reassurance as for the knight's. *Of course he's not. You would have seen signs of it.*

The large knight straightened, looking much like a metal tree, wide and hard, the firelight reflecting on his armored chest. Impossibly, his eyes grew colder. "There is a reliable witness to his crime. An Englishman. A man of God." He drove the words home, grinding them out. "I am Sir John Wynter, here on orders of Father Robert, Abbot of the Cerne Monastery, to return you forthwith for hanging."

"No!" Kadriya cried. Hatred burned, hot in the knight's eyes, scorching her senses. It was frighteningly clear that he had no intention of learning the truth. She sensed then that Teraf must be innocent.

She approached the tall knight and lifted her chin to meet his eyes, slit with disdain. "He has no such chalice. Who is his accuser?"

The knight shifted in his saddle. "So you know a smattering of English, do you, heathen? Well done, but it will not save your thieving man." He tipped his head in the direction of a small wagon and signaled the other knights. "Tie him up."

... end of Emerald Silk Preview Pages ...

Traitor's Moon – Book Three –1459-Tainted with a cursed womb, abrasive Nicole is known as the Goddess of Frost. The half-Gypsy Stephen weds her to make amends for leaving her family vulnerable, but can he survive her razor tongue, and when he's labeled a traitor, will she defy Queen Margaret to save him?
Copyright 2014 by Janet Lane

Chapter 1

August 28, 1459, Coin Forest, Somerset
Swallowing a string of oaths he chose not to express, Stephen Ellingham calmed himself and cantered his palfrey, Hingit, through the darkened village. His knights, Harry and William, rode with him through the quiet streets. Pitch lights fought the midnight gloom and failed, and the smells of the bonfires and roasting pits faded behind them.

"Tell me again why we're following Lord Faierfield," Harry said. "He's in the foulest mood, and he told us to go direct to Hades at least three times this eve."

"Drunk as sin," William said. "Fierce as a badger, and over nothing."

"It must be more than nothing," Stephen said. First night of the harvest festival, and his neighbor, Walter Faierfield, seemed keen on a fight from the moment he arrived.

Stephen's father, Richard, Baron Tabor, had suffered Faierfield's temper through three dice games and quit the table after a barrage of name-calling. Stephen had stayed—a mistake, for Faierfield's ill humor only worsened. He'd insulted Stephen, calling him a heathen Gypsy. They'd shared fisticuffs, then Faierfield had started complaining about the dam again, demanding that Stephen, who managed the mill, dismantle it. Deep in his cups, Faierfield slurred more charges, his accusations meandering and senseless. Then Stephen's knight, Warin, also fuddled, had laughed at him. Faierfield roared that he'd file a complaint at court, and dragged his long arms across the table, spilling all the die and chalices. In a glaring, cursing huff, he gathered three of his knights and left for his castle, some ten miles away.

But it was no night to be traveling. The country was split, in upheaval, rife with criminals and dishonorable mercenaries. Poor England was sliding into civil war as the Duke of York prepared to fight King Henry VI for the throne. Roads weren't safe to travel, and this moonless night made them the more dangerous.

"We're following Faierfield to protect him from himself," Stephen said. "He can sleep it off at Coin Forest and go home tomorrow in the safety of daylight."

William huffed. "After his insults, it's a puzzle why you care."

"He's going through a rough stretch." Stephen had heard about Walter's ship, the Bagyrell. It had sunk, loaded with cargo, financially devastating him. "He's a good man when he's clearheaded."

"He said you were on thin ice with the king," William said. "And you saw his face."

"Aye, red as a rooster's wattle," Harry laughed. "And that huge yellow beard of his, flopping like a mustard mop when he cursed your father."

Stephen ran a hand through his hair, tangled from the ride. "I am fixed to settle this before it escalates to a formal complaint." His family already had their feet to the fire with alliances unsavory to the crown. No need to make it worse with a local feud over nothing.

The river cut sharply away, disappearing into the brooding border of Coin Forest, heavy with dense trees, its shadows often a harbor of secrets.

They left the village lights behind them and turned onto the the less-traveled lane to Walter's castle.

Overhead, the sky shimmered weakly from stars trapped in a thin mist, the moon absent. Harry lofted a flickering lantern, no match for the darkness that clung to the earth.

Wheat fields trailed a musky sweetness and in his ears, music lingered from the harvest festival he'd so abruptly abandoned.

All due to his short-tempered neighbor.

Several horses burst from the trees, their whinnying weak enough that they must be some distance ahead and to the left. They thundered toward Faierfield and his knights. A man issued a blood-stopping cry of attack, followed by answering cries of surprise.

"Hell's fire! Brigands," Stephen said.

"Here?" William said, his voice rising in disbelief. This road was a peaceful, minor highway between their properties.

"Desperate times." Stephens said. His muscles tensed, anticipating the fight. Faierfield's and Stephen's families suffered a history of discord, but Walter was a fellow nobleman, and a good man. They must save him.

Beneath him, Hingit pranced, skittish. "*Na daran,*" Stephen soothed, "*Na daran.*" Do not fear. He listened, assessing. Faierfield and his knights, four. Harry, William and himself, three. In the darkness, sounds of struggle—and more horses.

"Come on!" Stephen and Harry raced ahead, closing the distance between the marauding outlaws and Faierfield's small party.

Unseen in the darkness, the outlaws barked at Faierfield to stop.

Faierfield uttered a string of obscenities, his high-pitched voice still slurring his words.

"Quiet, my lord." Faierfield's gravelly voiced knight, Samuel.

Faierfield had revealed his location, not just to Stephen, but to the criminals. Stephen guided Hingit in the chilled darkness, feeling the ground begin to drop. The rogues had run Faierfield into a ravine to the right of the road between the two properties.

Harry still carried the lantern. "Kill it," Stephen said. No need to be more visible than their foe.

The flame died. Voice low, Stephen gave Harry direction. "You and William advance, straight on, and distract them from Faierfield. I'll circle around."

The ravine filled with the sounds of clashing metal, bruising blows. A swarming mass of armor and horse flesh and men, all huffing in their effort to kill. Stephen closed in on a snarl of men. They flashed before him as they moved, dark grey ghosts against a backdrop of black, like bats fleeing from a lightless cave. He heard more struggle ahead of him and waited.

Faierfield's high voice rose again, almost screaming, threatening to draw and quarter them.

"He's over there. Get him," one of the criminals shouted.

Stephen made a calculated risk of his position and signaled Hingit. They rushed forward. Stephen stabbed outward and above saddle height. His sword found flesh. The brigand grunted in pain and slid off his horse.

3

"Dog!" Another outlaw rushed to his friend's aid. Stephen dispatched him, and he, too, fell.

"Oh, my God." To the right, William's voice, tight with pain. The thud of a man hitting the ground.

"William's down!" Harry cried.

God's blood. "William!" Stephen rushed toward the voices. "William!"

"Stephen!" Faierfield cried out from the left, relief in his voice as he realized his party was not alone. "Thank God."

A rider bumped into Hingit.

Hingit turned, bit the horse.

The horse reared.

Friend or foe? Stephen brought his sword back to his chest, desperate to know where to strike.

A sword sang, slashing his unprotected ankle. Jagged pain shot up Stephen's leg, taking his breath.

Dizzy from pain, Stephen danced Hingit from danger, rocking his foot in the stirrup to be sure it was still there. A dung horseman approached him from behind.

Stephen ducked as a club swung past his head. *My death day?* Stephen unleashed his fury, slashing his sword in the darkness, seeking flesh. "The hell it is!"

Another horseman appeared from out of the dark. Hingit sidestepped, giving Stephen a good angle. He shoved the man, unseating him. The man cursed and slid off, grabbing Stephen's leg.

Stephen slapped at the horse but the outlaw held on. Hingit reared and stomped. The sound of a breaking bone, the fallen man's screams.

Another one swooped in. Stephen dodged, but not in time, and hot fire burst in his side. "Bastard!" Stephen confirmed a fresh wound, turned, stabbed viciously forward. Met flesh, passed bone. "Take this to hell with you," Stephen shouted.

The man grunted in pain. "Stephen! In God's name…" A familiar voice, a pitch higher than most men.

Stephen's heart seized. "Fairfield?" *Oh, my God.* The night's intentions cracked like broken arrows. "Is that you?"

The man slid from Stephen's sword and fell.

Stephen bolted off Hingit, slapping his flank. *"Se duce,"* he said. Go. He hobbled toward the man in the inky darkness. Found

4

him, felt the warm blood flowing. He reached higher, traced the scar above the man's eyebrow and clenched his full, soft beard.

Horror blotted his mind. "Faierfield!" He held his neighbor as he released a long, tortured breath and his body sagged.

Stephen waited in the silence, his heart beating dully in his ears. *Have I killed the very man I was trying to save?* He listened, desperate to hear a heartbeat, feel a breathe of life.

Cold silence gave Stephen his answer.

* * *

Back at his home Stephen sat on a storage chest, leaning against the wall in the solar. The outlaws had escaped, Stephen and the survivors had returned to Coin Forest, and guards were sent to retrieve the dead. Outside, the grey light of pre-dawn outlined the southeast tower of Coin Forest Castle. Harvest festival revelers, sobered by the news of the highway attack, had viewed the dead and now gathered in the great hall below, their excited conversations audible even from here.

Stephen gulped his wine, choking on the truth. His young knight, William, dead. The Faierfield knights, Samuel and Peter, dead. His stomach churned. *And Faierfield, dead by my own sword.*

Across the chamber, his mother, Sharai, had moved ells of silk off the table to make room for roast chicken and breads, but no one was eating. The colorful fabric bolts sat like a mocking rainbow in the corner, too bright for the disaster they faced.

His knight, Harry, sat at the table, a cloth over one eye and his fingers bandaged in a large white mitt. Blood at his temple matted his curly hair. Father Lewis passed Harry a cloth. "Gentle," he said, "Mind the stitches." The priest was past forty seasons now, face flushed, his wild eyebrows furrowed.

Stephen's father, Lord Tabor, sat next to the priest. Like Stephen his father was over six feet tall. Age had streaked his black hair with grey, but had not claimed his wits or strength. His mouth tensed into a thin line, he looked at Stephen.

Tabor struck his fist on the table. "Faierfield should never have left in the middle of the night like that. His cursed temper."

Sharai stood before the fire. The years had dulled his mother's beauty, but a strong spirit still shone in her eyes. She had plaited her white-streaked black hair in the English style and it framed her brown face, now tense, strained. She held her dark eyes closed and moved her head in a slow circle, humming a Gypsy tune. A nervous habit, something she did when troubled.

She continued with her odd song, the notes unsettling. Stephen shifted, groaned from the wound on his left side. He willed his ankle, scraped to the bone by the outlaw's sword, to stop throbbing. His senses reeled from the healing salve his mother had dabbed on his wounds, a stench of earth, fish and rotting peat.

"Dranego en yekhipe, zor. Bater. Bater." Calling on her Gypsy roots, Sharai chanted the spell and tossed the remaining ointment into the fire, where it flared in black-tipped spikes.

Her spell crawled up his spine like a morning frost but out of respect for his mother he concealed his shiver. Over two decades ago she had quietly wed his father and settled efficiently into her duties, earning cautious acceptance in Somerset despite the color of her skin. She made spells only in time of peril, and even then concealed it lest she be burned for witchcraft. She had filled Stephen's childhood with laughter and songs, and she believed in her power to heal, yet her chants echoed in the chamber, unnerving reminders of her heritage.

My heritage. The shadow of his mixed blood tainted his family, and now disaster with Walter. "I must make amends."

His mother pulled her silk rosary beads from her purse, threading the globes through her fingers from hand to hand. She whispered Christian prayers on the top of her Gypsy spells, prayers to deliver them from this ill-starred night. "What can we do?"

Father Lewis rubbed the side of his round face, the soft skin at his jaw pouring over his hand. "His death puts Lady Faierfeld in a precarious position."

His mother sucked in a breath, her eyes wide. "Emilyne!" She looked to Tabor.

His father lowered his gaze, saying nothing. Years ago he had spurned Emilyne, Lady Faierfield, to wed Sharai. The resulting scandal had hardened Emilyne into a bitter enemy.

"His death is untimely," Father Lewis said. "Faierfield's fortune is spent and they have no heir."

"Alex is the heir," Stephen said.

"He's cracked," Harry said, tapping his temple. "Many in the parish will petition the king to claim the holding. Henry will grant it to the nobleman who bids highest."

"He's just twelve, a child. I will speak for him," Stephen said. "Given the king's own mental lapses, he should be sympathetic. Willing to wait until Alex reaches his majority."

His mother's dark eyes grew wide. "You forget the curse."

The curse. All of Somerset knew the curse. Faierfield's first son had slipped from Emilyne's womb missing a left hand and had died six days later. Her second born, Nicole, inordinately tall and hateful. Then Alex, daft. If Alex couldn't inherit, the manor and its land would revert to the crown. Emilyne and her children would be disinherited, all because of Stephen. He pondered options. He would gain audience with the king—and ask for what? A favor? Inaction, that he forego a sizeable boon during looming war as an act of generosity? Possible solutions landed in his brain like insects on the lake at dusk, only to be devoured by reality as he realized the futility of them. He finally spoke the only option that seemed fair to Faierfield's family. "I could wed the daughter."

"Nicole?" His father shook his head. "What would that help? And you'd be miserable."

"She is difficult," Stephen admitted. Even with her light coloring there was a darkness about Nicole Miles, as if she'd slammed the door to life and homed the bolt. "But I think it could work."

"The idea has merit," Father Lewis agreed. "We cannot tuck our heads under the sheets."

"Stephen is Gypsy." Apology softened Sharai's eyes.

"He's English," Tabor countered.

"Gypsies. Plague. They use the words together," Sharai said.

"In France, not here," Tabor said.

Father Lewis nodded. "People are ill at ease with it. Further, Faierfield and Stephen were last seen together fighting." The priest's face wrinkled in concern. "He threatened you, Stephen, and you threatened him."

Like an onion, the priest's words stripped Stephen to a new level of alarm. "We were angry. Faierfield was relieved when he knew we were there tonight. He knew I was trying to help him." *Before I stabbed him to death.*

The priest touched his arm. "If his family loses their holdings, this will be another cross to bear." Father Lewis turned to Tabor. "Think! Stephen is titled. By wedding the daughter, he can protect Alex until he can inherit. Emilyne will be grateful. More willing to forgive Walter's death."

"But what of Katherine?" Sharai asked Stephen. "She's been speaking of the future."

Yes. Katherine. Warm, passionate, a viscount's daughter, well-positioned in London. He knew Katherine was expecting an offer of marriage. He swallowed with difficulty. "She will find another."

"And what of the curse?" Sharai's voice trembled. "Think of your children, Stephen. To keep Coin Forest, you need to present an heir."

The thought of disfigured children brought an uncomfortable tingling in Stephen's feet.

"Let's appeal to a second born son of nobility," Sharai said. "We shall … compensate him for marrying Nicole."

Stephen's considered it. Why not? A second-born son could protect young Alex, defend England from the Yorkists and gain enough favor with his service to earn a title.

"What man would take such a chance with his own offspring?" Father Lewis asked.

That unsettled Stephen, but growing up as a half-Gypsy had exposed him to the oft-times irrational fears and misconceptions of wagging tongues. Stephen looked to his mother. "Faierfield's death … " his voice faltered and he strengthened it, " … was my doing."

"I will not allow this," Sharai said.

The strength in her voice brought Stephen a flush of comfort, but he had never hidden behind his mother's fears, and would not do so now. He lifted his mother's face and she covered his hands with her own. "It was an accident," she said.

Outside, a hint of dawn's light pierced the grey and a trace of blue appeared in the sky. The fire flickered gold on the worn fireplace stones, shining black from countless fires. The stones seemed to expand, enshroud him as the darkness had earlier in the ravine.

Stephen had seen Nicole occasionally at the parish church, her beauty marred by her mouth frozen in an ill-humored scowl, eyes cold with challenge and distrust. His stomach knotted. *But what else can I do?*

A pause settled over the solar and everyone looked to him.

Stephen took a deep breath. His and Faierfield's family's political positions were at stake. He must decide now or risk falling between two stools, finding no remedy by lacking the courage to decide. He stood taller. "I have cast them in need. I must defend their holding." His life had slipped into shadows of change and uncertainty, and honor demanded he step forward to face them. "I must wed Nicole."

... end of Traitor's Moon Preview Pages ...

Crimson Secret – Joya's obsession with Luke and her
struggle to save the queen
Crimson Secret
Copyright 2016 Janet Lane

*Master bridge builder Lord Penry is a traitor, committed to
destroying Joya's beloved queen so York can rule. Joya, a
noblewoman carrying blood mixed with Gypsies, is equally
committed to keeping King Henry VI on the throne. They're both
right, both wrong, both lost in the heat of unbridled passion and
growing uncertainties. It's a dance of imperiled love amid the War
of the Roses, and time is running out to reveal their true loyalties.
During England's several wars, battles were fought near and on
bridges. Crimson Secret is a story of one of them.*

Prologue

A herring seagull swooped into Luke's face, an assault of
wings and sharp claws. Luke swatted it and his rope ladder
teetered thirty feet above the water. Luke grabbed the rung and
tightened his hold, the stiff twining cutting his flesh. His grip
failed and the rope snaked from his hands. Panic crippled him and
his foot slipped. He wobbled like a stricken duck, right leg flailing.
"Hold still. Grab my hand." From above on the bridge, his
cousin Degory reached for him. "You're all right. Step up to the
next rung. Slowly. A little to the left and… there. You have it."
In all his ten summers Luke had never experienced such fear.
He felt his hose moisten and he avoided his cousin's eyes.
Deg laughed. "Don't worry. If you fall, so what? That's what
we're here for. If you do, don't dive. Go in feet first and swim to
the left like I told you. I'm going to let go now. Ready?"
Luke took a deep breath and let go of Deg's hand. What could
be so hard about swinging from a bridge? Certes, it was a high
bridge, higher, grander and longer than any Luke had seen back
home in Somerset. Its graceful arches reached high, as if made for
angels, as splendid as Wells Cathedral with its fine stonework
spanning the length of at least four tilting fields.
He hoped Deg hadn't noticed his hose.

His cousin, three years older, swung over the bridge and descended onto the other ladder, nimble as a mummer. They stepped down their ladders and settled on the last rung.

Deg started swinging, pumping his legs, leaning back until his arms were straight and his swing formed an aggressive arch.

A quick look up showed that the rope was still securely attached to the bridge. A cool thrill of courage shot up Luke's spine, and he ventured a gentle pumping of his legs. Far below, the river churned and Luke grew light-headed.

"Look up!" Deg said. "Get used to it first before you look down."

Luke swung, higher, watching the clouds and the bridge swing in and out of his vision. His uncle's home sat snugly at the end of the bridge, and the shops sprouted like mushrooms on the deck of the bridge. "I'm doing it," he shouted. "This is fine!" His toes tickled at the bottom of the swing's arc and his heart soared at the top, the shivering, light sensation as wondrous as sunshine after days of rain.

Up and down, up and down, defying the seagulls that still swooped toward them, protecting their chicks. They gave up and flew back to the roofs and crannies under the bridge where they nested.

Too soon, Deg called to him.

How long had they been swinging? A moment, an inch of the candle, a bell's time?

"Time to jump," his cousin said.

New courage emboldened Luke. "Ready!"

Deg rose to standing. "It's simple. Don't jump until after you reach the top of your swing and have started to drop. Go feet first. Use your arms to stay upright. Don't let the current take you past the fisherman's docks. Got it?"

Luke blinked in the flurry of instructions. "Got it."

Deg nodded. "Do what I do."

At the highest point, Deg stepped off the swing and into the air, arms circling to keep his balance.

Luke tried to imagine what it must feel like to fall that far down in the air. Breathing became harder.

A splash. Deg's black head bobbed to the surface, and he swam to the dock. "Come on!"

"Hey, Turtle!" A harsh, raspy voice boomed from above the bridge. Luke turned, and the air chilled. His brothers, Philip and Christopher. They weren't supposed to arrive from Somerset until later this eve.

A familiar blanket of dread fell over him, worse than the seagull's wings, one that always buried Luke when in his brothers' company.

Philip grabbed the top of Luke's ladder and tugged on it, making it keel to the side. "What's the worry, Turtle?" he taunted.

"Scared to jump, Turtle?" Christopher asked.

The nickname pierced his skull. He would not answer them, would not feed their appetite at shaming him.

"Here, let me help you." Christopher pulled his dagger and started a sawing motion on the rope that held Luke's ladder.

Luke yelled. "No!" Fear surged, but he struck it down. He would not let them see his fear, ever again, after the barrel. Gritting his teeth, he kicked his legs forcefully, swinging high, and jumped.

Luke plummeted down, the rushing air whistling in his ears. His body tilted to the right and he landed crooked in the water. The river slapped him, a massive blow to his body that took his breath and rattled his neck.

He cut through the water like a cannon, the water pushing his tunic up over his head.

Finally he stopped sinking and an image came to him of a watery grave and hungry fish.

Up, must keep reaching up. Luke clawed to the light above, lungs burning. He broke through the surface, gasping, and struggled to the shore.

"Bad landing," Deg said from the dock. "You all right?"

Luke's skin was on fire and his neck hurt, but he admired Deg and didn't want him to think, as his brothers did, that he was afeared or worse, weak. "Yeah."

"So was it not fine as I told you?"

Luke rubbed his neck. "Aye."

"Let's do it again."

Up at the bridge, his uncle had joined his brothers. Luke could imagine Christopher's smile, his mouth curved in cruelty. After what they had done to him with the pickle barrel, they could not be trusted. He turned to Deg. "Let's go again later. After they leave."

Chapter 1

21 years later
Somerset, May, 1460

Joya Ellington, second daughter of Lord and Lady Tabor, waved her hawking glove and bumped the bed where her friends slept. "Come, ladies. It's May Day."

Her friend, Camilla, stirred. "Not for two days."

"Aye, but you won't make me hunt alone, will you?"

From Joya's bed Camilla groaned, her blue nightcap flattened from sleep like a storm-tossed tent. "The sun's not even up. Be gone." She pulled the covers over her head and her crooked cap disappeared.

Beside her, Prudence sat up, her slender shoulders sagging. She held her head, her expression pained from yester eve's wine. "Off to the forest with a dozen men? You'll hardly be alone."

Joya turned to her table and pushed aside the heap of hair combs, rings and pins to reach the water bowl. Sifting through the scattered garments she found a cloth, moistened it in cool water and pressed it to Prude's forehead. "This will help. And don't make it sound so improper. I'll be with my father and my priest." She looked forward to hunting with her father, Lord Tabor. She would receive his warm gaze of approval when she captured a pigeon or two for the festival table.

"Your father, priest, and ten other men," Prudence said.

Camilla's blue nightcap reappeared. She tossed the covers aside and propped herself on one elbow, regarding Joya with a raised brow. "Dawn has not yet broken, but look at her."

Prudence straightened and turned to Joya. "She's a vision." She touched Joya's coronet. "Not one hair astray, and her gown," she said, touching it. "The finest wool, yellow as the sun."

A teasing smile broke out on both their faces.

Joya rolled her eyes. Now would come the chants. She withdrew and plugged her ears. "I can't hear you."

"Oh, yes you can," Camilla said. "Her gown, so bright." Camilla started the sequence.

"A sheer delight," Prudence spoke the words in a familiar sing-song pattern.

"So small, a sprite," Camilla said.

Prudence tapped her chin, thinking. "Um—a bird, so light."

"Eyes dark as night," Camilla said.

"A lovely sight!" They framed their grinning faces with their hands.

"Stop you now." This ritual of theirs left Joya walking a narrow course. Their affection showed in their eyes, but small needles of disapproval winked below the surface of their words. "I am but lucky that my mother is such a good seamstress." She whopped them with her feather pillow. "There is no crime in looking nice."

"Good," Camilla said. "By cause if there were, the reeve would be shackling you."

Joya steered the conversation from herself. "So Cam, you're wide awake now. Come join the hunt. Think of the men. This could lead to your wedding day."

"The men don't look past you," Cam said.

"I am not interested." Joya clutched Giles' betrothal ring, suspended on a chain around her neck. Her fiancé had died months before at Blore Heath, at the hands of the malicious, usurping Yorkists. She would never love again. "Ah, but you should be. George will be there." George, the young Lord Minton. Camilla had been casting sheep's eyes at him.

"Even he isn't worth getting up in the dark for." Cam snuggled back under the covers. Joya grabbed for Camilla's leg and missed. "Hmm, I could strap your ankles to a horse and haul you out."

"Don't try me." Camilla bundled her legs beneath her and growled. "I have teeth. Good teeth. Now be gone. Anon."

Prudence swept an assessing gaze over Joya's gown. "And change that gown before you go out in all that mud."

Joya smoothed her hand over her skirt, full and flowing to allow free movement on her horse, the sleeves snug so she could efficiently handle her goshawk. She opened her mirror to check her coronet, bright with woven flowers and a yellow scarf. One can never be too pretty.

Prudence held her head. "Enjoy yourself." She laughed, a soft undercurrent of affection lilting her voice and warming her eyes. "What am I saying? You always do."

Joya planted a quick kiss on her cheek. "Thank you, Prude. Remember the games later at parish. Be there on time." She reached across and rocked Camilla's hip. "And you, Sleepy. I'll tell George you said good morn."

Camilla swatted her hand away.

Outside, Joya hurried through the bailey in the pre-dawn grey, heading for the mews. Father Jeffrye and her father waited with his knights by the drawbridge. Her brother's hound, Seven, sat between them, panting, ready for the hunt.

Sir Peter, short in the saddle and long in the tooth, turned an eye on her. "Late. So like a woman." His words taunted but his eyes lingered in admiration.

Joya raised a brow. "Early. So like a man." She waited for the men's laughter to die down and smiled at Peter. "We shall see if you can hawk like a woman."

"Or if you can hawk like a man," Peter answered.

"Do not bait her, Peter. At hawking, she will win," her father said, regarding her with affection.

"For me, she has already won." Peter's voice held suggestive undertones that drew more laughter.

Joya shot him a warning look. She enjoyed the hunt, had always been comfortable with the knights and their teasing, but she would not tread on the path to romance. Ever again.

She quickened her walk. This would be a good day. She and Diana, her prize merlin, would impress her father and provide food for the May Day feast.

She hurried to the mews, still feeling Peter's gaze on her. He had position, good humor and the wisdom of years, but he was not Giles. She still ached for him, felled by the maggot-brained Yorkists.

Giles would have turned twenty-two this month. She took a fortifying breath and ducked to enter the mews. Inside the squat hut her merlin, Diana, paced on her caged perch. She danced from side to side in excitement, a splendid bird with her white head, gold-ringed nose, and proud bronze and black-feathered chest.

From outside came the sounds of a trumpet and horses. Several men greeted her father. Diana's head jerked toward the rumpus. Joya positioned the hawk on her leather sleeve, hooded her and hurried outside.

A contingent of five men under King Henry's standard lingered on horseback before her father and his knights. "Spread the word," their leader said. They left, passing over the drawbridge.

Joya approached her father. "What word?"

"York. Word from Calais is that he and Warwick are returning."

"Again?" York and Warwick had escaped to Calais, and Warwick had returned after Christmas and stolen several ships from the king at Sandwich. Queen Margaret had effectively exiled them in Ireland. It all meant more war, more deaths. An old, familiar fear echoed from the past and Joya swallowed hard, fighting the nausea that rose from the mention of Yorkists. *We should have killed them all at Ludford.*

"Traitors," Peter said.

"They don't dare travel this far inland, damn their souls. If they do they'll rue the day they stepped on my land," her father said.

"They've been condemned." Not that it helped. Being attainted by Parliament hadn't stopped their five-year campaign to unseat King Henry.

"We're to be watchful on the highways, especially to the north," her father said.

The threat of war made the sky seem darker. Joya's skin crawled and she yearned to slap the Yorkists for the hateful bugs they were and feed them to the river snakes. She lifted her chin. A pox on them. Bastards, all. She posed a serene smile. She would not let them spoil the day. "Let's hunt, then, and provision our tables for May Day."

Joya handed Diana to the cadger. He added her to the six other hawks on the cadge and shifted it securely on his hips. Subdued, the hunting party headed for the woods.

By mid-day, the morning chill and dampness had burned off and Coin Forest was fresh with spring. The streams ran clear and tiny white flowers winked on tall stems within the high grasses. Pine needles carpeted the forest floor, releasing their fragrant resins as the horses crushed them on the trail.

Peter and the other men had taken their saker falcons west in search of grouse. Joya and her father had chosen to hunt at their favorite clearing a few miles away. They walked with their horses while Seven sniffed, looking for the opportunity to flush some game. Diana perched on Joya's protected arm, the goshawk on her father's arm.

In the companionable silence Tabor drank mead from his flask and passed it to her. She took a drink, stoppered the flask and positioned the strap over her shoulder.

Seven's tail straightened. He lunged toward a thick bush.

Three coneys burst from the cover, long ears flat, running in hell-bent haste in all directions.

"Ho! Ho!" Her father shouted to his goshawk. He unhooded and released the bird, mounted his horse and followed Seven and the hawk.

The sounds disturbed a bush full of flickers and they fluttered from their cover. "Het! Het!" Joya cried out and freed Diana from her hood and released her. Wings spreading almost a yard wide, she took to the air in a soft jingle of her bells.

Joya mounted Goldie and they followed Diana, ducking the low branches and thick brush. Their movement flushed a family of hares and more pigeons. Mud flew from her horse's hooves, splashing the hem of Joya's gown. No matter. Must stay with Diana. She could already imagine the look on her father's face when she returned with some plump birds.

She reached another clearing and a large pond, thick with lily pads. At the water's edge Diana pranced, mantling her prey. Joya dismounted, tethered Goldie to the low branch of a sprawling oak and approached her bird. "Good girl," Joya praised, trying to peer through Diana's wings to see what she had caught.

Behind her, Goldie huffed and pranced, trying to break free. "It's all right, girl," Joya soothed.

Diana continued to cover her prize, protecting it. Joya spoke softly and approached her, respectful of her sharp beak and claws. With a swift movement she hooded the bird, lifting her away to reveal the bird's prize: a fat vole. "Oh, Diana," Joya said, keeping the disappointment from her voice. "Very nice, my lady. Very nice." Joya opened her hawking bag, unhooded Diane and gave her a treat. The vole would not do for their May Day table, but she bagged it any way. The stable cats would be pleased.

Behind her Goldie still paced, skittish. "There now, girl," she said, approaching her horse. "What's vexing you?"

Her palfrey strained her reins, eyes widened.

Joya lowered her gaze to the horse's legs. Behind them the muddy shoreline was churned by the hooves of many horses, the deep imprints filled with water. Unseen earlier in her rush to tend to Diana, blood glistened in the pools.

Fear tingled her neck and the ground beneath her shifted. She was alone. How distant was her father?

She met the white-framed eyes of her frightened horse and followed her gaze to the left. Visible by a wild rosebush at the base of the giant oak was a bloodied arm.

The pool of blood beneath the body was as large as a soldier's shield, and his face—early twenties, she guessed—had taken on a grey tinge. His armor had been stolen, all but his greaves. The man had expired.

What if there are more? One step back, then another. On her arm, Diana crouched to spring.

I haven't tethered her. She reached for the bird.

Goldie gave another sharp tug on her reins and the branch broke. The horse bumped into Joya, knocking her off balance. She fell in the mud, arms outstretched to break her fall.

Diana fell off her arm and rolled. When her hood fell off, she flew to a high branch.

"Diana!"

But the hawk was hunting again and flew off, bells jingling.

Joya crooned to her horse. Calmly mounting her, she reined her to follow the hawk. Something caught her eye again, an object near a group of diseased trees. A pair of boots and legs by a fallen tree.

Stay, or go? My hawk. But what if this one's alive? She would check. If he still breathed, she would assure him she'd return, get Diana and find her father. She pulled her dagger. If he tries to harm me, I'll defend myself and escape.

She swallowed the stone in her throat and approached.

There were no signs of blood on this man. He was a few years older than the other man, fine lines settling around his eyes. His powerful brow line suggested much contemplation or deep study, and clearly by his clothes he was a nobleman. New mustache and beard growth shadowed his face. Hair the color of sand, nice jawline, thin face, high-set ears that brought attention to a fine, sensitive mouth. No helm or breastplate. She kept her distance, dagger drawn, poised in front of her chest. "Who are you?" As soon as the words passed her lips, her heart jumped to a dizzying beat. Why waken a sleeping bear? Where's Father? She stepped back a safer distance. Hands shaking, she pulled her hunting horn from her belt and blew hard. Her father would hear her and come.

The injured man hadn't reacted to her. She tried to walk away, but decency held her. She approached, caution tensing her muscles, dagger still drawn as she knelt beside his head. "Don't move," she warned, "Or I'll kill you." She placed her hand beneath his nostrils.

Moist air blew rhythmically against her skin.

His face was thin, and beautiful. Like a soft breeze his breath awakened sensations that had long been sleeping, and she was acutely aware of his masculinity, his power. She should leave him, but she could not. She tapped his forehead and received no response. Slapped his face, nothing. Finally she rolled his head back and forth. "Wake up!"

He stirred and groaned, holding his head. His eyes opened, blue, compelling.

-- End of Crimson Secret Preview Pages ...

Pronunciation Key

Atira	a-TEER-ah
Circle	The hub of the camp, fires
Dody	DOE-dee
Dorina	Dor-EE-nah
Durrill	DURR-ill
Eiderdown	EYE-der-down
Erki	ERR-kee
Gadje	GAH-zhe
Gitano	Hee-TAN-oh
Hanzi	HAN-zee
Ito	EE-toe
Jardani	Jar-DAHN-ee
Jilé	Jill-AY
Kamav tut	Kah-mahv-TOOT (I love you)
Kennick	KEN-ick
Kumpania	Koom-pah-NEE-ya
Latcho drom	LAH-cho drahm (Good journey)
Marime	MAH-ree-may (Unclean, impure)
Melodia	Meh-LOW-dee-ah
Miri	MEER-ee
Misto	MEES-toe (Exclamation of joy)
Nais Tuke	Nice TOO-kah (Thank you)
Pesha	PESH-uh
Phuro Marko	FOO-roe MAR-koe
Rafa	RAH-fah
Rom Baro	Rahm BARE-oh (Tribal chief)
Roma	Roe-mah
Romanes	RAH-mah-ness (Roma language)
Rupa	ROO-pah
Ruslo	ROOS-low
Sabann	Sah-BAHN
Sandu	San-DOO
Ucho	OO-choe
Vai	Vie